BEYOND THE BLACK CURTAIN

OTHER BOOKS BY THE AUTHOR

Legends of the Flashback, Books 1-3

X-Ray Rider and 7 Other Dark Rites of Passage

The Devil Drives a '66 and Other Stories

The Place And 10 Other Stories from the Region Between

The Witch-Doctor Diaries and Other Dystopias

Napoleon

by
Wayne Kyle Spitzer

Hobb's End Books • A Division of ACME Sprockets & Visions, Inc.
Spokane, WA

Copyright © 2017-2023 by Wayne Kyle Spitzer. All Rights Reserved. Published by Hobb's End Books, a division of ACME Sprockets & Visions. Cover design Copyright © 2022 by Wayne Kyle Spitzer. Please direct all inquiries to: HobbsEndBooks@yahoo.com

All characters appearing in this work are fictitious. Any resemblance to real persons, living or dead, is purely coincidental. This book contains material protected under International and Federal Copyright Laws and Treaties. Any unauthorized reprint or use of this book is prohibited. No part of this book may be reproduced or transmitted in any form or by any means, electronic or mechanical, including photocopying, recording, or by any information storage and retrieval system without express written permission from the author. This ebook is licensed for your personal enjoyment only. This ebook may not be re-sold or given away to other people. If you would like to share this book with another person, please purchase an additional copy for each recipient. If you are reading this book and did not purchase it, or it was not purchased for your use only, then please purchase your own copy. Thank you for respecting the hard work of this author.

For my sweetheart, Trinh. And for my father.

Contents

Prologue | Hour of a Thousand Paths

Comes a Ferryman

I | Ceremony
II | Sun Engine
III / Caveam Cristallum
IV | View to a Kill
V | Dialogue
VI | Explosion
VII | Dravidian Before
VIII | Dream
IX | Aftermath

The Tempter and the Taker

I | Awakening
II | Crucible
III | Pursuit
IV | Threshold
V | New World
VI | Jamais Vu
VII | Valdus
VIII | Plato's Cave
IX | Shadow Theatre
X | Escape
XI | Exorcism

The Pierced Veil

I | Confessions
II | Reunion
III | The Cage
IV | Thesea
V | Lying in Wait
VI | Descent
VII | Return
VIII | Treasure Cove
IX | Between Two Worlds
X | Dravidian's Passion
XI | Mushroom Dream
XII | Luminis Sub Omne
XIII | Sthulhu

Black Hole, White Fountain

I | War
II | Sthulhu Returns
III | Betrayals
IV | Death is Come
V | Gondola
VI | Styx Flumen
VII | Dragger
VIII | Questions
IX | Cell Visit
X | Recollection
XI | The Polyhistor's Tale
XII | Tale, Interrupted
XIII | Black Hole

To the End of Ursathrax

I | Poised to Strike
II | The Calling of the Cloud of Witnesses
III | The Fire-eater
IV | Chantilly
V | The Man of Branigan
VI | The Children
VII | The Widow
VIII | Pepperlung
IX | The Ferrymen
X | Dravidian No More
XI | White Fountain
XII | Attack
XIII | Confusion
XIV | Trapped
XV | Rosethorn
XVI | Sihadi
XVII | Convergence
XVIII | Into the Depths
XIX | Betrothed to the Blade
XXI | Synergique Amore
XXII | The Revolutionary
XXIII | Different Paths
XXIV | The Boar Eels
XXV | Wrapped Around Him
XXVI | Epilogue

Prologue | Hour of a Thousand Paths

It was the first night of the Sacrificium, a night of sacrifice and death, a night when the black coins tendered in the Lottery would be tendered back. It was also the *Hora Mille Semitis,* the Hour of a Thousand paths—for that is the day the Sacrificium had fallen on this year—the hour when best friends might become enemies, when lovers of longstanding might betray oaths, the hour in which anything and everything was possible. And the alignment was felt: from the upper echelons of the capitol to the poorest quarters of the downriver provinces. For the message of Valdus' rebellion had spread—whether it was a tract nailed to a door before quickly being torn down or a blast in the night that caused the power to fail in entire regions. It was a night for dreaming and for huddled collusions, for the breeze to course through rustling leaves, for long dead hearts to awaken and start pumping blood. The Sacrificium had once more come to Ursathrax, but so had the Hour of a Thousand Paths, and Valdus' Revolution, and something else, something elusive but impossible to ignore, nebulous, but as real as the River Dire, which seemed to have stolen into the world on the wind itself.

Comes a Ferryman

I | Ceremony

The hooded and blinkered draft horse knew only the road before it. Of the alfalfa patches they had passed on the way to the ceremony it had shown no interest, although surely it had smelled the plants more acutely than any person. Even things that could have affected its very survival, such as the rawboned fox slinking through the willows along the River Dire, had garnered only a nervous whinny.

"Here we are, miss," said Dr. Terazza, sounding far away even though he was sitting directly beside her. She'd been so focused on the horse that she hadn't noticed they'd ground nearly to a halt.

She looked down through the porthole window of the buggy, past the edge of the coffin road and past the long, wide, descending steps (which were abutted on both sides with pews of onlookers, some of whom broke etiquette and turned to look at her). The sacrificial pier was there, ashen black amidst the fog, its dim lanterns maintaining an outline as it stretched away from land—so that when viewed from the road it resembled some Cyclopean, crescent-headed polearm, the tips of whose blade vanished into river smoke.

"Yes," said Shekalane. "Here we are." She stared at the pier vacantly. "The ride seemed shorter this time. Isn't that odd?"

"It seemed short to me, too," said Terazza.

She looked away from the pier to find him looking at her intently, but kindly. "Perhaps it was only the company," she said, and smiled at him warmly. "Thank you, Sestus."

"The honor has been all mine, Ms. Shekalane. It's a shame it took these circumstances for neighbors to get to know one another. I'll be sure to free Milkweed when you are well clear, and to look after her after, you have my word."

She gripped the cushion wing and stood slowly, mounting the short step delicately before proceeding onto the long step and finally the cobblestones.

"Ms. Shekalane ..."

She turned to face him.

"Whatever the Lucitor has called you home for, may your passage be a safe one."

She moved to respond but hesitated, finding herself drawn to the draft horse again, which snorted and hung its head. She lowered her makeshift veil. "Goodbye, Sestus."

He tipped his hat to her and snapped the reins, causing the carriage to lurch forward, the horse's hooves clattering against the stones as Shekalane stepped to the edge of the stairs.

"All rise and face the chosen," said the rector, followed immediately by a tumult of shifting bodies and thudding woodwork as the congregation rose from their pews.

The sound and the sight of it startled her—but sobered her, too, especially when the wind moaned and a silence fell. There were so many—where had they all come from?

She scanned the faces haphazardly, her attention flitting from one to another. Unklung was there, as she'd known he would be, nearly unrecognizable without his straw hat, and wearing a formal sash across his chest instead of his mushroom bag (all those hours together traipsing dry creek bottoms and shady, overgrown grottos!). Silentina was there, despite their friendship having cooled since her involvement with Valdus. And, to speak of the devil, he was there also—no. No, she could see that she was mistaken. The man in the green cloak and cravat was not Valdus.

"We love you, Shekalane," someone cried.

And another: "Hear! Let's hear it for our most beautiful teacher!"

Someone started clapping tepidly—then another, and another, until virtually everyone had joined in, and Shekalane realized she was misting up, even smiling, in spite of herself. The scene somehow touched her beyond words.

"The Lucitor won't have a jimmy to get up if you get your hands on 'im," someone shouted, and there was laughter.

"Not after what He's put you through!" Cheers.

"Who said he had a jimmy?" More laughter—which became a tumult, which, fueled by the jugs of liquor being passed around as well as everyone's pre-ceremony jitters dissipating into euphoria, became a crescendo, which quickly became boisterous and carried on too long and led Shekalane to search the crowd for Valdus yet find him nowhere.

And then a raven cawed and a red dot fell wavering upon the rector's ample forehead, causing those nearest him to gasp and cower, and this, too, spread throughout the crowd, as the dot swung in great but diminishing circles—touching everyone, it seemed, as though it were branding them—until the great, black bird alighted on its special platform and cawed again, this time with finality, ruffling its feathers, folding its wings, and staring coolly out at them with its one real eye and its one cybernetic one—beside which a scarlet light shown piercingly.

The rector fidgeted, and a bottle shattered somewhere amidst the murmuring crowd.

"Ah—yes, well..." He adjusted his robes and patted his torso, searching for something on his person. At last he withdrew a scroll from an inner pocket and spread it open.

"Who stands with this woman to express the good wishes of her family and friends?"

Everyone said, "We do!"

The rector made the sign of the inverted cross—tapping his left hip then his right, then his chest. *"Benedictus Lucidus.* Shekalane of Jaskir, you may proceed to the edge of the River Dire, whose waters are the sweat and the blood, the, ah, urine and the semen, of the Lucitor Himself, and present yourself to his courier."

The usual introductory notes sounded from the great and terrible organ which sat to one side of the pier, and Shekalane waited for the inevitable pause between those notes and the music proper to take her first step onto the long, maroon carpet. When the music started, its notes sounding somehow weaker and less substantial than usual, she couldn't help but dwell on why the melody was different for different groups of people—men from women, children from adult, the aged from all. But she knew why in her heart. It was because the men were going to fight for the Lucitor, the children were going to be trained, the aged and the infirm were going to die, and the women—at least those among them that a man or even a god might find pleasing—were probably going to be raped. How particularly perverse it was then that, as Valdus once explained, the music used for women had once been used to accompany brides on the happiest day of their lives.

She glanced at the player as she proceeded and took note of old Harianna—her wispy white hair fluttering in the breeze, and her little nose just visible beneath the hood of her ceremonial robes. How many such ceremonies had the old woman played, Shekalane wondered, in the expanse of her eighty years? A draft horse whinnied from the vicinity of the carriage lot as if to whisper for her, *Too many, Shekalane, including the ones for your son and your beloved Stachtyr, and now my back is curved and I see only the keys before me.*

Shekalane scanned the crowds one final time for Valdus as she approached the pier, and not finding him, focused again on the pier itself. The sight of it did not torment her eye or fill her with dread as it once had, when she'd watched from these same steps as big Stachtyr disappeared into a cloud at its terminus. Nor did it seem to suck the very breath from her lungs as it had when little Sihadi was called. She had lost everything so long ago that her own selection in the Lottery was merely an anticlimax; she would miss the ragged children she tutored on Solstice-days, and she would miss the passions of Valdus—although he, too, however indirectly, had been taken from her by the Lottery years ago—but she would not miss the woman who had loved them, or the world in which they had lived. Seeing the children that one last time had been good enough for her—for she had specifically asked that they not be allowed at the ceremony. And as for Valdus, well, she now had her answer as to whether he had ever loved her or not. What he knew of love was reserved for his rebellion—his Quixotic quest to kill Asmodeus and to unseat the Lucitor—she was but a thing to draw strength from.

And what of you, Shekalane? Did you not share his passion for this at first? Was that not the very genesis of the affair? And would you not still be colluding with him intimately as well as strategically were the situation any different? Yes, but ... She shook her head. As with the children, their last encounter had been good enough. That had been a lovely night, the night they'd stolen away in Grintherp's fishing boat to make stormy love beneath the Dire Borealis. Anything more, anything beyond his physical passion, any single thing expressed verbally or otherwise—would have merely disappointed. It always had.

No, at this point she wanted only to dash the cup of blood and sweat and tears to the ground. Black hole, white fountain, as she'd often expressed to her students. Death and rebirth. What was lost in this universe was lost; what was to come was not of this universe.

There was a commotion as she reached the bottom of the stairs and moved toward the altar—something that sent a ripple through the crowd and caused people to gasp and to express surprise. Shekalane turned to see a winged creature the size of her hand flying toward her erratically—an elfemale, its lithe, white form dancing bat-like through the hazy pools of light. It was Milkweed, and she was carrying something—something which, as the little creature fluttered wildly about her head, Shekalane recognized to be a tiny scroll.

But then the raven entered her frame of vision, cawing excitedly, and Milkweed dropped the thing to the carpet. The little elfemale darted away as the raven pursued, and what followed was an aeronautic dance above the transfixed crowd in which the ignudi tried to escape but was blocked at every turn by the raven. And seeing how distracted everyone was, Shekalane bent quickly and snatched up the parcel.

She turned it in her hands: the scroll was contained in an emerald ring which acted as a seal and bore Valdus' standard, which glinted in the lantern-light. She swooned a little looking at it—this despite her feelings just a moment before. It touched her somehow beyond words; it was almost as though he were proposing to her—here, now, in her darkest of hours, when it seemed all the world had abandoned her, and with a rush of emotion she pulled the scroll out and put on the ring, then quickly opened the note.

It read: *The emerald in this ring is a homing beacon, however its power source is limited. Activate it by pressing the emerald when you approach the Stygian Flowstones, or on my command (which will manifest as a vibration), whichever comes first. Stay alert. You will know what to do. Watch the gateways to the Forbidden Channels. Although he doesn't know it yet, the ferryman is already dead. Power to the Revolution!*

"Hear, hear," shouted the rector as the airborne combatants vanished into the fog. He tapped his scepter several times. "Order, I say!"

She quickly stuffed the note into her patched, green shawl.

At last the congregation settled. The rector indicated that Shekalane should join him in standing within the great black circle sewn into the carpet, a circle which contained the Lucitor's own standard—a giant, blood-red inverticus—which was made by connecting the dots of the inverted cross. She did so and he took her hand, then everyone bowed their heads.

"Our Lucitor Who art in His Mansion," he began, which everyone repeated, including Shekalane. "Tremble we who come before you. Thy kingdom has come, thy will has been done, in the earth and not the heavens. Accept from us this night our blood and souls. And forgive not our wills, as we forgive not our willful. And lead us not to the tyranny of choice, but deliver us one and all down the River Dire. For Thine is the choice, and the predetermination, and the terminus, forever. *Benedictus Lucidus.*"

"*Benedictus Lucidus,*" everyone repeated.

"Do you have final words to say, Shekalane of Jaskir?"

She shook her head. She had already said her goodbyes.

He turned her hand palm-up and unfastened his knife sheath as Shekalane looked up at him through the frayed veil—her greenish-brown eyes steady but not without fear—then slid out the knife and laid its sharp edge across her palm.

Shekalane nodded once. Still, he hesitated—until the raven came cawing back and relighted on its upraised platform, its piercingly-lit third eye seeming to focus on him and its tiny beam cutting through the gloom to paint the back of his hand with a scarlet dot. Swifter and more assuredly than she might have thought him capable, he drew the blade across her flesh—then quickly cut his own, re-sheathing the knife and clasping her hand tightly in both of his.

He held like that for several seconds, squeezing so hard his hands shook, then gently placed his palm on her head and just as gently pushed, saying, "Down," until she was on her knees before him.

"Lift your veil."

She lifted the veil.

"Good. Now, Shekalane of Jaskir, do—"

A great foghorn sounded in the blackness out over the river, a blackness so complete it might have marked the border of the world, and both he and Shekalane jerked. The distraction with Milkweed had put them behind schedule; regardless, no one was ever prepared to hear that sound, not if they'd attended a thousand such ceremonies.

At last the rector continued: "... do you, ah, if accepted as a bride to our Lucitor, whose bile is the bath of all things tarnished, promise to, to ..."

Shekalane was looking up at him from her hand—which was bleeding profusely—as if to say: *Is this how it's supposed to be?*

In his eagerness to please the raven's camera, he had cut her too deep. He fumblingly withdrew a cloth from his robes and handed it to her, his fingers trembling, which she quickly used to make a crude tourniquet. Then, his thoughts flustered, he withdrew a small, black book from an inner pocket and opened it to the mark.

"Very well. So, ah, do you, Shekalane of Jaskir, ah, promise to share all that He has bestowed upon you, including but not limited to your youth, your beauty, and your skills as a courtesan, and to support Him in all endeavors, big and small?"

The foghorn sounded again, as terrifyingly as the first. And although she knew it emanated from an earthly source—a dragger, one of the great and terrible ships from which the ferrymen launched their gondolas and which transported them upriver after they'd delivered their charges—it didn't sound earthly. She could only liken it to the sound a tuba made at its lowest note, but then that note changed to one that was slightly higher ... and lingered there, as though the universe itself were brooding over some alien and inscrutable purpose. As a tutor, of course, she knew there could be no such thing as sound in a vacuum. But if there were such a thing, perhaps in a place where all the laws of physics had been turned upside-down, she felt certain that the other-worldly horn was what a black hole itself would sound like.

She heard something pattering softly against the carpet and glanced up to see the rector gripping the book tightly within his wounded hand, trying to slow his own bleeding.

"I do," she said.

"And will you, if it is decided otherwise, and so that others shall not want for space or bread, submit to death by our Lucitor, whose enzymes and proteins are the building blocks for all Ursathrax, and do so without hesitation or recourse—"

The foghorn sounded again, as if angrily impatient. The signaling torches needed to be lit, yet she knew it was expressly forbidden to do so before the vows were completed. She also knew, as the second note faded back into whatever haunted realm it had come from, that there would be no fourth sounding. The ferryman was already on his way.

The rector tried to hurry things along: "... and do it without recourse to violence?"

"I do," said Shekalane, then quickly corrected herself: "I will."

24

"Then I now pronounce you one with the Lucitor, and forever estranged from those who are not. And what the Lucitor has torn asunder, may no man reconcile." He made the sign of the inverted cross, then raised his bloodied fingers, flicking them once, twice, a third time, spotting her face with maroon. "Rise and replace your veil."

The crowd shouted: *"Benedictus Lucidus!"*

She stood but gave pause, for amidst the chorus were the voices of children. Her children, she realized, seated right there in the front. The entire class was there, including round, red-headed Alana and mute, feral Lat, who had come to them out of nowhere—simply washed ashore one day—like a piece of beautiful driftwood. He sat slightly apart from the others as he always had, and seemed truly lost, just completely and utterly alone.

Shekalane glanced at old, bespectacled Mabellisa, unsure whether to love her of hate her for ignoring her edict; had she known the children were there, she would have given last words! Especially to poor Lat, who had no friends or family but Shekalane herself—for she had always bonded best with singular and unique personages, be they children or adults.

The music began again—a simple, transitional overture—as the great, gas torches built into the pier and along the top of the wide steps burst into blue-red flame; until, finally, an enormous gong was pounded three times, ending the music, and, save for the crackling of the flames, an eerie silence fell over everything.

How long it lasted would have been impossible to say. But at great length the dipping of an oar was heard—indistinct but growing amidst all the night and fog—almost as if some invisible person were walking slowly but purposefully toward them over the water.

"All rise," said the rector. And with a great shuffling and creaking of pews, all rose.

"Servant, you will face the courier."

Shekalane turned to face the long, pitchfork-like pier and the impenetrable river fog beyond it, and made a deliberate attempt to tamp down her heart rate, which had quickened at the sound of the oar. *I will not fear you, ferryman. Although I know you will wish me to. Although I have heard the stories. Although you will be drunk with your power over me and over others—I will not fear you.*

She fingered the scroll hidden in her shawl. What did he mean, "You will know what to do?" Did she dare hope that Valdus might marshal all his resources in an attempt to rescue her? Even were that so, could such an effort do anything but fail? No one had ever escaped the Lottery— save by death itself.

A shape emerged from the fog, a mere phantom at first, a ghost. But as it approached the dock's terminus it became more corporeal, so that she could just make out a hooded figure in a serpentine boat, which entered the circlet at the edge of the cloud bank and came to a stop with its starboard side facing them.

She swallowed as a nervous tremor went through the crowd, and the figure attached a hooked cable to an iron arm upon the pier before slowly turning to face them. She could just barely make out the bottom half of his face beneath the hood— although it wasn't his true face at all but an oddly stoic-looking skull, which she knew to be a mask, and which knowledge she used to try to comfort herself. And she was partially successful; she had seen all this before, had she not? What could instill any new fear in a woman who had lost everything—first her husband, then her son, then a lover, and now herself and the friendships she had formed and her beloved school children and even her familiar, Milkweed, who was either dead or lost in the miasma?

She jumped as the raven cawed suddenly and leapt from its perch, batting its wings furiously before gliding the remaining distance to the ferryman and alighting upon his shoulder. He leaned against his oar with a strange kind of grace as a group of robed figures emerged from the crowd and began prodding her forward with their cruelly-configured pikes.

She pivoted suddenly and faced the crowd—more specifically, the children—Lat, in particular, and said, "I have something to say to my pupils!"

"Silence and speak not," ordered the rector. "The time for last words has passed. Sentries!"

The sentries pressed forward, backing her onto the pier. The raven's red eye gleamed.

"It is only this ..." She looked directly at Lat as the red dot of the raven's camera fell wavering upon her hair and her shoulder, which she glanced over quickly to see the ferryman stirring behind her, abandoning his oar and placing a high, black boot on the bow. But he did not leave his boat.

"We spoke frequently of black holes and white fountains, did we not? Well, know then that though I go into a black hole now, I will re-emerge in a white fountain. As above, so below. Death is but rebirth! We will see each other again!"

One of the sentries reversed his polearm and shoved her hard with its butt, causing her to stumble backward as the barrier spikes rose quickly from the floor—separating them decisively—as well as along both sides of the pier. She stepped forward again almost instantly, gripping the bars and making direct eye contact with Lat; but he did not seem to acknowledge her, none of them did, and it occurred to her in a flash of horror that perhaps they had been drugged.

She allowed her hands to slide from the bars. It was over and done with, all of it. Everything she had ever known ... just gone.

She turned to face the ferryman. He just stared back at her stoically, as if in perfect stasis, as cold and serpentine as his boat. She began moving toward him slowly.

The music began playing again, causing her to look back at the departing crowd over her shoulder, and she saw Petrus, Paulus, and Magdalene in a pool of light next to Harianna, the two balding men strumming their citterns while blonde, beautiful Magdalene swayed and hummed. Petrus began singing, "He is now to be among you ..."

She saw, or thought she saw, the ferryman unhook something from his belt and cast it to the deck, after which a cloud of smoke bubbled up rapidly and completely obscured the landing platform. She paused hesitantly, but then continued walking, repeating to herself, *I will not fear you, ferryman. Although I know you wish me to—I will not fear you.*

She looked once more over her shoulder at the players and the crowds filing out—numbed almost comatose by the perverse contrast of it, the harmony of the music and the horror of what lay before her, until she entered the expanding cloud of smoke and all was lost in a swirling gray void.

She could not even be certain that she had cleared the corridor of spikes when she glimpsed a tall, indistinct figure standing amidst the smoke and the fog, a figure which had pushed back its hooded cloak and whose lanky but muscular form could now be discerned, especially his long arms, which were savagely sculpted as if from years of manual labor—one of which unhooked a thick handle from his belt and seemed to squeeze, causing a great, curved blade to flash out with the ringing of steel.

She stopped dead in her tracks, her heart starting to beat faster. Was this the truth of it? Was the Lottery and the pomp and circumstance surrounding it an even bigger sham than she had suspected? Is this what had become of her husband and her son? Had they simply walked into the gloom to be butchered like animals?

She took several tentative steps to her right, considering finding the edge of the platform and perhaps leaping into the water—but he merely countered her, striding confidently to stand before her and to prevent her from continuing any further. She froze again as she looked at his mask and into his eyes, the irises of which caught the light reflecting off his scythe and gleamed a sickly yellow. He stepped closer, calmly, in perfect control, and though she tried to tear her eyes from his impenetrable gaze, she found, at least momentarily, that she could not. Then she shrunk away in a rush of terror and hurried for the edge of the platform, which was just visible in the dissipating smoke, and he strode rapidly after her and blocked her yet again, but this time he gripped her wrist and wrenched her away, causing her to tumble to the boards in the direction from which she'd come.

She pushed herself up, her rich, brown hair having come undone and fallen over her face, and looked at him angrily, her heart pounding, all the pain and sense of loss smoldering now, but he only glared back at her intently, his own chest heaving, as though he might smite her with his weapon at any moment. Then her dark eyes flared and she launched at him in fury, colliding with him and beating on his chest with both her arms, again and again, until he hugged her savagely, preventing her from striking him any further, and scooped her up in his own arms. Immediately something fell to the boards, and Shekalane feared at first that it was Valdus' ring, but it wasn't—it was her tiny copy of *The Chrysanthemum Cage,* which she had used to inform her herself spiritually (as well as her students) since losing her son.

She saw the ferryman's head jerk to look at it, his eyes wide behind the mask and seemingly rabid with fury—for it was expressly forbidden to bring anything but yourself to one's coronation.

What happened next happened very quickly—as he carried her onto the boat and seated her on a cushioned bench, then slapped her in shackles, and finally stuffed a black hood over her head, at which point everything went dark and she nearly passed out, but was prevented from doing so by the muffled whinny of a draft horse somewhere on the shore.

II | Sun Engine

The dispatch runner arrived almost breathless and leaned close to Valdus at the bow gunwale. "Enemy spotted—a ferryman and his charge. They've just passed the Stygian Flowstones."

Valdus lifted his binoculars and peered upriver, saw a black speck just rounding the curvature of the great cavern wall. "Excellent, corporal. Lector, the sun engine..."

Lector looked up from his gauges and readouts and shook his head. "Still charging. The test burst drained more energy than we could have anticipated."

"How long?"

"At slow charge—about an hour, at least."

"Bloody hell ..." Valdus stood and paced the length of the machine. "And a fast charge?"

Lector and his assistant exchanged nervous glances. "As I said earlier, my lord, a fast charge could jeopardize the integrity of the containment field. And energized plasma is nothing to trifle—"

Valdus slapped on hand on his shoulder, his thumb touching his neck. It was a comradely but vaguely threatening gesture he used often. "How long, Lector?"

"I–it is difficult ..." He examined the complicated machinery. "About half that, if the hydrogen flasks seat properly. You must understand, my lord, that an incorrectly seated flask can cause the weapon to explode the instant it is fired."

Valdus tightened his thumb on his neck. "I don't speak the language of ancient machines, Lector. How long?"

"Gurn will help me with it. Perhaps ... one-quarter of an hour."

"Fast charge it, then." He looked at Gurn, who seemed suddenly frozen with terror. "I will be beside you. We shall share the risk, as we shall share the spoils of a free Ursathrax. The Revolution will not be won by prudence but by audacity."

A deep voice boomed from the stern, where reflected water danced in the dark. "And no one is more audacious!"

Valdus smiled as General Hirth strode toward him across the foredeck, his armor clinking, his weapons jangling, and saluted them, then motioned for his superior to join him at the starboard gunwale, where they both stood facing the interior of the cave.

"Look at what your leadership has accomplished, my lord. And this but one of twenty such bunkers ..." They watched as a group of men rolled a giant spindle of steel blasting net along the dock, where many other such spindles were piled, and Valdus nodded approvingly, especially when he saw Fenris swing his lantern up to inspect the great door winches. The massive winches were vital to opening and closing the Cyclopean rock door which had been dressed to blend with the cliff face on the outside. "So many weeks spent blasting out this largest port yet ... I would hate to see all that work come to naught, sir."

Valdus looked at him sidelong and arched an eyebrow. "You as well, Hirth? A man whom I once watched hijack a barge full of armed sailors by himself, and leave not a one of them standing?" He smiled rakishly. "You disappoint me, comrade."

"My lord, it's just that ..." Hirth turned and nodded at the sun engine. "Well, *look* at it."

Valdus did so, casually. Certainly the ancient machine was intimidating—with its great, gunmetal-gray barrel and its tangles of white-orange hot coils and its exhaust vents like the gills of some monstrous fish and all its cooling ducts and exposed wiring and gauges and readouts—but he did not see it as, how had Hirth put it earlier? "A thing not of this earth." He saw it only as a machine, no different, ultimately, than, say, the paddle wheel of a barge. But then, Shekalane had always said of him that for all his brilliance, there was a blind spot—a place within him where a poet might put words or a painter might put colors, but for him could only be filled with raw data. And what form that data took, she'd said, she couldn't begin to conceptualize. The statement had stung him, even though she'd made it within the context of a compliment to his strategic abilities. It stung him still.

"All I know," he said, pushing the memory from his mind, "is that Lector believes it capable of penetrating the shields of a ferryman's gondola. Which is something we are about to test."

Hirth gazed out over the water. "And the ferryman's raven?"

"I leave that to your bowmen," said Valdus.

"They're passing beneath the *orbis lunae*, my lord." —it was Crith, his second lieutenant.

"Indeed ..." Valdus strode back to the bow gunwale, where the lieutenant was propping himself up by his elbows and peering through binoculars at the River Dire. The man passed the scopes to Valdus, who snatched them eagerly and pressed the eyepieces to his face. "Let us see who our ferryman is transporting," he said.

The gondola swam into focus as he worked the thumbscrew, but because they were positioned at a wide section of the River both the boat and the figures aboard remained small and difficult to assess. Still, the petite form seated on the center bench *could* have been Shekalane—he'd still received no word from the dispatch runner he'd sent to Jaskir—but it was more than likely another woman, or even a small man, from farther upriver, Tanerune, perhaps, or Litz. Otherwise, why would she not have activated the ring?

Lector stepped up beside him. "There remains the problem with the focusing ring, sir. If they are not sufficiently separated, the ferryman and his charge ..."

Valdus lowered the glasses, thinking. "Narrow it as best you can. And hurry. Time is of the essence."

"If she is on that boat, it ... Plasma is not known for its neatness, my lord."

Valdus began to speak but paused, then raised the binoculars again. "You have your orders."

He watched the little boat, and as he did so, he reached down to his belt and triggered the signal for Shekalane to activate the ring. *If she has it,* he thought. For he did not know if his dispatch runner had been able to deliver it to Milkweed or not.

He adjusted the binoculars to focus on the great, iron door across the river, which he knew to be grated on the bottom to allow for the flow of water—one of the *vetitum portas,* the gateways to the Forbidden Channels. Such was the real reason for his insistence on killing a ferryman while the Lucitor's actual soldiers posed the greater threat; for he knew also that the ferryman wore about their necks the key to those very gates—although he had spoken of it to no one, not even Hirth. The power to be gained from accessing those channels, which some believed might provide a back door to the Lucitor's mansion itself, was simply too great to risk it falling into anyone's hands but his own.

I will rescue you if I am able, my love. But the benefit of all Ursathrax must come first. Power to the Revolution.

III / Caveam Cristallum

For a time, there was only her heart beating and the suffocating blackness and the sound of her breaths, which came and went in harsh, ragged bursts, and she feared she might hyperventilate. The hood had the effect of magnifying her awareness of her surroundings, strangely, and thus her terror—the sound of the ferryman's boots thudding against the boards and a sensation of rocking, the sound of something being placed beside her on the cushioned bench, the sound of iron clanking and water slapping against the sides of the boat. And yet there was something else, a vibration, a throbbing as she wrung her hands ...

The ring.

How had he said to activate it? *Press the emerald when you approach the Stygian Flowstones, or on my command, which will manifest as a vibration ...*

Then the hood was snatched off and she gulped the air greedily—as her captor mounted his dais at the back of the gondola and took up his oar, which he used to shove them off.

The raven, meanwhile, had taken roost on a tiny, upraised platform near him. Both were rimmed in dim light from the lantern swinging from the great spiral-like curl that was the boat's stern—a lantern that flickered as the ferryman touched something on his elevated control pad and the air briefly became charged with static electricity, which Shekalane presumed was a result of the shields being activated.

At length the ferryman mumbled something, or perhaps she merely imagined it, and she jolted as her right shackle opened. And, while her left shackle did not—it did seem to loosen somewhat, so it at least no longer dug into her flesh or pressed against her wrist bones so painfully. Then something familiar caught her eye and she looked down to find her veil lying next to her on the crushed red velvet seat, next to which lay her book.

She breathed deeply, her heart rate slowing, as she tried to process what she was seeing. Was this a trick? Was he baiting her with the promise that he was somehow different, a different kind of ferryman, one who understood how terrified his charges must be and who had some measure of empathy—only so he could perform some cruel reversal later and crush her spirit completely?

She dared a glance in his direction and saw him place his oar in the forked bough at his knee and begin rowing them out toward the middle of the river. He did not look at her as he did this but rather gazed up and to the side—at a minor hole in the ceiling of Ursathrax left by a fallen stalactite, which still dribbled sparks—while pushing the oar in great, robust circles, and at a surprisingly rapid clip, even as locks of his long, dark-brown hair, the bulk of which was gathered in a gold band at the back of his neck (the skin of which was ashen blue) alighted on the breeze and fluttered behind him.

From this proximity and without all the smoke—although wisps of fog were everywhere—she could clearly see the slightly distended profile of his death mask, which appeared to be made of thin bronze beneath its chipped and cracked pigment (itself the greenish-blue pallor of the dead) and also a single steely eye, which was recessed amidst the blackened eyelet and whose yellow iris caught the light from the bow lantern and gleamed.

He was like an apparition, and there were at least three things in addition to his mask that she had difficulty looking away from. The first were his arms and shoulders, again, clearly visible now that he'd swept his cloak back, which were enormous for such a tall and otherwise lanky man— especially his dead-blue arms, which were so muscular and ropey and vascular and rough-hewn that he looked as though he had been performing hard labor since the day he was born, and one of which had been branded with the sign of the raven.

The second was his strange clothing and accouterments, nearly all of it black: the cloak with its broad hood and exquisite gold piping, the Mandarin-necked tunic whose collar had been embroidered, also in gold, with what could only be described as a phallus (but with a human skull where the scrotum would be), the rosary of fine bones, like chick bones, around his neck, the great, golden cross with an arrowhead at the bottom which glinted beneath his chest, as well as the leather cummerbund bearing all manner of tiny hooks and lanyards (some of which supported small black spheres which she recognized as being what he'd thrown to the pier to create the smoke-screen) and finally the thick, wide belt with its large, golden buckle and its attachment for the strange weapon which hung heavy at his hip (along with yet another pair of shackles).

It was that weapon that intrigued and terrified her the most, with its great blade that was the same size and shape of the scythe she used to cut down the overgrowth behind her cottage, and yet was forged, or so it seemed, of solid gold, yet a gold with alien highlights, of blue and pink and lapis lazuli. The blade was attached via a serpentine tang to a thick, bronze cylinder about a half-foot long, a cylinder veined with intricate, flowing threads of a strange, bluish alloy she had never before seen. She gathered there was more to the weapon than could be ascertained on first inspection, though why she thought this, she couldn't say.

Perhaps it was the blood-red crystal, which was placed midway along the shaft as though it were a type of switch, and glowed from within with a kind of dark energy that filled her with unease, although, again, she would not have been able to explain why. Still, as much as she hated the Lucitor and his ferrymen—including this one, *especially* this one—she could not help but admire the economy and functionality of such a weapon, as the blade did not extend from the handle but rather lay parallel against it—until activated, that is, as it had been on the dock.

The ferryman turned to face her and she quickly looked away—as if an owl had suddenly focused on her in the dark. Now that they'd reached the trunk of the river, he had relaxed the intensity of his rowing to a more casual pace, and was allowing the current to do most of the work. (She didn't dare risk activating the ring now!) Instead she looked at the floorboards, and after a few moments, remembered the book lying next to her. She reached toward it habitually—but froze when the raven cawed loudly and its red beam fell upon the back of her hand.

A tense moment followed in which she looked from the ferryman to the raven then back again as her fingertips wavered over the golden cover. Then the ferryman motioned with his head, and the raven's light swung away and switched off. She picked up the book slowly and placed it on her lap.

There was a brief gust of wind and all of Ursathrax seemed to moan, and as the sound echoed away down the great cavern she looked up at the Dire Borealis and marveled, as she often had, at its shimmering beauty.

Slowly, she opened the book, and the hologram popped up immediately, like a horizontal green quasar. The voice of Montair, the wise and venerated but little known author, began precisely where it had left off when she'd closed it, the quasar elongating and constricting as he spoke: "I have answered you in full—the crystal cage, the *Caveam Cristallum,* is *you.*"

The ferryman turned his head—but the shadows were such that it was impossible to determine if he was looking at her or not.

"At least insofar as you imagine yourself to be. And the world beyond its bars, or its columns, if you prefer, is *pulchra illusio,* a beautiful illusion. But while I have answered you in full, I have not *questioned* you in full. And my question to you is this: Would you step from your cage—"

The raven squawked harshly and she snapped the book closed. But while she had assumed the hologram had annoyed the creature, she could now see that wasn't the case; rather, the black bird was poking its head this way and that as though it had heard something deep in the fog.

"Sthulhu," said the ferryman. "Scout." Oddly, his voice was not muffled by the mask but rather enriched and given gravitas by some technical means she could not understand.

Sthulhu launched himself into the gloom with a fracas of wings and they floated in silence for several moments. At last the ferryman said, quietly, as though he were speaking to himself, "'Would you step from your cage if you knew the door was ajar?'"

IV | View to a Kill

"My lord, the charge is complete."

Valdus looked up from his map table and smiled. "You see? And we are still here—with our limbs included. You worry too much, old friend. And the focusing of the beam?"

"I have adjusted the apex angles of the prisms so that the wave front should converge on the ferryman alone," said Lector. "But I must warn you, sire. The plasma core is only marginally stable; should any single constant become variable once the weapon is fired ... the results could be catastrophic—especially if the shields of the gondola create a mirror effect."

"There will be no mirror effect," said Valdus. "Lieutenant Crith, how long until they are out of range?"

Crith ground his binoculars. "They are moving slower than anticipated, my lord, although at this distance it's impossible to say why. Regardless, I'd estimate no more than five minutes."

Valdus expressed his satisfaction by placing his hands on his hips and exhaling. "We're ahead of schedule. You've done well, Lector." He moved around to the chair built into the side of the sun engine. "I'll sight the target myself. General Hirth, prepare your boarding party."

"Be advised, my lord," said Lector, "that I have not yet re-slaved the trigger mechanism to the sighting device ..."

"Then I trust you'll trigger it from your control panel precisely on my word. Watch me closely."

He settled into the chair and pressed his forehead against the sighting scope, activating the lead-measuring and rangefinder scales. "Everyone don your goggles. Men with no eyes make poor soldiers."

He worked the controls of the turret until the tiny boat slid into view, then zoomed in as close as he could on the ferryman's head, which remained hardly larger than an apple seed, before scanning right to the passenger.

Is it you, my elven-faced nursemaid and most preferred port of call? Why do you not activate? You should not assume I can see you, if that's the case. But then you have always assumed me to be perfect and infallible, not so much a man but a slab of granite for you to push yourself against. If only you knew to what lengths I have gone to ensure the success of the revolution, the lengths I intend to go.

He re-focused on the ferryman. *And you, Taker. Today I take from you. First, I will take your head clean from your body. And then I will take your gold-plated key ...*

A raven called from somewhere in the gloom, and he pushed the thoughts from his mind. "Lieutenant Crith, see to it that Hirth has assigned archers to monitor the mists." He ground his brow against the sighting scope. "If it flies, kill it."

"Yes, my lord."

"Today, my friends, we make history once again. Long live the Revolution!" He narrowed the sights on the ferryman's head. "Prepare to fire."

V | Dialogue

Shekalane looked up from the book, which she had been about to reactivate, opening her mouth to speak, but hesitated. The truth was that she was speechless. At last, she managed, "'And if, finding that the illusion outside also had a door ... would you seek to step through that as well?'"

The ferryman dipped his oar in and out of the black water. Finally, he said, "Montair ... I've hidden several copies of his works in the walls of the barracks ... but the *Caveam Cristallum* is the one I keep close at hand, always. At least while at home. We are not allowed such books, of course. But it's a risk I am happy to take."

Again she moved to speak but hesitated. Was this a dream? Had she consumed the wrong kind of mushrooms with her last meal so that now she fancied herself capable of communion with ferrymen as well as rocks and trees? Ferrymen who slept in barracks instead of the opulent villas everyone knew them to live in?

"I find that difficult to credit a high servant of the Lucitor," she said at some length. "Surely your indoctrination began at a very young age ..."

His oar splashed gently in the water. "Before being chosen to serve, madam, I spent part of my life as a civilian, just as you. My mother introduced me to his children's fables as a boy, and I moved onto his philosophical works as I matured."

She shook her head. "But it is so incongruous. May it surprise you to know that the priests would have us believe you are undead men created by alchemy ...?" She smiled wanly. "And while I have taught my students to reject such superstition, I cannot believe you are simply chosen by Lottery the same as everyone else."

"We have felt the black coin in our palms, madam, I assure you, most of us at a tender age. I was fortunate to be taken at thirteen by Asmodeus himself, then a young ferryman, after which I knew my parents no more."

She stared at him intensely as a chill crept up her spine. "But ... your eyes. Your *skin* ..." She tried to look away from him but found she could not.

"The result of ritalimortis injection after becoming a brownie." He turned to face her. "A ferryman's apprentice. It ...

41

has many effects, some intended and some not. All of them serve to alienate you from, and to intimidate, others."

Again she felt as though she had entered a dream. Her eyes were fogged over with it. "May I ask ... there's a reason. How old are you, ferryman? And do you have a name? A birth name, I mean?"

The ferryman faced forward, pushing his oar. "You must understand, madam, that we will not be able to continue this conversation once Sthulhu returns. Your veil, too, will have to be replaced before we become visible to others."

Shekalane looked at the floorboards. "I understand." She looked up at him. "It's just that ... my son. He was chosen at about the same age."

He rowed for a moment before turning to look at her. "I am thirty-four years old. And my name is Dravidian."

She felt a rush of relief, but was uncertain why. "I am Shek—"

"Madam, please." He pressed the grip of the oar during the return-stroke in such a way that the muscles of his arms seem to ripple, and it occurred to her that maneuvering such a boat to ensure it stayed on course was no simple task, but rather a delicate process requiring great strength and stamina, but also technique, style and experience. "It is no easy role, that of ferryman," he continued. "I do not wish to know those I escort to their fates. I dare not, for my own survival. No one goes willingly, not at heart, and if I were to see them as individuals—"

"You would know my name," she interrupted. "Or you wouldn't have sent Sthulhu away or quoted Montair."

He completed the return-stroke then pushed forward again, seeming to consider this. "I would know it, madam."

"I am Shekalane," she said. "I was a teacher ... before being handed the black coin. Now I don't know what I'll be. Dead, perhaps." She laughed a little. "We shall look just alike."

The ferryman drew on his oar and said nothing—but her intuition told her he was withholding something. Again the dream-like feeling stole over her, and she said, with a rush of realization, "You know—don't you? You know how it is I've been selected to serve ..."

He pushed forward on his oar and drew it back. At last, he said, "We are sometimes given special instructions for the handling of a charge. You are to be unharmed, or, if force is required, no marks are to be left upon your person. Based on this, I suspect that you shall want for nothing; and that you are not destined for either of the Twin Houses."

Shekalane looked at him a moment longer, then out over the gloomy river, turning this over in her mind, somehow knowing what it meant but not fully prepared to accept it. Being twenty-nine years of age, she had prayed to be spared indoctrination into the demidaines—the "brides" of the Lucitor. She began to speak but paused, having noticed a great structure materialize out of the fog—a door, of sorts, fully one quarter as high as the ceiling of Ursathrax itself. "Dravidian ... what is that?"

He followed her gaze to where the Cyclopean door was coming into view off the port bow. "One of the *vetitum portas,* surely you have heard of them. They are the entry points to the Forbidden Channels."

She suddenly recalled Valdus' note: *Watch the gateways to the Forbidden Channels.* This she did, peering at the willowed delta around the door and seeking for any sign of activity. *The emerald in this ring is a homing beacon ... you will know what to do.* But in fact she did not know what to do, other than to keep

Dravidian engaged, and thus distracted. Nor did she did activate the ring, although she could have done so easily. *The ferryman is already dead ...*

She pushed the thought from her mind.

"I don't believe in the Lucitor's religion," she said at length, referring to Dravidian's words regarding the Twin Houses. She glanced at him sidelong. "Sacrilege, he thinks. Blaspheming His great and terrible name like that."

To her surprise, Dravidian didn't say anything, just continued to row.

"Well, I don't. I remember a trip a friend took to the end of Ursathrax when I was a child—part of her indoctrination into the Sisterhood of Trappers. They travelled there on a big riverboat, like the kind you ferrymen use to tow your gondolas upriver. She was taken through the Tunnels of Light and Darkness, and given sweet things to eat at tunnel's end by the priests and priestesses. They lectured her on the Unholy Tabernacle, about how the faithful would enter the House of Peace, and it would look like the Tunnel of Light, only a thousand times more beautiful. Then they told her how the unfaithful would be put to pain in the House of Torment, which would look like the Tunnel of Darkness but a thousand times more horrible. And there they would suffer. Not just for the rest of their lives but for all eternity."

Something glinted in the shallows near the door and her eyes darted to it, but it was just water glistening on the back of a duck.

Shekalane laughed. "My friend didn't buy it then, and I don't buy it now. Even the sight of the Twin Houses themselves was not enough to convince her. They seemed fake to her, like mere facades."

Dravidian shook his head. "The House of Torment is real, Shekalane. I have stood in my boat outside its gates and listened to the cries of the Damned."

"But you have not been inside it," she said.

"No."

There was a brief silence. After a time she said, "Did you know there are some who believe the Lucitor to be dead?"

He turned to look at her sharply—disapprovingly, it seemed, although that may only have been her imagination, then slowly looked away.

"Others say he lives on as a great *computatrum* grown sentient. Do you know what that is? A *computatrum?*"

"No. Although it would seem to indicate a person, or, since you mention the development of sentience, a thing, that performs computations."

"That is correct. Still others say that He is human but has learned the secret to immortality, and that it has driven Him mad. They believe He established the Lottery hundreds of years ago to curb over-population, but that it has long since outlived its usefulness toward that end, and only goes on because He has forgotten what it was for, only that it was necessary."

"I'm afraid you confuse folk tales with serious conjecture, madam."

"Few folk tales begin as folk tales, Dravidian. Behind these, I suspect, lies a kernel of truth. How else would they grow? These are not imaginative times. And tell me, who but a madman would orchestrate the kind of grim pageantry represented by you ferrymen?"

His oar creaked as he worked it, as did his black leather gloves, which were laced to the elbows. "Who but a madman, indeed."

She looked at him and felt a sudden blush of conflicting emotions, as well as an unwelcome sense of nostalgia—most of which manifested as imagery: her son turning to look at her one final time before stepping into the smoke, little Lat showing up with not a friend or family in the world, Dravidian himself as a boy, with a shock of brown hair and rosy-red skin, perhaps turning to look at his own mother—before vanishing forever into the void. And something dissolved inside her, just melted away, not her anger and hatred for the Lucitor and His Lottery, but for this individual man, whom she now realized was as much a victim as anyone, even more so because he had been turned into a focal point for everyone's pain and outrage.

This beautifully-formed, ropey-limbed living-dead man with a headful of Montair, like little Lat all grown up ...

"What are the brides like, Dravidian? Are they happy? Are they sad?"

"They want for nothing, as I've said." He turned his head briefly to study her before refocusing on the river ahead. "I, too, saw being chosen as a curse in the beginning. But it is—you're aware of how Montair put it. A black hole which becomes a white fountain. You will emerge as something new."

"Once ... it is done ... I wonder ... will we ever see each other again?"

He shook his head. "Not like this, Shekalane."

And then everything turned white, and the world was split in two.

VI | Explosion

"Now," said Valdus.

And before there was even a sound, there was *light*. Not a light such as the kind created by a lantern, nor the green-white light—so harsh and so harmless—of a hologram, nor even the dazzling, yellow fire of a fully-functioning sun orb (of which so few remained); rather, this was a light that cancelled the world, a light so complete that it annihilated every color, line, and form, and for a fleeting moment matter itself seemed to cease to exist.

Then it quickly faded and the sound came—a sound like a thousand shields being activated all at once, a sound that crackled and vibrated and caused the glass in the lanterns and the porthole windows to rattle and clink into fine fractures—accompanied by a pulsing, flickering, ragged-edged blue beam, which didn't narrow as it grazed the ferryman's boat (first catching it on fire and then causing it to explode) but punched straight through into the opposite wall of the world, where it met enough resistance that most of its plasma fuel was depleted before something caused it to refract back, but at a fraction of its power, so that the sun engine was blown to pieces and the porthole windows shattered and Valdus and his men were thrown into the air.

They landed hard upon their backs, having been flipped like ragdolls by the blast, first Gurn, his head bloodied by shrapnel, then old Lector, who immediately curled into a ball, and finally Valdus, who was disoriented for mere seconds before he patted himself down to ensure he wasn't wounded and sprung to his feet.

"Water!" he cried, shielding his face from the flames of the sun engine's gutted wreckage. "All hands—quickly!"

He hurried to the bow gunwale as the others came running and quickly untangled his binoculars, then peered through them at the gondola's burning ruins. There was no indication of survivors; indeed, there was no indication of anyone on board at all. "Bloody hell," he cursed. "Someone find General Hirth. Tell him—"

"Here, my lord." He was standing in a skiff off the port bow, along with two other men. All of them were heavily armed.

"I shall accompany you," said Valdus, but paused before vaulting over the gunwale, turning to look at Lector, who was still curled into a ball and trembling noticeably. He rushed to him.

"Lector, my old friend, how grave is it ...?" He rolled him over. And, although he appeared to have sustained only minor injuries, cuts and bruises by the look of it, the elderly man's eyes were vacant and shell-shocked. No, it was more than that, they were the eyes of a man who had lost faith in the very ground beneath him, indeed, reality itself. They were the eyes of a man who had suffered a thousand cuts and bruises over the course of a long life, and survived them all, only to have been broken all in an instant.

"Someone see to him," said Valdus, then stood and hurried to the gunwale. "The Revolution cannot succeed without him."

And they shoved off toward the wreckage.

VII | Dravidian Before

Although they hadn't yet gained the top of the stairs, Dravidian could already see the feeding frenzy taking place outside the narrow door: the chaotic vortex of color as the little elfemales— who had come, as always, in response to the recorded mating call—flocked to avoid the hungry black shapes that darted in and out amongst them.

"Hurry, Dravidian, or we'll miss the feeding of the ravens entirely," said Pepperlung.

They burst out onto the foredeck of the dragger and took the scene in as it swirled around them, Pepperlung laughing and spinning in time while Dravidian stood calmly and observed the maelstrom. These ignudi were slightly smaller than those he'd seen baited elsewhere in the world, the spread of their delicate wings measuring no more than two hand lengths, if that. But what they lacked in size they just as surely made up for in the diversity of their coloring, for never before had he seen such lovely combinations of oyster and indigo, of apricot and rouge, of lampblack and lilac and lapis lazuli—all spun entwined between soft wings and nude bodies like swirling dyes in a textile maker's kettle.

Yet even among all that fluttering, exquisitely paired color, there was one flitting sprite that stood out from the rest for her very simplicity, for she was solid green from tapered head to cusped toe, as well as from wingtip to wingtip. And she seemed as drawn to Dravidian as he was to her, because she fluttered close and brushed herself against his mask, trilling and purring softly—before being snatched away by the beak of a raven, the violence of which caused the lenses of his facade to be dotted with blood.

After that, he saw only the beating black wings of the ravens, for they outnumbered the elfmales greatly now, and as he titled his head to watch them spiral, a fierce red blur entered his vision and he refocused to see Prefect Asmodeus standing at the rail of the superstructure in his scarlet cloak and mask, and with him the Bride Observer everyone had been talking about, who's yellow eyes looked down upon him through her black veil with serpentine indifference.

"Look at her, Dravidian," said Pepperlung, stepping close enough to rub shoulders. "She was chosen at a young age, you can tell ... and she wears it like a queen. I've never seen the likes of her."

Dravidian pressed the pads at his temple, loosening his mask with a little hiss of air, then took it in his hands and began cleaning its lenses, using a cloth from his hip, studying her as he did so.

She was dressed in semi-translucent clothes which seemed to suggest many shades of black all at once. The diverse garments were moved to whisper about her body by a gentle breeze, yet were cut and tailored in such areas as to conform tightly and highlight the finer aspects of her femininity. There were slits, for example, cut into the fabric at her thighs, which ran from her waistline to her knees and revealed blue-gray skin like polished river rock. How oddly statuesque she was!—especially compared to Asmodeus, who stood fully a head shorter and was bent slightly from age—as well as voluptuous. Her presence was like a column of black smoke which rose curling and twisting from the superstructure platform to what would have been Dravidian's height had he stood directly beside her. And yet her eyes seemed dead, and not just because of injection-induced ritalimortis. They were animal eyes, a doll's eyes, serpentine not because they were cold—which would have at least implied sentience—but because they were inhuman. Because they could see, but not gaze.

She said something casually to Asmodeus and he cocked an ear toward her before looking at them and saying something back.

Dravidian placed an arm on Pepperlung's shoulder and turned them to face the gondola davits. "I wouldn't stare too long, my friend. Besides, we have boats to prepare ..."

Pepperlung shoved against him good-naturedly, causing him to lose his balance and nearly fall. "Oh, I see. Now that you're about to be elevated to Master you're too good for mess hall talk." He laughed. "I shall have to tell the demidaines that you will no longer be accompanying us!"

Dravidian chuckled and looked at his boat—which, thanks to the skill of its builder, seemed to have more of a personality than the bride above. Indeed, it appeared almost to brood as it lay in its harness, the ferro on its prow stabbing at the ceiling of the world like a knife, its six bars for the six regions of Ursathrax lying under that like the teeth of a comb, its oily-black hull catching the light of the local Orb (now in Moonphase) and spreading it thin along its length, causing its gold trim to gleam.

"I'll miss them," he said, expanding his gaze to the other ships. "You get to know them like people over the years. Each with their own quirks and eccentricities." He turned to Pepperlung. "And I'll miss you, old friend. We'll still see each other at the Taberna, of course. And, yes, occasionally at the demidaines. But I'll have a reputation to maintain, as I'm sure you'll understand ..." He winked and grinned.

Pepperlung reached up and pressed the release pads of his own mask, then swung it around to his back. He forced himself to smile and said, "But it won't be the same." He inhaled and exhaled deeply. "I never thought this day would come. Take care of yourself, my friend." He glanced over his shoulder at the prefect and his tone became grave: "Beware, Dravidian. The bride is just sightseeing but Asmodeus is here for you. You are the only ferryman up for elevation this year. Watch yourself. There will be a test, surely." He put on a show for the prefect and the Lucitor's bride by shouting louder than necessary, "Your last run as a journeyman! Next time I see you, I shall have to call you Master Dravidian!" He clasped Dravidian's shoulder. "It's been an honor serving with you."

Dravidian returned the gesture. "And you as well, my brother. Black hole, white fountain. What dies only continues as something different." He turned his attention to the brownies running helter-skelter up and down the deck and singled two of them out. "You there, plug the drain and man the frapping lines."

"Something from one of your books?" said Pepperlung.

Dravidian paused with one boot on the gunwale and turned to face him. "You knew?"

Pepperlung grinned. *"Everyone* knew. You're not a very good liar, Dravidian. I'll be sure to keep them safe until you are able to fetch them."

Dravidian smiled with his eyes and saluted him, then placed the mask to his face and pressed the pads with his thumbs, sealing it, before raising his hood. "Release the monkey lines," he said, his voice transformed, and gripped the nearest one as it fell.

"Lines untied and grunts released!" called down a brownie.

"Proceed," said Dravidian—which was followed by the final hooks being disengaged and the gondola beginning to lower.

He continued to stare up at Pepperlung as the boat seesawed toward the water, although it was difficult to tell if he was looking back or not because of the climbing-net between them and the bright spotlights which rendered him a silhouette. He looked every bit a man in a cage standing there, and yet his boat awaited in which, for a brief time, he could be free, and Dravidian wondered, as the shadows of the climbing-net crept over his own mask and cloak, what it was going to be like to be a ferryman but no longer a gondolier; what effect would living in a tunnel of administrative work have upon a person? A final glimpse of bent-backed Asmodeus just before he disappeared behind the gunwale spoke of everything he feared.

He had little time to dwell on it, however, as Skylla and Sthenios were already there—greeting him eagerly by poking their slick, shiny muzzles over the gondola's gunwales the instant he touched down on the water and playfully demanding to be fed. He shoveled some chum at them from the little bucket hanging from his control panel and activated the shield, which didn't affect them because they were already within its radius and it didn't reflect slow-moving or low-impact objects, regardless. In truth, although he'd ordered the brownies to ensure there was chum onboard just in case, he hadn't really expected to see his adopted friends this time of the year, for it was known the hydrippoi migrated downriver during the autumn months only to mysteriously reemerge at the Great Falls and thus the beginning of Ursathrax in the spring.

He watched them jerk their heads back to swallow the salmon then excitedly ask for more, but instead took up the polished oar from its rack on the starboard gunwale and examined its blade. Then, finding it sanded and re-glazed to perfection, he looked up at the dragger and saw Zaluther watching him eagerly from a climbing-net. He saluted the brownie sharply and made a note to recommend him for advancement at first opportunity; then, as the youth beamed and waved, he released the final hooks from his control pad, shoved off with the blunt end of the oar, and placed its shaft into the oiled forcola at his dais.

And then he was floating free in a wide gap between river clouds, a gust of wind causing his cloak to crackle, rowing with powerful strokes toward the shore as the great foghorn sounded for the first time, frightening the hydrippoi away but only for a brief time, he knew. And all he could think about was how good it felt to be back on the River Dire instead of cooped up in a clammy barracks, to have the wind at his back (or his side, as it were), and to see the river birds reel and the clouds race above and the Orb seem to fade in and out as the brumes passed. He noticed several ignudi traps floating nearby and a wry smile touched his lips as he thought of how even now some lovelorn Jaskirians were using the dust harvested from the creatures' wings to enhance their passion and sexual prowess.

That's when one of the hydrippoi suddenly breached off the port bow, splashing him with water, followed immediately by the other doing the same thing off the starboard. He laughed and increased his pace, liking the power he felt in his own limbs, swishing the blade of the oar in a broad circle and rotating it ever so slightly on the return stroke so that its tip never fully left the water, watching the hydrippoi cruise and cross each other's paths just beneath the surface before taking turns once again to breach the froth, but this time angling their jumps so that they crested against the shields and bounced off with a sizzling pop, again and again until one of them crested all the way to the top of the field and just hovered there, seeming to fly in tandem with the boat until it slid moistly back into the swirling water. Until at last the foghorn sounded again, louder this time, as those on shore still had not ignited the guiding torches, and the horse eels peeled away as he entered a great river cloud, which he navigated blindly until the blue-red torches lit up in the gloom, and when he emerged from the miasma he saw the sacrificial peer glowing in the night, and he saw, too, a lonely figure standing at the bottom of the wide steps at river's edge, a figure so lithe it might have been a child, dressed all in green rags and a shawl, with a makeshift veil over her face, and a countenance which, after he pressed a pad near his temple and caused the lenses in his mask to zoom, he saw to be the most profoundly human mixture of dignity and fear he had ever seen.

VIII | Dream

"Once ... it is done ... I wonder ... will we ever see each other again?"

He shook his head. "Not like this, Shekalane."

And then everything had turned white, and the world had split in two.

Now she was elsewhere. And yet she recognized her surroundings immediately—nothing had changed save the season (it was spring). She was home, and in the beginning everything was as it should be: There was the sand and the sky (for Jaskir Minor was fortunate to have a section of sky, although great portions of it had collapsed) and the world was just as she had known it. There was the giant ferryman statue on its pedestal with its grim, masked visage and mysterious weapon; and there was the cyclopean architectural ruin with its cracked columns and creeping vines (and, atop that, the pediment she had observed since she was a child, with its scenes both sacred and profane carved in deep relief). There was also the words whose meaning she had puzzled over for so many years, spelled out in those towering letters of stone: CASINO MAXIMUS. And there were her footprints in the sand and her cottage in the twilit distance.

But there was also an aberration, an intruding element—a blurred shape against the dark water. An aberration that sank and climbed and bobbed amidst the current until it bounced off a basalt formation and headed for the land, and its true form was revealed to her in a sudden flash—a boat, or rather the wreckage of one, entirely green, ruined but somehow still intact, a thing both familiar and alien. And as it glided ashore and tipped over amidst the foam, it deposited there yet one more thing, one more aberration, which tumbled from its belly and lay unmoving on the sand.

That thing was a man.

And when she rushed to him, dropping to her knees in the sand and froth and rolling his short but muscular body upon its back, she saw with a pounding heart that, not only was he alive, but that he was a man unlike any other she had encountered since her husband had gone into the sacrificial smoke so many years before, never to return. Moreover, it was a man she recognized instantly from posters put up all over Jaskir—a man wanted for treason and for attacks against the Lucitor, but also by the women who happened upon his picture. A man whom she would come to know intimately but did not know yet in this elsewhere and elsewhen in which memory and dream coalesced like lovers in rain.

It was Valdus himself, the Prince of the Revolution.

Nor—after the initial thrill had passed—was she particularly surprised. A battle had reportedly taken place not far from the Twin Houses just two days prior and had been the talk of the village ever since. What *did* surprise her was her heart rate: her world, after all, had been barren since her son, too, had walked into the smoke. It was amazing to her that she could feel anything at all, much less her heart beating against her thin shirt. Had she thought, even for an instant, that anything new could come into it ....

She moved the hair gently from his closed eyes as she thought about it: No, not barren in the traditional sense. Indeed, her world itself had become beautiful again; the twilit purple sky and red-orange clouds and circling river birds were proof of that, as was the green and flourishing forest behind her cabin. Indeed, the world was more fertile than it had ever been.

It was barren only of a man.

She fumbled with the rawhide strap at his neck, tracing her fingers along it until they came to something jumbled amidst his cloak. It was an exquisite golden timepiece; one that, now that she thought about it, she had heard and sensed ticking long before she had physically seen or felt it. The handle of the great blade hooked to his belt was of the same exquisite craftsmanship, and something about the timepiece and the weapon caused her to peer skyward at the great statue, and turning the timepiece in her hands, she realized that the unconscious man lying beneath her and the gargantuan idol looming above were of precisely the same likeness.

For Valdus, Prince of the Revolution, had become the ferryman, Dravidian.

That's when he jerked suddenly, violently, enough that she nearly leapt to her feet, and began coughing up brackish water through the little grill that was the only mouth opening of his mask. The fit lasted barely a moment, after which she heard him struggling to form words—which became the repetition of a single word, "Shekalane."

And, fearing that he truly was dying, she pressed her flushed cheek furiously against his own, pleading, urgently but gently, "Stay with me."

"To the end of Ursathrax," she heard him mutter, his eyes still closed. And then he was unconsciousness yet again.

The door to her room groaned as she eased it open. It appeared to her that he had not moved at all since she had put him to bed; he still lay on his back on the wide, deep mattress, the blankets folded neatly back at his waist. Nor did he appear troubled as he had on the river bank; indeed, he seemed almost to be in a state of meditation. And so she crept forward delicately, not really understanding why she needed to be close to him, nor why she was repulsed by him and drawn to him all at once, or how it was that he somehow both terrified her and put her at ease, or how he could be death, indeed, and yet, somehow—for her—life. The gold timepiece, which she had hung from the kerosene lantern on her dresser next to the rest of his accoutrements, ticked softly as she moved.

She drew open the curtains and panes as she approached the bed, letting in cool air from the river as well as a distant rumbling, the source of which she could not identify, then stooped over his head, her hair hanging in his mask as she examined his own hair, which had yet to dry completely and was the color of acorns in the rain. She cocked her head, struck by the fearful symmetry of that mask, which was wholly different from the kind she had seen in pictures or at festive cotillions (she'd slid a hand under his head earlier to where the mask was tied with a leather thong and pulled one of the ends, but while the thong was loosened the mask was not; indeed, it would not come free even when she tugged upon it gently). Nor was it light and cheaply-made as such facades invariably were, but rather solid and expertly crafted, and when she ran her fingers along its edge she could both see and feel that it was lined in crushed velvet the color of blood.

She took special notice of the maroon diamond at the center of his forehead, which wasn't really a diamond but rather the shape one would expect if they were to draw lines connecting the tips of an inverted cross. Nor was it part of his mask; rather, the mask was designed to highlight it. She could not tell merely by looking at it if it were painted on or some form of tattoo, nor could she resist touching it, albeit softly, and decided that, indeed, it was some form of tattoo. And it was beautiful; he was beautiful, from the crown of his head to his hard, sinewy abdomen. But what the rest of him looked like she could only guess, for the blanket was there and she had not even tried to remove his trousers, which were quite rugged and had been sopping wet just a short time before.

The timepiece ticked and the rumbling intensified as she touched her fingers gently to his hair and twirled a lock between her fingers, marveling at its health and vitality. Such a contrast to the deathly pallor of his skin! She ran the silky lock through her fingers until it fell free, then lightly brushed the back of her hand against the cheek of his blue-gray mask.

He did not stir, only continued breathing in a slow, steady fashion. Emboldened a little by this, she traced around his mouth grill ever so slightly, then, emboldened still further, she allowed her fingers to follow the contour of his chin, which was sharp and almost feminine, and yet, like everything else about him, oddly robust, then down his neck, which seemed long to her for a man, as though he were a member of some race not entirely human.

Her focus shifted to the large raven tattooed upon his right shoulder. As with everything else associated with the stranger (for he was a stranger even though she knew his name), it was of exquisite craftsmanship and artistry, and she wondered now if perhaps her assumption that it was a kind of brand had been incorrect. Perhaps it was personal and unique to him alone, an expression of brotherly love toward his raven, Sthulhu, perhaps? If such was the case she found it endearing, to say the least. Just who was this tall, whipcord of a man, really? Was he singular and unique, the only ferryman to ever cultivate his own persona apart from his order? Or were there others just like him, an entire race of elven dead-men, all of them oddly regal, and yet foreboding, too?

She looked down to find herself toying with the hair of his chest, and immediately stopped, all the while peering at the Orb-lit water outside the window, and at the mysterious, rumbling fountain which had been there all along—but whose presence she only now internalized—a white fountain, a chaos of river water and foam, as though a giant were beneath the currents and blowing through an equally Cyclopean bamboo shoot. And she supposed it was time to ask herself, or at least admit that the question was a reasonable one: Was this all a dream? And if so, how long had she dreamed? Had she dreamed only since the world had gone white and split in two? Or had the ceremony itself been a dream? Her receiving of the black coin a dream? Her loss of both little Sihadi and big Stachtyr a dream?

She turned to the dresser upon which she had lain out his strange clothing and accouterments and saw through the window reflected in its mirror that the stars had winked on one by one and that the Orb, now purple as a Vampire rose, was beginning to take on the deep blue aura which blanketed Jaskir when the night fell; for the Orb's dark-half, the moon, did not rise in Ursathrax—it awakened.

She, of course, would take to the tattered couch next to the long, low tea table in the living room, but first she took a moment to examine his things by the candlelight, reaching first for the bronze-colored hilt of his weapon. She ran a finger along the device as she studied it, starting at the purplish tip of the blade and sliding it just above the deadly-looking edge before switching to the shaft itself and tracing around the sinewy blue lines until she came to the blood-red crystal, or whatever it was, which seemed to stare back at her like an evil eye, penetratingly, unblinking. She circled the crystal gently, round and round, first one direction, than the other, before delicately touching the gemstone itself, which she rubbed ever so slightly, until the device hummed suddenly and the crystal turned green and the great, golden blade swung out with a ringing of steel and a flash of reflected light.

She leapt back instinctively, startled, her heart suddenly pounding. When at last she had collected her breath, she inched forward once again, noticing how the tip of the blade had, such was its sharpness, sliced into the satchel beneath it upon opening, revealing a blood-red interior that was becoming a pattern among the strange man's accouterments. And she noticed one thing more—the golden corner of something inside the satchel, something she immediately wanted to touch and to slide out and to examine, but that, considering what had just happened with the weapon, wasn't sure if she should dare.

But she did dare. She dared so quickly it astonished her, closing her thumb and forefinger on the thing's hard, cold edge and withdrawing it quickly, so quickly that she was turning it in both her hands within seconds, feeling its embossed metallic texture, which was sumptuous beyond belief, and toying with the golden ribbons that served as a bookmarks. For that's precisely what this new thing was: a book, the *Caveam Cristallum*. And before she knew it she had opened it to one of his marks and the green-white quasar had popped up and the voice of Montair said, "Would you step from your cage if you knew the door was ajar?"

She shut it immediately, her heart suddenly racing, pressing her hand upon its cover as though the book had a will and sentience of its own and would fly open and consume her if she allowed it. That's when something glinted and she saw Dravidian sit up in the bed behind her, turning his head to face her, his eyes catching the emerald light from the kerosene lantern and reflecting it back.

She froze and focused on the cover of the book, which depicted a cage with its door hanging open, and her heart pounded.

She refocused on Dravidian as a gentle gust of wind caused the curtains to fly and the candles on the dresser to sputter, but he only stood there now in the dark, his mask an indistinct blur—a pale and greenish-blue shape which was eerily stoic. At last he moved toward her, silently, seeming almost to float, until he stood directly behind her, then placed his right hand gently upon her shoulder.

She turned her head to look up at him slowly, meeting his gaze with her own, and was struck by the queer contradiction in his eyes, for his was a gaze both confident and surprisingly vulnerable, no less so than her own, and still it was undeniably masculine, a thing youthful yet experienced, a thing as consistent and grave and implacable as it was beautiful.

He slowly reached for the corner of the book with his left hand, breaking eye contact only long enough to choose a mark—but she pressed down harder as he tried to do it. He paused and gazed into her eyes, coolly but warmly, infinitely patient, and she found herself falling into them just as surely as she had ever fallen in her life, and gradually relented as he gently turned the page and candlelight fell across the surface and the quasar hologram popped up before them.

"And if," said Montair, "finding that the illusion outside also had a door ... would you seek to step through that as well?"

She looked at him tentatively, expectantly, then turned the pages herself until she found what she was looking for and the shape of the quasar changed.

"*Synergique vrai amour,*" said Montair, "your true synergistic love—the one who opens all doors."

She looked at him expectantly.

Again, he broke eye contact just long enough to find his mark, then turned the pages once more, to where the chapters were separated by a musical interlude—an orchestral arrangement Shekalane immediately recognized as "Lovers Lost," perhaps the most romantic composition ever to be conceived, and yet one so few were even aware of. He turned her gently to face the window and the White Fountain.

"Do you know what it is?" he said at last.

She studied it, nodding slowly. "I think so. It's a doorway, of sorts. It's what awaits on the other side of death."

Dravidian nodded. "It is what Montair speaks of. Not death—but transition. For what winks out in one place winks on in another, always." He stared at the fountain, his eyes seeming to dream. "If I were to step through that door ..." He turned to face her. "Would you come with me?"

She looked at him longingly—at his fearsome mask—but hesitated. She trusted him, and yet, was this not how death would come? As a whispering seduction?

"I don't know yet," she said.

There was a soft hiss as he depressed the pad at his temple and swung the mask around to his back, then moved his lips to within a few centimeters of her own and paused, breathing slowly, seeming to draw her own breaths from her. "But you would consider it ..."

"But, Dravidian, where would we go? How would we survive?"

He cupped her face in his hands. And though he was too close for her to see his face clearly, his beautiful eyes with their golden irises and Stygian pupils drew her in inexorably, like black holes with golden linings, if such a thing were even possible, and she whispered, "I would step through it ..."

He took her in his arms and drew her slowly against him. "And would you find the strength within yourself to persevere even when the world turns its cold face against us?"

"Yes," she rasped.

"Then run with me, Shekalane. To the end of Ursathrax and beyond ..." And he gently but firmly locked his lips with her own.

She sighed and squeezed her eyes shut, marveling that his dead-blue lips should be so warm while Valdus', which were always so full of blood and life, had nonetheless been cold. Then, as he continued to draw her into him, she swooned, and her legs began to tremble.

Indeed, it was almost as if by opening the book she had opened herself—as though everything in her life had led to precisely this moment, and she was shocked to feel a tingling in her groin she had not felt since before Valdus had vanished into the southern woods, since that last time so many months hence that he had loved her, wrecked her, really.

And she said, "Show me the white fountain, Dravidian," as all thoughts of Valdus vanished and Dravidian scooped her up in his arms and carried her to the bed.

The timepiece ticked—not so much in her ear but in her mind and her very breast—as he lay her upon the bed, and the White Fountain rumbled. It was a personal eccentricity that she found the sensation of her own pulse loathsome—thus she avoided feeling it whenever possible—but she could no more escape it now than she could escape her own desire as he probed her mouth with his tongue and combed through her hair with his free hand and butted her lips with his own before brushing them over her chin and down the slope of her neck—his breath tickling her skin—at which point he sealed them about her own with precisely the right amount of pressure and caused her to moan.

Oh, Dravidian ... you have been alone but you have not been lonely, it is clear.

She gripped the bed posts and arched her back as he kissed down the length of her neck, unsure if she could withstand what was coming. She'd always been sensitive—her small breasts especially—what would she do when he—

She moaned and bit her lower lip as he puckered his lips back and forth along her collarbones—nudging the green straps of the dress off her shoulders—then down her solar plexus and between her small breasts, pulling the dress down with his chin—where he sucked gently, creating a seal. And then he was moving again, kissing his way up one of the slopes and dabbing her nipple with his tongue and swirling it around the areola—once, twice, a third time, after which he nibbled and bit softly while sliding a large and calloused hand up her thigh and in and out of her waist and up the side of her chest (pushing the flimsy sundress up as he went so that it gathered in a bunch about her abdomen) and wrapping his long, dead-blue fingers around the entirety of one breast, which he squeezed gently but firmly before closing his lips about the nipple.

She cried out briefly before stopping herself and looked down at him as he drew on her, at his bluish-green flesh pressed against her own—which, although pale (as was most everyone's in Ursathrax), was nonetheless pink with life, and returning her focus to the curtains blowing above the headboard, was struck by the surreal nature of it all, and a quote from childhood came unbidden to her mind: "Is all that we see or seem but a dream within a dream?"

And suddenly it seemed she *was* dreaming within a dream (for she was convinced now that's what this was), and she realized that while she was laid out upon the emerald sheets like a fine musical instrument in Dravidian's artful hands, she was also fifteen and swinging upon her swing near her mother's laundry line, the Orb-dappled clothes flapping like veils all around her, and the sunset-painted River Dire flowing red as menstrual blood nearby.

And as the White Fountain rumbled and the timepiece ticked and the curtains billowed in the first world, and the wood and rope of the swing creaked back and forth in the second, Dravidian moved from her excited nipples to her arched abdomen, and, placing his hands on either side of her stomach, began kissing it as passionately as he had her breasts, causing her to groan, even growl slightly, and to arch her back still more in the first world while knifing her legs and swinging higher in the second, at which point he took her buttocks into his great hands and pressed his thumbs against the back of her thighs and began kissing and nibbling his way up the inside of her legs, sucking gently at those liminal spaces where the leg met the genital area— that soft, vulnerable place that was so like the webbing between thumb and forefinger, or the tip of a horse's snout—before moving onto the soft petals of her labia, flicking and licking, finding the part among the folds, laying her open, lapping slowly, gently, up and down, before settling at last upon her clitoris, closing his lips about it as though he were truly kissing her there, flicking his tongue across it, gently at first than progressively harder, nibbling at it, sucking it gently, swishing her around in his mouth as though he were tasting a fine wine, flicking some more, faster and harder, finding his rhythm, doubling it exponentially—while the curtains and the hung clothes billowed, the swing swooped forward and back, the timepiece ticked, the sky swept in and out of her vision, until at last a circling raven appeared there and the White Fountain emerged from the blood red river and she came so suddenly and so powerfully that her entire body spasmed and began convulsing. Nor did he stop there but continued to draw on her, drinking her fluids without relent, massaging her pubis with his fingers, causing her to orgasm again and again as everything flared white and the world split in two ...

IX | Aftermath

By the time they caught up with the larger pieces of wreckage from the ferryman's gondola, they had moved downriver far enough so as to no longer even be in the same region; rather, they were now fast approaching the Archon Narrows.

"Mind your binoculars," said Valdus, his voice seeming raw and more agitated than usual. "Anything that glints, zero in upon it and do not let it leave your eyesight."

For he knew the keys were made of a light substance and were gold on the surface only—and would float.

Hirth glanced at him sidelong before exchanging looks with Lieutenant Crith—an interaction that did not go unnoticed by Valdus, who thought: *They think me callous to the fact that I may have killed my betrothed. And Hirth, at least, suspects an ulterior motive. But I for one do not believe she was on board. Why would she not have activated?*

Because she may not have received your message, said a voice, which he pushed from his mind immediately.

The important thing right now is the key, he told himself. And yet as his men examined the bits of wreckage (catching them with their oars as they were able and drawing them close) it was becoming increasingly evident that they might at last find nothing. And thus a new plan of attack would be needed, for one of the keys belonging to the ferrymen *had* to be acquired; nor would he abandon Shekalane to be raped by the Lucitor (for that was what was in store for her, surely). However cold-hearted and simple of purpose his men seemed to think him, he was not so single-minded as that.

His gaze landed on the opposite bank of the River Dire as he brooded, where an abandoned platform could be seen at the mouth of the Archon Narrows; then, after focusing on it briefly, he panned to the side of the river from which they had come ... and saw an identical platform. He squinted as an idea began to form, but his train of thought was interrupted by Crith, who said, simply, "A glint, my lord."

Valdus moved toward him so quickly that he nearly upended the boat, snatching the scopes from him as the man pointed and pressing them to his eyes. He zoomed in on the glint, working the focusing ring furiously, but such was the distance and the dark that he could not tell for certain. What he *could* tell for certain, however, was that something golden was floating in the water, something connected to a jagged-edged mass.

"It is what remains of the ferryman," he said, his eyes full of intensity. "And something is attached." He glanced at Hirth, who was already looking at him—suspiciously, it seemed. "A communications device, perhaps. Hurry. Steer us alongside it."

The men rowed vigorously as Valdus returned his attention to the platforms. *Yes ... it might work. The bigger question is ... do we have the time?*

He took the oar from the man nearest him as they approached the floating object, thinking, *I will rescue you yet, my love. And then I shall have you as well as the key to the Forbidden Channels ...*

He used the oar to maneuver the piece of debris along the starboard bow, but, as they had moved well past the *orbis lunae,* the darkness was near total. "Lantern! Quickly!"

Crith held a lantern over the gunwale as the object bumped against the hull, and they saw at the same time that it was not, indeed, the ferryman's remains, but a child's near-headless doll ... around whose neck a small, golden necklace gleamed.

Valdus looked up to find his men, almost to a man, staring at him expectantly.

Well, what did they expect? That there would be no more incidents such as the All Servant's Parade attack? That somehow all of their hands wouldn't run red with blood before this was all over? "It is not the first time," he said. "Nor will it be the last. You would all do well to remember that. Now man your oars, time is of the essence."

He reached for the doll—but before he could touch it a red dot fell wavering on its half-face, and his men let out a collective gasp as a raven called somewhere in the gloom.

The dot moved up Valdus' arm to his face, then quickly touched on all their faces one by one, cataloging them, marking them. A bowman managed to squeeze off a shot almost instantly, but the bolt missed its target and the raven's beam continued to swing in the fog, falling upon bits of the wreckage and at last targeting the base-cave itself.

"Row, men," said Valdus urgently. "Our lives depend upon it now. But do not fear!" He shot a glance at Hirth. "There is another plan."

The Tempter and the Taker

I | Awakening

She awakened with a rush, drawing in air which smelled like ammonia and pain, and found herself lying on the floor of the gondola while Dravidian crouched over her and Milkweed—Milkweed! She lived!—purred against her ear. The gondola's lanterns had been extinguished so that they floated in near blackness.

"My lungs burn," she managed, reaching up to pet Milkweed and realizing suddenly that both her wrists were now free of shackles.

"It's the smelling salts," said Dravidian. "It will dissipate quickly. How do you feel otherwise?"

"I feel—I dreamed of a white fountain." She looked into his eyes. "You were there with me ..." She drew her hand away from Milkweed and rubbed the ignudi dust (so prized for its qualities as an aphrodisiac) between her fingers. "So were you, Milkweed, it seems."

"There's been an attack," said Dravidian—then paused, holding a black gloved hand to his temple.

Shekalane heard a jumble of garbled voices emanating from his mask's circuitry.

"At least one ferryman and his charge have been killed," he said, "and power stations throughout Ursathrax have been sabotaged."

"A ferryman killed? But how ...?"

"I don't know. Early reports indicate the terrorist Valdus is using a new weapon—one capable of penetrating shields." He stood abruptly. "I must get us underway. So long as we drift we are particularly vulnerable."

"This weapon ..." She sat up on her elbows. "Is that what caused the white light?"

"Yes," he said, and mounted his dais. "As well as the shock wave that rendered you unconscious. I, too, lost consciousness briefly." His fingers danced across the control pad as he appeared to check readings. "I'm redirecting all power to the port and starboard shields. But with weaponized energy of that magnitude ...."

Shekalane thought of the ring and sat up the rest of the way, her senses rapidly returning. "Where are we? And how long was I out?"

He took up his oar and placed it in the forcola. "About an hour. You stirred once in response to smelling salts—you must not remember—then fell into a deep sleep." He turned his mask to face her as he began rowing. "Our charges often haven't slept for days prior to the Sacrificium—I estimated you needed the rest. As for where we are at, we are approaching the Archon Narrows."

She looked at the green ring. *Activate it by pressing the emerald when you approach the Stygian Flowstones ...*

"Dravidian, I—I've always wanted to see the Stygian Flowstones. And now—with our fates in the balance—I wish to see them more than ever. Will we be passing them soon?"

"I am sorry, Shekalane. But we passed them while you slumbered. Had I known of your wish I would have awakened you and rowed us close. It is a custom among us, some of us, to grant such last wishes when we can."

The magnanimousness of such a custom struck her, and she looked at Dravidian—pushing and drawing on his oar, harder even than he had before they'd gained the middle of the river, and realized he was doing it for them. For her. To protect her.

The ferryman is already dead.

She could not disregard that part of the note. And yet— was she herself not, in a sense, "already dead," if the near certainty of being forced into sexual slavery didn't drive her to act?

There is no choice, Shekalane. You must activate the ring.

But her conviction swayed like a tree in the wind. How could she possibly do that now that she knew her jailor as a man and not a monster? Now that she knew him as a man of uncommon depth for whom she felt—did she dare even think it?—a *stirring?*

Again the pendulum swung. It was all well and good to have met a kindred spirit on the way, but he himself had said they wouldn't see each other again after her deliverance. Certainly she had to consider her own survival first—wasn't it at least possible that Valdus would spare him if she were to ask?

A new weapon. One capable of penetrating shields.
The terrorist Valdus.

No. No, she was being a fool if she thought Valdus would spare an enemy, much less a ferryman same as Asmodeus, for whom his hatred was complete. Nor could there be any warning if such a weapon were being used; indeed, they could be stricken at any instant, and he (Valdus) had already shown his willingness to risk innocent life.

Again she looked at Dravidian, at the strangely earnest living-dead man intent upon his rowing, as well as the weapon hung heavy at his hip, glinting, and the answer came to her with such sudden clarity that she was amazed she hadn't seen it before.

Activating the ring was their best and possibly only chance for survival. Even Valdus would not risk the life of his own betrothed in order to simply kill another ferryman, she was sure. And thus he would be forced to approach them and penetrate the shields slowly, which would allow her an opportunity to negotiate or at very least give Dravidian a chance to defend himself.

She fingered the ring gently. *Forgive me, Dravidian.*

She had just started to press when Sthulhu came cawing back out of the gloom—urgently, frantically (causing Milkweed to dart away yet again), and alighted on Dravidian's upraised arm.

II | Crucible

"What is it, Sthulhu? Speak."

"Enemies," said the raven. "Port and stern. Many men, heavily armed, *awk!*"

Dravidian began to reply when a great sound tore the night—a sound so lumbersome and ultimately shrill that it could only be iron crying out in distress. It came at once from left and right, and was followed by what sounded like chains rattling—but hundreds of chains, *thousands* of chains!—as water gurgled and dripped, after which a third sound, a sound which clanked and creaked and ratcheted faster and faster, grew prominently amidst the cacophony.

Shekalane saw light from the *orbis lunae* glint metallically in the blackness ahead of them. Dravidian must have seen it too, for he triggered the bow spotlight, which shown whitely from the blade-like ferro and revealed an enormous blasting net—impossible—rising from the blackened waters. No, not one blasting net, Shekalane realized, but many, all conjoined so that they spanned the entire width of the Narrows!

"Enemy closing off the port bow," said Sthulhu, who had leapt from Dravidian's arm to the top of the ferro and trained his red beam on the shore.

Dravidian activated the port spotlight and Shekalane saw longboats with many oars approaching rapidly; she counted five, maybe six, spearheaded by a green lead boat—at the bow of which crouched a man in a hooded cloak of the same color.

She leapt to her feet almost instinctively. "It is Valdus!" she cried.

A bright light caught the corner of her eye and she looked behind them; Dravidian had activated the stern spotlight so that yet more boats were visible—a mid-sized vessel with a small cabin and two additional longboats—which were closing rapidly. All of the ships both port and stern bristled with men and arms.

"Dravidian—what do we do?"

He commanded: "Sthulhu, quickly, while they are blinded by the spotlights, locate the next *vetitum portas*. It should be near."

She saw the raven's beam swing in the dark—then lock onto something. "Exactly one nautical mile," he said. "As the crow flies, *awk!*"

They were again engulfed in blackness as Dravidian killed the lights. "Sthulhu, distract them," he ordered—and she heard the bird's wings beat furiously into the night. To her he said: "The key around my neck is to access the processing terminal at the end of Ursathrax. But it will also open the *vetitum portas*—the gateways to the Forbidden Channels—although we are forbidden to do so except in the direst emergency. You may have noticed there is no riverbank on our starboard side in this region, therefore there is nowhere else to go. I will angle us for the doorway but I can't promise I will judge the distance correctly or that I will be able to out-row our attackers. I—I have heard the rebels have begun capturing women and children for use as human shields. I will do my best, Shekalane. You are free to help me if you wish; there is an extra oar attached to the gunwale directly behind you. The decision, of course, is yours."

She watched as he began rowing with powerful strokes, her vision having grown somewhat accustomed to the dark, rubbing her wrist as she did so, then turned and looked at the oar fastened to the gunwale.

"It is the Hour of a Thousand Paths, ferryman!" Valdus shouted as he and his men approached. "The hour in which anything is possible! Our killing of your brother is proof of that! Prepare to be boarded and to leave both the girl and this world behind. Long live the revolution!"

She peered into the night and could just make out his form amidst the boats, her handsome and dangerous former lover come to rescue her, her darkling Prince of the Revolution who in the end had not forgotten her. They were too close now; the ferryman—*Dravidian*—as skilled and powerful as he was, would never outrun them. Her mind seemed suddenly full of nonsense now that the experience had ended and the outcome seemed certain, as though she had regressed to an earlier, infant state. It would be a short, brutal life with him—with Valdus—but it would be free, nor would it be without passion, at least when he wasn't tilting at his windmill or chasing his whale, and it would change the world forever so that no one need fear the ferryman or labor beneath the Lucitor's yoke ever again.

She looked forward at Dravidian, who was also a mere shape in the night, and her heart pounded as she watched him draw upon his oar. *Beautiful, undead stranger, who bid you welcome into my heart and made me feel for you almost as a lover? Will you not still deliver me to your Lucitor if you survive? Will you not use your key again to open the gates of hell at the processing terminal only to row away from me forever with your humane, dreaming eyes and your thoughts and quotes* of Montair? Who are you to me, ferryman, and who am I to you? Is it selfish of me to want to live even if that means you will surely die? And are you not doing the same? Life is selfish, only a fool believes otherwise; passion is selfish, and above all, love is selfish!*

She looked toward Valdus and saw that he was close enough to make eye contact with, and she did so lingeringly, seeing in his face something she had never seen there before, something eager and pure and almost innocent; he was as a child to her in that instant, and yet he was also as a stranger, like something from another life altogether, whereas Dravidian somehow shared her time and space and interiority, had done so, somehow, even before she had met him, and as she turned away from them both to ponder the extra oar she wondered how the word "love" had even come into her mind.

You try so hard just to make do and to get by, she thought, *You try and you try and you try. And some days, you succeed! But then comes a black coin to first your husband's palm and then your son's, and finally your own, and everything you thought you knew is suddenly up for reinterpretation. Then comes a lover who is obsessed for all the right reasons but still obsessed, then comes war and rebellion and the Hour of a Thousand Paths in which anything and everything is possible. And then, just when you think you can peaceably say goodbye to it all, when the numbness finally becomes libation instead of pain, then ...*

Comes a ferryman.

And it was at that moment and none before that she realized precisely what she had to do.

III | Pursuit

By the time Shekalane unfastened the spare oar (which was surprisingly heavy and more than twice her height) and began to paddle desperately, the rebels' boats had closed to within a hundred feet and the glinting tips of their weapons could be clearly delineated, even in the dim light of the distant *orbis lunae.* Nor did her initial efforts, performed under such duress, achieve anything but to disrupt their course.

"No, Shekalane," said Dravidian, seeming inhumanly calm given the circumstances, "you must row on the other side. Place it in the forcola—the rowlock. And mind your balance."

She did as instructed, placing the oar's shaft at random amidst the forcola's grooves and starting to pull and draw on it furiously—but the pole kept slipping, forcing her to spend most her time and energy trying to replace it in the rowlock, prompting Dravidian to shout, "Easy does it, Shekalane! Subtlety, not brute force! Hold the oar palm-down and don't squeeze, and follow it with your body."

Again, she did as instructed, and to her surprise, her movements began evening out and she became more surefooted.

"That's it," said Dravidian. "Row from your stomach. Think of it as walking on the water."

She did so, concentrating furiously, minding her footing, telling herself to breathe. She was doing something right; their speed had clearly increased. She spared a glance over her shoulder and saw Sthulhu hovering erratically in front of first one boat then the other, aiming his ruby-red beam in the men's eyes, causing the ships to slow and to lose direction.

"Mind your oar, Shekalane. We are almost there."

And suddenly they *were* there, and the gondola's steel ferro had served its purpose by clanging against the iron door and preventing any damage to the shell of the ship. Shekalane turned to see Dravidian whip the chain of the great arrow-headed key over his head and insert the instrument into an equally great keyhole, which glowed blood red inside and activated a green light on the console—which caused the leviathan door to shudder and groan and to begin rising.

"Dravidian!" Shekalane barked, seeing how close Valdus and his men were, and also seeing Sthulhu dive upon Valdus' face in a ferocious attack, which forced her former lover to grapple with the beast and to lose his focus, however temporarily.

Dravidian saw it too, and called harshly, "Sthulhu! Come!"

He steered them into the passage even as the great door with its widely-grated bottom began closing again, and the last she saw of Valdus after he had pressed the raven to the floor and slammed an inverted crate over him was the man standing suddenly and looking at her with an expression of complete and utter betrayal.

IV | Threshold

They found themselves in a blackness such as Shekalane had never known, a blackness which would have been total if not for a pair or red indicator lights—one directly beside them and one a couple hundred feet away—as well as an illuminated sign, which read, simply, 'Styx Flumen | Zone 49.' But there was something else too, a horrible smell, and it was not just because of the dankness, nor the curious phenomenon in which the loss of one sense will accentuate another. No, this was the smell of waste, as if they had entered into a great sewer canal. As if they had penetrated the flesh of the world itself and entered into the very bowels of Ursathrax.

"Dravidian—what is this place?"

She heard his clothes rustle as they drifted, as though he were distracted with something. "The Forbidden Channels, as I said," he whispered. "Forbidden to all, even we ferrymen—save for an emergency such as this."

"But how can that be? It is too narrow; our voices echo."

The lanterns came on both fore and aft, illuminating their surroundings with flickering light. They were in a kind of service corridor, the towering walls of which vanished into blackness and were punctuated every fifty feet or so with great, horizontal reinforcement beams. The beams were heaped with something resembling reddish-brown earth, some of which crumbled and splashed into the fetid, brown water.

Dravidian squinted, observing the outline of another door ahead. "You were right. It's a lock, perhaps." He began rowing them toward the other door.

Exactly midway between the doors a large, panoramic panel suddenly lit up beside them, startling them, and Dravidian pressed his oar against one of the rough-hewn walls, stopping the boat. On closer inspection the panel appeared to be some sort of directory: on it were unusual geographical terms (all preceded by the word "environ"), only one of which, *Novum Venum,* he recognized, for it was the name of the capitol and his home. The others—*Styx Flumen, Cuniculum Amoris, Somnium Nix, Magnum Ignotum, Cuniculum Terroris*—were foreign. The overall directory—if that's what it in fact was—was labelled 'Local Park Grid.'

Shekalane looked at him in the half-light of the lanterns. "What does it mean?"

Dravidian shook his head slowly. "I don't know. As for the other terms, they appear to be place names—in Latin."

She looked at him, confused.

"An ancient language. We are taught it in—"

"I know what it is, Dravidian. But it's been years. I wonder how they translate ..."

He continued shaking his head. "I think ..." He ran a dead-blue finger over the panel's surface, starting at *Novum Venum.* "New Venice—the capitol—River Styx, Tunnel of Love—"

She placed her finger next to his. "Yes ... Snow Dream, The Land Unknown, Tunnel of Terror. If these are destinations, I think I'll pass on that one."

The display went dark as suddenly as it had come on, and they looked at each other. He rowed them a little further to the next door, which had an illuminated sign next to it that read, 'Cuniculum Amoris | Zone 27.'

She looked at him again. "The channels you spoke of?"

Dravidian shrugged. "I presume."

The door enticed Shekalane to fanciful speculations. "Why do you think they are forbidden, Dravidian?"

He studied the door. "Legend has it that they run parallel to and expand out from Ursa Major, like rings in a tree trunk, and that they are worlds still being manifested by the Lucitor—not to be seen by human eyes until the time has come. And that they are full of forbidden knowledge."

Shekalane's face beamed with excitement and she touched his arm. "Then there is hope! As above, so below!"

"What do you mean?"

"Dravidian, don't you see? If the channels mirror Ursa Major than it's likely they'll have gateways just as the one we've entered. Thus we can circumnavigate our attackers and re-enter Ursa closer to the processing terminal." She lowered her chin and gazed up at him in a way she hoped was compelling. "Besides, don't you want to know what's on the other side of that door?"

His eyes lit up with curiosity and he seemed tempted—after all, he had a questing, explorative nature no less than she, and indeed, who could say what lay beyond such a threshold?—but fear quickly replaced it. "A test," he muttered quietly. "I am being tested."

She looked at him with something like pity, feeling an onrush of sympathy for him. It was clear to her by his change of expression and the way his eyes had begun darting nervously about the chamber that he was experiencing an abrupt and profound conflict between precisely that questing nature and his indoctrination as a ferryman; indeed, he suddenly looked as though he were witnessing a blasphemy—like he was seeing his god naked for the very first time.

"We dare not go further, Shekalane," he said. "We should not be here—should not be seeing this. We must return through the door from which we came immediately." He started rowing them back.

"But they are still out there!"

"We don't know that."

"I do—because I know them." She fingered the homing beacon in her pocket as he stopped rowing and glared at her. "They—they have quartered in my village outside Jaskir several times. We haven't had a choice, you understand. And I can tell you they are men of singular purpose. They have you outnumbered, Dravidian. And they will not go away. That I can promise."

"You forget Sthulhu. He will not go away, either."

"Sthulhu has been captured. It happened while you were opening the gate. He cannot help you now, Dravidian." She lowered her eyes. "Just as Milkweed cannot help me. Nor I, her."

This took him aback, but only for an instant. "Then it is even more imperative that we return." He continued rowing with renewed vigor.

She shuffled close to his dais. "Please believe me when I tell you these are killers, Dravidian. You cannot win this fight. Not alone. And certainly not without your raven."

His rowing slowed as he weighed her words. At last he stopped completely and said, "Then we will outwait them. Sthulhu will have transmitted images of the attack by now, and reinforcements are surely on their way. We have only to stay near the door. Time is on our side."

Shekalane looked at him forlornly. "Is it, Dravidian?"

Something rustled and chirped above them and they both froze.

"What was that?"

Dravidian lifted his oar and, utilizing a specialized hook on its shaft, took hold of the aft lantern. He raised it slowly.

The ceiling of the chamber was covered with inverted bat–*things,* for they couldn't be called bats, surely, as each was half the size of a man, and they seemed more like small people, monkeys, perhaps, than any flying creature Shekalane had ever seen.

"That settles it, then," she said. "Time is definitely not on our side."

Dravidian lowered the lantern slowly, whispering, "Who is he to you? A lover? That would vouch for a man of broader character than many have presumed. If he is a good man with a terrible purpose, such a man can be reasoned with."

"Of course, you would say that." She regarded him warmly. "No, Dravidian. Not a good man with a terrible purpose. A bad man who once had a good purpose. His motive is revenge, pure and simple."

"He has lost someone to the Lottery, then."

She shook her head. "If so, he has never mentioned it. That's what's so odd. Revenge for all Ursathrax, I suppose."

He seemed to be thinking about this when static and garbled voices began emanating from his mask again—seeming very loud in the silence—and he switched it off.

She followed Dravidian's gaze as he teased the light upward again, and noticed what he was noticing—a slight gap amidst the bats, as if one was missing. Had it been that way before? She continued: "And I am and have been alone, just like you."

He looked at her—even as a bat-thing swooped from the dark, attacking, its flailing claws tearing the key from his neck, causing it to drop into the water. He struck the creature repeatedly with his fist—the violence of which surprised her—until it shrieked and broke off, flying back into the dark as quickly as it had come. She looked up to see more creatures waking, and at least one dropping into flight—then jumped as Dravidian activated his weapon, causing its golden blade to swing out and its full, curved shaft to extend.

He swung as the thing fell upon them, cutting off one of its wings, and it fell into the water on the other side of the boat even as Shekalane leapt onto the dais and manned the oar. The flailing creature immediately tried to climb aboard; Dravidian swung again, decapitating it, causing yellowish white blood to spray—a spurt of which sprinkled across his mask and burned, hissing.

Several more creatures attacked as Shekalane tried to row them toward the new door, but the boat only careened off first one wall then the other as the things swiped and bit at them—missing in all cases, as the two of them were ducking and twisting—but relentless in their assault. At last Shekalane righted the boat and moved them to the door, where she punched a button next to the red light.

The door grated upward as Dravidian dispatched the creatures one by one, saving Shekalane more than once as she rowed them through the opening but accidently striking the door's control panel during the melee, causing it to explode—before his scythe was knocked from his grip and he tumbled into the water, grappling hand-to-hand with the last of the beasts.

Shekalane paused, uncertain for a moment, then snatched up the scythe and smote the creature in two. She then dropped the weapon and extended to him the oar. Dravidian looked at the burning control panel as the door began to close—rapidly—then at his key, which was bobbing in the water just a few feet away. She shouted to him as though reading his thoughts, "Don't try it, Dravidian! There isn't time."

He locked eyes with her, hesitating—then gripped the extended oar and climbed aboard as the door slammed shut with finality.

V | New World

She was crouched next to Dravidian with a hand on his back, helping him to recover, when she first noticed the change in the light—which shimmered upon the floor of the boat like the Dire Borealis but was different in kind, so that when she raised her head to identify its source she saw that, indeed, there was no single source, but rather a hundred of them and yet none at all. It was a light that came from everywhere and nowhere all at once, ethereal, multi-colored.

And while some of its individual sources were recognizable—lamps and lanterns along elevated boardwalks, a blue *orbis lunae* (two, actually, one nearby and another more distant), the illuminated windows of stacked rowhouses and grandly terraced townhouses—others were fabulously alien, such as the forests of candles, each the approximate mass of a man but varying in height from a few feet to a few hundred, or the great curtains of water beads, or the glittering points of light that covered the enormous stalactites—could they be windows, even?—as well as the stalagmites which covered the riverbanks, or, more spectacularly, the Cyclopean chandeliers and other glowing glass forms which hung helter-skelter amidst the helictites.

"My God, it's beautiful," said Shekalane, sensing Dravidian standing slowly beside her, gazing up with her. It was such a contrast to the Ursathrax they knew, which was always so gray and choked with gloom. Here you could see forever, and furthermore, you could see everything clearly, so that she found herself awed speechless by the lights, the beauty, and the wonder of it all. And there was *so much* to wonder at, because it was so much bigger here than from where they'd come; the circumference of the world itself was bigger, so that the distance between the port wall and the starboard—both of which were embossed with spirals and mandalas and all manner of labyrinths—as well as from the water to the ceiling, was more than double that of the previous world.

And the music! There was *music* playing from somewhere, *everywhere,* like some Cyclopean orchestra, an orchestra of behemoths. And what they were playing became clear to Shekalane as she listened, for she had heard it before, indeed, so many times before, most recently in her dream—"Lovers

Lost." Also, there was a roaring sound somewhere, and she could feel warmth emanating from someplace ahead.

She glanced back at the shut door, but it was clear to her now that they were on their own.

She offered her wrists to be re-shackled. Dravidian shook his head. "No, Shekalane. So long as we are lost, let us at least be free."

She smiled wanly, then looked around again until her gaze fell upon the stacked rowhouses and terraced townhouses. "They're not real—are they?"

He shook his head. "Not the upper floors. See how they grow smaller as they rise, to create the illusion of height. Mere facades, Shekalane. The same as so many in our Ursathrax. And look, see how the real ones are dark and abandoned. I'm afraid we'll find no help there."

She looked at him thoughtfully, moving aside a lock of her hair. "What will we do?"

Dravidian gazed off to where the world itself curved gradually out of sight, and said, "This region, though larger, seems to curve and to run parallel with the Ursathrax we know. So the only thing I can think of is to follow the current and hope that somehow it will lead us back home." He looked at her sidelong. "All rules are off until then, but if we find the way back—then we must do our duty."

Shekalane nodded. "I understand."

He picked up his weapon and deactivated it, causing its blade to fold in and its shaft to retract, then hooked it to his belt and retook his dais and oar, and began moving them forward.

"Curious," he said at length. "The lower dwellings seem to have been part of a genuine community at some point, but where is the sacrificial landing?"

Shekalane responded absently, gazing in wonder at the giant chandeliers: "The what?"

"Where do ferryman pick up their charges?"

"The Lottery does not exist here, Dravidian. It never has."

She could see, as they floated forward, how this new world expanded, becoming ever more magnificent, and was growing increasingly mesmerized by it. The Dire Borealis shimmered as the curious roar she'd noticed earlier increased and their hair began to dance in a warm wind. She watched him for a moment as he guided them absently, seeing that he, too, had fallen under the place's magic spell, and said, laughing a little, "I'm sorry I rowed us in circles. Would you show me?"

He drew on his oar, regarding her, then, as they passed a giant vent which blew warm air and set his black cloak to billowing, he motioned her to join him on the dais.

"Lash oar," he commanded, causing a curved part to pop from the forcola and to secure the oar against it, then positioned her in front of him and put the oar in her hands, over which he rested his own.

"The art of rowing from the back is similar to rowing from the front," he said. "Only you have to steer, as well, which, as you've discovered, is not as easy as it looks." He gently pushed her hands forward. "The forward stroke is the same ..." He steadied her as she completed the movement but stopped her when she started to push down. "But instead of withdrawing it from the water you keep it submerged, and rotate it, like this—so that the flat of it is horizontal."

He drew her wrists back while slightly applying downward pressure. "Then you push down—easy does it—while drawing back. This compensates for the motion of the initial forward stroke. Do you understand?"

"I think so," she said. The music mesmerized her.

"And you repeat ..." He pushed her hands forward again. "Now back—good, keep it in the water—rotate, down slightly, and draw back."

She did so, repeatedly, and such was the harmony of the ship, Dravidian's assured, patient guidance, and the music, even the water and the labyrinthine patterns all around, that her strokes were perfect and she fell into a sort of trance.

"To steer right, you rotate the blade toward the bow at the end of the forward stroke—that's it—for left, you push harder on the initial stroke—then bypass the compensating move. Like this ..."

"But how can the boat turn all by itself?" She cocked her head, examining the length of the gondola. "It's bent." She craned her neck to look up at him. "Isn't it? It's asymmetrical by design. That's how you can row with one oar."

He nodded, the ethereal light causing his eyes to sparkle.

"Your eyes," she said. "They dance."

He gazed at her a moment, then moved his face closer to her own. "What did you mean, Shekalane, when you said, 'Of course I would say that?'"

She smiled. "It is human nature to project onto others what is in our own hearts."

He looked confused.

"Don't you see? You are the good man with a terrible purpose."

There was a long beat as they made extended eye contact, and it was clear from the look in his eyes that he had never been spoken to in such a loving manner.

"No one has ever spoken to you that way—have they?" She gently touched his mask. "As a man—not a symbol."

She started to pull its thong slowly—until he placed a hand over hers, softly resisting. At last he relented and moved her hand to the pad at his temple, which, realizing the strap was just for show, she pressed gently, causing the mask to hiss and release. She eased it down carefully.

And somehow, curiously, his face looked precisely as she had expected, precisely as it had appeared in her dream: a thing youthful yet tempered with experience—feline rather than blocky, whose dark brows swooped at an angle toward a slender nose and sharp chin, and whose cheekbones were pronounced as they were in the most beautiful of women. And yet, as in her dream, again: it was a face utterly masculine, a thing as consistent and grave and implacable as it was beautiful.

She traced the contours of it slowly, until he swung his mask around to hang at his back and moved his face still closer, and they kissed for the first time while passing a great heating duct, at which point he abandoned the oar completely and embraced her fully even as the ring on her finger started vibrating incessantly and a great light shown upon them, and they looked up to see another boat approaching.

VI | Jamais Vu

They were being signaled with a lantern. Dravidian immediately readied his weapon and re-secured his mask while Shekalane raised her hood.

"Ahoy, who goes there?" shouted Dravidian. "Be advised that we are armed and prepared to defend ourselves."

A baritone voice responded: "You have no need to defend yourselves from me, dear friends."

A man emerged from the river smoke at the bow of a larger boat, a boat which appeared to have a mechanized paddle wheel, but that he was steering with a long pole against the current. He killed the mechanism and stopped rowing nearby—so that their boats were parallel to one another—taking them in, taking Dravidian and his frightful mask in. His eyes were magnified by thick glasses, the round lenses of which were huge. "Oh, dear," he said. "But have I to fear you?"

Hardly, thought Shekalane. The bearded man was built like an ox.

Dravidian looked at him for a time, then removed his mask and collapsed his weapon, re-securing it to his belt. "You have no need to fear me, fellow traveler." He extended a gloved hand. "My name is Dravidian."

It was the first time she had heard his voice without it first being filtered through the mask, and Shekalane found she liked it, a lot, for it was so much less perfect, so much less theatrical, and so much more merely human.

The man glanced at his hand, then gripped it firmly. "Jamais Vu," he said, robustly—but quickly lost his focus as Shekalane lowered her hood, and he took special note of her. "By Thesea ... and who might you be?"

She smiled and bowed slightly, then offered her hand. "Shekalane."

Jamais leaned forward and kissed her fingers. "Your charms would drive any man in Ursathrax to distraction, Shekalane."

She noticed a key such as the one they had lost—but platinum—hanging from around his neck (as well as a Nautilus seashell), and glanced at Dravidian, who acknowledged her with a look. Jamais adjusted his cloak to conceal it as if it were second nature for him to do so. He straightened suddenly as though something had just occurred to him, and Shekalane could see the wheels turning as he studied them, his eyes flitting back and forth.

"Indeed," he said. "A curious and beguiling pair. The Tempter and the Taker!"

She began to grow uncomfortable as he looked her up and down, stroking his beard, and gripped the neck of her garment modestly. Likewise, Dravidian placed a hand on the hilt of his scythe.

"What is it, Jamais?"

He seemed to snap out of it. "You'll forgive me, it's just that—the madam is an uncommonly beautiful woman." He met her eyes. "You have that quality the French call *Jolie laide*—it is in the melancholic air about you and the vaguely awkward way you inhabit your body."

Shekalane smiled and blushed a little, but wondered who the French were.

He studied Dravidian. "And you—I have seen one such as you before. You come from ... *Styx Flumen.*"

"I have recently become acquainted with that term," said Dravidian. "But we come from Ursathrax. I from Novum Venum—the girl from Jaskir. And we are lost. Can you tell us where we are?"

Jamais started chuckling, which became a bellicose laugh. "Why, you are still in Ursathrax, of course! There is more to the world than tiny *Styx Flumen,* you know. More precisely, you are in the region known as *Cuniculum Amoris.*"

Dravidian and Shekalane glanced at each other.

"But never mind that! What I want to know is—how did you come to be here?"

Dravidian shook his head. "We aren't entirely sure. We were being pursued. I had a key, like yours—which we used to enter the Forbidden Channels. But we were attacked by creatures I have never seen before ... and it was lost in the melee. Now we are marooned."

Jamais straightened. "A key, you say. Like mine ..." He fingered his own key through the folds of his clothes.

"Yes, sir. Gold instead of platinum, but otherwise the same." He paused. "I—we saw it when you kissed Shekalane's hand."

Jamais half-turned, processing this. "You are perceptive, the both of you. Gold, you say ..." He appeared lost in his own thought, but popped out of it suddenly. "Ah! Well! It could not have been like mine—yours appears to have served an actual function, yes? This—this is mere junk jewelry. I sell it." He changed the subject: "These creatures you mentioned ... what did they look like?"

"Like bats," said Dravidian. "Only bigger."

"Much bigger," said Shekalane.

Jamais nodded, rubbing his beard. "The *Lamia Simia*. They have become quite a problem in the service channels—the Forbidden Channels, I mean. They were from *Cuniculum Terroris,* originally, but have now spread throughout the super structure ..." He paused, as though having chosen his words poorly. "They have spread everywhere, I meant to say." He exhaled. "I dare say they have made my work more difficult." His tone became upbeat. "Come, my friends—I have just brewed some fire-tea!"

Dravidian and Shekalane regarded him hesitantly.

"Come along, I won't bite ..."

He dropped anchor as Dravidian tied off against his ship, and they climbed aboard.

Shekalane touched a hanging pan, ducking under it, as she stepped onto the deck. "Your boat is a carnival, Sir Jamais! What is it you do?" She looked around the ship, which was hung and cluttered with all manner of merchandise, then at a wooden sign suspended over the cabin. She read it aloud: "'The

Peddlin' Pair.'" She looked at the sleeping compartment just below it. "But you are alone."

"Alone? Nay, I am never alone." He fiddled in the galley, preparing the tea, having switched to a different pair of glasses for up-close work. "I have the memories of loved ones, always, as well as friends and trading partners in a dozen different—" He paused abruptly, as though he had said too much. "I have been rowing the River Dire for a long time—years, decades, who knows? That's the way of it in the Land of No Clocks!"

Shekalane moved between the rows of baubles and trinkets, some on shelves and some suspended amidst strings of lanterns, observing hookahs of every size, shape, and color, exotic shells, framed quotes in languages she didn't recognize, a basket of snow globes labelled 'Genuine *Somnium Nix.*' "But why? And how have you survived? What do you eat?"

"Plenty of food along the River Dire, if you know how to look. As for why, well, to reach Thesea, of course."

"Thesea ... you keep saying that. What does it mean?"

She touched a dangling item, gently—a golden locket—as Jamais handed her a cup of tea.

"You do not know, of course. The Great Ups? The White Fountain?"

She focused on him, still touching the locket. "What did you say?"

"I was speaking of the Great Ups—the White Fountain—which exists at the end of Ursathrax. Are you aware of it?"

"I have dreamed of ..." She paused, shaking her head. "No."

"Thesea is the world beyond Ursathrax," he said from the galley as he poured Dravidian's tea. "The world of many directions. Meaning it isn't a sluice like this one, but rather expands out in all directions ..."

She opened the locket as he carried on and saw a picture of a much younger Jamais in the company of a beautiful woman. She nodded at Dravidian, indicating he should have a look.

Jamais returned with Dravidian's tea, blind to everything but what was a foot in front of him because of the glasses. "It exists. But first one must find the door out of Ursathrax, the main one, anyway, at the end of the River Dire." He returned to the galley and began preparing his own drink. "There have always been whispers, of course—myths—perhaps not in *Styx Flumen* but elsewhere—of other doors along the way, short cuts, you might say ..."

Shekalane showed Dravidian the locket as Jamais left the galley and moved toward them. "Wormholes that fold the world—the underworld, at any rate, and that stand ajar for those who can find them."

She thought of her and Dravidian as she looked at the tiny picture. Were *they* a couple?

Jamais leaned close to them, oblivious to what they were looking at, and paused for emphasis before saying, "I believe I have found one."

She came out of her reverie in time to see him raise his glass.

"A toast! To fellow travelers and well-met friends!"

Dravidian and Shekalane exchanged glances, hesitating, then clinked glasses with him. "Hear, hear," they said.

He bolted back his drink, and they followed suit. "And to sharing the adventure," he added.

Dravidian puffed his cheeks and pursed his lips as he swallowed the strong liquor, as if to say, *That was interesting.* When he recovered he said, "What do you mean?"

Jamais looked at them, rosy-cheeked from the alcohol, and began pouring them another round. "I am on an errand which requires a timely diversion—something you two could provide in abundance, I'm sure. I was returning to Traumnovelle to hire helpers when I met you. I will pay each of you one-hundred aurums for your time—enough to fund your journey for the foreseeable future and beyond, I think. It won't take long, and I don't expect there should be any real danger, but it will require that you abandon your present course, for a day, at least, possibly more." He held up his glass again. "What say you? Will you share the adventure, and the spoil, with me?"

Shekalane looked at him, then at Dravidian, her eyes betraying her excitement. Dravidian looked back at them, then stepped toward the side of the boat and gazed on. "Where we come from all of Ursathrax is but one circle—and the River Dire flows back to whence it came. That is the only world we know." He turned and reestablished eye contact, first with Jamais, then Shekalane. "And the one to which we must return."

She held his gaze a few breaths longer then looked away, attempting to hide her disappointment.

"Furthermore," he continued, "I believe your key to be genuine and that you can assist us in going back—but that you hide this for fear of being robbed." He gripped the man's massive shoulder, and shook it gently. "I ask you for your trust, dear friend. Our entry point is not far. We have just come from there, as I've said, and can show you the way. If we assist you with your errand, will you use your key to let us back in?"

Shekalane looked back and forth between them, not liking the direction in which this was going. "Dravidian ..."

Jamais looked at him gravely, somberly, then suddenly became animated again. "Back to *Styx Flumen?*" He laughed heartily. "Why in Ursathrax would you want to do that? May as well try to crawl back into the womb!" He indicated the key.

"This is junk! There is no 'back,' only forward! Forward upon the River Dire, which flows inexorably to Thesea ..."

There was an enormous mechanical sound which echoed like thunder in the distance, and Dravidian and Shekalane looked up and around, as did Jamais. It was followed by a deep, bass rumbling, which built into a trembling, which built into a swelling and rolling of the water and a burst of wind which caused the lanterns to flicker and the pans to clatter and some glass baubles to fall and break, as well as the key beneath Jamais' tunic to glow and to pulse—in perfect unison with the flickering moon globes, as though they were all of a piece, all wired into the same source—until at last the tumult subsided.

At length Dravidian said: "Then what of sideways travel, Jamais? Perhaps we should speak of that."

Jamais started to say something but paused, and the wind howled through the channels. Everyone glanced at everyone else. At last he sighed and sat down heavily. "Alone? Yes. Ever since ..." He took out the key. "Aye, it is genuine—and forged of the same maker as was yours, I am certain. Gold, did you say?"

Dravidian nodded.

"One of the minor, environ-specific keys, perhaps. Those are the most common—good for opening the gates to the service channels in one region only." He leaned close. "This one ... will open them all. All the doors in all the worlds, except for the *Cyclopean Porta*."

Dravidian furrowed his brow. "The *'Cyclopean Porta?'*"

Jamais nodded, slowly. "The giant doors that separate the regions of Ursathrax. If you have been to the end of *Styx Flumen* you have seen one, although you wouldn't have been aware of it."

Dravidian shook his head. "I have been there many times—there is only the Twin Houses and the processing terminal, to which we deliver our charges."

"Nothing else?" Jamais' tone was rhetorical.

"The shipyards for the draggers, of course. Beyond these stands a great wall, beneath which the River Dire disappears." He paused, thinking. "There is a great symbol on the wall, like this ..." He circled his thumbs and forefingers and held them together.

"Aye. It means 'infinity.' That's no wall, Dravidian. It is a door—as tall and as wide as Ursathrax herself. Thick, too—too thick for a man to swim beneath and come up on the other side. I know ... I have tried. *Styx Flumen* ... it is not a good memory." His thoughts were clearly elsewhere.

Shekalane placed a hand on his leg and said softly, "What happened to her?"

Several breaths passed before he said, "We were traveling peddlers, my wife and I, as the sign indicates. For fifteen years we traversed these waters, as inseparable as the hydrippoi—which is, of course, as you will come to understand, somewhat ironic. We were drifting off the very door you speak of, drinking wine after an excellent dinner, as I recall, and feeding the horse eels what remained, when Sarabella got it in her mind to join them in the water—which is temperate enough to swim in near *Novum Venum,* as you know. They are such amiable creatures that I didn't at first see the harm, but, well, Sarabella being who she was, so full of life and fire, always—she took to riding the back of one of them." He laughed at the memory. "They put on quite a show for me that night, beautiful Sara and her shining, white steed—until the hydrippoi decided to turn all together and at once, and swim for the door, and before I knew it they had vanished beneath the surface, and I had dove into the water and tried to follow."

He paused, looking at them. "The *Cyclopean Porta* are grated beneath the surface, just as the *vetitum portas* are, so I was able to swim well beneath the door before turning back for lack of air. But though I attempted the reach again and again, I couldn't do it, I couldn't follow my Sarabella. The doors are too thick—a hundred feet, at least. I didn't have the lungs—large as I am. But I *heard* her call out from the other side; sometimes I think it was just my imagination. And I thought I heard her call, "There is another world, my love! I await you there!"

A silence fell over them as he finished the story, and Shekalane felt a deep sorrow for him, feeling as though she understood him completely now. So this was how he had gotten started on his quest—what had motivated him initially and motivated him still.

"Another world ... and that was this—Thesea?"

Jamais started. "Uh? No, no. That was just the start, the cracked door, so to speak. There are many worlds, many regions, each larger than the previous. And the River Dire flows through them all—to Thesea."

"I don't understand."

"Nor did I, for many years. Until the key came to me—and changed everything. Since then I have been moving back and forth through the walls of the world—the worlds—charting the varied regions—attempting to decipher the grand design. I survive by trading items from one to the other. How I wish I could share with you, with someone, the amazing things I've learned." There was more silence. "But since you insist upon returning from whence you came; yes, I can help you with that. Nor will you have to retrace your steps. I know of another such channel—this one is recessed, and it is hidden from view by a breaker-like rock. It presides in a small grotto in which I store surplus goods. I will show you."

Dravidian and Shekalane looked at each other before nodding tentatively.

"And we shall help you with your errand, Jamais," said Dravidian. He raised his glass and was instantly joined by Shekalane. "To sharing the adventure," he said. "And the spoils."

Jamais looked at them for a moment, then burst into a jovial laugh. "Wunderbar! Then let us discuss the plan over a table of good food—which we can find in abundance upriver ..." He gestured in that direction. "In Traumnovelle." He looked sidelong at them almost menacingly. "The City of Fleshly Delights."

Then he opened a compartment and removed a great scabbard, which was emblazoned with a red monogram (his initials) and seemed to contain scrolls as well as a sword, whose long, black handle caught the lantern light and briefly displayed highlights of a dozen alien colors, adding, as he swung the sheath around to his back, "Her name is Rosethorn ... and she discourages trouble."

At which point Dravidian and Shekalane looked at each other—already wondering if they had made the right decision.

By the time Dravidian had maneuvered the gondola around and began following Jamais' ship—which jangled and clanked with all its wares—a silence had settled between the ferryman and herself that Shekalane knew was mostly her fault. She couldn't get past how easily he had reverted to his former self once realizing they could return—as if nothing had happened between them at all and she was still merely a charge to him.

But what had she expected? That he would abandon twenty years of indoctrination merely on a whim? For she understood it more than she wanted to admit: Having been chosen at such a young age, his thirst for love and freedom and exploration was bound to conflict with his training of so many years—whereas she didn't have that; no, what she had was the growing terror, however much she'd sublimated it, that she would be turned into a concubine to the Lucitor. Surely he could say something, anything, to alleviate her fears and doubts, were she to simply ask him?

At last she said, "Would you still see me given against my will to another, Dravidian? Even a god?"

But he didn't say anything, just looked at her deeply as he rowed.

She thought of Valdus and his single-minded purpose—was Dravidian no different? Given to an abstract ideal over love?

Finally he said, "I must know the way back, Shekalane. Whatever our fates from there, let it be we who decide. Each of us."

And, at least in the moment, she found that was good enough for her.

VII | Valdus

Valdus exploded from the dank water and gasped for air in the blackness, squeezing the light sphere to activate it—which lit up like a little sun in his palm, illuminating the narrow chamber and casting stark shadows everywhere.

So, this was where they had disappeared to, something like a sewer sluice cut into the side of the world, and yet ... where were they now?

He looked up at the red light next to the door and the gold button below it, as well as the illuminated panel which read, 'Styx Flumen | Zone 49.' What did it mean? Then he held the light toward the far end of the chamber and noted a second red indicator (and another button, surely, for something gleamed), and another panel, although he couldn't read it from this distance. He also noticed something—several somethings—floating in the water, and when he swam closer he realized they were the corpses of animals; no, not animals, *things,* for he had never seen anything like them in all his travels throughout Ursathrax.

Perhaps it was his movements that activated it, for a long panel suddenly lit up in the dark along the wall closest to him, and he was moving to examine it when he heard a digging and a shuffling, and looked up to see a white ignudi emerge from a debris-choked pipe placed just above the door he had swam under.

It was Milkweed, of course, and as they were familiar with each other from the times he had called on Shekalane, he whistled after her and she flew to his shoulder without hesitation. They stared up at the long panel together as Valdus tried to make sense of it, but as most of it was written in an alien language, he could only surmise that it was some sort of guide—and this only because he recognized the name of the capitol, *Novum Venum.*

He looked sidelong at Milkweed as she gazed at the display, her little head cocking this way and that like a bird's and her pink, albino eyes (in which the panel's colors were reflected) blinking.

"It is a mystery, little one," he said, and smiled. "Not for the likes of us to understand. Perhaps Lector will know what it means."

He peered at the far door again, wondering what lie beyond it and not being able to imagine—yet knowing Shekalane and the ferryman had gone through it. And everything in him wanted to pursue immediately—for the buttons below the red lights were surely how the doors were opened from the inside—but to what end, strategically? They'd had an ample head start—it was possible he would never find them. And what of tactically? After all, he was alone, and armed only with a knife ...

He scanned the corpses of the creatures. *Aye, you've left behind quite a mess, ferryman. Alas, we shall see how you fare against a battalion of well-armed and well-trained men ...*

He petted Milkweed gently, knowing also that if he were to trigger the far door she would be gone instantly, and knowing, too, that because of the pair-bond between domesticated ignudi and their masters, she might be his only hope of locating them.

And that's when he noticed a golden, crossbow bolt-like (but much smaller) key floating not six feet from him—and surged toward it instantly, startling Milkweed into flight.

Now we shall show the men that Valdus has not failed, he thought, gripping the device tightly. *That accidents—sacrifices—such as the child do not happen in vain. That, though the road to a free Ursathrax may become a river of blood, it is still a river which leads somewhere.*

And yet another thought nagged at him, one that begged answering now that he'd obtained the key: How would it benefit the revolution to pursue them further?

He moved back toward the door, thinking on this. *Because you still do not know if she has betrayed you or if she is being coerced.*

He rebuffed himself immediately: *And what if that were so? Is she now so important that you would jeopardize everything you have worked for in order to save her? That you would violate your own edict to your men to put the revolution before everything, including their wives and children?*

No; no, he couldn't justify it based upon his feelings for her. But if it was true—if she had betrayed him, moreover, if she had assisted the ferryman *willingly*—then she would have to be punished. Surely this would be his edict were it anyone else—

No. That also was not true. His edict, were it anyone else, was laid out in his own charter.

Death to the enemies of the Revolution.

Death to anyone who colluded with them.

VIII | Plato's Cave

Shekalane gazed up at the inscription on the gigantic archway—which extended from one bank of the River Dire to another—and read:

WELCOME TO TRAUMNOVELLE
"Abandon All Inhibition Ye Who Enter Here"

She glanced at Dravidian as they passed beneath it—who looked back at her and raised a single, swooped brow—then gasped aloud as she saw what was on the other side: for there were two bronze statues there, one on each bank of the river; a male and a female, both completely nude, and each fully half the height of Ursathrax so that they towered like Titans in the mist, and such was the beauty and sumptuous symmetry of their faces and bodies, and so graceful was the way they reached out to each other, their great fingertips not quite touching, that Shekalane couldn't help but think of something she had seen in a picture book one time, which had depicted similar figures painted on the ceiling of what the caption had called the 'Sistine Chapel'—'God creating Adam,' if she recalled—by someone called Michelangelo.

But as they followed in the foamy path of Jamais' paddle wheel, she saw that there were more titanic statues, at least a dozen or so, and that, unlike the ones near the arch, these were what many would call profane. Indeed, what they seemed to be witnessing—from a cat's eye-view—could only be described as an orgy; nor did Shekalane flagellate herself for blushing as they rowed past a giant man and woman engaged in the Yin and Yang position—it wasn't every day that one looked upon a handsome giant with his tongue arched in the sheath of a goddess, or gazed up at a goddess while she fellated a titan who's mettle was tall as a ship's mast.

She spared a glance at Dravidian and saw that he, too, was gazing transfixed at the tableau, his face strangely sanguine, as if he'd stumbled upon a great oasis amidst the desert, and she supposed her face bore the same expression, as she could feel her nipples poking firmly against the fabric of her tunic.

The city itself was reminiscent of the town they had seen upon entering *Cuniculum Amoris*—but on a massive, denser scale—in that it was comprised largely of stacked rowhouses and terraced lofts (all of which were adorned in gold) that diminished in size as they climbed the walls of the world, and yet these were clearly occupied, even some of the fake, miniaturized ones higher up, and shown with what seemed a thousand lanterns glowing in their windows.

And yet despite all the opulent decadence of the place there was a quality of squalor just beneath the surface, as was evidenced by the demidaines calling to them from the lower windows—many of which were broken, she now realized—or the bearded man fishing from his terrace, which was itself hung with raggedy clothes.

At length Jamais steered his boat beneath another, smaller archway and they followed him into a great cove, which appeared to be the city's beating heart and commercial hub. Now in Traumnovelle proper (as distinguished from the city's facade), they found it to be a wild, packed, dangerous place—a chaotic and seemingly lawless world which, if it had once been intended as an erotic wonderland, was now anything but. And as they docked their boats outside a place called Plato's Cave, Shekalane found her earlier titillation turning to simple fear and trepidation.

She observed as Jamais bartered with the dock attendant and then motioned for them to come aboard, which they did after Dravidian had tied off and secured the gondola, and he was immediately handed a high-collared, oil-slick-colored poncho and black, wide-brimmed hat.

"In the interest of not drawing any unwanted attention," said Jamais, as Dravidian took off his cloak and put it on.

To his surprise, it was a perfect fit, and hid his accouterments as well as the mask hanging at his back nicely.

"I concur," he said, and placed a hand on the small of Shekalane's back—who was already being ogled and catcalled from every corner—as they disembarked. He offered his hand and she took it, and the catcalls stopped, for he was an imposing figure even without his cloak and mask.

They entered Plato's Cave where the trio was greeted by a hostess in sensual dress, who led them through a lantern-lit catacombs of rough-hewn rock and crackling fire pits, during which time Shekalane noticed an arched doorway beyond which she glimpsed black-robed figures standing before powerful lights—before a curtain was drawn, blocking the view.

"You've come at the perfect time," said the hostess. "The show will begin any moment."

They came to a rounded booth next to a fire pit, where Jamais insisted on sitting with his back to the wall so he could see the door. "We don't intend to stay long. Have you any recommendations?"

"The vesiculam," she said. "It's freshly harvested and can be prepared quickly. I'd suggest pairing it with a pallida ale." She glanced sidelong first at Dravidian then at Shekalane, who were seated across from each other with Jamais, who was at the end of the table, in the middle. "I'm given to understand it goes well with the show."

Jamais lifted the great scabbard's strap over his head. "The vesiculam, then. With ale."

He watched her go, then opened a pocket in the sheath (which was full of what seemed to be charts and maps) and removed a small, leather-bound journal. The book was well-used and appeared to be packed with notes written on all manner of stationary, including napkins, and was secured by a worn band. He put on his readers and pulled off the band, then rifled the pages in search of something.

"It lies in the village of Flax, about an hour upriver to the Caprona distributary, and about an hour in. Unfortunately, I was not able to get as close to it as I would have liked, and could only see the top of it. But I am now convinced that it is precisely what I suspected it to be. Here ..." He pushed the book toward them, which he had opened to a hand-drawn diagram of what appeared to be a metal enclosure, and they examined it.

"It looks like a cage," said Shekalane, and looked up at him. "But why?"

His glasses were so thick that they magnified his eyes twofold, and, finding it comical, she distracted herself by refocusing on the expanse of rock behind him, the contours of which were highlighted by the lanterns.

"Look closer. Note the rock formation just behind it. You can see it ... here. And here." He slid a small, torn sheet from the journal and positioned it next to his hand-drawn diagram. Printed on the sheet was a daguerreotype: it depicted a cage with an identical top alongside a similar rock formation. Next to the cage was a large, flat surface with an enormous red cross on it. The cage and the flat surface were near the edge of a great cliff, beyond which could be seen a powerful light, like a thousand sun orbs condensed into one, which appeared to be sinking into an expanse of water. The daguerreotype had a profound effect on Shekalane, as she had never seen anything like it.

Dravidian touched the light image and circled it with his dead-blue finger. "What is it?"

Shekalane indicated the ocean. "And this ... the River Dire? How can that be? It has no end."

Jamais sat back in his chair, studying them, firelight dancing on the side of his face. He leaned forward and pointed to a spot on the diagram. "There's more. Using my telescope I was able to discern this ..." They looked at what he had indicated closely. It was a numerical designation: EML 421. Jamais slid his finger to the daguerreotype, where the same designation could be seen.

Shekalane shook her head. "But I don't understand ..."

"It is the same cage ... only in different places."

Dravidian started. "The myths—"

"Of other doors along the way. Short cuts ... that fold the world."

"The underworld, you said."

"Yes. I—" The hostess returned with their food and drink and began setting it down.

"Ah. Ah! Thank you." He gave her what looked to be an exorbitant sum and she bowed slightly, looking into his eyes seductively, then Dravidian's, but also Shekalane's, and glided away.

Jamais leaned in. "I believe that is precisely what Ursathrax is." He took a slim sheaf of charts from the scabbard and began spreading them out on the table. "This is only the tiniest portion of it ... my life's work since I lost my Sarabella. More than a hundred charts so far, and at least as many grimoires, authored over the course of thirty years."

Dravidian and Shekalane poured over the documents.

"Now you see why I was so protective of the key ... it alone has allowed me to move back and forth between the worlds." He ran his hand slowly across the maps. *"Styx Flumen ... Cuniculum Amoris ... Cuniculum Terroris—*all the inner circles of Ursathrax. Also the middle worlds: *Cuniculum Venatus, Blood Libidine, Cuniculum Epicurea* ... Aye, even *Magnum Ignotum,* the first of the outer realms."

Shekalane attempted to translate the words in her head as she studied the maps, managed 'games/gambling,' 'war/bloodlust,' 'the Land Unknown ...'

Jamais continued: "She has revealed herself to me, Ursathrax, I mean, one lovely and terrifying layer at a time, but still the layers come, each one greater and more seductive than the last. She is as a fabled statesman of another time and place once said, 'a riddle, wrapped in a mystery, inside an enigma.' And yet, thanks to this key, I have begun to unlock her secrets. The existence of the *Cyclopean Porta* is one of those secrets. The existence of the *Imperium Locus* is another."

Dravidian cocked his head. *"Imperium Locus.* Control room?"

"Yes ... at the end of Ursathrax, before the last porta. It is there, some say, that the great doors between regions can be opened once again."

An awkward silence followed as Dravidian and Shekalane glanced at each other, and she wondered if he was beginning to doubt his sanity as well.

Shekalane looked at him with something akin to pity. "You speak as if Ursathrax were a person. A lover, perhaps."

Jamais laughed. "I suppose that's true. It is the hallmark of lonely people, to anthropomorphize. They do it to their pets quite frequently. But that is just one of her secrets ... for while not a person same as you or I, she is, I believe, sentient. She is self-aware. Surely you have felt it, on those days when the leaves of the trees rustle even though there is no wind? She is alive ... she has her moods and her trespasses, like every living thing. And also like every living thing, she is mortal. By which I mean she has a beginning, a middle, and an end, as do all things ... and that, after five-hundred years, she is nearing her end."

There was another long pause, and Shekalane looked at Dravidian, who said, "No. That is not possible. The Lucitor would not have created something so frail and temporal ..."

Jamais studied him for a beat. "And yet the sky is falling, is it not?"

Dravidian didn't seem to know what to say.

Jamais leaned close. "What if I told you that Ursathrax was created not by your Lucitor but by human beings such as ourselves? That it was designed centuries ago not by a god but by a man, who made a machine to administer it that came to believe itself a god? That it is all ... *pulchra mendacium,* a beautiful lie?"

Dravidian sat back in his chair. "I suppose, if you were to tell me that, I would think you quite mad."

Jamais was not daunted. "Or that ... it was designed as a kind of grand escape—from the real world, which is outside, and above—a dark-ride through many imagined environs? But that something happened to that above world ... something terrible. And such was the violence of it that all the *Cyclopean Porta* were closed, sealing off Ursathrax not just from the surface, but from its own regions one to the other. And that, over the course of many generations, its people came to forget that first world ever existed?"

Dravidian gestured in exasperation. "Madness, assuredly."

Shekalane was looking at the charts. "I suppose you mean to tell us that this upper world is Thesea."

"Yes."

"But where is it? It isn't even on the maps."

Jamais looked at her and smiled mischievously. He tapped the daguerreotype. "It is right here, of course. You were only partially correct in saying this could not possibly be the River Dire. Rather, it is what the River Dire *becomes.*"

Dravidian and Shekalane just looked at him.

He touched the nautilus shell around his neck, then held it out in front of him, fingering it thoughtfully. "I believe the underworld and all its regions ... all of Ursathrax ... to be a great spiral. Not the potter's spiral, what some call the spiral of Archimedes, which expands linearly, each turn being equidistant to the previous, but a logarithmic one ... *Spira Mirabilis* ... which expands exponentially, its circumference becoming greater and greater. Like this."

He held up the pendant. "This takes its likeness from the shell of a nautilus, a mythical creature similar to this vesiculam. Note how each turn is wider than the last, doubling, tripling, quadrupling. Some have called this the Fibonacci Sequence.

Others, the Golden Ratio. It is within this, they suggest, that one can divine the fingerprint of the creator Himself."

There was a distant rumbling and the lanterns flickered, as did Jamais' key. The glasses rattled briefly.

Shekalane stared at him a moment, then back to the charts. "So the spiral is the River Dire? And it becomes ... Thesea as it gets wider?"

Jamais nodded. "In theory, yes. I believe the River Dire enters our world at *Novus Venum,* at the Great Falls, and spirals out ever wider until it reaches the last and the largest of the *Cyclopean Porta* ... beyond which lies the Great Ups ... and Thesea."

Dravidian laughed. "The Great Ups? Jamais, you ask too much of us! Are we to believe now that water runs up hill?"

"Let me just say that, based on my reading, it's possible the ancient engineers found a way to marshal something called the Leidenfrost Effect, but on a massive scale. The important thing is, before the *Cyclopean Porta* were closed, one had but to follow the River Dire to reach the upper world. Now, however, that route is shut to us ... the River may reach it, but man may not. As I said, the keys will not work on the *Cyclopean Porta,* not even this one. Our only hope, it would seem, or rather my own, since you insist on returning, are the cages ... such as the one in Flax. And the only hope for mankind, in general, is to reach the *Imperium Locus."*

Shekalane stared at the charts and shook her head slowly. "But you still haven't explained how this ... upper world ... differs from our own. What is this Thesea?"

Jamais sat back, contemplating this. At last he said: "If the river could be said to be our jailor, our slave master, which is what Montair suggests, a thing forever goading us forward along a predestined path, than Thesea is its opposite. A place where the bars of our prison become so spread out, that the prison ceases to exist. The channel spreads, the water moves slower, until eventually all walls disappear. And as a result, one moves in any direction they choose. That is Thesea."

He released the pendant, lost in thought. "What I call freedom. And it is worth pursuing, indeed, it must be pursued, the worsening Ursaquakes are proof of that—regardless of your lack of faith. Dixi."

He lifted his glass and bolted back his drink. Dravidian and Shekalane looked at each other, then bolted back their own. The lanterns throughout the establishment suddenly dimmed, leaving only flickering firelight—which was greeted by applause.

He leaned in again, his cheeks red. "I tell you it is a grand illusion, all of it, and Ursathrax a grand artifice!"

There was more applause as projected beams appeared everywhere, casting a hazy-edged spotlight on a hundred different surfaces—including the expanse of hewn rock behind Jamais—accompanied by mysterious, sinewy music.

Shekalane glanced from the hewn rock to Jamais himself, who had returned to his charts and paid the show no mind.

"We must gain entrance to the cage in Flax," he said. "And I think I know precisely how to do it ..."

And then the strange drink began to take effect, and he was all but gone to her.

IX | Shadow Theatre

First there were the balls—or rather the performers curled into balls—which rolled in from both the left and right and coalesced in the center of the spotlight, then rose up two by two until they had formed a fountain of the kind one would expect to find in a courtyard—which was accentuated by performers from offstage reaching in with splayed fingers to form the boughs of trees, while yet another, utilizing a prop, formed a shining sun-globe.

The drink continued to take effect, making her feel buoyant, weightless, giddy ... mischievous. Her thoughts unspooled in a manner completely alien to her. She felt as though she were floating.

(*I could simply rise, could I not?*)

A hooded figure entered the spotlight from the right, followed by another on the left, and they met in the middle (in front of the fountain), where they dropped their robes to reveal a man and a woman, both of them nude, he wearing only a pointed hat of the kind Valdus sometimes favored, and she only a veil.

And something about the two—perhaps it was the primal angularity and aggressiveness of her breasts, or the way in which his manhood hung heavy and curved and at half attention—awakened her libido with such a sudden intensity that she immediately slipped off a shoe and (as the man and the woman in the spotlight began kissing) began brushing the side of her foot up and down one of Dravidian's boots ... then continued up his leg, moving around to the inside, searching for him ...

(*there you are*)

... as he reached slowly beneath the table and unbuckled his boot, his expression showing that he was feeling the effect of the drink no less than she—as the shadow play continued on the wall behind them and the woman began gesticulating angrily and the man touched her face gently before turning and walking away.

Shekalane bit her lower lip as the ball of Dravidian's foot touched her undergarments and began moving up and down.

(*yes ... like that ...*)

She glanced at the wall, saw the woman in the spotlight sink slowly to her knees with her face in her hands as the sun orb became a crescent moon and performers offstage held stars aloft on little sticks.

(*harder ... find me as I have found you ...*)

He found her. She pushed her head back slightly against the booth's cushioned backrest, continuing to rub her foot up and down Dravidian's metal, trying not to moan as he used his toes to massage her clitoris through the fabric of her panties. She glanced at Jamais—who was pouring over his documents, but, more so, appeared to be frozen in time—then at the ceiling, where the play was also being projected.

The shadow woman laid down on the side of the fountain and seemed to shiver as leaves blew through the spotlight.

Shekalane placed on a hand on her forehead, then over her mouth, and realized with a mixture of horror and fascination that her hand had become transparent, smoke-like, ghostly. (*but my hands are on the table!*)

(*have I died?*)

Came a centurion on a horse, his faceplate down, who ordered the woman to leave, pointing. She did as commanded, her head hung in sadness, after which the centurion carried on, exiting the spotlight as well.

Shekalane gasped a little, or thought she did, as Dravidian continued to massage her.

The shadow woman crept back into the spotlight and laid on the side of the fountain. But again came the centurion, who arrested her this time despite her animated protests.

The tree bows retreated and the performers comprising the fountain melted to the floor, then rose again, re-coalescing as a horse upon which the centurion and the woman rode. Other performers moved scenery on sticks to indicate they were travelling, until again everyone melted to the floor, and rose as a table and a cage. He put her in the cage and locked the door, then sat at the table and began reading. At length she extended a hand through the bars, not for want of bread, it seemed, but—

He pulled his chair up to the cage and began reading to her.

(*oh, Dravidian ... how I wish to be closer to you*)

At length the woman lay down and fell asleep, and the centurion did likewise, lying so close as to nearly be touching her.

(*I am here ... mere inches away*)

(*and yet ... how is it you come to me while your body remains across the table? how is it you kiss me like smoke upon the lips? how is it we rise together ... that our bodies have become as ghosts ... that we billow about the lanterns like swirling smoke?*)

(*we dream together, Shekalane*)

The moon orb turned and vanished from the spotlight; the sun orb returned. Came another centurion, who awakened the first, arguing with him and gesticulating angrily—

(*where are you, my love ... your eyes gaze but do not see*)

(*Dravidian?*)

—until a fight broke out between them and the second centurion was defeated. The first centurion opened the cage, but the woman did not step out. He sunk to one knee and pleaded with her ... until at last she took his outstretched hand and went with him. The cage and the table melted.

(*they are us*)

(*yes*)

(*they tell our story and do not know it*)

The horse returned, and with it the woman and the centurion, and the scenery blew past.

Shekalane lowered her chin, looking at Dravidian, gritting her teeth, her pleasure turned to something more aggressive, a need for release, a need to ...

(*I want you inside me, Dravidian ... in every way a man can be inside a woman, I want you inside me*)

But now the man with the pointed hat returned, as well, on his own horse, and swept the woman away from the centurion.

(*no, no!*)

The spotlight went black.

Again came the fountain. And again came the centurion, alone and distraught. He laid on his side, shivering, as leaves blew through the spotlight.

(*where are you, Shekalane?*)

The shadow woman returned, holding a knife which dripped blood. She dropped it and fell upon him next to the fountain, making mournful gestures before laying her head upon his stomach. At last she sat up and pointed her finger at the sky, as though having conceived a great idea. Then she uncovered his steel and began coaxing it to life.

The audience laughed uproariously and applauded, their voices strangely distorted, as if slowed down.

(*I am below you, lover ... just as you came to me over the table, I have come to you from under ... can you feel my smoky hands upon your steel?... my hungry kisses ... my greedy tongue?*)

(*yes ...*)

And then, somehow, the dream became something akin to reality, and she was rising from beneath the table (more as a flesh and blood woman than a ghost) and climbing into his lap even as the shadow woman did the same and the audience clapped and cheered, although when she glanced about the room she saw that they did so as if in slow-motion and Jamais still poured over his documents as if frozen in time. And yet she and Dravidian could still hear one another's thoughts.

(*can you feel me risen into your lap?*)

(*yes ...*)

(*and can you feel me gripping you ... guiding you in?*)

(*yes*)

(*oh! ... as I can feel you parting me ... filling me ... sliding in and up and touching my deepest place ... make love to me, Dravidian ... fuck me ... while we are here in this place and can!*)

(*I have wanted to from the first moment I laid eyes upon you*)

(*then come inside me now, Dravidian ... unleash your white fountain ... oh! ... see how even my buttocks fits your hands ... my synergique amore, my one, true synergistic love!*)

And then they were being called back somehow, and it was over.

But not before Shekalane had had her second orgasm for the day.

X | Escape

"Do you understand what I just told you?" Jamais looked at her as though baffled by her unresponsiveness.

Shekalane came out of it as if from a dream, said, "Mm."

To Dravidian he said: "That isn't much of a weapon, if there's trouble. I assume you are handy with it?"

Shekalane continued to rub him with her foot. "There's more to it than meets the eye."

Dravidian gazed off as though still feeling the effect of the drink. "As ferrymen, we are trained to master our weapon." He looked at Shekalane, who met his gaze. "If subtlety is required, I assure you, I can use it to ... part a peach, smoothly, in total darkness. If, however, brute force is desired ... I have been trained to ... smite an opponent again and again: fast, hard, unrelenting ... without tiring ... and with devastating res—"

There was a commotion elsewhere in the room: something—a flying creature, of some sort—was fluttering through the inn erratically, knocking over glasses and causing an uproar, and being pursued by men with nets. It arrived at their table in a flurry and Shekalane immediately recognized Milkweed as the little ignudi hid in her hair and dropped a small, green note-cylinder into her lap.

The men converged upon them and Dravidian stood slowly. "Halt, and step no further," he said.

One of the men said, "The white ignudi ... she belongs to us."

Shekalane removed the note hastily and read it as Dravidian and the men exchanged words. It said: *Do not forget that the ferryman's sworn oath is to deliver you to the Lucitor. We are in Cuniculum Amoris and await your signal. The choice is yours. Love Eternal, Valdus.*

She looked up in time to see one of the men knock off Dravidian's hat—and he responded instantly with an upward stroke of his scythe, the effect of which wasn't immediately clear. The man and the others stared at Dravidian's dead-looking face; people gasped. One of his friends said, "Brutto ..."

Brutto looked down ... and saw his hand lying next to Dravidian's hat on the floor. He looked at his wrist—saw blood jetting from the stump.

"Go!" commanded Dravidian to Shekalane and Jamais, and they all fled while the men were distracted with Brutto's wound; however, when Shekalane glanced over her shoulder she saw that the men had regrouped quickly and were giving chase.

They were headed off by yet more attackers before they reached the door they came in, and, remembering the arched doorway she had peeked through earlier, Shekalane parted the curtains and shouted, "Dravidian! Smoke screen!" At which point he threw one of his smoke bombs against the floor and masked their escape.

The trio scrambled through a brilliantly-lit chamber which gave Shekalane the impression of being the source of the images being projected throughout the establishment ... and she quickly realized that the performers weren't human but rather artificial beings designed to look like humans (but in disrepair so that their inner mechanics, so clearly artificial and yet curiously organic-looking, as though the beings were full of white onions and egg noodles, were visible in various places.)

At last they burst through another door onto the docks and gained their boats, quickly shoving off as the group of men, now grown to a mob, crowded the planks. Dravidian saluted them with his scythe, still feeling buoyant from the strange drink, while Shekalane, also still feeling its effects, peeled off her garments and struck a majestic pose.

And then they were on their way to Flax, a village in which they were to perform something precisely according to Jamais' instructions—not a single word of which they had heard.

Sthulhu flopped and batted about beneath the crate as the device strapped to Valdus' wrist suddenly illuminated and began beeping. Clever old Lector had done it again—this time by fashioning a homing beacon that would be activated the moment Shekalane removed the note from the cylinder, which she had clearly now done.

"They are not far," said Valdus, studying the illuminated map, even as the last of their ships cleared the *vetitum portas* into the new realm. "We shall have them before nightfall."

XI | Exorcism

By the time they'd been shown the other gateway back to *Styx Flumen* (which lie well-hidden in its grotto just a little downriver) and backtracked to land at the ramshackle dock near the rude farm in the rude village where the cage stood, having left Jamais' boat tied off just around the bend, Jamais had debriefed them on the plan and they'd all donned their disguises: Jamais as the exorcist in Dravidian's black cloak, Shekalane as the prostitute in a midriff-baring Samhain Eve costume from Jamais' inventory (one shoulder of which had already been damaged by Milkweed's little claws in the creature's desperation not to be separated again), and Dravidian, bound with his own shackles, as the possessed, afflicted man with his oil slick-colored poncho and green-gray, dead-blue skin.

The background of the plan and the need for it was as simple as the plan itself: Having been shot at with a bow and arrow the first time he had tried to approach the property, Jamais had made enquiries at the local tavern and learned that the land was owned by a poultry farmer named Parvus Periver—a paranoid and miserly man known to visit the local brothel obsessively and to have long since lost his mind to ignudi dust. Thus they would present themselves behind the safety of the gondola's shields and pretend to barter Shekalane for the use of his cage in an emergency exorcism. Then, once inside, it was hoped Jamais' research would allow him to activate its lift mechanisms. As for what would happen after that—who could say?

And yet no arrows came, even when Jamais called out in his booming, baritone voice, and when Parvus emerged at last from his shambles of a cottage he seemed more curious than anything.

"Dravidian, you are possessed," Shekalane reminded him, and he immediately began tugging at his chains and gnashing his teeth.

"We are in need of your help, good sir!" cried Jamais, wrestling with Dravidian, who was shackled to the boat. "I see you have a cage over yonder by the cliff face that could contain this poor afflicted man while I sprinkle Holy Water. May we use it?"

Parvus looked from Jamais to Dravidian to Shekalane to Jamais again ... then back to Shekalane, who made a point to appear small and separate as though she were with them against her will. Milkweed had curled into a ball amidst the jumble of her hair and was not visible save for the tip of a webbed wing, which Parvus appeared to take special note of.

He looked at Jamais dubiously. "Have never seen holy man with sword at his back. And why need cage for shackled man?"

Jamais moved to speak then paused, raising his eyebrows. He glanced at Dravidian and Shekalane. "The man's affliction ... has imbued him with superhuman strength. Once, ah, the Holy Water flies ... he will surely break his bonds. As he has done before. As for my weapon ... I may be a holy man, but I am no fool. It's a dangerous world."

Parvus studied him, and it occurred to Shekalane that for a man who had "lost his mind to ignudi dust" he seemed awfully cogent.

"That cage full of chickens," he said at last. "Where else I put them while you do this thing?"

Jamais hesitated, affecting deep and troubled thoughts as he struggled with Dravidian, who hissed and spat at him. "It would entail a loss if you were unable to recapture them, I understand. But I have money and will pay you generously. How ..." He struck Dravidian with the back of his hand. "Settle, damn you! How much will you take?"

The man glanced at Shekalane, who shook her head slightly.

"I have money, preacher," he said, and gestured with his arm to indicate 'No.' "Who is woman?"

"This ..." Jamais indicated Shekalane but paused, thinking. "This is Jolie Laide. 'Beautiful ugly,' as the French say ..."

Shekalane put a hand on her hip and arched an eyebrow.

"A good woman with a vile trade seeking reformation. She owes me a life-debt for liberating her from a cruel master of demidaines. I hope to deliver her to the nunnery upriver, that is if they will take her with her familiar, from which she is quite inseparable. Show yourself, little one ... he will do you no harm."

Shekalane reached around and roused her, and Parvus' face lit up as Milkweed's tapered head poked out from her hair and looked at him with sleepy, slanted eyes. White dust billowed slightly as Shekalane drew the drooping shoulder of her garment up.

"Hello, little one ... fear not," said Parvus, wetting his lips slightly. "She make lot of dust, that one. So, ah, white, and pure ..."

Dravidian cried out suddenly and groped for the elfemale, causing her to squeal and to take flight briefly—directly to Parvus' shoulder, where she alighted without clawing him and began to coo against his neck.

"Alas, money is all I have to trade," said Jamais, and took up the oar. "I am sorry we disturbed you."

"Wait!" said Parvus, touching Milkweed's wing and running a white finger beneath his nose. "I have idea, preacher."

We could be a theatre troupe, though Shekalane with a wry smile as they all played their parts: as Jamais circled the cage, rustling chickens aside and flicking Holy Water into it from his silver flask (which she would have bet good money was full of whiskey), and Dravidian hissed and yanked at his shackles within (which had been secured to the cage using the extra pair from his belt), and she herself —rather, Jolie Laide—stood beside her new guardian and teased his stringy hair playfully.

"Now it is safe for me to enter and finish the process," said Jamais, and triggered the cage door, which whirred as it pushed out and slid sideways.

Shekalane distracted Parvus while Jamais examined the control board.

"I will need the young woman's assistance," he said at length, and she quickly went in.

He was just about to power up the control box (which Milkweed had alighted on), when a group of Valdus' men burst upon the scene—yanking Parvus aside and activating the cage door, which moved sideways and seated inward. They searched him for weapons roughly and found the key to the cage on his belt. A henchman held it up: "Is this for the cage?"

Parvus nodded, and the henchman used it to lock the door, looking up from the lock at the same time as Shekalane and making eye contact with her. Milkweed flitted to a lever near the ceiling of the cage and looked on.

The men quickly surrounded them, aiming their crossbows. Someone shouted, "Hold! Valdus comes."

Jamais indicated the power switch to Dravidian and Shekalane with a nudge and a nod, then reached for it slowly. One of the men snapped forward, aiming his crossbow directly at his head.

And it was it this moment, oddly, and none before, that she noticed the golden plaque secured to the bars, and on it the unusual inscription: "Is *all* that we see or seem but a dream within a dream?"

Now what in Ursathrax is that supposed to mean? thought Shekalane as the shadow of a man in a cloak and pointed hat grew upon the wall, and when she at last turned around she saw Valdus' eyes glaring back at her, and she saw, too, that any innocence those eyes had ever expressed was long gone.

The Pierced Veil

I | Confessions

Valdus arrived and paused outside the bars, taking the scene in, trying to figure out what was what, then began circling the cage slowly, making extended eye contact first with Shekalane and then Jamais—whom he paused in front of. His dark eyes flicked to the platinum key and back. "Who are you, sir?"

"I am a man of the cloth, as should be obvious," said Jamais. My name, if you must know it, is Jamais Vu."

Valdus just stared at him. "I do not trust you. Remove the key from around your neck and toss it between the bars." He added quickly: "Not your weapons—any of you. Do not so much as think about them. We will deal with that in good order."

Jamais hesitated, trying to pretend it was nothing, but quickly realized the ruse would get him nowhere. He surrendered the key and Valdus put it on his belt, then continued circling. He stopped in front of Dravidian and they stared at each other.

"I have confessions for you, ferryman. Would you like to hear them?"

Dravidian stood slowly, sliding his shackles up the bars, and glared at him flatly.

"The power stations, for example. All the work of my men and me ..." He paused, cocking his head, and Shekalane saw his eyes virtually sparkle with pride. "But, of course, you and your Lucitor already knew that, didn't you?" He continued to walk slowly around the cage. "The barge assaults. Again, my men and me. Indeed, on at least one occasion it was but one of my men— General Hirth here. Likewise, it may interest you to know that we've established supply chains and weapons caches throughout

Ursathrax, some in the capitol itself. It was not difficult; the people support our insurrection. Of course they are not happy when loved ones get caught in the crossfire—who could blame them? But it is important that the Lucitor understands that we will stop at nothing to achieve our ends."

He circled around to face Dravidian again and stopped. "The All Servants' Day attack, for example."

Shekalane did a double take to make sure she had heard him correctly, for the news of that dreadful event had reached even the likes of Jaskir.

Dravidian glowered at him. "Many women and children were killed in that. They were watching from the crowd as the flotilla passed. The flotilla was shielded, as you must have known. The onlookers were not." He paused. "I was there. The body parts burned as they hit the shields. You are nothing but a murderer, Valdus. And your revolution will meet the same fate as the others."

"Perhaps. And perhaps not. But I am a murderer no more than you. I just do so directly, and for a just cause. Such is the price of a free Ursathrax." He ended the conversation abruptly. "Put something on the girl and take her to my boat, and prepare the block. Pray to your Lucitor, ferryman. It is almost time." He whirled to leave as they removed Shekalane from the cage. "Watch them carefully."

And as they spirited her away and she locked eyes with Dravidian over her shoulder (then saw him exchange glances with Jamais), she could only wonder what the two men were thinking.

II | Reunion

They went to where Valdus' boat was moored, after which he told the guards to leave and the only sound was the river gurgling against the bank and the creaking and chipping of wood—which Shekalane quickly realized was Sthulhu trying to break free from the crate.

At length he said, "Why?"

There was a long pause.

"I thought he might be my son."

"Your *son?*" He paused for a beat. "Do you think me a fool, Shekalane? He is too old to be your son. I guess him to be no less than ... thirty."

She turned and took a couple steps toward the edge of the dock, then looked out across the river. "I know. I knew it when he told me his name."

Valdus' tone became menacing: "Why would he tell you his name, Shekalane?"

She felt him glaring at the back of her head. At last she said, "He wants to run."

There was an even longer beat before Valdus chuckled bitterly, then laughed. "You mean to tell me a ferryman is running?" More laughter. "To where? A chicken coup?"

Shekalane didn't say anything.

"Is that why you were half-naked in a pen with a mask-less ferryman and a fat, old priest?"

She gazed into the depths, trying to sort her conflicted thoughts and feelings. It seemed to her as if she had been awakened from an enchanted dream and snapped back to a rude reality. Her thoughts and emotions swirled like the water. "There are times when a woman can accomplish more with ... allure ... than a great man with a great army, Valdus."

Another silence.

"What do you mean?"

"You were correct in not trusting Jamais' response. We met him immediately after entering *Cuniculum Amoris.*" She tried to think fast on her feet, thought of the 'Peddlin' Pair' sign on Jamais' boat. "He and his wife are thieves. They steal rare and valuable objects and sell them up and down the River Dire. The peasant, Parvus, is in fact quite wealthy. Jamais spoke of a chest he keeps in his bedroom, a chest full of precious gemstones, the key to which only Parvus knows the location. We were running a distraction for Jamais' wife ..." She thought quickly. "A master lock pick. In return we were to be given portions of the spoils. The ferryman planned on using his to run as far away from the Lucitor as he could."

"And you with him, Shekalane?"

Yes, she thought, *a thousand times, yes!*

"No. No, of course not. My intention was to contact you once he was gone."

There was a long pause as Valdus considered everything. "Is that all it was?"

Shekalane said, softly: "Yes, my love."

"And there is nothing between you and this ... ferryman?"

"Only friendship ... which began as a misunderstanding."

She watched his shadow pace to a nearby tree and pause. "Only friendship. With a monster." The water gurgled; Sthulhu struggled within the crate. "You have become as a starving woman then, indeed." He turned around. "The ring ... do you have it?"

She fingered the hoop hesitantly before facing him again. "I've obtained information we could not have dreamed of, my love. You must hear me ..."

Valdus was holding out his hand.

She took off the ring reluctantly and placed it in his palm.

Valdus sighed. "I am not the thick brute you seem to think me, Shekalane. I realize there would have been a period of time where you may have been ... conflicted. It is a conversation for another setting." He cupped the side of her face in one hand. "I have not been a very attentive lover, I know."

Looking into his eyes, she was surprised by this rare insight into her on his part, as well as the admission, and began to feel her old feelings for him stir.

He began playing with her hair gently. "One day, when this is all over ..." He slid his hand around to the back of her head and began pushing slowly, moving her face closer. They kissed, softly at first, then more and more passionately. Alas, she found herself thinking about Dravidian, again finding it odd that his dead-blue lips should be so warm while Valdus'—flush with life—were cold. Thus she found herself mentally pulling back even as he pulled her harder against him, pressing into her intensely. She could feel his arousal through their clothing, and she felt something else, as well—Jamais' platinum key. The key to their eventual escape from Ursathrax.

Her head hung back as he began kissing her neck, and she sighed, wondering at all the beautiful lights in the great stalactites above.

"I confess, I feared you had betrayed me at the gate," he said. "But now I realize how invaluable the information you possess will be." His kisses petered off. "Tell General Hirth everything you have learned so that he may cross-reference it with our attack plan."

Shekalane slowly came out of it, lowering her chin and looking at him dazedly.

"A dragger comes, aboard which we have learned is Asmodeus himself," said Valdus. "I intend to abscond with you in the ferryman's gondola, wearing his own accoutrements, and put us back upon the River Dire—directly in the path of the prefect's ship. Naturally, upon detecting us, they will bring us aboard, as you and the ferryman are being searched for even now. Then, having circumvented the dragger's defenses, I will cause its shields to be lowered ... and signal my men on the shore to attack. Once the ship has been secured, we will continue on course to *Novum Venum,* where we will lay siege to the Grand Port ... and the House of the Lucitor itself."

Shekalane just stared at him, completely sobered from what she was beginning to feel a moment before. She shook her head slowly. "How will you do this thing? How will you cause the dragger's shields to be lowered?"

As she spoke he used his knife to pry the green stone (the original homing beacon) from the ring; he held up a new one, a near-duplicate of the first, slightly darker. "This is a shield bomb. Its primary components are a shield generator and a highly directional explosive. To use it you have only to point its face at the target, like this ..." He demonstrated. "... and shake it three times, which will activate a timer. You must shake very hard. The bomb will blast outward, away from you ... killing everyone within fifty feet, and causing the ship's shields to go into emergency shutdown. At the same time, a temporary body shield will be generated, which should protect you from the blast. The prefect will want to question you about your disappearance, as well as your ties to the insurrection—"

"About us? How could he know that?"

"Perhaps you should ask your ferryman." He looked at her penetratingly. "I only know that he does, or suspects. You are being hunted, Shekalane. And when they find you, they will interrogate you. And when they do, you must detonate the ring."

"But ... why me?"

He finished seating the device in her ring, then held up his hand, a finger of which bore an identical hoop. "Because your role in this is that of a fail-safe. I do not know what will happen once we are brought onboard, or whether we will be in proximity to one another. What I do know is that Asmodeus will want to question his ferryman as much as he'll want to question you, perhaps more. When he does, I will lower my hood and reveal myself to him. Then I will kill him. Alas, there are too many variables and the stakes are too high to leave this to chance. If the task falls to you, I ask only that prior to detonating the ring you call out, 'For Valdus.' By this I will know to hit the deck, after which my men will attack ... and slaughter the survivors." He paused. "Fear not. I think you know which option I'd prefer. You are merely a redundancy, Shekalane."

She just looked at him—the relational aspect of his statement not lost upon her. She looked down and realized the ring itself—which she had first taken as a sign of love—had always been utilitarian. "From a homing device to a bomb," she said. "Never a token."

He looked her in the eyes intensely. "From a wife-to-be to a seductress. We are at war, Shekalane." He held up her hand, said, "It is because you wore this that Ursathrax will be saved. You have done well."

"What is to become of the ferryman and Jamais?"

"This ... Jamais. Will he talk?"

She shook her head. "He has no interest in the affairs of *Styx*—of our world."

Valdus nodded slowly, thinking. "I will interview him, and we will take it from there. As for the ferryman ..." He chuckled. "Do you need to ask? He must be killed, of course. Immediately." He turned to leave.

"He's just a pawn. He was conscripted into service just as I."

Valdus paused. "Your persistent concern for him is ... troubling. It engenders questions of faithfulness ... of loyalty."

"I am loyal," she said.

He turned around—as though a lantern had been lit—appearing hopeful. "Prove it. There is a way."

She bowed to her knees at his feet. Looking up at him, she said: "I did not activate the beacon. You must hear me out as to why."

"Yes, I know. My last message contained a new one, the cylinder itself. It was activated when you removed the scroll."

She looked at him as though wounded. "So you did not ... never mind. I understand why you may have doubted."

"But why did you not activate?"

"Because I knew you would kill him if you found us."

She thought she saw a red dot flit across his waist, but when she looked at the crate it was black.

"Yet there is still so much to be learned, Valdus. He has told me so much. And I can promise you he will tell me still more. But I need more time." She lowered her head. "The choice is yours, of course."

He lifted her chin gently. "You have carried out a brilliant deception for the cause, my love. But time is a luxury we are running out of fast. I ask that you wait here while I attend to something."

She looked up at him. "And I ask that you make time for me. This one time." She began kissing his fingers and the matching ring. "Help me to help you."

She unbuckled his breeches and freed him.

"Shekalane, there is no time ..."

"You must make time. And know that I will be by your side, always. Have I ever failed to finish what I've started, lover?"

He grunted and gasped as she stroked him. "And if I refuse? Will you have the stomach for what comes next?"

"Let me show you what I have the stomach for ..." She took him into her mouth.

He put back his head, and she snuck the platinum key from his belt.

Valdus said, "Your skills as a courtesan ... remain unrivalled. It is no wonder that—"

Sthulhu cawed and his mood changed abruptly ... and he stopped her.

"Whatever strength I have left, it is not to be spilled upon the dirt. Wait here."

He tucked in and strode off, leaving her dazed and confused ... and strangely conflicted. On one hand she felt like perfect filth; on the other ... She touched the key (which she had hidden in her cleavage) as she watched him go, then got up and ran after him. "Valdus! Wait!"

He ignored her even as Sthulhu started gnawing at the slats of his crate. She caught up to him on a grassy rise beneath the trees and turned him around by the shoulder. "Stop and listen to me for once! The ferryman knows of a hidden corridor which leads directly to the Lucitor's cathedral. He only spoke of it once, but suggested that if His enemies were to gain access to it ... they might circumvent all of the Mansion's defenses."

Valdus stared at her for a moment. "Then a full-frontal assault might not be necessary ..."

"He said it was protected by a key-code, but that the ferryman are privy to it. I can get this information for you, Valdus. Go and search Parvus' house for the peddler's wife and the chest ... but return me to the cage so I can milk him for the code. And before you say you will extract it from him yourself, know that the ferryman's hatred for you is complete now that he knows of your involvement with the parade attack—as complete as yours is for Asmodeus and the Lucitor. He is not going to tell you anything."

He glared at her, uncertain how to respond. At last he said, "Very well. You shall be returned to the cage for a period of one hour. But guards will remain at a distance, and I expect a full report when I return."

She shook her head. "We deal for that, as well as all the other information."

For once, Valdus appeared almost speechless. "What is it you want, Shekalane? You want that I should just set the ferryman loose so he can warn his brothers? The wall between this world and our own is thinner than you presume, dear lady. As is the wall between wanting to run and wanting to return." He sighed. "You ask too much of me. You knew who I was and what I was sworn to do before we ever became betrothed."

She inhaled deeply. "But I did not know the lengths to which you would go." Her eyes were serious, his almost apologetic. "People change, I know," she continued. "The ferryman wants to be free of his servitude, for example. But I do not believe you have changed so much as to murder an unarmed man while the woman you love begs you to show mercy. That is not the Valdus I love. That is not a Valdus I could love."

This seemed to reach him, at last. At length he said, "I will consider it, Shekalane. For you."

She caressed the side of his face gently, then glanced at the glittering stalactites once more. "Have you looked at them? Like an upside-down city ... Everything's so much bigger here. Do you think people live in them?"

Valdus looked up, briefly. "I'm sure we will never know."

She watched him, waiting for him to say more. But he only looked back at her somewhat blankly. "My focus ... is on the Ursathrax from whence we come. I—I am not like you, Shekalane. I exist in only one world."

Something crossed her mind, a mixture of adoration and pity. She pecked him gently on the lips. "I know."

III | The Cage

They returned to the cage at the base of the cliff wall, all eyes upon them.

"Put the girl back in with the others," said Valdus, then ordered two men to stay behind while he and the others searched of the area. "You come with us," he said to Parvus.

They were in the process of exiting the scene, and the henchman from before had unlocked and caused the door to open, when an Ursaquake rattled the clearing ... at which point Shekalane snatched the keys from the henchman's hands and got into the cage—triggering the door shut behind her and reaching through the bars quickly to re-lock it.

"Now, Jamais!"

Jamais hit the switch.

There was an electrical hum as the control panel sprang to life, lighting up like an ornamental tree, as well as the sound of machinery activating—immediately followed by a *hiss* and a *scree!*—which startled them. Shekalane noted a large, wide, horizontal lever that was flashing blue in the 'STOP' position, and shouted to Jamais, who gripped it in a beefy hand. He glanced at Dravidian and then Shekalane, both of whom nodded. Then he pushed forward on the lever, to 'UP.' There were three quick, hard beeps, followed by a clunk and a shudder as the cage began rising—rapidly.

Shekalane peered between the bars at Valdus, who, having heard the commotion, turned around—appearing flabbergasted by what he saw. He took a few steps toward them, clearly riveted, then froze, surely seeing the platinum key glowing at Shekalane's chest. He reached for it on his utility belt ... before locking eyes with Shekalane as the cage continued to rise—then came out of it suddenly, calling: "Crossbows!"

His men opened fire as the cage increased speed—unleashing a flurry of bolts, some of which ricocheted off the bars while others passed between them, including one which struck the control panel resulting in a shower of sparks and the cage ascending even faster. Shekalane felt her stomach drop as she gripped the bars—saw river smoke become treetops which became open sky which became the great glass formations which became Cyclopean stalactites, in the glowing windows of which she thought she saw people moving.

Within seconds they had breached the shell of Ursathrax where it began to curve and were engulfed in a breezy blackness. She happened to look downward through the porthole window in what appeared to be an escape hatch in the center of the mesh floor—saw the light shrinking below as their speed increased and wind whistled through the cage, tossing their hair, ruffling their clothes. As the light shrank away to nothing she thought: *Everything you have ever known, vanished like smoke ... just wind through a keyhole.*

There was another *screee ...!* which continued as Dravidian voice-commanded his shackles to release, shouting: "Free bonds!" But they did not open.

"If they are voice-activated, that won't work with this noise!" shouted Jamais over the screaming sound. "Try another command!"

"Right bond release," snapped Dravidian—and his right shackle released. "Left bond release!"

His left shackle did not release.

"Left bond release!"

"It may be that we are already too far from the mainframe," exclaimed Jamais, his eyes never leaving the control panel, which chimed for each invisible floor passed, growing in rapidity, while a digital readout ticked off numbers: 2,000 feet per minute ... 3,500 feet per minute ...

There was a rumbling sound, like heavy cloth flapping rapidly in the wind. Jamais studied the panel, ran his fingers along an illuminated row of switches labelled 'LIGHTS.' He flicked one on, and immediately a bank of powerful spotlights illuminated the iron scaffolding flashing past on one side—giving Shekalane a tantalizing (and terrifying) glimpse of Ursathrax's innards, the grand machinery behind the world itself.

She gasped and cried out: everything seemed gargantuan and vaguely threatening. Jamais hit the other switches, activating spotlights on all sides of the cage, including the roof and bottom. They were moving at dizzying speed through a seemingly endless infrastructure. Again, there were three quick, hard beeps. Then, suddenly, the cage slowed, causing their stomachs to leap into their throats— and stopped.

They all looked at each other, still gripping the bars, the hair hanging in their faces. There was a near total silence save for their labored breathing and a kind of vast and vacuous moaning.

"Shekalane, the other shackle," said Dravidian. "Try pulling—"

They all jumped and Shekalane gasped as a great wheel with vertical tracks began turning just outside the cage; she glimpsed giant gears, teeth, black oil, mercury-red fluid coursing through transparent tubes. The disk rotated into a horizontal orientation, and locked into position. Something decompressed loudly, followed by more beeps, and they began moving again—horizontally.

Now they were able to get an extended look behind the stage curtain, the grand illusion. They saw great air ducts and what appeared to be a leviathan boring machine.

They were peering transfixed at these sights when they passed through a series of huge spider webs, which stuck to and covered the cage. There were large fly-like creatures caught in these webs, most of which had been cocooned, but some of which were still alive and struggling. One of these was at Shekalane's eye level, and she was both horrified and mesmerized by its grotesque nature and its frantic movements, until the bulk of the webbing was torn away by the lift's velocity.

She watched the webbing dance away behind them before locking eyes with Dravidian, and her face must have looked traumatized because he tried to bring some levity to the situation by saying, "I wonder what the peasants are doing tonight," and smiled.

This made her laugh in spite of everything, and she was just starting to gather her wits when she felt something crawling up her leg, and she looked down to see a spider the size of a grapefruit scurrying toward her head. She shrieked and batted it away—but it only landed on the floor nearby and quickly righted itself before aggressively scrambling back up her leg. She backed into a corner, batting at it wildly—regardless, it had reached her throat and had placed a leg on her chin before Dravidian snatched it by its carapace, his fingers sliding between the creature's legs, and slammed it against the bars—which accomplished little but to enflame it further. He slammed it again, and it became so angry that it nearly freed itself from his grip. He held it there while it struggled ferociously and shouted, "Shekalane! My scythe! My belt has twisted ... I can't reach it ..."

She rummaged quickly beneath the oil-slick poncho, originally mistaking his cock for the weapon, then whipped the handle free and looked at it, depressing the blood-red switch and causing the great, golden, purple-hued blade to swing out with the ringing of steel. She sliced vertically between the bars, up one side of the spider and down the other, severing its legs, the stumps of which shot gouts of yellow-white blood. There was another series of beeps as Dravidian dropped its body to the floor and she looked down at it resolutely, the hair hanging in her eyes ... and the cage suddenly slowed, grinding to a halt, throwing Dravidian against the bars, and her against him, so that they were eye to eye and nose to nose.

They both jumped again as another mighty wheel started rotating rapidly outside, gears grinding, teeth ratcheting, oil glistening. The disk circled until its tracks had returned to a vertical position and locked into place.

Jamais said: "Hold on to something. We're going up again."

Dravidian and Shekalane looked up—saw two, no, three spiders on top of the cage. Something decompressed loudly, followed by yet more hard beeps, but this time one of the tubes burst, spraying the floor of the car with red fluid as they rose. Two of the spiders fell between the bars, one dangling by a single leg while the other lowered quickly on a strand of web. Shekalane cried out and grabbed Dravidian tighter, dropping the scythe—which clattered against the floor.

The insect landed a few feet from Shekalane and moved about uncertainly as Dravidian reached for his weapon, which was just out of reach. Then the thing moved away from his hand and began scrambling up Shekalane's back. Dravidian's fingertips brushed the handle of the scythe, causing it to spin sideways ... and to be even further out of reach. Shekalane cried out again as the arachnid scurried up her long hair. Dravidian strained to reach his weapon, his wavering fingertips almost there, even as the spider began crawling over Shekalane's head, and she screamed. Dravidian gripped the handle of the scythe and swung it up decisively—stabbing the insect straight in its abdomen. The grotesque, yellowish fluid rolled down his arm as the thing shuddered and died, and he flicked the blade—hurling the creature against the far wall. He was staring at it when the other spider suddenly dropped in front of it, inverted, its legs dancing wildly. Dravidian jumped—even as the dancing subsided, and more yellow-white goo bubbled up from the corpse. He looked up and saw Jamais sheathing his knife.

The cage shook as it picked up speed—metal rattling, small parts ringing—on and on and up and up, faster and faster, until the scaffolding and machinery suddenly gave way to solid rock. There was a sound like gravel under horses' hooves as earth and stone blurred past all around them—like papyrus belts spinning at unbelievable speed—the lights on the sides of the cage playing along the rock, reflecting back. There was a sound like a rockslide, an avalanche, which became a roar! Wind blasted through the cage vertically; the temperature started to get cooler and cooler.

Dravidian and Shekalane clung to one another desperately, still covered in a fine lair of webbing, their eyes squeezed shut, his cheek pressed against the top of her head, her cheek pressed tightly against his chest. She could feel his heart beating: it was accelerated, of course—but not like hers, which seemed about to punch through her breast. She found it unbelievable, impossible, that she could feel so comforted even as the world shook and roared and seemed to fly apart around them. She couldn't get close enough, wished she could climb right inside him.

Take away the light, she thought, *and all the world is just hearts beating in darkness. Beating alone! Blind! How could one be sure that they themselves even existed? And yet the beats of one in close enough proximity to another pinged back, didn't they? Like the signals of bats. And they said: you are alive; you are not a wraith, not a vampire, not a thing without a reflection! Not a thing alone in the darkness. Any two were a cathedral.*

Her reverie was interrupted when she noticed dark-red blotches, almost maroon, spattered over the mesh floor, at first taking them for the machinery's fluid, but then realizing how much darker they were. She followed them with her gaze—to Jamais' boot which was covered with the stuff, then up the leg of his trousers which were streaked, and realized with horror that there was a crossbow bolt lodged in his side, and that he was bleeding.

The cage shook violently, loudly, as their speed increased, and Dravidian shouted, "We are out of control! We're going to crash through the ceiling of the shaft!"

Jamais pulled the lever back to 'STOP,' but nothing happened.

Shekalane observed another lever start blinking on a panel above his head, and shouted, "Above you, Jamais!"

He looked up and reached for it—then cried out suddenly, touching his side. When he turned his palm out it was covered in blood. Above him, beyond the bars of the roof, beyond the tube flashing by with dizzying, almost sickening speed, a pinpoint of yellow light began flashing.

Shekalane's chin trembled and her feet went numb, and her ears popped furiously. Every portion of her body had become heavier, even her face. Her head sagged forward and down, and her brain felt as though it was suffocating; she felt as though her heart itself had become a heavy stone.

She looked through the mesh floor briefly—found it difficult to look up again. When she succeeded, she saw—through a reduced field of vision—that the flashing yellow light had turned red, and was twice as close. She poured all her energy into standing, grasping a bar to help pull herself up, finding it nearly impossible, and reached for the lever—but such was the gravitational force that her arm and hand no longer wanted to obey her commands. She pushed herself to the extreme as the light grew larger and her vision shrank to a tunnel, then grasped the lever in a final, desperate lunge, and pulled it. Immediately a portal irised open, flooding the shaft with light, and her stomach leapt into her throat as the cage slowed abruptly and they emerged into a world of all-encompassing white light ... and stopped.

Valdus was still peering up at where the cage had vanished into the ceiling of the world when something caught the corner of his eye at ground level, and when he focused on it he saw it to be something about half the height of an average man and covered with a drop cloth. He strode to it immediately and yanked the cloth off—revealing a podium with a curved stand and what appeared to be a control panel on top.

"Where is Lector?" he said hastily, sensing an opportunity.

"I am here, my lord," said the old man, joining him at the console.

"What is this thing?"

Lector studied the panel before pressing a button labelled 'POWER' and causing it to light up with a variety of glowing indicators and levers, some of which were burned out and inert—including a darkened lever clearly labelled, 'DOWN.'

"I believe, my lord, that it is an exterior control panel for the cage." He pulled on the lever to no effect.

"Can you fix it?"

Lector looked up at him slowly, confidently, even cockily, seeming his old self for the first time since the explosion of the Sun Engine.

"My lord," he said, bowing. "You may consider it done."

IV | Thesea

Shekalane remained frozen for several moments, uncertain where they were, or even if they had completely stopped moving. Her stomach was no longer in her throat—and yet the air was still restless, ruffling their hair and clothing gently.

There was a familiar hiss followed by the sound of robust mechanisms as the door pushed out and slid open. She covered her eyes partially in the blinding whiteness, her vision slowly adjusting, as Milkweed fluttered out erratically, blinded as she. She could hear a vast and airy sound, as though an impossibly large giant were inhaling and exhaling, and the squawking of birds.

Their surroundings began to materialize as the blinding light withdrew into a dazzling, searing disk, impossible to look at directly. They were in a new world—not merely a new environ of Ursathrax but an entirely new dimension—one that extended in all directions for as far as the eye could see.

They had emerged at the top of a towering cliff at the edge of a vast body of water—a towering cliff among other towering cliffs, most of which were still taller, so that layers of shale-like rock in varying colors were exposed spectacularly in the fierce orange haze. Even through her dizziness, Shekalane had a sense that the differently colored bands told a story, somehow, like the layered pages of some great book. Water birds roosted and circled and reeled in breezy flight patterns everywhere and she followed one of them as it launched from its nest among the neighboring rocks and dove to the base of the cliff—where it vanished beneath the waves crashing mercilessly against the rocks— then saw it emerge with a fish in its beak before shifting her gaze out across the depths, which rippled and shined and were divided by bands not unlike the cliffs, past the water stacks, all the way to the horizon.

Her eyes weren't used to seeing so far—this world opened up layer after layer, each more faded than the last, so that it achieved a depth that was virtually impossible in the underworld. It was, she reaffirmed, in every sense of the word, truly a new dimension. And the clouds! There were entire ranges of them, entire inverted landscapes, hanging above—like red-orange mountains in the sky.

Jamais stepped out, grunting, holding his side, looking on, and Shekalane followed, also looking on. Again, Dravidian spoke the command to open his remaining shackle—but it still didn't work. A red indicator light that usually remained solid now flashed repeatedly. He stood slowly, sliding the shackle up the bar. Shekalane heard the sound and turned to face him, then took a step closer. Dravidian indicated Jamais with a nod of his head—who was limping around and still gazing off in awe, and badly wounded—said, "Please ... help Jamais."

She placed the palm of her hand on the side of his face, then hurried toward Jamais, calling his name. But he didn't seem to hear; he was too distracted by the wonders around them. She too found herself once again glancing at the light: it was hot, blinding, too much—and yet she wanted to grow toward it, be closer to it. It was a little like her feeling for Dravidian—and Valdus, too, to an extent—something that overwhelmed and terrified her, but also drew her to itself.

And it was decidedly male, she thought, that great, burning disk. It sought to penetrate her, to give her life— but also to burn her to a cinder with its great shafts of light, as it did the clouds. And such shafts of light! Of course she'd seen rays through clouds before, in Ursathrax—*Styx Flumen*—but these were different. They—the light, the cliffs, the water, this entire world—it didn't feel created. It didn't feel designed, constructed, as did everything in Ursathrax. It felt ... *uncreated.* Uncreated by man that is.

Her distraction was so great that she stumbled and ran right into Jamais, who pivoted to support her with both arms, crying out in pain, before quickly covering his wound with a hand. They looked at each other and she realized there were tears streaming down his face ... and blood through his fingers. A lot of it.

"It is Thesea," he said, deliriously. "I was right ..." Milkweed fluttered about behind him.

Shekalane nodded and put a hand on his shoulder. "Yes, Jamais. You were right."

"She is close ... my Sarabella. I can feel her. She saw this." He glanced around, gasping in the wet breeze—then nodded to himself, as though to confirm. "She saw this. The True, Great Work. She is a part of it now."

Shekalane smiled up at him warmly, almost motherly, her eyes misting up. She put her free hand on his other shoulder and encouraged him to sit down on the rocks, then unclasped Dravidian's black cloak at his neck and pulled it off him, maneuvering it around the scabbard. She yanked the knife from his belt and tried to cut the cloak into a bandage ... when it would not cut or rip, she pulled her top over her head—but the sun immediately seared her impossibly white skin, causing her to cry out. She grabbed Dravidian's cloak and clasped it about her shoulders, began ripping her top into a strip ... then started wrapping his torso with the material as the wind gusted powerfully.

"She beckons me to join her ..."

She made a knot in the bandage, jerking once, twice, as Jamais grunted. Then something dinged loudly and she looked to the cage—saw Dravidian leaning toward the control panel, which was just out of his reach.

"By the Lucitor," he said.

"What is it?"

"Valdus! He's ordered the cage back down."

Shekalane and Jamais glanced at each other and the big man seemed cognizant for a moment. "Get out of there, Dravidian!" Jamais shouted.

Dravidian rattled his shackle to indicate he could not. Shekalane scrambled to her feet and rushed to the lift, but the instant she reached it the machinery hissed, exhaling loudly, and the hatch began to close. Dravidian grabbed its moving edge, trying to stop it, but to no avail. He glanced about quickly before his gaze settled on the door frame itself, then groped for his scythe under the oil slick-colored poncho, unhooking it from his belt, and held it out, pressing the button to extend its shaft.

He stretched toward Shekalane with the pole. "Block it with this ..."

She just looked at it, dazed.

"Quickly!"

She snapped out of it and grabbed the handle—but it was already too long to fit between the jamb and the moving door.

"The blue rocker," said Dravidian. "It adjusts the length ..."

She pressed it, extending the shaft even further, then again, causing that same shaft to collapse back into the handle. The door was only about a foot from being closed when she jammed the handle length-wise between it and the jamb, stopping it.

They lowered their heads in relief. They'd scarcely had time to catch their breath when a harsh beeping began, and a robotic voice said: "Warning. Door unsecured. Lift will resume motion in 90 seconds. 89 ... 88 ... 87 ..."

Dravidian said, "Tend to Jamais ... I will return."

Shekalane froze, looking up at him. The wind buffeted her hair.

"Do it! I'll be back. But I'll need my weapon."

She looked at him, then back at Jamais, who was standing again, roaming, gazing at the sky—then beside him, at what appeared to be a podium ... or another control panel. She looked back at Dravidian. He looked at the device tentatively—"77 ... 76 ... 75 ..."—and nodded briskly.

She ran to the podium and found that it was, indeed, an exterior control panel ... alas, it had been exposed to the elements for 500 years, and was merely a ruin. She ran back to the cage, steadying herself by gripping the bars of the door, and lowered her head in exhaustion. "No good ..."

The countdown continued: "68 ... 67 ... 66 ..."

Dravidian reached between the bars, covered her pale hand with his own dead-blue one. "Jamais ..." She began shaking her head. "Someone has to make it, Shekalane. Someone has to survive."

"61 ... 60 ... 59 ..."

She looked up at him, shaking the hair out of her teary eyes, and felt a desperation she had never known. "Not without you! I can squeeze through and belay our descent with the panel ..."

Dravidian stared at her intently, earnestly, and said, "It is too late, Shekalane."

There was a buzzing sound which faded quickly and he looked at the panel, the lever of which no longer glowed.

"Look, see? The lever has gone inert."

She stared back at him, nodding slowly, as though beginning to accept the situation—then suddenly ducked under the handle and squeezed through. She turned away before he could respond and called to Jamais through the bars: "We will return for you, Jamais!"

This time, he did turn around, and stared at them in a daze, at least initially. But then he seemed to focus, looking at them in much the same way as when they first met upon the River Dire. He laughed gently, holding his side, and began taking difficult steps toward them.

"You still make quite a pair ... the tempter and the taker! I somehow knew, the moment I first saw you emerge from the gloom, that we would become great friends. And I knew ... that you belonged together ... like my beloved Sarabella and I. *Synergique vrai amour,* your true synergistic love ... the one who opens all doors."

Shekalane said, "Try not to move any more than is necessary, Jamais. We'll be back."

He shook his head. "No, no. I shan't be here. I am where I belong, my friends, where I've always belonged. It is where you belong, too—where all Ursathrax does." He slid the scabbard which contained his beloved charts around to the front and caressed it dazedly with bloody fingers. "Alas, would that it could be so without the key. Wasted, it is. Everything I have done."

Shekalane reached between her breasts and tearfully revealed the recovered platinum key to him, causing a glint to reflect off his tunic. He looked up and saw it ... and chuckled briefly. "A synergistic triangle is now complete. Return you must, then ... but not for me. Do it for all the world. And bring with you all who will listen."

The robotic voice continued: "31 ... 30 ... 29 ..."

"In the cabin of my ship you will find a trunk full of journals ... the key is in the teal bell-jar at the stern. These will help guide you through Greater Ursathrax should you be unable to return in the cage. Between these journals, the key, and ..."

"24 ... 23 ... 22 ..."

He suddenly lifted the sheath over his head and off his shoulder—crying out in horrendous pain.

"Jamais, no!" cried Shekalane.

He took a couple more steps toward them but found he could not continue, and pressed the fist containing the sheath to his side in pain.

He caught his breath. "This, like your love for one another, is a gift ..." He grimaced. "Neither are to be squandered ... nor treated lightly. The sword, Rosethorn, is of particular consequence, as you will see. I wish I had more time to explain. Use them to create something that transcends the both of you. Give birth to a new world. I have left what other clues I may."

He held the scabbard out to them, but they only stared at it in a daze.

"11 ... 10 ... 9 ..."

"It is important to me that you take it. Please. Let my own love not to have been in vain."

Shekalane reached for it with tears in her eyes—had just brushed it with her fingertips when Jamais collapsed onto his knees, the blood gushing from his torn dressing. He fell forward, the sheath tumbling to the rocks, as Milkweed fluttered desperately about him.

"2 ... 1 ... maglevs engaged."

And the lift dropped back into the earth.

V | Lying in Wait

Lector looked up from the control panel and smiled. "The cage is on its way. The floor scale indicates it is carrying approximately two-hundred and seventy-five pounds."

"Shekalane and the ferryman," said Hirth.

"Or the thief," said Valdus. "See to it the elevator is locked into place when it arrives." He turned to his men with crossbows. "Take your positions. You will fire on my word only. Do I make myself clear?"

The men with crossbows took up their positions as the lift continued down, and the machinery hummed with power, seeming to grow louder with each passing moment.

Valdus thought: *What spell has he laid upon you, Shekalane, that you would betray me—betray us all—in such a way? Do you cleave to him just to hurt me? Was my absence this time so long, me devotion to the cause so complete, that you felt yourself scorned? If thus, than you have lied from the start when you said your passion against the Lucitor was universal, not personal. You lied all those nights we lay together after exhausting our passions and discussed until morning the beautiful ideal to which we strove—the destruction of Asmodeus and the Lucitor, the ending of the Lottery, the reorganization of all Styx Flumen into a free and sovereign democracy!*

Hirth said, "Even if he is still partially shackled, the ferryman may throw his blade, if he has it. I have seen it done."

"On my word only," repeated Valdus. He sensed disagreement and looked up to see Hirth and Lector exchanging glances. He locked eyes with Hirth. "You have your orders, mister."

VI | Descent

The sound of the surface world was lost very quickly and Shekalane felt as though they were hovering in empty space—before the cage shook violently and her heart skipped a beat. She quickly became conscious of her respiration—realized she was sucking in air and exhaling it in rapid bursts. The fact that they were plummeting now became evident due to external sensations, such as the rush of air past her body and the pressure against it.

She heard a low-pitched fluttering noise and a whistle of varying intensity and pitch, like that which occurred when one blew air through relaxed lips while moving their tongue back and forth. The whistle became a roar, like a giant fire—snapping, popping, crackling. The lights of the cage on the passing walls of rock even looked like flames—as if they were plunging into Hell itself—as they sank faster and faster amidst a rhythmic shuddering and rolling.

Her eyes were irritated by the slip stream and she felt a steady pressure on her body from below. The rock flashing past became iron scaffolding. There was an ear-piercing *skreee!*

followed by a shower of sparks and a tremendous heat against her face, which she assumed to be from the breaks, and she smelled something burning.

Dravidian began shouting something, which she couldn't make out over all the noise. Meanwhile her feet had gone numb and she closed her eyes as they reached terminal velocity. She had no internal sense of falling with her eyes closed, but the sensations caused by the pressure on her frame, the twisting effect of the slip stream, and the ear noise caused her to feel that they were still plunging and plunging fast.

I was wrong; this is how it truly ends, she thought, and held onto Dravidian desperately. *Either dead in the impact if the brakes fail, or dead by Valdus' hand.*

For if there was one thing she was certain of, it was that he would not forgive her again. *Black hole, white fountain,* she thought, her mind reeling. But there would be no white fountain, no blooming like some great and terrible flower into a new world, a new lover, a new self. There was only this, only the making of fast friends to lose them faster, only meeting your one, true synergistic love to be killed beside him—or worse, to be spared while he alone was killed— only birth and death and pain and loss. There could be no rebirth, no phoenix rising from the ashes, no Thesea, not just for poor Jamais or themselves, but for anyone. They were lost, all of them: every person, every soul, in Ursathrax, even Valdus—especially Valdus! And the most horrible aspect of it was, she no longer cared. It was a total eclipse, a complete annihilation, a perfect surrender to the irresistible hunger of the black hole. And it all would have been assured if Dravidian had not pulled the handle of his scythe free of the door, pressed his lips to her ear, and said a simple, potent series of words.

And those words were: "I am free of my bonds."

VII | Return

Valdus said to Lector: "E.T.A."

Lector looked at his readouts. "Level 16, and slowing."

Hirth unhooked a sphere-bomb from his belt.

"No bombs," said Valdus.

Hirth raised a shaggy brow. "Shall we throw flowers, my lord?"

Valdus didn't say anything, only held his gaze, then turned to face the lift.

They doubt your willingness to do what is necessary when it comes to Shekalane. You have entered the time when allegiances might be reevaluated and faith to your leadership questioned. Would you see the Revolution jeopardized owing to your attachment to a woman who no longer loves you—worse, who has actively betrayed you?

"Level nine."

Or, again—would you make of her an example? After all, who would question the commitment of a man who had killed his own betrothed for the cause?

"Level seven."

The time is coming, Valdus. A time for killing more than just the Lucitor's servants or whatever innocents get in the way. The time is coming to kill your own friends, if necessary. No one said it would be easy, this doing of the impossible, this disruption of the Lucitor's complete and total hegemony over everything and everyone. And yet you have done it—have you not? You have done what no man had so much as dreamed, and you have done it with so very little, with virtually nothing but your own will at first. But history will judge you either hero or mass murderer on the outcome alone. Nothing must jeopardize the success of the Revolution—nothing!

The cage appeared suddenly—easing onto the lift pad in a plume of smoke, hissing, and everyone stood at attention. There was a shuffling and clinking of weaponry. At last the hatch opened, pushing out and aside as smoke poured across the floor, and Valdus' men fidget anxiously.

"Hold," he said. "I command it."

They all watched raptly as the smoke began to clear, until two figures began to resolve, one much taller than the other, with its arm upraised—

"Fire!" shouted Valdus.

And everyone did so, their bolts clinking and clanking off the bars and ricocheting off the stone wall behind. Yet the figures remained standing, the bolts passing through them as though they were ghosts, and when the smoke cleared Valdus saw that Shekalane and the ferryman were not there and that they had only punched holes in a handful of garments attached to the rear bars: a black cloak (as well as what appeared to be the ferryman's mask and other upper accouterments) and an oil slick-colored poncho.

And Valdus saw something else: a gloved hand reaching up from the floor and drawing a hatch closed.

"Those with bombs, follow me," he said quickly, and rushed forward.

He entered the cage and lifted the hatch in time to see the tip of Shekalane's garments disappear into the service tunnel.

"Run from him, Shekalane! Save yourself!" And to his men he said: "Drop your bombs and get clear."

Shekalane heard the explosions even as Dravidian opened the hatch and scrambled out of the chute, then offered his hand and pulled her up and out.

They had emerged not twenty feet from the gondola, and as the explosions rocked the ground beneath their feet Dravidian closed the hatch quickly, revealing it to be disguised as a giant toadstool.

THUMP–THUMP–KER-THUMP-THUMP-THUMP! went the explosions as Dravidian untied them and shoved off, and neither of them could resist pausing to gaze at the columns of fire and mushrooming smoke.

Shekalane's eyes misted over. "It's lost to us now, isn't it? Not just Jamais ... not just Milkweed ... but Thesea."

"I fear that it is so, Shekalane," said Dravidian.

She watched the plumes of smoke rise. "He fights a mirage, a lie, and does not know it."

She looked at Dravidian as the glow of the explosions played upon his face.

"I suppose I will never see her again," she said, and felt tears arcing down her cheeks.

"And yet you may," said Dravidian, indicating the toadstool with a shake of his head. "There are doors, my love. Now ... help me to row. The grotto Jamais showed us ... we shall hide there."

VIII | Treasure Cove

"Dravidian," said Shekalane after he had rowed them skillfully into the blackened grotto (and she had taken advantage of the dark to re-don her green garments). "Do we dare to use the lanterns? How close do you think they are?"

"I spied the lights of their boats before we entered the cave," he said. "Very small in the distance. I think we have time."

He activated the bow lantern, and there beyond the gondola's blade-like ferro lay a veritable treasure trove of Jamais' surplus wares: chests heaped with silver and gold and pearl necklaces, sacks spilled over with rubies and sapphires, chalices and decanters of a hundred varieties, furs and pelts and exotic textiles stacked like cordwood and draped from oversized vases, crates of full of ornamental candles, of incense and myrrh, of swords and knives and halberds and pole arms, of colorfully-wrapped fireworks and foreign liquors and exquisitely-blown pipes and hookahs.

Dravidian and Shekalane looked at each other, then back at the cornucopia.

"I suppose we will have to stay here tonight," said Dravidian.

"Mm." She nodded absently. "I suppose."

Nor were Jamais' riches all the grotto had to offer, for it was overgrown with every manner of mushroom—all of them enormous—blue buttons and purple paddy straws, great, golden morels, gypsies with rounded, phallic caps and towering portobellos the size of small trees. Some had flat caps and some conical, some were covered with silky fibers while others had scales, some had gills that were creamy-white or pale pink while others were of deepest blue and oozed black liquid. It was a veritable multicolored forest of domes and gills and stems, and yet, to her surprise, Shekalane knew them all, or most of them, from her days traipsing dry creek bottoms and shady glades with her friend Unklung.

And finally, just as Jamais had promised, there was the door, unique from the previous ones in its appearance but bearing next to it the same control panel—a panel that was darkened and inert.

Shekalane fingered the platinum key, looking at the door, then lifted its chain over her head. She handed it to Dravidian. "It is safer with you. Will you return us to Styx Flumen?"

He turned the key in his hands, shaking his head. "Indeed, I wish to never let you go, Shekalane. And yet ... my honor pulls me in two directions at once." He paused, thinking. "You were right about him. He is a very haunted and dangerous man. I confess, I feared you had been lovers once. But I see your soul now. No, deliver you to the processing terminal after what we've experienced?" He shook his head again. "I am a monster, but not such a monster as that."

He swung the rope of the platinum key over his head.

"Dravidian, I ... there is something I must—"

His placed his fingertips to her lips. "If the mouth of the cave is spotted, we may both have to flee back into *Styx Flumen* temporarily. Let us test the key and douse the lights. There isn't much time."

This they did—but upon insertion the panel remained inert. He tried it several times and several ways to no effect. They looked at each other.

"Could he have been lying about it," said Shekalane, "or taken leave of his senses?"

He shook his head slowly. "I don't think so. Remember how it glowed when the Ursaquake hit. Twice; first aboard Jamais' boat, and then in the cage. No ,,. it is a problem with the door itself, I think." He looked at the crates of weapons. "The mouth of the cave is narrow. I will fortify it as best I can with those." He nodded to indicate what he was looking at.

She followed his gaze but instead focused on the crates of candles (and the boxes of matchsticks atop them), then the stacks of furs and textiles. "I'll light some candles so you can douse the lantern, then prepare us a place to sleep."

IX | Between Two Worlds

By the time the lanterns of the search boats began moving past in the inky dark, they were as ready as they could be: Shekalane having prepared for them a thick bed of furs amidst the mushrooms and Dravidian having fortified and booby-trapped the cave mouth with all manner of spiked weaponry. They watched by candlelight as the questing boats sent up flares, which shot toward the stalactites and exploded like fireworks ... before trailing down, white-hot and sputtering.

Dravidian said, "They are free to move about in a way they never could have in *Styx Flumen*. One dragger would have been the end of them."

Shekalane shook her head almost wistfully. "A dragger ... a great ship, powered by slaves." She gazed at the stalactites, which shown in stark relief by the harsh light of the flares. "Like Ursathrax herself, I suppose."

She turned to Dravidian. "They have a plan to capture one ... to use it as a Trojan horse. To attack *Novum Venum*."

Dravidian looked at her. "Is that what you wanted to tell me ...?"

She hesitated. "Partially. But there is something else ... something—what is it, Dravidian?"

The flares had apparently borne some result, for a single boat had broken off from the rest and was slowly moving toward the mouth of the cave. Dravidian activated his scythe and Shekalane gripped her pole arm tightly.

Dravidian said, "I will take one side of the opening while you take the other. If they enter, we shall catch them in a pincer movement."

Her pulse quickened as she took up her position, and yet she was amazed at her overall placidity, and she suspected that the true fear, the kind of fear that set one's legs to trembling and emotions to crack under pressure, would come after—if they survived.

"When the time comes," said Dravidian from the other side of the opening, "strike and fear not. And do not stop striking until everyone who would harm us is dead upon the water. We ... we have no choice now, Shekalane."

She nodded determinedly.

And yet, as the boat continued to close, she began to doubt herself as well as the outcome, and with her doubt came a warbling and a quaking in her stomach, a shaking in her arms, and she questioned her ability to fight at all, much less to sink a blade into her former lover if he were among their attackers.

A light shown onto their position and they shrank back amongst the shadows. It wasn't until fine sediment began sifting the air between them that she realized it wasn't just she who was shaking, but the cavern and the world itself. And she realized, too, amidst the quake, that the platinum key around Dravidian's neck had begun to flicker and glow—as had the control panel near the door, which now read: 'Styx Flumen | Zone 72.'

"Dravidian," she snapped, indicating it, and he immediately strode toward it and inserted the key.

The door between the worlds decompressed instantly and slid upward along its tracks, and she was about to go through when Dravidian stopped her.

For the boat, now bobbing precariously upon the water, appeared to be turning back. Indeed, it was being signaled by the others even as they watched, and Shekalane felt a great relief wash over her as it completed its turn and began returning to the group. And at last they were gone, moving on down the River Dire.

They stood before the doorway and gazed out at *Styx Flumen,* at its smaller circumference, its smaller stalactites, its narrower waterway.

"How oddly comforting it seems just now," said Shekalane.

Dravidian nodded.

"Like a nursery," she said. "The orbs themselves just ... toy suns. I feel like I could fall asleep beneath them and never wake up." There was a silence. "You said the capitol was beautiful ..."

"Yes," he said. "Beautiful. But small, although I always thought it large." He smiled, shaking his head in deep thought. "I know nothing. Not even myself."

Neither spoke for several breaths.

"What will you do, Dravidian?"

When he didn't respond, she touched his face gently. "You want to warn your fellow ferrymen, don't you?"

He nodded.

She looked back at *Cuniculum Amoris,* and took a few steps toward it. "Strange, isn't it ... how one world can be so gray, so lifeless, yet safe, except for the Lottery. While another can be so beautiful ... and yet savage."

She turned to face him. "I asked you once what the brides were like ..." She returned and took his hand. "But I never asked you what your fellow ferrymen were like."

She looked at their clasped hands, struck, as always, by the contrast: his so blue, as though dead, hers pink and full of life.

"They slumber and do not know it. They are at peace, I suppose."

"As are all dead things." She moved her face in front of his. "As I was, when I met you ..."

He leaned in to kiss her—as an enormous stalactite broke loose with a shower of sparks in *Styx Flumen* and fell crashing into the water, the impact of it rattling the ground in both worlds, causing one of the glass structures in *Cuniculum Amoris* to fall as well.

Dravidian turned and took a step in that direction. "Thus will go the whole underworld in time," he said.

She watched the stalactite slowly sink in *Styx Flumen,* burning, until water started jetting from places all over the ceiling and the weather beyond the door became a downpour.

"Is it up to us to save them?" she asked at last. "The things we've seen ... what we know ... are we responsible now?"

She felt his hands on her shoulders, and angled her face toward his ... and saw in his grave, earnest eyes the answer she knew to be true, and they kissed in the liminal space between worlds, softly at first but then more and more passionately, until his hands were on her breasts and her legs were trembling and they sunk into the pelts and textiles she had piled and laid out as the door slid slowly shut behind them.

And as they lowered something came over her—spirited through her—a kind of playful demon; and she twisted him so that he fell upon his back amidst the furs and pillows and she upon him, her dark hair tumbling over her face, and began playing with the hair of his chest, kissing it around the key—not with abandon but with a slow, meditative quality, for she wished him to know that she was about to set out upon an exploration of his body but knew they had all the time in the world ... for the time being.

For the key had come at a price. And, rightly or wrongly, she felt a debt was owed for the betrayal.

Perhaps he sensed this and wished to spare her (although he need not have, for she wanted him; in every way a woman could want a man, she wanted him), because he took her face gently in his hands, and, nose to nose with her in the flickering dark, asked, "Are you scared?"

She glanced up and down his face. "Of what has been put before us?" She shook her head slowly. "Not so long as we face it together." She wiggled against him, shivering slightly. "It has grown cold; the great vent we passed upon first entering *Cuniculum Amoris,* and the others we have seen? It is as though they blow cold air ... as though the quake has disrupted something in the bowels of Ursathrax herself." She moved the hair away from her eyes. "I want to warm you, Dravidian. I want to be warmed by you ... from the inside. I want to please you and to feel your essence slide through me." She touched her fingers to her larynx, then slid them delicately between her breasts. "Do you understand?"

He gazed into her eyes, the fine folds around his own crinkling in a way that made her want him even more.

"I would please you first," he said softly, kissing her once on the forehead, once upon the nose.

"I am dirty ... and it is too cold to expose my shoulders," she said, lying.

He picked up one of the fur coats and helped her into it, then stroked the hair next to her temple, laying his head slowly back against the pillows. He gazed up at the gondola's steel ferro (which loomed above them for the ship was right behind him and the flat-bottomed boat's prow rested well above the waterline), and said, "Take hold of my ship's ferro, Shekalane. And hold on tightly."

She looked at the great black and gold ferro, which pointed like a scimitar at the ceiling of the cavern, and its comb of seven tines, six pointing forward and one back, then back at Dravidian, whom she kissed before pushing herself up by her arms and, with the assistance of Dravidian's big hands on her waist, gripped the topmost tines, the forward of which was etched with the word 'Jaskir' and the backward of which was etched *'Novum Venum.'*

She looked down at him as he hiked her frayed dress up along her dirty thighs and realized she was breathing far too heavy and fast, and tried to calm herself by observing the grotto around them, the piled treasure, the phantasmagoria of mushrooms. But then his cheek grazed the inside of her thigh and he began kissing her leg softly, and she surrendered all pretense to being in any sort of control.

X | Dravidian's Passion

His years of rowing had given him the hands of a masseuse—calloused, to be sure, but soft somehow, too, managing to be both solid and supple, and imbued with equal parts iron and finesse. She sighed as she felt them glide up and down the small of her back beneath the fur and her tunic, even while his breath and lips kissed the inside of her legs. Her grip upon the steely tines relaxed as the metal warmed to her touch, and she could feel the tension leave her like so much cold liquid as he rubbed his fingers gently but firmly into her flesh.

"Talk to me, Dravidian ..."

"Relax," he said, playing along. "As though you were in my gondola ... floating lazily down the River Dire on a summer afternoon."

She laughed a little at her own request.

"I can see it. I trail a hand languidly in the water ... while you row, standing tall and straight as a spire."

He slid his hands down around her haunches and squeezed gently, then rubbed his fingers softly up and down her tail bone, dipping into the area where the cheeks began to form.

"And you lay across the cushions and gunwale like an exquisite bolt of silk." He ran his tongue meanderingly up the inside of her leg. "The contours of your drapery in this vision invite me to warm speculations, Miss Shekalane. I would abandon my oar."

She sighed, pushing her haunches tight against his hands. "I wear no undergarment. Abandon it and speculate not."

She laughed, but it was a nervous laugh, as she knew she was open to his full scrutiny now, and, although she had groomed herself carefully in preparation for the Sacrificium, they had been through much since.

Again he ran the tip of his tongue along the inside of her leg, this time the leg opposite, but on this occasion he did not stop, causing her breath to hitch as he sucked gently at the soft flesh between the leg and her vulva and began kissing and licking, harder now, along the perineum.

Again her breath hitched. "Oh, Dravidian! I think you are a torturer and not a ferryman."

He placed his hands upon the insides of her thighs and gently but assuredly spread her legs further open, almost to the point of discomfort, then swept the flat of his tongue up slowly and firmly, from the bottom of her perineum to just short of her clitoris.

"Oh, oh ...!"

She moaned as he slid it down again, nearly to her anus—then up once more, flat and wide over her labia (still sparing the clitoris), again and again, causing her to shudder almost violently and dew up like the mushroom heads all around them.

"Close upon me, Dravidian," she said, and very nearly growled. "Close upon my little manhood and smote it again and again. I—I command it."

She laughed.

"Not yet," he said, and began alternating his strokes so that they covered the entirety of her vulva; and such was her spending that she felt embarrassed by it and more than a little sorry for the mess she was making ... and yet he did not seem to mind, but in fact lapped at her as though thirsty.

Oh, Dravidian, she thought, her entire body veritably quaking, *my sweet, devilish Dravidian. Never would Valdus spend so much effort nor lavish such attention upon me, never in a million years ... you are not the taker, indeed. And this in the full knowledge that I was prepared to please you with my own mouth, to de-venom you completely and to rest upon your stomach while you dreamt—having expended no energy at all.*

She envisioned them lying naked in Dravidian's gondola as they floated lazily downriver, but from a bird's eye view, as Sthulhu might see it. They lay on their sides, he behind her (and fully inside her), holding her in his arms, and she curled away, a perfect yin and yang. She moaned as, in the vision, he thrust his hips slowly in and out, while she pressed her haunches against him, ground them into him, her face contorted in ecstasy. It was only then—as though sensing she was in that mystical space only sex could engender, and thus ready—that Dravidian passed his tongue over her clitoris.

She gasped and arched her back, her heart pounding, her chest heaving, her nipples hardened to river-polished pebbles as he swept over the swollen bud again and again—then stopped suddenly and wiggled his tongue against it.

"By Ursathrax, it is too much," she exhaled. "I could come right—"

He stopped as though on a coin and pulled his head back, allowing a couple breaths to pass, then pushed forward again while wiggling his tongue, repeating this each time she was about to orgasm, as though he were in her thoughts, in her mind, inhabiting her very body. Until she could take it no more and grasped his head in both her hands and held it against her as tightly as she could, at which point he began sucking on it and nibbling at it even while sliding his hands up her body to her breasts, which he massaged in a circular motion while teasing her nipples with his thumbs.

And then he had at her with abandon, licking, sucking, nibbling, lapping at her, lapping up her spending, bearing down upon her like an animal—until, feeling as though a circuit had been completed and that electricity were coursing through her entire body, she came powerfully, as though she were in a canoe and shooting the Great Falls themselves, the force of it rolling through her like waves, from his tongue to her clitoris to her buttocks and up her spine, to her heart, where it seemed to explode out of her and leave her in utter ruins.

And it was at that very moment, as she shuddered and trembled in the aftermath of what had been multiple climaxes, that she observed the conical, vermillion head of a familiar mushroom—the *somnium carnales*—which she had harvested many times in Jaskir, but which she had eaten only once (with Valdus) ... and knew precisely the pleasure she would bestow upon Dravidian.

"Tell me what you are feeling ..."

He moved to respond but could not find the words he'd thought in his possession. Now that he'd ingested the mushroom pieces, he suddenly felt imprisoned, stifled, as though his thinking had become just so much muddy water.

She must have had some idea of the helplessness he felt, for she spoke to him as one might speak to a pet, or an infant.

"I didn't mean for it to confound you," she said, and giggled like a little girl. "But women like their men confounded, did you know that? It brings out or maternal instincts, I think."

She had begun nudging the fur and her top garment down one pale shoulder.

"Shekalane, I—"

"Have I told you how handsome you are beneath your mask?"

"But Shekalane ... I feel ... Surely ..."

"You will have a vision first, which some say is a dream while others claim it to be a different reality." Her warm hands had run down past his navel. "The vision may show you something significant ... Be mindful, lover. Then you shall find yourself here again but in a heightened state of pleasure."

"But ... how will I know ..."

"Relax," she whispered, and began kissing his stomach.

XI | Mushroom Dream

She rose suddenly and took him by the arm. "Come with me," she said, and turned to leave.

Was this the vision?

He remained. Their arms tugged against each other.

She turned to face him. "It is the vision, my love. See how you are fully-dressed and wear your mask, which you know to be still in the cage."

He looked at her, saying nothing. She released his hand and crossed the room, glancing at him alluringly over her shoulder every few strides—until disappearing behind a green veil.

He followed her. If pressed, he could not have explained what he was thinking; he wasn't, really. At least not in any way he was accustomed to.

He brushed the veil away and stepped from the cavern, entering a torch lit stairwell which contained a spiral staircase leading down to semi-darkness. He could see no trace of her nor detect any sound of her descent. Nevertheless, he followed the metal steps down and around, his own footfalls hurling metallic clanking sounds deep into the tubular stairwell, where they reverberated off the stone walls to echo like thunder.

He had not descended far when he happened upon a door cut into the damp stone wall. It hung wide invitingly, opening onto an oddly lit room from which tapering green veils bellowed forth to dance restlessly in the flickering torchlight, the semi-translucent tapestries casting strange and languid shadows on the faces of the rough-hewn stones. It was altogether curious; for, as the winding steps had only led him further below ground, he could not guess where the breeze might have found its origin. Mystified, he gripped the scythe's handle and entered the room, brushing aside veils.

It was like wading through a dense forest. And after wading through it for perhaps a quarter mile, he was no longer certain he could find his way back. He pressed forward regardless, and found at last what could only be described as a clearing. It was a large area in which the beautiful emerald hangings were spaced further apart. He assumed it must be the center of the room, yet for all he could see the forest of blowing veils went on forever and contained many such spaces.

Be that as it may—he'd obviously found someone's sleeping quarters. For at the clearing's center was a low-lying bed, round of design and exquisitely crafted. It was heaped with white cushions and throw-pillows (save one which was entirely green, dark enough in shade to be nearly black), and draped with bolts of emerald silk. Someone had placed a basket of green apples on the floor beside its headrest, and next to that a bottle of green wine, which caught the light and glowed. Everything was echoed by cheval glass mirrors, rocked back on their pivots to stand vertical in their frames. One of them was moving as if turned and instant before. Yet there was no sign of Shekalane.

Cautiously, he moved forward. And as he neared that little oasis of soft things and polished glass, he discovered at last where both the breeze and the light were coming from. For his eyes had suddenly registered the chamber's opposite wall, which was not really a wall, but rather a grid, beyond which he could only make out vague hues of green and brown. The outside world. That odd light was merely sunlight filtered through green veils.

The grid itself consisted of simple wrought-iron piping but was adorned with great, flat, metal cut-outs which were painted green and seemed to be imitations of veils in the breeze. When glanced at casually, the illusion of depth was nearly seamless. He ruminated on this overlong, perhaps, but it occurred to him that one could live the entirety of their life in such an illusion and never know of the vast, real world beyond. Indeed, wasn't that what everyone in Ursathrax ...

Something caught his eye and he turned to face the fringed, green-black pillow. And here was a curious thing, for it had been embroidered in gold with the phrase, "Is *all* that we see or seem but a dream within a dream?" There was something else about it, too—something protruding slightly from beneath it. Slowly, he reached out for its edges and lifted the pillow away.

A thick, curved blade lied in wait against the sheets.

He breathed deeply, his eyes fixed on the gleaming weapon.

"Here, ferryman."

His scythe was in his hands and swinging at the speaker's legs with its shaft fully extended before he'd spun around enough to see that there was no danger. It completed its deadly arc and he feared for an instant that he'd taken the legs of an innocent person. But Shekalane's bare feet slapped against the floor and he realized she'd leapt above its path. And then one of her feet was gone into a blur and his scythe was no longer in his hands. He heard it clatter against the floor a short distance away.

And somewhere in all that surging adrenalin and racing blood their eyes met, and they realized what had happened, and the laughter came so suddenly and was so overpowering that they fell against each other for support and seemed to flow together like two liquids, and he wanted to lock his lips about her own so desperately but couldn't because of the mask, and he wanted to squeeze her tight against him and run his hands along her body yet couldn't because of the gloves, and realizing this, she took his hands carefully in her own, saying, "Come to me."

And then she pulled him to the bed and the vision was ended, and he was back amidst the furs and textiles where he'd began, and his breath hitched as he came powerfully, so powerfully that she gasped and *Mmmed* but did not relent, until it felt as though a primal circle had been completed and his strength and essence had been transferred into her.

Perhaps they'd been equally eager to please, she and him. For surely no less than three minutes had passed before she at last left him and lay upon his stomach. By that time he felt as though he'd been drained of more strength than he had indeed possessed to begin with, and it was an awful, frightening, delightful sensation.

"You came a lot," she said, her throat clicking thickly against his stomach.

"I—I am sorry, Shekalane. I—"

She rubbed his chest. *"Shhh.* I wanted it this way. I ..." There was a silence. "I think I'm in love with you, Dravidian."

He stroked her hair softly, saying nothing, then gently lifted her chin. "And I, you." He continued stroking her hair with his thumb. "Alas, what lies ahead ... it will be no easy road."

She shook her head slowly. "The road will be what the road will be." She lifted herself slightly and lay her head upon his chest. "Let us speak no more of it. Just hold me. And let tomorrow fall where it may."

Such was their disposition until her eyelids began to droop and her consciousness began to fade, and she fell asleep in his arms, which along with his shoulders were one of the few aspects of his physique possessed of much mass, and this only from so many years rowing.

He laid awake for some time, gazing at the stalactites on the ceiling and listening to Shekalane's breath against his chest. Rationality had returned at last, and he examined the various elements of the vision, which she had said to be mindful of, with a troubled brow: a thick, curved blade lying in wait against the sheets ... a multitude of veils ... a fringed, green-black pillow embroidered with, 'Is *all* that we see or seem but a dream within a dream?' It was a vision that spoke of mystery ... and whispered betrayal.

And yet, ultimately, he decided that the vision was mere phantasmagoria and that he'd continue to trust her. To do any less in the face of what they'd shared would have been cowardly and paranoid. He believed he understood Shekalane. There were certain women who kept that special place within themselves, the mysterious wellspring from which all things deeply personal flowed, hidden forever behind a shroud of fog no man could ever fully penetrate. But since the need for this place to be accessed from without was nearly as great as the need to keep it hidden safely within, they learned early to let flow certain streams in certain directions, to be sifted by certain hands. One man was lover, the other; friend, still another; father figure. The cards were dealt at the start of the game. And a man could no more trade his hand for another's than he could trade his very soul.

Perhaps, he reasoned, it was merely because of their shared path that she'd taken him as a lover. Regardless, he accepted the card she offered gladly, for it was a fine one indeed and his hand had been empty for a long while.

XII | Luminis Sub Omne

When Dravidian awakened, he found the temperature had dropped still further and that he could now see his breath. He also found one more thing—which was that Shekalane was no longer by his side ... and, realizing the implications of this, he sat up with a start.

But though he scanned the chamber thoroughly, he saw no sign of her—although he did observe a darkened recess in the cavern wall that could have been a doorway. It was curious he hadn't noticed it before.

He put on one of the great fur coats, shivering, and investigated—found that it was, indeed, a passageway. Moreover, it was a *warm* passageway—strangely, a hot wind blew through it—

equally strange, it was illuminated, although the source of its red-orange light was clearly at a distance.

He hadn't progressed far when he came upon Shekalane's shoes and fur coat, abandoned on the passageway's rough-hewn stone floor. He stepped over them and continued, coming next upon her green shawl ... then her camisole, then her garter belt and emerald stockings, until at last he rounded a corner and entered a large chamber and beheld her standing naked before a Cyclopean, rounded, vertically-positioned grate, beyond which, in the inky blackness, burned a red-orange disk, itself as tall as one man standing on the shoulders of another.

And yet Shekalane's lithe, beautiful form was not the only figure in the room, for all around stood statues depicting humans of every size and shape, posed just as she, with their arms spread wide and their palms turned up, their fingers splayed, some upon the floor and others upon alters and inside coves, and scattered among these were baskets of fruit now withered and fallen to rot. So, too, had someone piled Jamais' finest pelts and textiles all about. Had Dravidian been pressed to explain what he saw, he would have offered that the red-orange disk was some ancient device tasked with regulating the temperature of the world, similar to the great warming vent they had passed upon entering *Cuniculum Amoris,* but a thousand times more potent. And as for the statues, they were representations of worshipers, perhaps, and the fabrics and baskets of fruit, offerings.

He read the words chiseled crudely into the stone above the grate: *'Luminis sub omne.'*

"The light ... under all." He looked at Shekalane as she turned around. "What does it mean?"

"I'm sure I don't know," she said. "But I feel something has changed ... something in the mechanics of Ursathrax itself. What blew cold last night now blows hot ... as if the world has ... corrected itself." She turned and gazed at the inscription. "Perhaps it refers to a kind of mirror image of what Montair calls the demonic sublime—are you familiar with that?"

"Yes," he said, then shook his head, shirking off the fur coat, allowing it to crumple to the floor. "And no. In truth, I have never really understood that aspect of his thought."

"It refers to ... a dark intent ... that underlies all things. What my father used to call *sub umbra,* the shadow behind."

"I'm afraid I don't understand."

She turned to face him again, then glanced him up and down, appearing to admire how he looked in only his boots and trousers. "You have a demonic sublime. It ... shows through ... not only through your musculature and how it forms fearful and compelling patterns, but in how you are looking at me right now."

She took several steps toward him, utterly confident in her nakedness, her chin held high, her dark eyes full of resolve. "What would you do with me, Dravidian? My own demonic sublime ... it calls to you. Can you hear it?"

She lowered to her knees before him and pulled on the thong that secured his trousers, then loosened the laces and pulled the sturdy, black garments down just enough to free his metal, which rose to meet her mouth almost gracefully, its beautifully-formed, dead-blue head crested with a dewdrop of precum.

"I feel as though we commit a sacrilege, Shekalane ..."

She paused, looking up at him. "Then let us commit it."

And she pulled him down upon the pelts and fabrics as he gave into the seduction, realizing he could no more resist taking her than he could change the fate the Lucitor had given him.

He could not lie.

The truth was that from the moment they hit the bed of sumptuous textiles, and he knew her sultry face and languid body would be his to ravish, the question of where they were no longer existed in his mind. Carnal selfishness overrode all else. He wanted her, and he would have her. There was no room for questions of honor, ethic or duty in the equation.

Perhaps sex is a divinity, as some would say, he thought. *For do not divine configurations always function above the confinements of right and wrong?*

She traced her fingers over his face as he pecked at her lips and pulled back, repeatedly, roughly. "You are youthful-looking for a man of thirty-five," she whispered, then added, "But the gauntness of your face hints at the rugged and weathered man to come. You really are quite desirable. And those eyelashes—Dravidian, have you ever had anyone tell you that you would have also made a lovely woman?"

He started to say that he had not when she cupped his cheeks in both her hands and drew him into her bosom.

XIII | Sthulhu

Free at last, Sthulhu flew.

But he did not fly as his captors had intended—for he had heard their exchange clearly, and knew they had fitted him with a beacon and expected him to fly straight away to his master ... and thus betray his position.

Instead, he flew directly past where his circuitry informed him his master was ... and beat his wings onward.

Toward the end of this new region, wherever it may lie (for only then would he remove the beacon, and he knew just how to do it, and return to his ferryman, having first set their pursuers on a false course). Toward the end of the River Dire ...

    To the end, if need be, of Ursathrax itself.

Black Hole, White Fountain

I | War

Shekalane knew. She knew somehow what the smell was even before they rounded the bend and began floating past the village of Flax on their way to Parvus' homestead. It was an acrid smell, an obscene smell, a smell at once coppery and metallic, but also earthy, oily, a smell that was unnatural and acidic and yet cloying, musky, sweet.

It was the smell of human flesh burning. She knew it even before the great bonfire of corpses came into view, for the smoke coated her mouth and nose, and she knew, also, that it would never leave her, not if she scoured herself a thousand times with soap and myrrh. Dravidian knew it, too, based upon his expression; at least so much of it as she could see, for they had disguised themselves in rich clothing and wide-brimmed hats from Jamais' store (and concealed Dravidian's gondola nearby) for their re-entry into the village.

But the pile of burning corpses, which the villagers were adding to even as the pair walked past, was not yet the worst of what appeared to be the aftermath of a violent battle. Rather, it was the four severed human heads which had been mounted on pikes near the waterline, above a plank upon which had been written, in blood: 'This is what resistance to Valdus looks like.'

Dravidian craned his neck to examine the heads as they passed them, and, although he remained calm (as always), she could see in his eyes that, like her, he was having difficulty processing what he saw. "Did you realize he was capable of this?" he asked.

And there was something about his tone, something bewildered and outraged—a thing unintended but palpable—a hint of judgment; that when combined with the memory of what she'd done to get the key, as well as the horrific reality of the death masks, smote her completely ... so that she fell to her knees in the shadows of the heads on pikes and vomited violently.

He waited patiently for her nausea to pass, rubbing and patting her back, before saying, "Jamais' boat, Shekalane. The charts ... We must get to them." —then helped her up with the assistance of a passing villager in an eyepatch, whom he asked: "What happened here?"

The old woman straightened and answered gruffly, "What do you think happened? Marauders ... pirates. They came in the middle of the night and began kicking in doors. They were looking for someone—a man and a woman ..."

She paused, scrutinizing them with her one milky eye, and Shekalane quickly turned Dravidian by the chin to gaze out across the village. "Look at the carnage, my love. It's terrible."

She hoped the repositioning of his face away from the old woman would discourage further scrutiny, which it did, at least momentarily, as the three of them looked on. The village, meanwhile, lay nearly razed beneath its canopy of towering mushrooms, the rising smoke from its smoldering dwellings catching the shafts of late afternoon light between the treetop-like mushroom caps and causing a funereal glow.

"Some resisted and were killed," said the old woman. "Most the villagers still strong enough to fight were conscripted, and their loved ones taken hostage. The attackers were merciless ... they struck our mightiest limb from limb, some while they still slept. Their leader, a man named Valdus, spoke of a great war, and said it had come now to *Cuniculum Amoris.*"

Shekalane nudged Dravidian away from them. "Where is he ... this Valdus? Where are his soldiers?"

"Oh, they have left," said the woman. "He said they were not interested in capturing territory, only in unseating a tyrant. In truth, I do not remember much of what he said. It seemed to me he spoke long but said nothing, as such men often do."

"They left no garrison, no detail of soldiers?"

"Only bodies ... in a place where even the dirt is too poor to inter them."

"Shekalane, look," said Dravidian, peering upriver, and she followed his gaze to where a single column of smoke rose billowing beyond the village—in precisely the place where they'd left Jamais' boat.

II | Sthulhu Returns

The cage, like Jamais' boat, was completely destroyed. Dravidian had returned to it (while Shekalane scoured the ruined ship for any surviving charts) to retrieve his cloak and other accouterments, but he had secretly hoped the lift might yet be salvaged. It was clear to him now that that was not to be.

He sat down upon a boulder amidst the still smoldering ruins and contemplated their situation, wondering if Shekalane were doing the same, and knowing somehow that she was. He was looking at his now tattered and arrow hole-ridden cloak (still attached to the rearmost bars of the cage) when Sthulhu alighted upon a nearby branch.

"*Awk,*" squawked the bird, his feathers ruffling as he folded his wings.

Dravidian looked up as if from a dream. At length he said, "Is it really you, Sthulhu?" He glanced at the plaque attached to the bars: *Is all that we see or seem but a dream within a dream?* "Or just some cruel mirage come to haunt my darkest hour?"

"It is I," said Sthulhu. *"Awk!"* He turned his head sideways and regarded him with his cybernetic eye—its ruby red beam falling upon Dravidian's naked face. "Is it *you?*"

Dravidian touched his bare cheek, suddenly reminded that his mask still hung at the back of the lift. "It is I, old friend. Although ... I dare say, you have never seen me like this. Much—much has changed since we last saw each other. We have a new directive."

Sthulhu cocked his head as though consulting hidden data, which, considering he was connected one and the same to at least a fraction of the Lucitor's vast mind, Dravidian supposed he was. "Incorrect. Directive remains the same. Pick up and deliver recipients of the black coin to processing terminal at *Flumen Finem.*"

Dravidian stood slowly and approached him. "Your master commands a new directive. From this point forward we are charged with delivering *all* of Ursathrax to Thesea, the processing terminal beyond *Flumen Finem*. This—this directive comes from a higher authority than the Lucitor ... and must supersede all others."

He looked at Sthulhu hopefully; even so, his hand wandered close to the hilt of his scythe. "It is feared the capitol has fallen," Dravidian said. "And that the enemy now speaks with the Lucitor's voice. Our position must not be betrayed under any circumstances. Do you understand?"

Sthulhu did not move, but remained frozen with his head cocked.

Dravidian closed to within striking distance and paused. When Sthulhu still did not speak, he said, "I must know that you understand this directive, Sthulhu."

He moved his hand slowly so that his fingertips just grazed the hilt of his weapon.

At last Sthulhu reoriented his head and his cybernetic eye changed color from red to a greenish blue-white, and a hologram appeared amidst the smoldering wreckage. It depicted Valdus and Shekalane at the edge of the River Dire, he standing and she bowed upon her knees before him.

"Yet there is still so much to be learned, Valdus. He has told me so much. And I can promise you he will tell me still more. But I need more time." She lowered her head. *"The choice is yours, of course."*

Dravidian cocked his head, watching, listening.

Valdus lifted her chin gently. "You have carried out a brilliant deception for the cause, my love. But time is a luxury we are running out of fast. I ask that you wait here while I attend to something."

She looked up at him. "And I ask that you make time for me. This one time." She began kissing his fingers and the matching ring. *"Help me to help you."*

She unbuckled his breeches and freed him.

Dravidian moved closer to the projection, staring at it intensely.

"Shekalane, there is no time ..."

"You must make time. And know that I will be by your side, always. Have I ever failed to finish what I've started, lover?"

He grunted and gasped as she stroked him. "And if I refuse? Will you have the stomach for what comes next?"

"Let me show you what I have the stomach for ..." And she took him into her mouth.

The hologram faded away and a silence fell over the glade as Dravidian reseated himself upon the rock. Sthulhu remained respectfully silent. In his mind's eye Dravidian saw Pepperlung on the deck of their great dragger, *The Vorpal Gladio,* saw him glance over his shoulder at the prefect as his tone became grave: "Beware, Dravidian. The bride is just sightseeing but Asmodeus is here for *you.* You are the only ferryman up for elevation this year. Watch yourself. There will be a test, surely."

The ground trembled suddenly and the remnants of the cage rattled as a minor Ursaquake shook the glade, and the sun orb went from gold to orange. A horse whinnied in the distance and Dravidian looked out across Parvus' homestead to see a great steed leap up in its corral. The slightest push against the dilapidated boards would have freed it—but the creature either did not know or did not care. The horse, however mighty, knew its place. It knew in its primitive yet tamed wiring what Dravidian, in his advanced and now liberated own, did not: that nothing lay beyond its cage that did not already exist in abundance within.

"Sthulhu, go to the boat and await me there," he said, and watched as the raven launched into flight and flapped away.

He entered the husk of the lift and put on his black upper garments: the half-sleeved hauberk and tunic-belt, the padded, vest-like jerkin with its high collar and broad, Manchurian-style shoulders. The jerkin was filthy from their adventures since entering the Forbidden Channels. He brushed the dust from its blue-black velvet with hands that were blue-white and dead-looking. That done, he scooped up the exquisite leather girdle from the floor of the cage and secured it snugly about his abdomen. Finally, he clasped his habit about his shoulders and donned his mask—it was reassuring to feel the façade's velvety lining against his face once again. Then he drew a gold circlet from a sheath in his boot and placed it on his head to keep the hair from his eyes.

He was grateful for the distraction the familiar ritual provided—as always, it allowed him time to think. *Was it true, then? Had she been in league with the terrorists all along?*

(If so, look at what her allies had wrought!)

And not merely in league with—in love with. She loved the Prince of the Revolution, it was clear.

A blue ignudi flitted past and he snatched her in his fist, holding her before him as she struggled and squirmed and regarding her coolly. He now felt certain that Shekalane had been sending Valdus messages ever since they'd gone through the gate—via Milkweed, perhaps, whom he had adored. His heart became steel again as it all came clear to him. Her love for him was like so many other things in Ursathrax, just another illusion, another lie. He thought of all the tests he had passed on his ascendency to Master, and realized *this* was his final test: the greatest temptation of all. He released the elfemale as his mind reeled with the implications.

Illusions within illusions! Tests within tests!

And, such was his thinking, that when he looked once more upon the engraved plaque riveted to the bars—*Is all that we see or seem but a dream within a dream?*—he knew all in an instant what needed to be done.

III | Betrayals

When he returned—mounted upon the horse from the corral—to where the wreckage of Jamais' boat was moored, he found Shekalane fast asleep, curled into a ball on what remained of their friend's bed (which had somehow been spared the same fate as the rest of the ship). But, having much thinking to do still, he chose not to wake her after he'd dismounted.

Instead, he stroked her hair in silence for what seemed a long time, and attempted in that time to convince himself he had done no wrong—that it was too late for regret in any case, and that he could simply transport her back to the gondola and they would be away. He tried to tell himself that his actions had been justified; indeed, that he could have a clear conscience regarding *all* his decisions. After all, it was not easy for a ferryman to resist the caresses of a lover, for those women bold enough to love him were rare. And, certainly, it would not have been easy for any man to resist the caresses of a lover such as Shekalane.

She woke, then, and rolled her head on the sooty pillow to regard him.

"Nice mask," she giggled sleepily.

Oh, beautiful mirage! He wondered if anyone else in Ursathrax had ever lain with someone who might just as well have materialized from their dreams—although, sadly, he knew few ever did in all their lives—only to have to reconsider them in such a way. And he wondered, too, to whom he would even tell the tale—of what he had experienced in this chimera-haunted world, and how badly he had wished to remain with her amidst its sundry illusions, nor how deeply it had hurt to say what he knew had to be said next.

"Shekalane," he rasped, and had to clear his throat before continuing: "We must go ... back to *Styx Flumen.* I—I fear I've lost my direction."

She stopped smiling, then, the sense of playfulness draining from her face like bathwater bled from a basin, and he noticed for perhaps the first time how pallid her face was, how strained her eyes were behind the glittering allure.

There was an extended silence, longer than any that would be considered appropriate in a polite conversation, and just as he was about to repeat his statement, the woman who had claimed to love him spoke again.

"Dravidian," she began, her voice little more than a whisper, "when I get up, I want you to lift the pillow beneath my head and consider what you see there. You are an intelligent man. You will understand the significance of what you find."

She slid around him and stood.

Confused, he looked to her expectantly. She only gazed down at him solemnly, saying nothing, her mussed hair hanging in her eyes.

He turned to face the fringed, soot-covered pillow. Slowly, he reached out for its edge and lifted it away.

A thick, curved blade had lain in wait for the duration of their encounter.

He breathed deeply, his eyes fixed on the gleaming weapon.

"So ..." he began, resigned. "The vision was to be true after all. You are—"

"I am Shekalane, who once loved the man named Valdus," she finished, then added, "nothing more nor less, although I do not expect you to believe that. Know that I observed your raven's projection just as you did, but from this location. Know, too, that, because I know how it must appear, and how hopeless my situation has become, I had fancied slaying you once you returned ..." She paused briefly, toying with her braided lock of hair, twirling it between her fingers. "But I found I could not. I found I could not pretend you weren't as human as I. Nor could I pretend I hadn't come to care for you deeply." She laid a hand on his shoulder. "Shall you extend to me the same respect, or will you deliver me after all into forced servitude, sexual slavery, even death?"

Slowly, he turned to face her.

Suddenly and undeniably, he was gazing into the eyes of his charge again, and not, after all, the woman with whom he'd spend the rest of his life. What's more, he was gazing into the eyes of the enemy—someone who had been on the most intimate terms possible with the very man responsible for all the bloodshed. Someone who—it was clear to him now—had used him toward her (and *his,* Valdus') ends.

He marveled at how he'd managed to ignore the utterly obvious: her use of the white ignudi as a kind of courier during their sojourn, the emerald ring which he now noticed was unusually large and had surely contained a homing beacon before its limited power source would have rendered it inert, the obsession with the color green—Valdus' trademark—all part of a deception so obvious it had been invisible.

Should he have expected anything less from a desperate woman in a desperate situation than a predatory instinct for survival? Indeed, he should not have, and yet he had. For in the final reckoning men saw only what they allowed themselves to see, only what they desired to see. And the astute predator, whether natural-born or moved by circumstance, knew this well.

Several breaths passed and finally he stood, facing away from her. "You should have killed me, Shekalane," he croaked. "While you had the chance."

He said nothing more. The moments passed and still he added nothing.

A rustle of clothes indicated she had turned away from him too. "Then it seems I will live free just long enough to regret my decision, won't I, Dravidian?"

He hid like a coward behind his mask's fearsome countenance, offering nothing. No solace. No wisdom. Nothing. He was filled from head to toe with nothing.

His silence enraged her.

"You really are a gruesome bastard, aren't you?" she sneered at last, and whirled him around to face her. "How easily you succumbed to my overtures! How easily I could have ended your life! You are indeed fitted well to your profession, Dravidian. I thought you were more, fool that I am. Fool of fools!" She laughed as though amazed at her own naiveté. "You are what you are, what you have always been, what you will always be ... death. And not even your own kind of death, as is Valdus, but—but ..."

Her face froze suddenly and her eyes welled up, and her steely expression melted. "Oh, Dravidian, I am so sorry. I didn't mean that. You know I didn't mean that ..."

He might very well have struck her an instant before; now, he retreated to the far end of the ship to brood alone among the hanging pots and pans, before kneeling in front of a cheval glass mirror in a corner of the prow. Gazing into its surface, he found the deathly face of his mask glaring back at him—its darkened, down-slanting eyeholes betraying tiny glints of yellow. Beyond that, and beyond the fall of his own brown hair, stood Shekalane, vulnerable and alone in the hazy light. Gone was the velvety allure she had exhibited hours before, gone was the air of glamour and finesse which had so enthralled him in the cave. Gone were all those things and yet it was at that very moment and none before that he realized how much he loved her.

Indeed, how could it be otherwise? he thought. *For while the facades we erect around ourselves and others—as well as those imposed on us as children by The Lucitor—can be beautiful to behold, it is the naked, imperfect soul we love when we truly love another.*

And knowing what he was—just as she'd said, what he had always been and would always be—the thought chilled him as could no other, and he forced it from his mind with an inner violence that chilled him still more.

He stared at the deck of the ship.

I am the ferryman, he told himself in the silence. *I will be no more, indeed, can be no more. I am only the ferryman.* And he repeated it over and over as if doing so would make it true again.

"Please believe me when I say that what I did, I did for us," Shekalane said at length, her voice sounding distant and insubstantial through the din of his thoughts. "How else could I have recovered Jamais' key? Or convince him to return me to the cage? We were in an impossible situation, my love. *I* was in an impossible situation. Damn Sthulhu for having so little faith in my motives. I should have slain him while I had the chance!"

She paused, and he glanced up to find her looking at him through the mirror.

"Sacrilege, he thinks. Killing one of the Lucitor's ravens like that. Well, they should all be killed. Perhaps if others did the same, in time there would be none of the beastly things left to forward the Lucitor's tyranny."

He pretended to be unmoved by this. Seeing that, she added: "I'm sure you do not share this sentiment. That is because you no longer live in the shadow of the Lottery."

She fell silent then and offered her wrists.

He crossed the length of the boat and took out his shackles, put them on her.

"The Lottery casts its shadow over all, Shekalane," he said at length. "Even we ferrymen. I feel its darkness now as I must ask you to accompany me to the River."

IV | Death is Come

He rode into the village at full gallop—with the hooded, black cloak of his calling flapping wildly about him (so that it appeared Shekalane, who was seated behind him, wore a cloak also) and the horse's hooves churning up clouds of orange-red dust in their wake. Schools of ignudi exploded skyward as he drove them into the heart of Flax, the little winged women making their entrance a dramatic one—which served his purpose precisely, for it was his belief that, given that there was no other route back to the gondola save through the heart of the village, their best hope at passing unmolested was to do so forcibly.

Only when they had gained the main thoroughfare, where merchants had begun resurrecting their tents and stands and shops, did he slow to a more casual gait. Walls of color and scent flanked the street here much as the Barrier Walls flanked the River Dire, and thus the world. Slabs of fresh meat had again been lined up, as had their buyers. Krogg segments were piled high next to stacks of venison and bear. Briny bins spilled over with giant emperor crabs, sold whole or by the leg by burly vendors, at least one of whom was missing an arm. Women in dirty robes watched over tables heaped with vegetables. Aromas drifted through the nostrils of his mask: fresh baked bread and roasted foul, vinegar, garlic, fecund fish.

Yet even among all that activity, their arrival had hardly gone unnoticed. Heads had begun to turn and a silence had set in that said one thing very clearly: *There are strangers among us again.*

These strangers, of course, bore them no malice. But even had they known, that would have surely accomplished little to comfort the suddenly white-faced townsfolk (croppers and middle-men mostly), who averted their eyes and scurried indoors as Dravidian and Shekalane passed.

"Hurry along now," he heard one old woman wheeze to her ward. "Death is come."

He wanted to reach up and remove for a moment the skull mask of his order—but the sight of his dead-blue skin and yellow eyes would have only driven them to greater fear.

As always, the facades humans erected around themselves and others, and those imposed on them at birth by The Lucitor (and later by the Lottery), fascinated him. It was true enough that he wore the habit of a ferryman; it was also true that, like all ferrymen, he'd been injected with ritalimortis serum at a young age and drained of his natural color. But such was the curse of every child delivered into the cult of the raven—Free Will had nothing to do with it. Surely then, without Free Will, a man could not be defined so easily as by the nature of his profession or the façade behind which he enacted it—could he?

"The Lottery does not exist here, Dravidian," he remembered Shekalane saying. *"It never has."*

He would recall this much as coming from behind him; first the lone voice of a man, which stirred the chill air like a grinding stone: "With so much blood in the ground, the very weeds will refuse to grow at this harvest."

And joining in, another man: "Indeed, those already sprouted will wither and die."

And still another, close to the first two, this one literally choked with hate: "A man and a woman, he said. The woman very beautiful and the man pale as the dead. Perhaps we can trade them for—"

At that Dravidian whirled on them, jerking the reins of his mount and forcing it to pivot around in wild accordance. The thrashing of its hooves against the road sent orbset-illuminated dust billowing skyward, enveloping himself and the mare in a roiling red haze. What ignudi had returned abruptly fled again.

"Silence!" he boomed, attempting to proclaim his authority in the most decisive manner possible.

Then, glaring wild-eyed through the death mask's eyelets, he shifted his gaze—just as his mount shifted beneath him with the sound of restless hooves—from cropper to cropper among the offending three, and added, dryly, "Or sick or well, chosen or unchosen, to the River you will go."

The countrymen recoiled at the proclamation. Then, in the space of perhaps two or more breaths, they turned and fled with wild abandon. He had reached for his belt and gripped the scythe suspended there.

Again he thought of the facades human beings erected around themselves and others, and those imposed on them as children by The Lucitor ... if for no other reason than the very power such facades could either endow men with or rob them of.

Yet as he righted his course and continued along his way, he became acutely aware of the many men, women, and children now ogling them from the dark recesses of their dwellings, their faces blue-white with fear as if steeped in moonlight. Facades or no, perhaps they were right. How hideous he must have looked in their eyes; could he hardly blame them for their cowardice? He, who bore the exaggerated, slanted browed visage of Death itself? Who, slender as a leper in his ebony garments and billowing black cloak, rode arrogantly through their midst? Whose hair, long to the shoulders and wildly unkempt, whipped sidelong across his mask to dance fiercely in the dust-strewn wind? Could they not have been terrified?

He thought then, as he so often did, of how good it would be to move among his fellow humans when night came ... as a man, and not as Death. For he was required to play Death only as long as the cropper should tend his fields or the merchant should sell his goods. By night he moved silently through the lamp-lit streets of the capital, which bustled with others in The Lucitor's employ and bore little threat to an off-duty ferryman (he'd long since taken to wearing colorful clothes as a means of departure from his work, thus his presence among the flamboyant residents went largely unnoticed).

Such was his life beyond the oar, a life of reading in the barracks, of reflection at fountain side, and of wanderings about the city while his ferryman's cloak hung tapering and silent, lost amidst the fellowship of its brothers in the catacombs beneath the Lucitor's mansion and cathedral. (These dank galleries belonged to the ferrymen, but the upper levels of the mountainous structure were home to but the Lucitor had His ravens and had never been seen by human eyes. Only the ravens, whose shadowy shapes came and went from the place both night and day, knew for certain what lay within.)

Onward he rode through the emptied streets of Flax, alone but for the company of his brooding mount and the ignudi returned to scavenge once more. Hoping to shake the black mood fallen on him, he turned his attention to the Lilliputian elfemales, and, watching them dance and flit about in the dusty air before him—how ecstatic they were by this chance to plunder freely!—felt his spirits gradually rise until a thin smile touched his lips behind the mask's grim countenance.

"Ghastly pig!"

He turned his head slightly, rolling his eyes upward within the now shadowed eyeholes of his mask, to see a grotesquely obese woman leaning precariously from a second-story window. She was holding a plump, red tomato in one hand, and as he watched, she cocked back a beefy arm and sent the bulb hurling toward him. He jerked his head clear of its path and it whistled past an ear—exploding against the street in a protracted, bloody smear. The assault left the ignudi nearest them reeling and struggling for balance, and, watching dispiritedly as they fled back into the shadows, he felt a blackness fill him yet again, just as it had filled him earlier. It was a liquid blackness which began at his toes and swelled steadily upward, steaming and boiling like so much hot oil.

Very well, then.

"Hang on to me," he told Shekalane.

Then he kicked the mare in its flank and charged south toward where his gondola was moored, thundering past tents and abandoned mule carts (some laden with produce, others with corpses). And as he rode, with the wind blasting through his hair and the power of his steed flowing like wildfire up the reins and into his arms, he threw back his head and laughed, shouting: "You are right to fear me, Flax! Tremble and hide, then—for indeed, Death *has* come! Death has come to *Cuniculum Amoris!*"

V | Gondola

They passed through the remainder of Flax unmolested. They rode in silence, for there was little to be said between the Damned and Death itself. Somewhere in that silence Dravidian vowed to perform his duty in spite of what had occurred. He would not fail himself again.

As they passed beneath the arch at the edge of the township, he noticed someone had scrawled "Death to Valdus, and death to those he pursues" on the stone. For want of a distraction, he searched the purple haze for ignudi, but found none.

Circumnavigating a great section of fallen sky (which had been marked, comically, "Mt. Charon" via a wooden sign), Shekalane told him of a similar "mountain" of violent origin in Jaskir. From that she attempted to back into a discussion about Ursaquakes, but he simply ignored her until she fell silent once again.

At last they reached his boat, floating lazily against its tether beneath a bridge of crumbling stone. He helped her into it as gently as he could, choosing to release her from her bonds as an act of good faith (which he reasoned would make them both feel better), but wary, too, of Sthulhu's watchful eye.

The boat rocked precariously as they positioned themselves respectively, with the prisoner Shekalane seating herself on the crimson bench in the middle, and Dravidian pausing to activate the lanterns both fore and aft before taking up his oar at the stern.

He watched absently as a young squire, tasked with guarding the bridge, perhaps, emerged from the cottage nearby to regard him coolly and the horse, tied to a nearby tree, in particular. The look upon his face told Dravidian he might just as well kill the beast now that it had been polluted by an outsider's touch.

"I will return for the horse shortly," he lied to the youth authoritatively. "See to it that she is cared for until then."

He pressed his oar against the bank and shoved off, setting the black, ornately crafted boat adrift, its lanterns jangling dissonantly and their glowing elements casting rectangles of orange-amber light onto the water where the shapes danced distorted like shimmering ghosts. Then, gazing beyond the now-battered ferro, he looked to where the currents vanished into the gloom and soon lost himself in reverie.

VI | Styx Flumen

He returned them to the gateway through which they'd entered *Cuniculum Amoris* and they passed through it back into *Styx Flumen*.

All was silence for some time save for the gentle splash of the oar against the water and the melancholy songs of the ignudi, now fluttering overhead once again (but left un-harassed, if not unremarked, by Sthulhu on Dravidian's order, who scanned their numbers in search of an albino like Milkweed but found none in the kaleidoscope of dancing colors).

When he had rowed a substantial distance from shore, and they were well upon their way down the black waters of The River Dire, his charge spoke to him at last in the cautious tones of the helpless.

"Will it be merciful?" she asked, her green-brown eyes focused solely on the water. "My death, I mean, if that is what is to be. Will it be quick?"

He had heard the question countless times before. Usually he assured his charge it would be, for such is what he'd always been told. Yet the Lucitor's ravens were far more than mere couriers of the Lottery's edict—they were His eyes and ears, as well. Surely the Lucitor would torment one who had bestowed such a favor upon the Prince of the Revolution, would He not?

Still, she hadn't run, and that was the only certain means in his experience of condemning one's self to torment instead of peace.

He wanted to ignore her query, but in light of the unusual circumstances, he felt obliged to offer something—anything, really, so long as it would silence her.

"I have no way of knowing for certain, ma'am," he said. "But the *sapiens noctuam* tell me it usually is. They say—"

"You've *spoken* with them?" Her eyes widened with surprise. Her mood had lightened, and he quite foolishly interpreted this as an acceptance of her fate.

"They've spoken to me," he said, referring to the human-owl hybrids said to populate the giant tree boughs which overhung the River Dire near its end. "I but listened." In fact they had done no such thing.

It was cold, and she crossed her arms over her breasts in order to grasp her own shoulders. She stared up at him with the same eyes she had used to seduce him at the altar of the *Luminis sub omne.*

"They say only the blessed receive messages from the *sapiens noctuam*," she said. "Are you blessed, Dravidian?"

He rowed, listening more to the roiling of the water than the queries of his charge. Again, he was failing to calculate his responses in accordance to his profession.

"I wear a mask and push an oar," he said. "By what definition might I be blessed?"

He realized how inappropriate the remark was as soon as he'd said it, and attempted to remedy this further breach in credibility by adding: "Perhaps serving the Lucitor is blessing enough. After all, isn't He the final authority in all matters?"

She looked at him with sparkling, mischievous eyes, as if she'd won some minute yet vastly important victory. "But no authority is absolute, is this not true?"

The oar dipped in and out of the water and he ruminated over what she'd said.

"This authority will be absolute enough for you, I'm afraid," he said, and hoped the finality of the statement would discourage further discourse.

203

It didn't.

"What if I were impregnated?" she asked with a renewed zeal. "Would you not be ushering your own offspring toward its doom, or at least forced servitude?"

The woman was tenacious. She might gain her freedom yet, or a slim chance at it, anyway, for he feared he might end up pitching her overboard long before they reached their destination. Still, he thought about what she'd said, and responded in kind.

"Certainly, one cannot destroy something which has never existed." He turned the skull-face of his mask to face her. "And never will."

She stared at him a moment longer before turning away to gaze into the depths again. He rowed, saying nothing.

In spite of himself, he found his attention drifting back to her as he worked, and shifted his eyes so that he could study her through the mask's eyelets—while appearing to stare straight forward—watching as she lowered an arm over the boat's prow and allowed a languid hand to drift lazily in the water. She hung her head gently to one side as she did so, and he noticed the mischief brewing in those strange green-brown eyes before she even spoke.

"But it would haunt you, would it not? After all, you would never know for certain if you had denied the world of its next great genius."

She didn't look at him as she said this, but continued gazing into the water, where her eyes shown blank and wide, awaiting a response.

"Madam, I find it difficult to believe that my loins should be capable of producing such a savant. In any event, I'm not at all certain the world needs more genius, nor any more people at all, much less a ferryman's son ... or daughter."

There was a sum of moments during which neither of them spoke. At last Shekalane broke the silence by saying, in a soft and meandering tone, "'The Ferryman's Son.' That has a nice ring about it, does it not?"

He riled a little at the suggestion. It had always seemed to him that some women made it their chore to wholly underestimate the perceptiveness of the men with whom they related. As if a man was—by definition—merely some unmovable slab of granite: no more capable of reading a woman's intonations than he was of identifying her manipulations. That she thought she might sway his conviction further with such a lame attempt at irony left him agitated and insulted.

"Perhaps the madam will choose to compose an opera as her final wish," he said. "And title it just such."

Unfazed by this, she lifted a bare foot with delicate ease, and, smiling playfully, began toying with the dark folds of his cloak—as if to inspire another encounter such as the ones they'd shared in the treasure cove and at the altar of the *Luminis sub omne*. He noticed the nails of her toes, like those of her fingers, were painted green, identical in shade to the cypress trees and singe grass lining both sides of the River—narrower here than perhaps anywhere else in its endless stretch.

He resisted the urge to swipe her foot away, realizing, rightfully, that such an action would be no less unprofessional than if he were to give into her advances out right. Instead, he took a moment to gather his thoughts, and said, finally, "I pity you, Madam Shekalane. It has become increasingly clear that you will deceive yourself until the very last moment. You will be delivered to the processing terminal tonight, madam. Nothing can stop that now. All orders sent down from The Lucitor are final. Please, do not test my patience further."

She dropped her foot, but the mischievous smile remained. Not for the first time, it occurred to him that it was a mannerism better suited to a girl than a woman.

Again, her restless eyes shifted toward the water, and after a time she said, "I could swim ashore, could I not? Surely you've had charges attempt just such a feat. It really isn't much of a reach. Shall I try, Dravidian?"

"If you like."

He knew she would not.

Still, she climbed to her feet in the now deep blue light and seemed to contemplate the notion, squinting her eyes and pursing her lips while she estimated the distance. And, although it was true the River was narrower here than most other places, the reach to which she referred was still substantial enough to give even the strongest of men second thoughts.

She lolled her beautiful head to face him, and said, quizzically, "And you wouldn't try to stop me? Perhaps by slashing open my loins with that ... *thing.*"

She dipped her head to indicate the scythe.

"Why should I?" he said. "You must understand, Madam Shekalane, that these waters are infested with—"

Something flapped out of the gloom suddenly, hovering between them for little more than an eye blink—a ghostly white figure about the size of a full-grown bat. No, *two* figures, one white, the other black. Dravidian saw that they were holding something, something long and dark—before Sthulhu squawked and launched from his perch, chasing the specter back into the mists.

And yet Dravidian had had an image burned into his retinas from the encounter: a red emblem, or monogram more properly, consisting of two letters, like someone's initials.

"Dravidian, it was Milkweed," said Shekalane. "And I think she had Jamais' scabbard." Her expression suddenly changed and she became elated. "The maps, Dravidian! Don't you see? Don't you see what that could mean?"

He looked at her gravely.

She was fumbling with her braided lock of hair when the foghorn of a dragger sounded ahead of them. He peered beyond her but could see only blackness. Gradually a distant light appeared, a light so vague he might have imagined it. It gained solidity as he rowed, expanding and dividing into individual points, and he recognized the pattern as belonging to the *Vorpal Gladio*.

Moments later he could hear its monstrous paddle wheel churning the water. The ship's great stained-glass lantern winked at them: two short bursts—a summons to signal.

He reached above him and gripped the lever of his signaling lantern, then triggered the shade thrice, acknowledging them, before stilling his oar and awaiting their response.

A moment later it came: one short burst, one long— *Prepare to come aboard.*

"Charon's vanity," he cursed, and replaced his hood.

He locked the oar into its forcola and stepped down from his dais, his shadow falling over Shekalane.

"I must replace your bonds," he said, and loosed the shackles from his belt.

She shrugged away from him, gripping her braided lock of hair. "Why? What's going on?"

He reached for her arm. "Inspection."

She inched beyond his reach. He stared at her through the mask's slanted eyelets, his gloved hand wavering in the air. "Shekalane, please ..."

Then he leaned forward and gently took her arm.

VII | Dragger

Even from his dais, he could see Shekalane trembling as the dragger approached.

He could not blame her. That they employed such vessels to ferry their gondolas upriver was commonly known, but it was doubtful that Shekalane—who had been born in Jaskir and hence was no less a creature of the inland forest than any bear or coyote—had ever seen one up close. He tried to imagine it through her eyes: the dragger emerging from the swirling gloom like some hellish apparition—its sides laden with black gondolas and its derricks strung with mock shrunken heads.

The juggernaut slowed to a virtual crawl and dropped its anchor, which seemed a hammer of the gods as it struck the water, and he set them on a parallel course, so that they drifted between the chain of that anchor and the dragger's portside. After passing beneath the scuffed bottoms of several gondolas, he spied a free derrick further down and heard brownies run along the deck above them. They appeared atop the vacant derrick seconds later, a gaggle of apprentices in brown masks and brown clothes, and lowered the harness until only its floats remained above water. He maneuvered them into position over it and secured the yaw-lines. A young voice called down: "We're bringing you up!"

"Hang on to something," he told Shekalane.

Iron rattled above them as the brownies cranked the hoists, and the gondola began climbing in fits and starts, swinging to and fro.

A figure came into view as they rose above the bulwark, at least so much of one as could be viewed in the darkness, and

Dravidian studied it, hoping against hope to find someone other than Prefect Asmodeus. But the man was standing with his back to them, his hood drawn over his bowed head and the ends of his cloak splashing to the deck around his feet, and seemed but a dark obelisk. Nonetheless, Dravidian could tell from his modest height and crooked posture that it was, in fact, Asmodeus.

He was surprised to see a large cage standing just beyond him, taller than the prefect himself and nearly twice the length of his gondola. It was cruelly configured out of twisted iron and curved spikes, and tightly meshed to preclude a man reaching in or something small slipping out. Colors fluttered within like the brilliant stuff of chaos itself (as if someone could actually cage the Lucitor's own building material!), and he realized suddenly that the cage was filled to capacity with chortling elfemales.

The rumors of Asmodeus' sadism were true, then. For never before had he seen ignudi caged in such a way only to be fed to the ravens later; generally it was considered sport only if the creatures had responded to the recorded mating call of their own free will.

They jerked to a halt and he stepped from the gondola, motioning for Shekalane to be still. The two brownies secured the derrick and took up their positions facing him, one to each side so that they framed the prefect and thus made a triad.

He knelt and awaited his inspection, recalling memories of his own apprenticeship, when he, too, had worn a brownie's dull uniform, and went about his work behind a dung-colored goblin mask. How important he'd felt when first a ferryman had knelt in his presence, while he who was but a dockhand remained standing!

Protocol, of course, required his chin be bowed, and bowed it was. But he was more adept than most at observing without moving his head, and so was able to watch in sporadic glimpses as the prefect lingered by the ignudi cage. He seemed almost to be reaching into it, or fumbling with the lock—he couldn't tell through the cover of his cloak. But it was clear he was doing *something*.

He started to turn around and Dravidian lowered his eyes, listening as the man's boots paced slowly across the boards toward him, setting the wood to creaking. They came to a halt within his limited field of view, shining in the light of his gondola's lantern as if coated in black oil ... then turned and paced away again.

"Rise and be inspected," he said, his voice that of an exalted serpent—a voice at once raspy and slippery—one that, once heard as a young apprentice, could never be forgotten. It was a voice that, over the years, had earned him a nickname—inspired by the Devil himself—'Old Scratch.'

Dravidian stood, lifting his gaze as he did so, and found the prefect as he'd first glimpsed him over the bulwark: facing the cage in his long, black cloak, but a Stygian pattern against all that color. The man turned to face him slowly, fully revealing his bent spine and hunched shoulders, as the lamplight caught his blue-stained death mask and seemed to set it afire. His pale eyes met Dravidian's own.

At last Asmodeus moved toward him, his right arm bent at the elbow and loose at the wrist, fingertips dangling, his knotted white hair hanging from the shadows of his cowl to sway in the breeze like egg-laden spider webs. He stopped in front of Dravidian and his yellow eyes sized him up from behind the corpse-blue mask, the folds around them pale as the dead. There was an insanity in them Dravidian could not define.

"Ferryman," the prefect greeted him, and motioned to the apprentices. "Leave us."

As the juveniles scrambled off, Dravidian glanced beyond him at the cage—and noticed a white ignudi among its occupants. Surely it could not have been Milkweed; for, even had the ghostly shape been her, as Shekalane thought, she couldn't possibly have been captured so quickly. Then again—

Jamais' scabbard. The master maps to all of Ursathrax.

—the presence of so many ignudi on the deck of a dragger (and amidst so many ravens) at any time other than the mating broadcast was impossible itself. Unless, of course, the dragger had intercepted smugglers after his launch and seized their contraband. That seemed entirely likely when he recalled the ignudi traps he'd seen coming into Jaskir. These ignudi did bear the same striking colors, and they would have undoubtedly fetched a fine price as dusters downriver.

"You must be curious," Asmodeus said at length, "if I have approved your elevation to Master."

Dravidian froze. He wanted to run, to hide, to look to Shekalane for guidance. Instead, he lifted his chin firmly and said, as confidently as he could, "Yes, my lord."

Asmodeus looked at him for what seemed a very long time. At last he glanced toward Shekalane and leaned in, whispering, "And you shall find out ... in my cabin. Away from Valdus' whore. Come."

And to the brownies waiting at a distance he shouted: "Take her to the cellblock for now. And erect a curtain around this area."

VIII | Questions

Asmodeus led him to a narrow, gloomy, private cabin in the rear of the vessel and shut them in it. The shutters were partially open—enough so that the dim lights on the River's opposite bank were visible but not enough to alleviate the room's generally oppressive nature. The air was thick with incense.

"Be seated," said the prefect, and vanished into a rear sanctum which, aside from the candles on his crowded desk, was the only source of light, and this hardly more than what a modest fireplace would have provided. He shut the iron door firmly behind him.

Dravidian seated himself across from the desk and waited, studying its cluttered surface as he did so. A flare went up outside the shutters—which were unusual in that their slats were positioned vertically rather than horizontally—which caused the room, however briefly, to resemble nothing more than a cleric's cubicle, its desk overflowing with stacks of paper, placed in the center of a jail cell. He could hear the prefect praying in what he imagined was the secret language he himself would begin to learn as a master.

If, that is, he was still to be a master.

At last the door to the inner sanctum was opened and the prefect emerged with a candle in his hand. He was hoodless and maskless now and the door was closed at once behind him. He stood near the bulkhead and studied Dravidian for several moments.

"We've no need of our hoods or masks here," he said. "You may remove yours also."

Dravidian gazed at him for several breaths. At last he removed his hood and placed his fingertips to the temples of his mask, decompressing it, then swung the strap over his head and sat the façade upon the desk. Asmodeus approached slowly, set the candle on the table, and sat down.

At length he said, "Who art thou?"

Dravidian just looked at him. "I—I'm afraid I don't understand, my lord. I am the ferryman, Dravidian. Surely you—"

"Yes, that is your name. But since entering the Forbidden Channels and seeing what was on the other side ..." He leaned toward him, gazing into his eyes intensely. "Who *art* thou?"

Dravidian was about to say that he was the same person as before when the prefect preempted him. "Don't answer, be silent. I know too well what thou would say. But you have seen through the veil, or so you think. And now you are in two worlds wherever you may be." He traced his dead-blue fingertips over a dusty gold statuette in the form of a man whose skin and musculature had been selectively cut away, revealing his heart and brain and other organs. "On one world, this one, is written 'Determinism.' While on the other, the one from which you have returned, is written 'Free Will.'" He dropped his pale hand and regarded Dravidian coolly. "You, like many young men, have become infected with the latter—surely thou does knowest it. Is this why you have considered conspiring against us? For thou hast considered conspiring against us, and thou knowest that also."

Dravidian opened his mouth to speak but stopped, understanding in a rush that the prefect might well know—somehow—everything. For while he had assuredly reviewed Sthulhu's recordings (which, while revealing much, would still have left gaps), who knew by what other means the Lucitor might watch as well as listen? Indeed, might not the trees, the rocks, his gondola itself, be instruments to this end?

"It is the girl, of course," said the prefect almost to himself, then leaned toward him across the table yet again. "But does thou know what will be tonight? I know not the extent to which you have betrayed your duty to satisfy your loins, and care not to know, to speak the truth; our mission as ferrymen has never been what we teach the brownies and journeymen. But tonight I shall condemn the woman and torment her unto death as the worst of heretics. And the very whore of the rebellion who has today kissed thy feet will, at the faintest flick of the lash, cast all her spittle and venom upon you, who will have proven the conviction of the order and put the lie to Valdus' Free Will forever. Knowest thou that?" He levelled his gaze at him. "Yes, maybe thou knowest it,' he added with thoughtful penetration, never for a moment taking his eyes off Dravidian.

"The girl was the catalyst," said Dravidian at last, and, lying, added, "nothing more. I was sworn to deliver her safely—which I have done—but in order to do so I had to enter the Forbidden Channels. The Code itself permits this. But I could not have anticipated what I saw there, not in my wildest—"

"Stop your speaking," Asmodeus hissed, and added, curiously, *"Ego non mentior.* Hast thou the right to reveal any of the mysteries of that world from which thou hast come? No, thou hast not. Thou mayest not add to what has been said of old—that anything beyond *Styx Flumen* is but the Lucitor's work in progress, new realms manifesting, dreams within dreams. I know too well what thou would say: that the Other Side is like unto the back of a stage, and that beyond that lie a real world undreamed of in our philosophies. Well, what if it were so? That Other Side lies in ruins while this one dreams in peace; who are thee to question the wisdom of the Lucitor and his clerics combined? And thou hast questioned it, but thou shall question it no more, no, not ever. *Ego non mentior.*"

At length Dravidian was able to translate the phrase: *Ego non mentior. I am not a lie.* He glanced at the gold statuette; its bones and tendons gleamed.

"Do not think me finished," the prefect went on, looking sternly at him. "For what wouldst thou have said to the world if thou had left us and thou hadst a voice?" He added quickly: "And by 'world' I mean this one, the only one, *Styx Flumen.* Wouldst thou have said, 'Follow me and I will make you free?' If so thou art no different from Valdus. But now thou hast seen these 'free' men; now thou hast seen the heads on pikes they leave behind—it's possible thou has even seen the destruction their progenitors wrought, ah, beyond the curtain, if you like." He rose suddenly and began pacing. "Yes, we've paid dearly for it, this so-called Free Will thou hast considered. For twenty-four centuries we wrestled with it, but now it is ended and over for good. Dost thou not believe that it's over for good? Thou lookest blankly at me and deignest not even to be wroth with me. But let me tell thee that now, today, people are more persuaded than ever that they have what bread and space they need, even though they have brought their freedom to us and laid it humbly at our feet. That has been our doing, we ferrymen, yours as well as mine. And what hast Valdus didst? Sabotaged our infrastructure so that the very people he claims to champion have suffered? Slain the innocent men who contract our barges? Blown up cafes and public squares and parades, yes, even mounted heads on pikes as scarecrows to his enemies? Is this thy 'freedom' for which you would have renounced your oath?"

Again Dravidian opened his mouth to speak but was silenced with a gesture. "Not yet." The prefect turned his back on him and moved to the partially shuttered windows, where he peered between the slats and seemed to gaze off into the night. "No science could give them bread so long as they remained free. So it was after the *Magnum Exitium,* the Great Destruction. In the end they laid their freedom at our feet, and said to us, 'Make us your slaves, but feed us.' They understood themselves, at last. And they understood that freedom and bread enough for all were inconceivable in this new reality, for never, never would they be able to share between them. Not so little and in such a confined space, surely. They were convinced, too, that they could never be free, not again, for they were, and remain, weak, vicious, worthless, and rebellious." Asmodeus half-turned, staring sidelong at him. "Thou wouldst, for a time, at least, have promised them the bread of a new world. But that world is but the old one, the one before the Great Destruction, born anew but as savage as before; can it compare with the relative safety and assured bread of Ursathrax in the eyes of the weak, ever sinful and ignoble race of man?" He turned back toward the windows. "No, it cannot. For the Lucitor has recast it in Thine own image and improved upon it in every way. Thou dost know, thou canst not help but to know, this fundamental secret of human nature: that so long as man remains free, he strives for nothing so incessantly and so painfully as to find someone or something to worship, in order so that he may be unfree. That is true. But man seeks to worship what is established beyond dispute, so that all men would agree at once to worship it. For these pitiful creatures are concerned not only to find what one or the other can worship, but to find community of worship. For the sake of common worship they've slain each other with the sword. They have set up gods and challenged one another, 'Put away your gods and come and worship ours, or we will kill you and your gods!' And so it will be to the end of the world, even when gods disappear from the earth; they will fall down before idols just the same. Thou didst know, thou couldst not but have known, this fundamental secret of human nature, but thou didst reject, while on the Other Side, the one infallible banner which was offered the world to make all men bow down to the Lucitor alone—the banner of His Lottery; and Thou didst reject it for the sake of freedom and the bread of woman." He whirled to face him. *"A woman!"*

Dravidian just looked at him.

He paced slowly around him, disappearing from view. "Behold what Thou didst further. And all again in the name of freedom. I tell Thee that man is tormented by no greater anxiety than to find someone quickly to whom he can hand over that gift of freedom with which the ill-fated creature is born. But what happened once you crossed over to the Other Side? Instead of strengthening your resolve to take men's freedom from them, as thou was sworn to do, thou didst desire to make it greater than ever!" The floor creaked as he paced. "Didst thou forget that man prefers peace, and even death, to freedom of choice? For while nothing is more seductive for man than his freedom of conscience, nothing is a greater cause of suffering. And behold, instead of remaining faithful to our firm foundation for setting the conscience of man at rest forever, thou didst choose for a time all that is exceptional, vague and enigmatic; thou didst choose what is utterly beyond the strength of men, acting as though thou wert the Lucitor Himself. But instead of taking possession of men's freedom, thou wouldst have increased it, and burdened the spiritual kingdom of mankind with its sufferings forever."

The prefect circled back to his desk, placing his fingertips on its surface, and stared down at him. "Thou didst conspire to become a martyr, a messiah, is that it? Thou! And did thou expect man's loyalty and that he should follow thee freely? Yes, thou didst. And thou didst decide that in place of the rigid ancient law, man would thereafter with free heart decide for himself what was true and what was false, having only thine example before him as his guide; is this not so? But didst thou not consider that, even if this were to come to pass, he would at last reject even thy example and thy truth, if he was weighed down with the fearful burden of free choice? No, thou didst not. And well thou should have, for they would have cried aloud at last that the truth was not in thee, and that they could not have been brought to greater confusion and suffering than thou had caused, laying upon them so many cares and unanswerable problems."

Dravidian lowered his head. It was true, in a sense, all of it, however much he had tried to atone. And the prefect knew it. Why then did he not simply send him to the cellblock and be done with it?

The prefect hitched his robes and reseated himself. "And by not considering it, thou wouldst thyself have lain the foundation for the destruction of thine vision, and no one would have been more to blame for it."

At length he reached for a great tome, opened it to the mark, and began reading.

How much time passed Dravidian could not have guessed; it seemed a very long time, indeed. And although he knew the record of his service was exemplary—perhaps better than anyone's, even Pepperlung's—the thought brought him little comfort. Asmodeus knew; however misplaced some of his grandiose projections were (for while Dravidian had considered, or failed to consider, all those things, he had not done so nearly as consciously as the prefect thought), he *knew*.

At last Asmodeus closed the book and laid it on the desk, whereupon Dravidian saw that it was not in fact a ledger of service records but something called *The Brothers Karamazov*, by Fyodor Dostoevsky.

"Hear me now, Master Dravidian ..."

Dravidian looked up sharply.

"They are not now, and have never been, worth such a vision. Do you understand?"

Dravidian could only look on, dumbfounded.

"Oh, of course, thou didst fall proudly and well," Asmodeus continued, "and yet you've recovered, like a ferryman; but the weak, unruly race of men, are they ferrymen?" He leaned forward for emphasis and his chair creaked. "I ask again, are there many like thee? And couldst thou believe for one moment that men, too, could share such a vision? Is the nature of men such, that they can reject divine authority, and at the great moments of their lives, the moments of their deepest, most agonizing spiritual difficulties, cling only to the free verdict of the heart? Surely thou didst know that thine deeds, if successful, would be recorded in books, would be handed down to remote times and the utmost ends of the earth, and thou didst surely hope that man, following thee, would cling to his newfound humanism and not ask for the Lucitor's divine authority ever again. But thou didst think too highly of men therein, for they are slaves, of course, though rebellious by nature. Look round and judge; twenty-four centuries have passed, look upon them. Whom amongst them hast raised up like thyself? In awareness, I mean, not arms. I swear, man is weaker and baser by nature than thou hast believed him! Can he, can he do what thou didst? By showing him so much respect, thou didst, as it were, cease to feel for him—for thou would have asked far too much from him. Respecting him less, thou wouldst have asked less of him. That would have been more like a savior, for his burden would have been lighter. He is weak and vile. What though he is everywhere now rebelling against our power, and proud of his rebellion? It is the pride of a child and a schoolboy. They are little children rioting and barring out the teacher at school. But their childish delight will end; it will cost them dearly."

He ran a pale finger along the cracked spines of the dusty books next to him. "It must be so. For we have taken the sword of Caesar, and in taking it, of course, have rejected Free Will and followed determinism. Oh, ages are yet to come of the confusion of free thought, of its science and cannibalism. And yet, with our victory over Valdus, all will be put to sleep again. They will no longer rebel nor destroy one another as under his, but no longer thy, freedom. We shall even persuade them that they are better off than before—once they renounce their arms and submit to us. And they will be convinced that we are right, for they will remember the horrors of war and confusion to which his so-called freedom brought them."

He sat back in his chair at last, regarding him with something like compassion, and a silence settled over the dusty room.

"Dravidian, listen to me. Dost thou truly think that thou art the first to cross over the forbidden threshold?" It seemed he tried to smile, but his face somehow wouldn't allow it, and quivered strangely. "For thou art young and foolish indeed if thou thinkest that."

Dravidian just looked at him, unable to move, unable to breathe.

"Aye, know that I, too, have been in the wilderness; that I, too, have lived on mushrooms and vesiculam." He nodded slowly, noting Dravidian's incredulity. "Yes I, too, once prized the freedom with which thou didst become infected, and strove for a moment to stand among the elect, among the strong and powerful, thirsting for a new world and a new beginning."

Dravidian looked at the spines of the books: at the trail left in the dust by the prefect's wandering fingertip.

"But I awakened and would not serve madness. I turned back and joined the ranks of those who have corrected the so-called True Work. I left the awakened and went back to sleep, for the happiness of sleep. So, too, will you. As will all the world."

He stood slowly and moved around the desk toward him. "Valdus' Revolution will not come to pass, and our dominion will be built up. But I need you and all who serve to be present and committed. And in return for your renewed loyalty I shall spare the woman's life."

He stared down at Dravidian, who could not help but to notice a strange, whitish fluid trickling down from the man's hairline.

"Indeed I shall not torment her unto death as promised; but I will interrogate her, and when I am finished, *if* she has been cooperative, I will render her unto our Lucitor and request that she be given leniency."

He placed a hand gently on Dravidian's cheek. "Wilt thou agree to this? In thy heart, I mean, and not just in manner. For if thou wilt, thou will surely find thyself ascended to prefectship in good order; and all will be as it was, as it should be, as it must be, forever."

IX | Cell Visit

Permission would not have been granted, nor did he ask; instead, he went straight to the detention block after his meeting with the prefect and located Shekalane's cell. It was easy to do, for it was the only one with a light beneath its door. Indeed, it was the only one in the entire cellblock that was occupied.

"Shekalane," he whispered, crouching, and braced the meal flap open with his finger. "It's Dravidian."

At last she said, sounding distant and utterly confused: "I cannot see you. Opening the flap triggers a light: It—it hurts my eyes, and burns the skin of my face. And yet it is *cold*—the cell, I mean. *So cold.*"

He withdrew his finger, allowing the flap to close, and thought he heard her teeth chatter. The dragger's great paddle wheel churned.

"Why have you come to me, Dravidian of the ferrymen?"

"You are about to be interviewed by the prefect himself, Asmodeus. During this interview you will be asked about your involvement with Valdus and his revolution. Answer him truthfully—names, dates, tactical information—he has assured me personally that you will be spared if you do so. Do you understand?"

A silence followed. "Spared. That's a curious choice of words. I trust by this you mean I will not be punished or killed ... but that I will still be delivered into sexual slavery."

"Shekalane ..."

"I've had a great amount of time to think, Dravidian. It's—it's in our nature; we women, that when faced with a closed door yet another door opens ... in our minds. And I've decided that Valdus has been right all along: the Lottery must end." She paused as the great ship rumbled all around them. "And I've decided something else; which is that his methods are justified, after all. Indeed, what is death—physical death, I mean—when compared to imprisonment and the suffocation of one's soul? The former at least provides an escape; but the latter .... No, Dravidian, I will not cooperate. Not even if I am tortured unto death."

"You don't mean that, Shekalane."

"What know you of what I mean and what I do not? You, who mistook a ploy, and a successful one, for an expression of love for Valdus? You, who in turn used that to retreat into your former self and turn your back on all that we have learned and experienced? No, I tell you plainly that I will not submit, and you—your order—will be forced to destroy me. Now please, go away. For, although I love you still, I cannot abide by what you have done."

At last Dravidian lowered his head. "Nor can I abide by what you have done, Shekalane. For by aiding and abetting Valdus, if only in bringing him comfort, you did also turn your back—on all his crimes and victims. And you would aid him still." He stood and swung his mask around on its strap, prepared to put it on. "It would seem we are at an impasse, at last. Whatever our fates, then ..." He fingered the façade's velvety lining. "Know that you, too, are loved."

Then he whirled to leave and, whirling, came face to face with a brownie in a dung-colored goblin mask and holding a tray—who quickly looked away and just as quickly looked back, as though recognizing him as someone personally significant to him. Dravidian stared at him for perhaps two breaths, taken aback by the directness of his gaze, and sensing, too, something—well, he could not define it, and quickly placed his mask to his face and depressed the pad at his temple, sealing it with a hiss.

The fact was, however cool she had played the encounter with Dravidian, she was anything but, and when the brownie slid the food tray through the slot she immediately snatched it up from the platform and hurled it against the wall.

It wasn't until she had paced furiously back and forth several times that she noticed the note, which had been secreted into her cell beneath the tray. Picking it up, she recognized the scrawl instantly, and read, somewhat breathlessly:

There is still a chance to make things right: the ring. Remember, get as close to the prefect as possible. Its activation will throw a shield around you and blast outward. I will be waiting on the bank to start the attack. You have a choice. But it is not dependent on what we shared. You may join me in the battle, or I will assist you into the Channels. —Love Eternal, Valdus

X | Recollection

"A detour through the cellblock, aye, Dravidian?"

It was Pepperlung. He was standing at the top of the stairs when Dravidian emerged from the detention level. It was a tone of voice he had not heard from his friend in at least ten years.

"It's a shortcut," said Dravidian, and added, casually, "as good as any other."

"I'd allot it is," said Pepperlung, stepping aside to let him pass—hesitantly, it seemed. "Ah, but you always have been one for scenic detours."

The men looked into each other's eyes briefly, their faces close, before Dravidian continued onto the deck.

"You shall have to tell me the tale sometime, Dravidian!" Pepperlung called after him. "As it stands now I have only the rumors to go by. And those are the stuff of which polyhistors might concern themselves."

Dravidian paused, understanding that Pepperlung had just rendered explicit what he had previously only implied, and he nearly whirled on him; it being in his mind to pull rank and correct him by saying, *"Master* Dravidian."

Instead, he continued along the deck to the great ship's prow—the place in which he had always done his best thinking—for he had much thinking to do, and Pepperlung's words had only further engendered in him the need to revisit a painful past episode—something triggered by his encounter with the brownie below deck, although he didn't know why.

Even now it was difficult to believe that ten years had passed since he had first been tempted from the Way—ten years since he had first doubted the wisdom of the Order, and doubted it, as with Shekalane, because of the love of a woman. He wondered as he watched the black water crash against the dragger's mighty prow if she still existed, although he saw no reason why she would not, and if she could still be found amidst the stacks of the Bibliotheca. And he wondered what Chantilly would think of the man he had become, more so the adventures he had experienced, and as he did so the past rose up like spray from the water and manifested so clearly and profoundly that it seemed no time had passed at all.

XI | The Polyhistor's Tale

"You love her *madly* don't you, Dravidian?"

They walked along the bustling west quay: Ripipin, Pepperlung and he, through the cool shadows of the exquisite dragger prows which towered above their heads, and Dravidian felt as though he were being jostled about like a ragdoll between his two prodding brothers—inebriated, the whole sorry three of them, with the euphoria of Sacrificium Eve: the eve before they would once again begin ferrying those chosen in the Lottery down the River Dire.

"I love only the fear in her eyes when she sees me!" Dravidian shouted, and leapt forward to swat at the ignudi gathered upon a mooring cable.

The elfemales exploded skyward in a dazzling cloud of color.

"Aye," said Pepperlung, "spoken like a true ferryman, I'd allot." He levelled his yellow pupils at Dravidian. "But is it true?"

"True enough for a fellow Bone Man," said Dravidian, and matched his pale gaze, smiling. "I'd allot."

Pepperlung snorted. "I don't hide in books, it's true. And why should I?" He touched eyes with a girl in rags as she passed. "When life is so much more interesting?"

The girl shrank away from his serpentine gaze, and, gathering the hood still tighter about her face, shuffled off quickly down the length of the dock.

Ripipin laughed. "Her pappy must've warned 'er about ferrymen."

"He's warned her of fools at the very least," said Dravidian, and slapped poor Pepperlung upon the shoulder.

"Women are for quick conquest, Dravidian," said Pepperlung humorlessly. "They are but cities of pastel towers, full of booty and fine jewels. We are the grim-faced reapers, who topple the towers and plunder them. Such is our lot. Such is theirs. To keep captured territory, to continue to occupy foreign soil, this is not good. Doing so can only invite treachery and betrayal."

Dravidian looked at him with frank surprise. "That's an impressive metaphor ... but misguided."

He spied a civilian gondola floating at dockside, opposite the great ships, and whistled to its oarsman, who gave him a courteous salute and stood to man his oar. (Civilian gondoliers could usually be counted upon to keep their prejudices in check, because they understood both the joy and the pain the oar had to offer, and so seemed almost brothers, although in fact they were as divided from ferrymen in their loyalties as kin divided by civil war.)

As Dravidian stepped into the gondola, Pepperlung said, "I only speak thus because you are a brother ferryman ... and my friend. For your own sake, look to your life at every turn while you are involved in this."

Dravidian looked at him after he'd sat down. "I appreciate your concern, but Chantilly shall not betray me."

The driver pressed his oar to the dock and shoved off. As they moved away, Pepperlung said, somewhat softly, "It's not her you should be concerned about."

Dravidian was laughing recklessly as he saluted him.

The Bibliotheca was like most structures in Ursathrax in that it climbed a Barrier Wall (in this case that of the east) in much the same manner as ivy will climb the dilapidated facades of old buildings. Its various rooms and corridors followed no specific pattern save that of the crude rock against which they'd been constructed, and thus their expanse seemed not so much a thing built by men but more of an outgrowth conceived of by nature itself—or the Lucitor, depending on one's theology.

He came upon the girl in one of the dimly-lit upper corridors, in that area where the more anachronistic works had been piled, the collections of epic poetry by Pynchion and Familaust, Reginal and Openwise, yet he didn't venture from the shadows to greet her immediately, for fear of startling her. Instead, he watched her for a time from the end of the hall, and so deep in the endless catacombs of ink and parchment were they, that the world seemed silent save for the occasional brush of mildewed paper as the girl turned the pages of the tome in her hands.

He leaned against the wall of crudely-bound volumes beside him after a while, merely to redistribute his weight, and the old books shifted against his shoulder ever so slightly, which caused her to look up.

"Is that you, Dravidian?"

He looked to his feet as to conceal his eyes, fearful to step from the dark.

"It *is* you," she said. "Please, come forward ..."

She closed the book and stood. "It's a shame, you know, that only ferrymen receive ritalimortis injections. Otherwise we might wink at each other in the dark like cats ..."

He stepped forward at last.

"You shouldn't talk of that here, Chantilly."

She shrugged. "We're alone. Father's on the third tier blacklining, everyone else is in meditations. Most are probably unaware this tier even exists; it's almost impossible to find without a guide ...."

"I found it," he said. "Remember?"

She appeared to think about that. "You were searching, there's a difference."

He tilted his head and considered this, and Chantilly giggled.

"And besides," she said, "it *wanted* you to find it." She lifted the book for him to inspect. "I found something you'll like."

He continued forward and lifted the volume from her hands, read its cover: *"The Man in the Iron Mask."*

She watched him in silence as he did so; nor did this trouble him. For it was true that people came away from relationships, whatever their context, with an added facet to themselves; and what he was learning from Chantilly was to never fear the silence, nor apologize for it by marring its perfection with trivial words.

At last he met her eyes over the rim of the book.

"Explain, Chantilly," he said, perplexed as to what affinity she presumed he'd have for such a title.

There was a flicker of disappointment in her eyes, and she said, "It's about a man condemned to a single room. His captors put a mask of cold iron about his head, I suppose merely out of cruelty, and he spends his days watching ships appear and disappear on the horizon, bound up in chains and his spiked helmet, seeing only as much as its thin slit will allow."

Now he understood.

"Ah," he began, feeling clever with enlightenment. "And you hope that by my reading this, I shall come to understand the hopelessness of my charges ..."

The prospect intrigued him.

She looked at him with what seemed almost pity. She smiled, then, apparently in spite of herself, and he realized with some embarrassment that he was tilting his head again, a mannerism she had always said 'looked for all the world like an infant contemplating the world beyond the crib.'

He straightened up and said at last, "Judging by your expression, it seems to me that I have misjudged the book's purpose ..."

"Dravidian," she said, seeming to shift tone, "have you ever wondered what it would be like, your life, I mean ... if you weren't a ferryman?"

A moment passed before he could respond. "But I *am* a ferryman." He took her shoulders in his hands. "These eyes, Chantilly—my skin, they cannot be changed. I will always be that which you see, that which the Lucitor has made me. 'What-ifs' and 'might-have-beens' can only cloud my thinking. I am what—"

She cupped his cheeks and kissed him before he could continue.

A moment later she said, "It is always the unworkable which attracts us the most, isn't it?"

Then she pulled loose the straps at her shoulders and slipped from her dress.

There was a thud at their feet and a rifling of pages, and he pulled her to him, locking his lips with her own. And it occurred to him—not for the first time—that the secret to happiness, for the person bound up in thoughts, could sometimes be as simple as knowing when to let the book fall; then, kissing and sucking, he descended her long, warm neck and buried his face between her breasts—her hands grasping the back of his head, her long, narrow fingers fondling his hair. He ran his tongue up the slope of one breast and swirled it around an erect nipple, then flicked at it, back and forth, again and again, before taking it into his mouth and applying pressure, tugging at it gently with his teeth on occasion.

She shifted against him, her mouth forming silent words, as he moved to the other breast, kissing and stroking. Then he slid downward, his lips tracing a path from the arches of her heaving bosom to her soft, quivering belly and beyond—coming to a rest at last upon her Mons pubis, where he paused briefly amidst the wiry thatch and lifted his yellow eyes to meet her own ... before slipping his tongue beneath its vermillion hood and engaging her suddenly and without mercy.

"Oh, Dravidian!" she gasped, and threw a leg up on a shelf.

He rose instantly and swept her off her feet, then quickly carried her around the corner to a work nook where he used her body to clear the table of books—causing her to giggle and to laugh—before setting her down and laying her back, back, until her narrow, sleek form was laid out like a bolt of gossamer cloth before him.

He kissed her, soft as a feather at first, then deeper, wilder, his free hand placed gently but firmly on her cheek, cupping the curve of her face ... while their mouths worked in unison, tongues dancing and twirling, flicking, probing intensely but never intruding to the point of being grotesque.

At last their mouths parted and he met her eyes again, but this time whole worlds seemed to swirl there. He pressed his lips to her cheek once more and flicked at her ear with his tongue, then moved to the end of the table and pulled her toward him by the hips. She lifted and parted her cream-colored legs—opening them slowly, majestically, like the unfurling wings of some great, resplendent bird—and he slid his hands over them, first on the outside, from her thighs to her toes, then on the inside, tracing along the tender flesh to her place before stopping short, so that her head lolled and her teeth ground with anticipation. Then he lapped at her from anus to cowl, once, twice, a third time, as she crisscrossed her ankles behind his head and wrapped her hands up in his hair, drawing him in.

"Yes—Oh, God, Dravidian. Yes!"

She leapt suddenly as he rediscovered her clitoris and began wiggling his tongue back and forth. He cupped the cheeks of her buttocks and lifted her pelvis as he did so, and so invigorating was the musky-sweet smell of her, so delicious the briny, bittersweet taste of her, that he nearly lost himself. He avoided it only by switching focus, nuzzling his tongue deep inside her and seeking depth as she pressed herself against him almost violently.

Her breath hitched once, twice—and, sensing she was near, he withdrew suddenly and renewed his efforts upon her clitoris, licking it back and forth, up and down, flicking and teasing, sucking it into his mouth, until she cried out rapturously and her entire body shuddered and quaked and there was a deluge of spending followed almost immediately by a pronounced dryness, after which she slid off the table and dropped to her knees before him, and, unbuckling his trousers in a veritable white heat, began stroking his steel while moving her lips up and down— rapidly, artlessly, hungrily—until he came so powerfully and voluminously that she gagged once and had to remove him from her mouth so that he finished at last upon her chin and her breasts and her thighs.

XII | Tale, Interrupted

"... art thou listening?" the prefect was saying.

Dravidian straightened. "Very much so, Prefect," he lied.

"Clearly thou wert not. I just told thee to meet me at your gondola in one quarter of an hour. Yet you have not taken a single step."

"I would not presume to walk before you, Prefect."

Asmodeus smiled. "Ah, very good." He began moving in that direction. "I understand thou visited the cellblock ..."

Dravidian thought quickly. "I—yes. I had considered speaking to her in private ... in the hope of encouraging her to submit. But I changed my—"

"Therefore my promise has been rescinded."

Dravidian looked up sharply—saw only the prefect's hunched back. "The girl shall be put to torment. Therefore it's possible she shall live, and it's possible she shall not. That depends on the both of thee. Thou wilt be present for the excruciation, Master Dravidian."

XIII | Black Hole

He had arrived slightly early, he knew, but was about to enter the brightly-illuminated tent anyway when he heard a pronounced and prolonged sniffing—and stopped dead just outside the open door-flap, after which he turned away slowly, delicately. He wasn't sure what the sound had been; but he could see his master's shadow far beyond his own on the deck before him, and Shekalane's, too: she knelt between his gondola and the ignudi cage while the prefect again lingered by its door, and this time, Dravidian was quite certain that Asmodeus was reaching into it, at least until he moved away from it at last and appeared to circle Shekalane slowly.

"Fear not, dear woman," he heard Asmodeus tell her. "We are not as harsh as we look."

Dravidian stared forward as the River breathed around them like a giant.

"Such a beautiful creature," the prefect went on. "What a pity thou should be ... *wasted.* We prefects can, of course, grant amnesty."

It was a lie. No one could undermine the Lucitor's authority, not even a prefect of the ferrymen.

Asmodeus stopped in front of her at length. "Surely, thou dost know what I mean, yes?"

She did not answer and Dravidian saw him pluck gently at her hair.

"Oh, come, such doors have been opened before thee before. Unless, of course, thou art too pure. Tell me, beautiful creature, art thou too pure?"

When still she did not answer the prefect continued, "Thou playest the enigma, and deignest not even to be wroth with me.

But I tell thee clearly: a purity such as that would bear fruit somewhere in the record. And I have such a record right here."

There was a rustling of pages as the prefect appeared to consult his ledger.

"Ah, yes, here it is. Shekalane Ravencraft ... tile number 232-77-7217 ... chosen in the autumn tumbling, notified by courier on ...." He trailed off abruptly. "Oh, now ... what is this?"

Dravidian's pulse quickened as a flickering green-white light filled the tent. A hologram. *The* hologram.

"You have carried out a brilliant deception for the cause, my love," he heard Valdus say. *"But time is a luxury we are running out of fast. I ask that you wait here while I attend to something."*

Then, Shekalane's voice, as smooth and vespertine as the twilight: *"And I ask that you make time for me. This one time. Help me to help you."* —followed by the sound of trousers being unbuckled.

Asmodeus broke his silence. "Well now, isn't this interesting?"

"And if I refuse?" Valdus again. *"Will you have the stomach for what comes next?"*

"Let me show you what I have the stomach for ..."

"Tell me, Shekalane," Asmodeus whispered at last, appearing to watch intently. "What was going through thy mind as thou bestowed this great affection upon our mortal enemy?"

"Yes, Shekalane ... like that ..."

"Was it appreciation for the hundreds killed in random attacks across Ursathrax in the last year alone?"

"Oh, God, yes ..."

"Or was it for the love of the suffering and starvation caused by his relentless raids upon our barges and farmlands and supply ships?"

"*Yes ...*" Grunting and moaning. "*Your skills as a courtesan ... remain unrivalled ...*"

"Or was it just ... base carnality ... perhaps even pure ignorance ..."

"*Ahhh ... Ahhhh ...*"

Asmodeus closed the book slowly.

Dravidian's head ached as the prefect paced around her once again.

"And thus we return to the heart of the matter. For if it was the former, I dare say thou knowest what comes next. He, our Lucitor, will feed thee to thyself bit by bloody bit—only to resurrect thee and do it again. But if, say, it was the latter ... Surely thou dost knowest—a beauty such as yours could not help but knowest—that there are ... options. Options which bear with them an official writ of amnesty and freedom from the Lottery forever."

Dravidian could listen to no more. Asmodeus had grown drunk on the dust and sought to rape her! His mind reeled from the realization; it all made sense now: the prefect's passion and grandiosity during the bulk of their conversation in his cabin ... his gradual mellowing as the dust released its hold—a prefect of the ferryman had become a common addict!

And now Shekalane was in danger not just of torment and death but of the ultimate violation—indeed, of the very thing she feared the most, the very thing which had made service to the Lucitor so repugnant to her. The notion filled him with despair: Was there nothing in Ursathrax that was not decaying? Must the integrity of the ferrymen wane also?

"I would rather open my legs to a snake," he heard Shekalane hiss, and it sounded as though she spat at him.

He saw the prefect's outline backhand her, heard Shekalane crumple to the deck. He could see their shadows clearly now: a bent, witch-like figure with its arm held out and its fingers dangling ... and the subtle curves of a woman, writhing near the floor. The two outlines lay parallel along the boards like creeping shades as he glared at them in disbelief.

It appeared she grabbed his ankle—and bit it. He swiped the back of his hand across her face again. *"Rebellious Whore!"*

Dravidian's heart knocked against his chest. He saw her shadow crawling toward the gondola but tried not to watch, choosing instead to focus on the silhouettes of the ignudi, who careened about their cage furiously, frightened by the proximity of the violence.

She cried out and he nearly burst into the tent; instead he again looked to the shadow-play in front of him: the prefect had grabbed her by the arm and was wrestling her from the boat. She resisted vigorously and he threw her to the deck; it looked as though he stepped on her throat.

"What a sweet beast thou art," he said, and added, "I'm sorry, did I say 'beast?' I meant, of course, *bitch* ... Dravidian? Is that thee loitering outside the flap?"

He froze. "I—yes, my lord. I heard a commotion ... and didn't think it my place to—"

"Stop your speaking and enter."

He entered the tent ... and could only stare at her, for she was bleeding from lacerations to her forehead and right temple.

Asmodeus said: "Behold how frightened your charge is, ferryman. Didst thou terrorize thy poor thing? If so it has made her ... willful." He studied him carefully before shifting his eyes to Shekalane and back. *"Easy,* ferryman. That is none of thy concern. I tried to offer this striking young woman her life. But instead she resisted ... and now we shall proceed with the excruciation as planned." He held out a set of keys. "Go to the cage and bring me an elfemale."

Dravidian noticed that his pale lips bore hints of golden glitter. It was quite obviously ignudi dust. Staring into his eyes, he could tell the prefect had been corrupted by it. He hesitated even as Asmodeus rattled the keys impatiently.

For he knew now what the prefect intended, and did not know if he could stand by while such an abomination unfolded. Indeed, he knew nothing save that he loved Shekalane and had betrayed her beyond any hope of redemption; that no matter what he did now it was far too late, and that the darkness, the *sub umbra,* the shadow behind, would win out at last. And that this total annihilation, this consuming of all light and sound and thought, was precisely what he deserved, although it was not what Shekalane deserved, not what Chantilly had deserved, not what the boy or his father from so many years hence had deserved—not what anyone born of any time and place did. And yet surely that was the way of things, it had been since the beginning of time, and he knew also that any salvific action on his part or any other's would have to wait until the next life, the next age, when the all-consuming dark might once again explode into a new age, a new epoch—a once and final chance to set things right.

Black hole, white fountain.

To the End of Ursathrax

I | Poised to Strike

It had all come down to this; everything which had come before was preamble. And now, standing at the vanguard of an army numbering in the thousands, Valdus was ready. In a sense, he had the ferryman's raven to thank for it: the creature had led them on a jolly good goose chase to the end of *Cuniculum Amoris,* but they had used that detour to extract conscripts from every village, town and city along the way. And while the quality of recruits was not always what he would have liked, their numbers alone would prove valuable beyond measure; for the Revolution would not be won by the tip of the spear alone—that is, his original army—but also by a sturdy shaft with which to drive it. And now that he had that, he knew the Revolution might yet prevail.

Even now he found their reversal of fortune after the debacle in Flax almost too amazing to believe. Who among them could have imagined that they would more than quadruple their numbers so soon after? Or that a spy once thought lost should suddenly reestablish contact and alert him to the fact that a turncoat ferryman and a beautiful woman in green had been apprehended on the River Dire—by Asmodeus himself? And while he had no idea why Shekalane and her ferryman should return to *Styx Flumen,* the fact that they had had allowed him to salvage most of his original plan.

And yet many uncertainties remained, foremost among them: Would Shekalane detonate the ring? For if she did not, they would have no choice but to storm the dragger while its shields remained intact, which meant their archers would be useless (for the fast-moving bolts would merely bounce off the fields). More importantly, it meant Asmodeus would still be alive and thus coordinating a response to their attack—and that, Valdus knew, could be the difference between success and failure. Nor was it merely the success or failure of a single battle which concerned him; for Hirth was correct in asserting that they would never get a second chance at such an operation.

So it was with sweaty fingers that Valdus gripped his binoculars and adjusted the focusing ring—seeing the dragger's outline clearly as it rounded the curvature of the world, but not, as yet, able to make out any details. For he knew that two things needed to happen in order for the attack, and by extension the Revolution, to succeed. First, their brownie had to deliver his message to Shekalane (as well as disrupt any outbound communications once the attack was under way).

And second, Shekalane had to find it within her to forgive him ... if not completely than at least enough to act on behalf of the Revolution in spite of him.

II | The Calling of the Cloud of Witnesses

Dravidian took the keys and walked to the ignudi cage, where he opened the little door and reached in, catching a red one by the tip of her wing, then drew her out, shutting the hatch. In his despair he forgot to latch it, much less to lock it. He walked back to the prefect and handed him both the keys and the creature.

Asmodeus took the elfemale and held it close over Shekalane, rubbing its wings with his thumb so that ignudi dust fell glittering into her hair, and onto her face, and over her entire body. When he was done he allowed the red ignudi to fly free.

"There we are, much better," he said, then rose his hand and snapped his bony fingers, shouting, "Drop the curtain and play the mating call."

Dravidian heard brownies shuffling along planks and immediately the black curtain surrounding them dropped and the strange call began emanating from the dragger's speakers. A moment later he saw the first raven zig by in the dark beyond the bulwark; then another, and another, and soon there were many, as they began alighting on the netting one by one and turning their heads this way and that, searching for the usual cloud of color and sustenance but finding only Shekalane.

And as the murder of crows congregated, a clock began to tick in Dravidian's ear; not a literal clock but rather the gears of memory awakening yet again—and he somehow sensed that many paths were converging all at this moment; that the dead hand of the past had suddenly squeezed its fist and reopened, and that it was drawing open the curtain on both the first act and the last. So, too, did a memory of Chantilly's texts come unbidden to his mind: The Calling of the Cloud of Witnesses, from something called *The Bible*. And he remembered the man, a fire-eater by trade, and the boy, and how he had come to meet them only hours after he'd made love to Chantilly amidst the stacks ...

III | The Fire-eater

Although he was many miles and hours away from her now and once again standing beside his gondola at the end of a fog-shrouded sacrificial pier (as he would be doing repeatedly over the month-long course of the Sacrificium), he was still thinking about his night with Chantilly when something moved amidst the gloom.

Only after a moment did the silhouette of a man emerge, and such was the size and build of him that Dravidian immediately unhooked his scythe and tapped his mask—it being his habit to confirm that his face was protected, for the mask had already become like a second skin even in his short time as a ferryman.

But the man did not step forward, and instead addressed Dravidian from precisely where he stood. "Are you dutiful? Honorable? Do you define yourself by such attributes? Do you love, and are you loved by others, even if it's but one or two in all the world?"

Dravidian froze, mentally and physically.

"Know that I was, too," said the man. "And know that I was dedicated to my work just as you are—that, indeed, we bore much in common, for I wore a costume and awed the masses also. I was a fire-eater, and I breathed it, as well, and I entertained thousands over the course of my life, up and down the River Dire. Know, too, that I paid a price for my dedication; and that, while it did not cause my wife to lose her love for me, it lessened it, and I mean in such a way that cannot ever be fully repaired. Know that everything you have ever felt and thought ... I felt and thought, too. For I am not just a number upon a tile, and this you must know before I submit to stepping forward."

Dravidian said, "I know it now, fire-eater. And while I am still young and foolish in many ways, I ... I believe I understand you." He gripped the handle of his scythe tightly. "Now come forth and submit to your bonds."

At length his charge stepped forward, revealing himself—in bulk, for they were of approximately the same height—to be even more of a giant than Dravidian had anticipated. It was sweltering hot, and the man loosed the blue scarf from around his thick neck and swiped it across his forehead ... before allowing it to drop, his expression uncowed. And yet something happened to his firm, noble gaze as he continued to behold Dravidian—something Dravidian had come to expect since his ascension to duty as a ferryman. Something he could only attribute to the design of his accouterments, or the pale of his skin and eyes. Regardless, the giant seemed to shrink noticeably all in an instant, glancing nervously at Dravidian's meat hook-like weapon and then over his own shoulder into the mists—before resuming eye contact and beginning to breath heavier than before. And, fearing his charge was about to flee, Dravidian strode toward him immediately and loosened the shackles from his belt.

He needn't have bothered. For after closing to within a few feet he saw that the giant was hyperventilating and clutching at his chest, and it became clear that he was suffering a seizure, perhaps even a heart attack, as he collapsed to the boards at Dravidian's boots and began writhing in pain. Dravidian could only look on as the man rolled his eyes up at him—his red hair soaked in sweat and matted against his forehead, his mighty limbs trembling—before he dropped to his knees next to him and set the bonds aside (but not his scythe), and, laying hands upon him, said, "Easy does it, easy, just breathe. Do not be afraid. Look, see ..." He pressed the pad at his temple and released his mask. "I am just as you are, as you said so yourself. It is all a charade, mere stagecraft. Relax. I have some water in my gondola ..."

But the fire-eater's eyes had become murky ponds and only quivered with fear and revulsion—until at last they went completely blank, and Dravidian set about reviving him with a fevered intensity, alternating, in the manner in which he'd been trained, between blowing into his mouth and pumping his chest.

And it was at that moment that there was a commotion on the shore and the sound of someone running along the planks toward them. An instant later a boy burst from the fog, and, seeing Dravidian looming over the dying man, stopped dead in his tracks ... before a pair of sentries arrived with a rattle of armor and wrestled him back into the gloom. But not before he'd swept up the blue scarf and his eyes met Dravidian's square on and he shouted, "A curse on you for killing my father! A curse on the ferrymen!"

IV | Chantilly

Recounting the episode to Chantilly in the Bibliotheca, he noted her expression take a turn toward the pale and asked if perhaps she were feeling ill.

"No," she said, tentatively, then added, "and yes. It's just that ... it's so horrible. That he should die at that moment, under such circumstances ... and that his son should bear witness." She leaned against her cart as though suddenly tired. "He must have thought you killed him ... were killing him. Oh, Dravidian, don't you see? How for every person chosen in the Lottery a dozen others are impacted? Don't you see how the Lucitor's enemies will breed like flies until, until ...."

"Until what, Chantilly?" His tone was earnest, not argumentative.

"Until the people rise up. Until they topple the Lucitor once and for all." She squeezed a handful of books into a gap in the shelf. "There, I said it. I just hope that when that day comes it won't mean your head on a pike, as well." She stopped sorting long enough to read one of the tome's covers: *"The Libidinous Librarian,* by the Jester. Ha!"

She passed the slim volume to Dravidian, who thumbed through it absently as he leaned against the shelves. At last he said, "You are a mystery to me, Chantilly, in your desire to spend time with me. I'm not colorful, either in character or physically, I cannot even look at you with a man's eyes, and I'm certainly no comedian—"

"I'm not interested in comedians, Dravidian," she said abruptly. "Commend to me *one* great contribution to this world by a jester ..."

He said nothing.

"You can't, can you? No, of course not. That is because loose-lipped men with curly shoes and bells on their hats come cheaper than the lowliest of fish. It is easy to be a fool, Dravidian. It is much harder to be the type of man you have revealed yourself to be in your letters ... and the drawings! You have a gift, my love, one that has given me much to speculate on."

"Surely," he began, "you would prefer the company of one whose insights could bring you laughter instead of reverie ..."

"Too many people—especially women, I dare say—use laughter as a surrogate for thinking."

He could only stare at her blankly.

"Chantilly—you are *extraordinary.*"

"Just aware." She knelt and scooped up the books at her feet. "I'm going to give you some things to read. You haven't yet made the discovery that it is your very isolation that ennobles you; it is what makes you interesting." She handed the books to him. "These are works of heroic literature ... tales of courage and obstacle by a dozen different men, now long dead. But you will discover, upon reading them, that they share certain sensibilities ... I believe they may indeed open a few doors."

He looked at her, confused.

"For example," she said. "Most great men, throughout history, have had an artistic sensibility. Do you know what art is, Dravid? I mean, really is?"

He believed he knew precisely, but he shook his head, only because he preferred the sound of her voice over his own.

"It is the ordering of chaos," she said. "Although some would say it is in the chaos itself that art becomes manifest."

She stepped away from the bookcase and kicked at a low shelf—causing the books there to tumble to the floor in a plume of dust and mildew. "There. Now ... have I created a work of art, or have I simply made a mess?"

He stooped to pick up the books but she urged him to disregard them with a quick gesture of the hand.

"If we say I've created art by knocking the books to the floor, then is not a barbarian an artist when he hacks his way through the enemy's lines? Wouldn't the spilling of blood then become simply another aesthetic element?"

Dravidian shook his head. "There would be no purpose."

"Exactly! Chaos, of course, is just chaos. Art is the *ordering* of such chaos into a pattern with a purpose. These great men I speak of, Dravidian, understood this. They perceived certain elements ... then drew lines in their head, connecting them. When they stepped back, they realized the lines formed a pattern. And the pattern they formed was nothing short of the answer for their times."

She grinned wryly. "Ah, and not a jester among them. You may find a man full of jokes in any field, on any ship, bending to any task. You will find a man of vision but once in a millennium, if then." She ran a finger back and forth over his shirt. "Sometimes I think I see the seed of such a man in you."

He felt perhaps as if he were being flattered undeservedly, and, since the sensation was a pleasant one, he decided to take his leave of her, for fear the truth might be exposed.

"I should go," he said, and began moving away.

"Dravidian ..."

He looked to her expectantly.

"What if I were chosen?"

He shrank deeper into the shadows, saying nothing.

"Would you do your duty and commend me to my doom?"

Silence.

"That is an unfair thing for you to ask, Chantilly."

"But ... would you?"

He whispered in the blackness, "Yes."

"And if I resisted? Would you employ brute force ... even your scythe?"

At last, he said, "Yes."

"Do you love me?"

"Yes."

More silence.

"Goodnight, Dravidian."

"Goodnight, Chantilly."

V | The Man of Branigan

The next morning found him once again garbed all in black as he emerged from the cathedral in the usual trappings: the slant-eyed death mask, the hooded cloak, the dark gloves not yet stained with anyone's blood (which he considered a badge of honor, although he knew that for most ferrymen, Pepperlung, for example, the opposite was true).

He was to receive his charge at the Festival Saltus in Branigan, which lie just north of the capitol, amidst the Old English communities of the Ruby Wealth, hence he'd be back in port by orbset with his charge's cooperation and fortune of currents. Nor did he anticipate any trouble; for the lawfulness and agreeability of the region was well known amongst the ferrymen, and it was of little surprise that a place that lie in the virtual shadow of the Lucitor's Cathedral should be so well-behaved. And yet, as he was beginning to learn, a ferryman's life was beset with complication from the moment he launched from the dragger—and this day, alas, would prove to be no different.

It was an unfortunate reality that sometimes the 'invited' had to be wounded so that they could be drug with little resistance to the boat. In doing so, he had missed the intended vein when he'd nipped the man with the tip of his scythe and had cut instead a major artery—causing the man to scream out and his blood to spurt about in tremendous quantities, even as his wife and children broke the barriers and were dotted with crimson as they tried to free him of his entrapment.

Dravidian glanced down at the man's face as he dragged him toward the boat, saw the sun orb bouncing off the blade of his scythe and stabbing him in the eyes. Already he had begun to look pale; how could he explain to the man's family that the sooner he got him into the gondola the sooner he could stop the bleeding and dress the wound?

"I will tend to your wound once we are on board," he said to his charge. "In the meantime a word from you may calm them."

But the man didn't hear him; he heard only the shrieks of his family, saw only their tormented faces which were spotted with his own blood.

Sentries and numerous onlookers had gathered about them now and Dravidian feared for a moment that the mob might overpower the guards and fall upon him. Through all the confusion and wailing he heard someone bark: "Stand aside! The Lucitor's will must stand."

And then they were in the boat and away, Dravidian shoving off before he had even tended to the man's wound, while the horrified woman and her children looked on and the sentries began to herd the crowd back to the riverbank.

VI | The Children

The faces swirled about him in what he had begun to suspect was a dream: pale as his own, swollen, webbed with bulging veins—all of them betraying quivering eyes full of abject terror which converged into one and filled his field of vision so that he saw in its iris the reflection of a man.

It was himself, Dravidian, and yet it was *not* himself. Rather, it was the black-clad ferryman, hidden behind his boney mask (now sprinkled with fresh blood), while the previously whirling faces (some also marred with blood) had been those of his recent charges and their families: the fire-eater and his son—who again cried out, "A curse on you for killing my father! A curse on the ferrymen!"—the man from Branigan and his wife and children .... And yet, were not those his—Dravidian's—own eyes looking back now? No, no—for these were not a man's eyes at all; rather, they were those of a devil—their pupil's sickly yellow, their whites spider-webbed with veins.

Images came unbidden to him then and he could see hearts beating in chests: in that of his charge and those of the man's children and wife—who looked like the kind of woman who's love of family could only be likened to a general's love of war, so seldom shared by his soldiers, or Dravidian's love of books. So, too, was he aware of his own heart beating—pounding—for nothing in his training had prepared him for what he now saw himself doing: dragging a bleeding father from his wife and children—children whom he, Dravidian, wished only to comfort.

But that had been wholly impossible, as had been the entire cursed affair, so much so that when the man later collapsed (and died) at the processing terminal, Dravidian collapsed also—to be revived only by smelling salts administered by Pepperlung himself, who had a good laugh at the thought of a ferryman being so sensitive and squeamish.

Now he was no longer dreaming but remembering, and as thunder cracked he found himself fully awake next to Chantilly in the Bibliotheca, in her little bedroom among the ceiling-high stacks, and he clung to her as normally he would not—shaking her awake at last only because he could not do otherwise, and telling her, breathlessly: "Chantilly ... I must go."

She rolled her head against the pillow to regard him sleepily. "What is it, Dravidian?"

"It ... it is a start," he said, then got dressed and took his leave of her—plunging into the stormy night and stealing a boat from the south quay, where he began rowing ... for Branigan.

VII | The Widow

It was as he'd hoped. The man's wife was still awake ... sitting as though mummified by a modest hearth—her blank face become the forum for the flickering firelight. Nor did she run or even gasp—indeed, she seemed not to notice him standing there in the shadows at all, at least not at first. At length she must have noticed the amber gleam of his eyes, and said: "Why have you come?"

He stepped from the inky darkness and knelt before her.

"I have come to atone," he said.

"He is dead, then."

"Yes."

She sat by the fire and said nothing. At last she asked, "How did you find us?"

"Branigan is small, madam ... I made inquiries. But that is not important. What is important is—"

"Atonement," she interrupted. "Closure."

Dravidian hesitated. "More than that. Will you submit to hear it?"

She looked into the fire. "Speak."

Dravidian gathered his thoughts. At last he said: "Madam, you know I have not chosen to be what I am. And you should know also that I bore your husband no malice, but fulfilled only my function and duty to the Lucitor, who's authority binds us all. However, since I find I cannot shoulder the burden of such misery as I have helped inflict upon you and your offspring, I will offer you my life now as collateral for the injustice done by those I serve ..."

He reached into his blue cloak and drew forth a dagger, then extended it to her.

She did not even look at him.

"I hold in my hand a dagger," he persisted. "I implore you, madam—you should not ignore this opportunity. The years do not mellow a hurt such as yours; they can only pour salt upon it and enflame it further. That course leads to obsession, and obsession always destroys. And I do not wish to see you destroyed, as your husband was destroyed. Please ... take the weapon."

Finally, she said, simply, "I will not, ferryman."

He waited for her to say more and when no more was forthcoming, he added, "My name is Dravidian. And I did not come here as a ferryman, but as a man. See? I wear colorful clothes, just as you—"

"To me you can only be the ferryman—servant to the Lucitor, part of the brotherhood of death and slavery—killer of my husband. I cannot and will not forgive you, boatman. And taking your life would be a forgiving thing to do. No, it is not by my will that you shall be redeemed. You are a silly young man with a selfish motive; and if I must live with the pain of having lost my husband, it is only fitting that you should live with the pain of having killed him. Now please, go."

"If he had not resisted so furiously, madam—"

"By the gods, just go!"

He turned and left the tent.

He was lost to confusion (less to her behavior as his own, for he felt cowardly and self-serving) as he rounded its edge and headed for the quay once again, until the voice of a child brought him to a halt, and he turned to see the widow's youngest daughter, who had emerged from a flap at the rear of the tent, gazing up at him.

"Why did you come here?" she asked him—in what seemed a surprisingly casual manner.

He knelt in front of her. "To explain why I took your father ... and to try to make amends."

She shifted her weight from one foot to the other, examining him. "Mother says bad men always take what isn't theirs. Even other people's lives."

"You will understand, little one, when you are older ... this is my hope." He plucked a purple flower from the grass and slid it behind her ear. "You have not been born into a free world. In time we all must do what the Lucitor wills."

"My mother says that your kind are less than human and should be shunned."

"There may be truth in that. But what does your heart tell you?"

She was appearing to think about this when a shrill voice cried out: "Tamarin!" —and he spun about to find the widow glaring at them from inside the tent's entrance. "Come inside. Now."

The little girl trotted in (he couldn't help but to notice she was still wearing the same dress from earlier in the day, the one with her father's blood on it), and he looked to her mother in the lamplight. "It's a sin to school a child in prejudice, madam. Hating me shall not bring back her father."

"No, but it will keep the girl warm in his absence."

All was silent save for the canvas of the tent dancing in the breeze, and Dravidian nodded, saying nothing. It seemed only fair.

It was only later, lying in the barracks, that he finally conceded to himself that some acts might lie beyond redemption. Nor was it in the face of the great atrocities of the history books that he thought this—but rather in light of the smaller things men and women did every day in the name of obligation or guilt.

VIII | Pepperlung

He told Pepperlung nothing of his visit with the widow, nor did he discuss it with any of his other brothers. He retreated into himself; and, because he'd never been inclined to spend much time in the company of any one niche or group of people, his further alienation from friends and colleagues went largely unnoticed.

It was to be a time of discovery. He delved headlong into the books Chantilly provided him and his readings always culminated in a long conversation with her concerning the meaning of the letters he'd read. Soon old ideas and viewpoints began to fall away—even as the auburn leaves began seesawing past the barracks' windows, and by the arrival of winter he'd undergone a stunning, if incomplete, transformation.

But his gradual enlightenment was not to proceed unchecked. The first such obstacle came on the eve of the Sodfest Brine, when a group of visitors not unfamiliar (but wholly unwelcome) came to call among the musty stacks of the Bibliotheca—where Chantilly and himself had been seated on the floor with a large volume spread across their laps, engaged in some mirthful cuddling.

They had been discussing the concept of 'empathy,' by and large the very nucleus of Dravidian's metamorphosis of thought, when Pepperlung and Ripipin emerged quite suddenly from the blackness just beyond their kerosene lantern—and called to him not by name but by professional title.

"We would speak with you, ferryman," announced Pepperlung, his greenish, blue-gray mask appearing to hang suspended in the dark, looking little different than it did when it hung from its hook in the cathedral's armory.

"Ferryman ... busy," joked Dravidian, and laughed. (He had assumed his brother joked, too, for he was not on duty and rarely did they address themselves so formally save in the presence of a prefect.)

"Your assessment of our purpose here is incorrect, ferryman," Pepperlung said coolly, and turned his mask toward

Chantilly. "I beg your forgiveness, madam, but his presence is required elsewhere."

Dravidian stood slowly and deliberately so that his naked face was only a few feet from Pepperlung's façade. "No .... No, it is you who is 'incorrect,' I fear." He shook his head. "I am not on duty and shall not accompany you. If there are matters of import to confer than I suggest we do so in the morning, in the armory or on the quay, where such matters are discussed."

At length Pepperlung breathed deeply, and his pale eyes gleamed within the mask's blackened eyeholes.

Ripipin said, "Leave him, then. We've done our share."

Pepperlung ignored him. "Dravidian, if you would spare yourself further—"

"The answer, friend Pepperlung, is still 'no.' Please, do not take me to task on this; I am more familiar with the Code than the both of you, by far, and am fully aware of where my personal rights begin and end."

Chantilly stirred beside him as if suddenly cold and touched his leg. It would not occur to him until many years later that there were few assets more commonly ignored than the gentle guidance of a prudent woman, especially in the face of a lover behaving foolhardily.

"Perhaps you should accompany them, Love," she said. "We can continue our debate another time."

"Debate!" Ripipin hissed.

Pepperlung nudged him into silence. "The girl knows something about the tenor of our situation," he said to Dravidian at last. "Perhaps you should listen to her."

"Yes, listen to her," said Ripipin. *"... Love."*

Turning toward her, Dravidian said, "Chantilly, understand it is not I who breaches etiquette, but my misinformed brothers ..."

Pepperlung took a step toward him. "Being a sycophant does not become you, Dravid. Please ... come with us now. The girl will wait."

Reseating himself, Dravidian said to Chantilly, "I believe we were discussing empathy before my fellow ghouls crashed our study ..."

Pepperlung sneered. "Empathy ..." He moved to take his leave of them but paused. "It is too late, Ripipin. Our dear Dravidian here has succumbed to the Madness. He has spent too much time in the words of the madmen who writ their misguided philosophies while in drunken stupors, or bedeviled by opiates—men who like carnie geeks slumped over their pathetic little scribblings muttering delusions to themselves while the real world flowed past them and real men saw to its needs. And like them, he has found an excuse to hide like a coward from his duties and say to his peers: I am better than you, oh simple friends. And so do not trouble me with your trilling and your squeaking. Aye, he sees us as mice, I'd allot."

He stood half in darkness and sighed. "Very well, then." He turned to go and Ripipin followed.

A moment later he called to Dravidian a final time: "It'll be quite cold out tonight, old friend ... see to it you take your leave of here before the Orb turns." And, quieter, he added, "I can do no more. Fortnight."

And then the two were gone, as suddenly and as silently as they had arrived.

IX | The Ferrymen

He left the Bibliotheca well after the turn of the Orb, stepping not into daylight but the cold blue glow of the *orbis lunae*. He held in the crook of an arm yet another stack of texts suggested to him by Chantilly, and as he walked along the deserted boardwalk he made something of a sport of trying to read their covers in the darkness.

Alas, the transport he usually relied upon to ferry him back to Greater *Novum Venum* had already departed ... and so he would have to walk around the bay to return to the barracks, a difference of about five miles. Regardless, he wore a heavy coat and the night was not as cold as Pepperlung had predicted, and he found himself whistling as he jauntily made the trek, wondering if any ferryman had ever run before, or simply disappeared, and wondering, too, if Chantilly would accompany him if he were to ever attempt such a thing, and how they would survive, to say nothing of his appearance and the great difficulty they would have in maintaining a low profile. Such were his thoughts when he heard a dog begin barking excitedly and scanned his whereabouts for its location—and stopped dead in his tracks.

They stood in a shadowy semi-circle further on down the planks, their amber pupils like cats' eyes in the pools of dark beneath their masks' slanted brows, their scythes in hand—the blades of which flirted with the moonlight to create ghostly twists of light which rippled and danced like water along their honed steel. And for perhaps the first time in his life he knew the fear of his charges when they looked to their fate and found not a man come to take them, but a devil.

He acted with no special bravery whatsoever. Indeed, he had barely heard the crash of the books against the dock before he was whirling around and scrambling in the opposite direction, his heart pounding, his thoughts racing.

He ran, bolted, jumped, *flew* along the boardwalk, and on those occasions when he dared look back, he saw the lot of them scrambling in pursuit, their scythes flashing and their black cloaks flapping frenziedly and their boots pounding along the worn planks like the blows of bludgeons.

Oh, what a wild chase it was, this midnight fox hunt! For its first few moments he sprang distances he would have thought impossible and wove through barriers great and small; until, as was often the case in such pursuits, his exertions left him entirely bereft of strength—ready, even, to surrender—and he collapsed upon the boards finding his breath no longer available to him.

They fell upon his prone form an instant later—and all was impact and blinding flashes as the cruel words flowed free as his blood (which flowed freely, indeed) and the handles of their scythes left bitter wounds upon his head and face and torso.

When it was over, Pepperlung leaned toward his ear and whispered, "Your transgressions will bring punishment upon us all. Desist your relationship with the polyhistor, forget what you have learned from her, and rejoin the fellowship of your brothers. You will not speak of this to her or anyone. You were lynched by friends of the fire-eater."

And then he was gone. *They* were gone, leaving him alone on the boardwalk, deliriously running his fingers through the beaded pools of his own blood.

X | Dravidian No More

"Why are you masked?"

She did not hurry to greet him as usual, but seemed to shrink into the corner as if frightened of him.

"We must end what we have begun, Chantilly," he said, and threw the books onto the floor between them.

"Dravidian, what in Ursathrax ..." She came toward him in a rush, her face flushed, her eyes wide with confusion and fear.

He took a step back.

"Do not come any closer, please."

She hesitated. "What's happened to you? Your voice, it's ... Dravidian, you mustn't do this—"

"Dravidian does not live behind this mask, Chantilly. In fact, *he does not live.* There is only dead flesh and yellow eyes behind this façade, nothing more."

She stooped to gather up the books.

"They should be burned," he said.

He could not have been more cruel even had he struck her across the face. Tears came into her eyes as she placed the volumes back onto the shelf.

"You have poisoned my thoughts with your books and your ideas and I have paid dearly for it," he continued. "It is a cruelty, Madam, to enlighten the beast as to what lie beyond his cage. He will only resent you for it."

She reached toward him and he stepped back yet again.

"Why are you so angry—"

"Not angry! Caged! You have made me aware of my confines where before I was not and—"

She lunged forward without warning and swiped away his mask—which slid along the floor and came to a rest, face up, in the corner—then stared at him aghast for a very long time. At last she touched his shoulders—and to her surprise, he allowed it.

"Dravidian, I am so sorry ..."

He stared at her in the silence. "The bruises and fractures will heal, this time. I have no doubt the next time will bring a harsher beating."

At last, she said: "Your cruel words are designed to make our parting easier ..."

He said nothing.

"That's a coward's way, Dravidian."

"We are all cowards," he virtually hissed, and took his leave of her.

XI | White Fountain

The ravens squawked furiously as they exploded into flight, shattering his reverie, and converged upon Shekalane's crumpled form—precisely as would buzzards on some carcass.

He took a step forward as they began to tear at her flesh, but the prefect stayed him with a gloved hand. "Remember who you serve, ferryman," he warned, "not *how* you serve."

That's a coward's way, Dravidian.

He watched aghast as the ravens dug their beaks into her hair, her face, her body—everywhere the dust had settled. She smacked at them savagely and one of them fell upon its back on the boards, its legs kicking wildly. "Dravidian!" she screamed. "Please!"

He gazed down at her through the slanted eyelets of his mask.

"She knows thee by name," said the prefect. "That can be forgiven, ferryman ... if thou cooperate."

That's a coward's way, Dravidian.

From farther down the deck he heard the sound of men marching: a few in boots but many more barefoot. It was a column of slaves being herded from the stockade to replace their tired brothers in the coal pits. Surely, Dravidian thought with relief, this would end it; the ravens would disperse and hopefully lose interest before the commotion subsided.

But the ravens did not disperse, nor did the prefect so much as look up from the excruciation, and a moment later the boots of three ferrymen pounded past, followed by a line of slaves, which divided them—himself on one side while Shekalane and Asmodeus remained on the other—like some fleshy caravan. He tried to keep the two in his line of vision but saw only the slaves' bodies and crossed wrists, which were free of chains. (There was no need, a master had once explained, because they had been chosen in the Lottery and immediately conscripted into slavery as children, and so believed themselves bound whether physically shackled or not.)

He waited for them to pass, and, watching as their blank faces filed by, couldn't help but to wonder what each and every one of them was thinking—what each and every one of them might have been had the Lucitor not singled them out as slave material so young. And then they were gone, as were the ferrymen bringing up the rear of the column, and he could see Shekalane and the prefect clearly again.

"Dravidian!" Shekalane screamed as a raven took up her single dreadlock, seeming almost to want to drag her skyward by it, and she batted at it desperately.

"This, too, serves the Lucitor's design," said Asmodeus.

Shekalane cried out, *"Is this* what you serve, Dravidian? Rape and chaos? Is that what your mask represents?"

Then the birds pecked at her throat and she fell silent; and it was at that moment that a series of events and revelations began to unfold that would change the history of Ursathrax, indeed, the entire world (Thesea, included) forever.

She remembered it—suddenly, out of nowhere—as if it had happened only moments before: Valdus using his knife to pry the green stone (the original homing beacon) from the ring—then holding up a new one, a near-duplicate of the first, and saying: *"This is a shield bomb. Its primary components are a shield generator and a highly directional explosive. To use it you have only to point its face at the target, like this ... and shake it three times, which will activate a timer. You must shake very hard. The bomb will blast outward, away from you ... killing everyone within fifty feet, and causing the ship's shields to go into emergency shutdown. At the same time, a temporary body shield will be generated, which should protect you from the blast."*

And, remembering, she grasped for the ring as the ravens tore at her flesh—and twisted it from her finger. For she would not kill Dravidian even if it meant beheading the very snake—Asmodeus—at the core of the ferrymen. And having removed it, she reached through the bars which formed the bulwark of the dragger ... and dropped it, or intended to, into the River.

But it never reached the water, only bounced off the riggings and gondolas further down—once, twice, a third time.

Dravidian froze, paralyzed in a way he had never known, for having seen her do it—having seen her use what were likely her last breaths to renounce Valdus once and for all—he could not unsee it.

And then the sound of marching came again and he half-turned: it was the coal pit workers the rested ones had replaced, led by a trio of ferrymen as before. He watched them approach, secure in the knowledge that—now that Asmodeus' aged frame veritably trembled from the effects of the dust and Shekalane's excruciation had reached its grotesque climax—the precept's corruption would be exposed to all.

But the caravan did not stop; the ferrymen merely marched on by, paying no note. He followed them with his gaze, trying to look through them as they passed, but found his view of Shekalane and Asmodeus hindered once again—at which point his attention was drawn up slightly and to the side, where he saw, in sporadic glimpses, the ignudi struggling in their cage. And he noted clearly, in the brief gap that opened between guards and prisoners, that the little door to the ignudi cage stood ajar—that they could have flown out easily had they'd only known it—and he noted this with such lucidity that when the slaves began filing past, all but blocking his view, he found himself staring at their crossed wrists once more.

Again, no chains gleamed in the lantern-light like bitter fire ... no cracking lashes spurred the men on. Glancing to his own wrists, all laced up in black leather, he saw that there were no shackles there, either—even as an enormous stalactite broke loose with the sound of thunder (for the aural signature of skyfall was always unmistakable) and fell crashing into the water, and he peered upward to find the great Orb nearest them hanging askew and showering sparks, beside which a ragged hole briefly burned brighter than the sun of Thesea, so that he averted his eyes and saw, with the image still imprinted on his retinas, Shekalane reaching out to him with love in her eyes ... and remembered the words chiseled into the stone above the underground temple: *Luminis sub omne*—the Light ... under all—and realized, too, that Milkweed had dropped Rosethorn and her map-sheath directly at his feet.

He looked to the prefect as the ferrymen bringing up the rear cleared the scene—and found him already staring back at him, his greenish blue-gray mask appearing ghostly in the dull light of the lanterns. "Thou hast still much to learn about being a ferryman," he said, and turned back to Shekalane, chuckling mirthlessly. "All in time, my young friend, all in time."

Shekalane covered her face with her hands even as the ravens attempted to peck out her eyes. Her screams split the night as Dravidian reached out ...

"Dravidian! Please!"

The prefect hung back his head and began chanting in the ancient tongue—and then his head was falling all the way back and rolling from his shoulders and something thumped against the floor, causing at least some of the ravens to erupt into flight.

Dravidian glanced down to find the sword Rosethorn in his hands, its blade covered in white blotches—for the prefect's head was gone from his shoulders, replaced by a fountain of white blood—then strode to the bulwark where the convulsing body had wandered, reaching and groping, and placed his boot in the small of its back—before shoving the robotic corpse over the rail.

Then the sword was clattering against the deck—even as the prefect's body bounced off the riggings and gondolas to finally splash below—and he was drawing up Shekalane; who threw her bleeding arms about his neck and fell against him, sobbing ... as he stroked her blood-streaked hair and a mighty explosion rocked the ship.

XII | Attack

Valdus ground the binoculars intently, amazed that he had been able to locate her, yet wondering why she did not simply activate the ring. Asmodeus was right there! Surely she had not come to hate him—he, Valdus—so much that she would ignore this unique, fleeting opportunity to rid Ursathrax of one of its chief administrators of terror—to what possible end? Merely to spite him?

Or was she unable to? For clearly he was torturing her, although the railing of the ship and the frenzied ravens made it difficult to ascertain how, precisely. And then he realized that she was on the move, albeit crawling, and that she was moving *toward* Asmodeus, not away from him. And as the relief flooded through him he thought, *You close the gap to ensure our success.* That's when it struck him—the reason they had returned to *Styx Flumen*. The ferryman had betrayed her. *Oh, my errant lover!* He thought deliriously. *Did I not warn you? Did I not say that a servant of the Lucitor could never be trusted? But look now ... you return unto the fold. Now you are like me and your heart is such as steel for the ferrymen and their prefects. Do it, my love, now! You are close enough; did I not say that it would kill everyone within fifty feet? Do it and call out my name as you do so, and we shall come to your rescue and the rescue of all Ursathrax!*

But, having reached the prefect, he saw now that she was continuing on, continuing toward the ship's railing, and before he knew it she was reaching between the slats and appearing to drop something into the water far below. That's when he noticed a ferryman standing amongst the shadows nearby, watching the scene unfold, and before he could even process what he was seeing the boatman snatched a weapon up from the deck and, utilizing the cross stroke that was so much more difficult to master than the horizontal, smote the prefect's head clean from his body.

He lowered the binoculars, only to raise them once again to confirm what he was seeing—saw the ferryman kick the prefect over the rail and the body bounce off the gondolas to finally crash into the water. And then he saw him swipe off his mask and scoop Shekalane up from the deck, embracing her in the way only lovers embraced, and knew in that instant that the ferryman had not only robbed him forever of his revenge upon Asmodeus, but of Shekalane's love, as well. Then there was a mighty explosion near the waterline, and, looking up from his binoculars, he saw that the situation was worse still—for the explosion had punched a gaping hole in the dragger's hull.

"The shields are down," he snapped, loud enough for all to hear. "General Hirth, prepare your men. Spare only the slaves ... and *the two*. I want Shekalane brought to me and the maskless ferryman isolated. Lector!"

Lector scrambled to his side.

"Assessment," said Valdus, and handed him the binoculars.

Lector peered through them intently. "It isn't low enough for the ship to take on water ... but a fire burns inside it. See for yourself." He handed back the magnifiers. "And that machinery—it's part of the original engineering, a Mobius loop reactor. If it gets hot enough—"

"But the ship is coal-powered ..."

"It's been retrofitted to run on coal, of course. But the reactor remains."

"And will blow as the fire intensifies, is that it?"

"Yes, my lord. Which will surely sink the ship."

Valdus seethed. He scanned the lines of their own boats. "The supply skiffs ... we'll use them to ladle water. We'll enter the hole and put out the fire; then attack the ship from the bottom up."

"My lord," said Hirth, alarmed. "The ferrymen, too, will investigate ... and cut us to ribbons as we enter."

"Only those not picked off on the deck by your archers," said Valdus quickly. "The rest will be overwhelmed by our conscripts, who will attack from the top." He grinned at him devilishly, as in the earliest days of the conflict. "Sheer numbers, my friend. The ferrymen are few."

Gurn was dubious. "The conscripts are a mob. If you think they can be trusted to capture—"

"If not, then so be it. As for any ferrymen guarding the hole ... I trust you and Gurn have not lost your talent for storming ships." He squeezed the man's shoulder, smiling. "Now let loose the bolts and launch the conscripts. Today is V-Day."

But his smile was a forced one—the truth of it was, he felt suddenly tired. And while he looked forward to killing the ferryman with his own hands before the day was finished, he no longer saw a reason to meet him on anything like a level field—or to meet him at all, if it came to that. No, the only thing that mattered now was the taking of the ship (if indeed it was still seaworthy after such a mighty blast below decks), and, by extension, the taking of the capitol.

He would throw the conscripts at the dragger like a wall of blades and flesh. Only then, when the smoke had cleared, would he and his men move in. He had wasted enough time and energy as it was. It was time for the endgame, time to exact his revenge not on Asmodeus or Shekalane or even her pale-faced lover ... but the Lucitor Himself.

It was time, he thought—as the arrows flew and the bodies began falling and the conscripts' ships rapidly moved out—for him to take his rightful place as the ruler of Ursathrax.

XIII | Confusion

They'd wondered aloud whether his ferryman's blood would flow red as their own, and with the third strike of a club they received their answer. The coarse wood lacerated his neck—flayed away the skin so that warm red blood drizzled beneath his collar to soak clean through the black velvet jerkin. He fell to his knees in the middle of the deck and had just begun to feel the rough planks through the fabric of his trousers when he was again borne up and onward by the strong arms of his antagonists.

The attack had come without warning and without mercy, and those ferrymen who had survived the initial onslaught had quickly disappeared—not out of cowardice, he was certain, but to regroup in the face of such overwhelming numbers—leaving the crowd to focus all their bigotry and bloodlust on him. Now he was being paraded about the ship like a floppy-limbed scarecrow, grabbed at and his clothes torn asunder—fed upon, it seemed, as if here were a crow-man stuffed with money and not straw.

Somewhere Shekalane was screaming, and when he craned his neck to search for her, he saw that she, too, was being jostled and prodded through the mob. He knew not what ends to which they were being ushered, only that the edge of the ship was growing closer with each cruelty. He resolved then not to look away from her, for who knew if it would be for the last time or not? His only hope now was that she would answer his gaze with her own, and they could say goodbye, the girl from Jaskir and himself.

And then came another blow which sent black pain flushing through his skull and he reeled for balance, twirling like a drunken dancer through the throng of flesh and noise. It was as if he were caught in the vortex of a dust-devil, with twisted faces cycling all around him. There was a glint of pale bone as his skull mask blew past, not on the wind but on the face of a stranger. It passed from view and then back again, and he realized that the stranger was holding it to his face, laughing and frightening the women, waving his hands which now bore his own black gloves, pretending to be a monster. Pretending to be him. On yet a third revolution he saw the man swipe off the mask and stick out his tongue, waggling it at the women as they giggled and shrieked. Then there was but swirling sky (rather, Cyclopean stalactites hanging in the gloom) and the now burning orb, and his back impacted against the boards, crushing the air from his lungs.

"Get him up, come on!" a gruff voice barked, and then beefy hands were again taking him by the collar, by the armpits, by the hair.

"Let him die with this around his neck," he heard someone say, and felt the strap of his mask being worked over his head.

He was hoisted onto a wooden platform, the rushing of the River Dire suddenly thundering in his ears. He sucked up the misty air in great inhalations, trying to coax breath back into lungs newly shrunken. A handful of men followed him onto the platform, their boots pounding the boards like drums, and by the time he realized what was going on, they had already shackled a great weight about his ankle and had begun forcing him out along the plank. He spun upon them without hesitation, driving his shoulder into the point-man's breastplate and toppling him against his fellows. They all shuffled back like a single giant centipede, retreating to the platform. He moved toward them in spite of his weakness, dragging the ball and chain, and had cocked back a bony fist to strike when an entirely new adversary shouldered past the others.

He was a balding, warty, potbellied troll of a man wearing heavy armor, with fat, grimy cheeks and eyes full of petty ambition, and even with the steel ball in tow, Dravidian would have gone through him as easily as driving a horse through light rain (the heavy armor notwithstanding) had he not gripped Rosethorn in a single, pudgy hand.

Dravidian must have looked shocked, indeed, for the crowds gathered all along the deck erupted into laughter.

"Drive him off, Blotto!" a lone voice cried out, and the sentiment was greeted by mass applause.

The man they called Blotto smiled, his grimy cheeks swelling and lifting and hardening, like ripe tomatoes. He took a step forward, Rosethorn at the ready. Dravidian inched back accordingly, stalling for time, gathering renewed strength.

"Drive him off!" a new voice shouted, and he took his eyes off Blotto long enough to scan the crowd of faces below, looking not for the man who had just cheered for his death but for the woman with whom he'd made love in the grotto and again in the temple of the *Luminis sub omne,* and for whom he'd come to care for more than he did himself.

For bigotry was nothing if not hypocritical, and though these crude conscripts would think twice before placing their lips after his on the rim of a cup, they would extend no such disdain to placing their lips after his on the body of a woman. And so he looked for her when he might have tried for Rosethorn, hoping to find her unharmed and unmolested now that the mob's attention had focused entirely on him.

He could find her nowhere.

And then Rosethorn's tip prodded him in the chest and he was forced to take a step backward along the plank, dragging the metal ball. The people of Valdus' revolution roared with approval, and a few here and there began to beat their steely gauntlets against the dragger's wooden railings. He watched unmoved as others joined in, banging bludgeons and dagger hilts and everything else imaginable against the weathered wood. The strip of timber beneath his boots sent powerful vibrations creeping up through his legs, and within moments the sounds of metal on wood had merged to become a single, unified chorus, which doubled itself and became at last a beast all its own, a quaking and trembling which was not unlike the spasms of Ursathrax herself.

And then the chanting began.

XIV | Trapped

"Drive him off! Drive him off! Drive him off!"

As a ferryman, he was unimpressed. He could only stare down at them in utter contempt, his lids drooped in boredom, his expression sardonic, and a smile crept across his face as a little of the old arrogance awoke, reminding him of days when he and his brothers strode like gruesome princes through crowds much like this one, their masks slashed ceremoniously with gouts of fresh blood, their black cloaks billowing like storm clouds about their bodies, their necks hung adorned with wreaths of golden flowers, and always their bearing proud and terrible as they marched past hateful onlookers in celebration of All Servants' Day. In those days the protests of the crowds had shook buildings.

Still, it was a reminder, and it *was* building nicely. And so they chanted their little chant, and he perked an eyebrow and delighted for a time in the hatred he'd inspired.

His reaction to the crowd had apparently unnerved his dear friend Blotto, who'd made no move to prod him further in many breaths. Then the man seemed to screw up his courage to some extent, and with a smile all his own began inching toward him once more over the board's crude surface.

Again Dravidian was nudged by Rosethorn's tip, and again he retreated cautiously along the plank, which began to wobble up and down as they played out still further along its length.

When at last he afforded a quick glance behind, he was not really surprised to find the end of the board not two paces off. He saw the blue-black currents and frothy white caps of the River Dire rushing past, a hundred feet below at least, and such was the vertigo that he had to spin around quickly in order to avoid stumbling—so that he faced away from his antagonist.

Now the sword poked urgently at the small of his back, nudging him to the very tip of the plank, the great ball of steel scraping over the wood behind him. He stared down at the water as if in a trance, noticing that his shadow was there (for the Orb burned brightly), many feet down and looking not like a man but merely an aberration, growing like a tumor from the side of the dragger, and he knew that there would be no escape for him this time.

A warm wind whipped up around them with very little warning, lifting his hair as it might bear up pollen and causing it to dance and ruffle wildly. Slowly and with a heavy heart, he turned to face Blotto once again, who wasted no time in lifting Rosethorn so that her exquisite tip just kissed Dravidian's heart.

He looked along her oil slick-colored blade and met Blotto's eyes with his own. And his were terrible eyes, more terrible than if he'd been injected with ritalimortis a thousand times over. He was reminded of his ascension to ferryman and how he'd felt upon first seeing his masked reflection in a mirror—how he'd felt upon gazing into his own yellow eyes, keen with humanity yet trapped in the face of death—and realized suddenly that looking at Blotto was exactly the opposite. For here were the eyes of dull death in a human, and such a juxtaposition terrified him more than he dared admit.

Then the man smiled, and his rotting teeth shown yellow-black in the play of fire-light and shadow, and realizing his time in that fire-light and shadow was over, Dravidian looked beyond him to the howling crowds below ... and saluted them.

And a woman shouted.

"Dravidian!"

It was Shekalane's voice, so raw and terror-distorted that he hardly recognized it; moreover, it might have come from anywhere, thus he could only shift his eyes about helplessly, searching in vain for its owner.

"Dravidian! I love you!"

He scanned the crowd desperately, his arrogance falling away like old shackles. *Where was she?*

At this time there came another sound, just a whisper among the bigger roar, yet seeming to him to ring a significant note. It was a moist, threshing, yet somehow dry sound, like wet boots running through bramble, and it seemed to be coming from right in front of him, from where the fat man stood with Rosethorn in his grip.

It seemed to be coming from Rosethorn herself.

XV | Rosethorn

He refocused on Blotto just as the smile faded from the man's lips and his mouth drew tightly closed, as if he were desperately trying to stifle a belch. His eyes shown suddenly wide and intense, yet their expression had not changed so much as become frozen in stasis. His shapeless body jerked once, his flesh seemed to roll as does water in a boat's wake, and then his fat lips were parted by what first seemed his tongue, but was revealed to be a budding red rose, which emerged into the fire-light and blossomed its petals, spilling blood onto the gangplank and filling the air with scent. Glancing to the hand with which the man gripped Rosethorn, Dravidian saw that she'd sprouted thorn-studded rose stems, which had penetrated Blotto's beefy wrist and chewed their way through his body.

His heel lifted off the wood and his ankle seemed to lock with paralysis, and then his body listed to the right and he began to fall. The rose imploded as if growing in reverse, retracting into his mouth which fell shut with the clacking of teeth, and an instant later Rosethorn fell to the plank and Dravidian stooped to snatch her up. Blotto's body fell into the void.

"Drive him off! Drive him—"

The chanting and banging stopped.

He stood erect slowly, purposefully, rolling his eyes to face the men on the platform, who squirmed and flopped over one another like frenzied maggots in their haste to get away. He watched them go, then turned and regarded the crowd with cool resolve.

The wind blew. All else was silence save for the moist sound of Rosethorn as she shifted and writhed in his grasp. She had changed color from oil slick to red-black, and was presenting the onlookers with a show of force, roiling like water as she changed her configuration, sprouting rows of jagged thorns which melted and gave way to hooked spurs, which in turn became cactus needles and sucker-knots and poisonous-looking buds, then became smooth again like breathing red steel. And he remembered Jamais' words: *The sword, Rosethorn, is of particular consequence, as you will see.*

Gasps and accusations of deviltry sprang forth from the mob. He smiled broadly at the whole sorry lot of them and shouted in the silence, "What? No applause? And after I've provided you with so much entertainment?"

Silence.

Then, from somewhere in the crowd: "Murderer!"

And from somewhere else: "We were right to persecute you!"

"Ah, yes!" he shouted. "The witch floats!"

"Death! Death!" chanted someone near the front, and began pounding his weapon on the railing.

But there was something else afoot now which kept the others from joining in, a rustling and a murmuring through the heart of the crowd, and the chanter petered out fairly quickly, feeling a bit silly, Dravidian imagined.

"If you like!" he nevertheless answered him, so that he might not feel alone in the world. "Death must claim his souls, after all, and you didn't expect the sword and I to perform for free, did you?" Then he laughed. "Not with such a surplus of pure souls at hand, surely!"

Now the commotion had moved to the very edge of the ship, where the last row of onlookers stood pressed against the bulwark, and he watched in confusion as these people drew aside like rustling stage curtains to reveal a tallish figure standing alone.

Then, in clear mockery of that strange force which bound everyone to Ursathrax's bosom, the figure leapt—shooting into the air as if sprung from a trampoline. The crowd gasped as the jumper twirled up and over the platform, exhaled as his bare feet slapped against the crude wood of the gangplank—where, inexplicably, he dropped a flower, which hit the edge of the board and rolled off, to follow the corpse of the man they'd called Blotto into the cold dark of the River Dire.

When Dravidian looked to the man who had landed in front of him he saw that he was not, in fact, a man ... but an adolescent. Moreover, although he was bare-chested and barefoot, he wore the dung-colored trousers of a brownie. A brownie who, even now, was bowing to the mob with the flourish of a seasoned performer.

And it was in precisely that instant that Dravidian realized he had seen this youth before—regardless if he had been masked, he knew it nonetheless—in the corridor outside Shekalane's cell.

XVI | Sihadi

"Hear me, thy people of Valdus' Revolution!" the juvenile announced at length, his voice as dramatic and flamboyant as his entrance and his posture, then raised a fist to express his solidarity. "I am Sihadi ... and like you, I have dreamed of this day for a very long time. Know that I, too, have served Valdus—but have done so until now only behind the enemy's lines—and yet I ask of you a simple favor: commend to me this one ferryman to do with as I please. Do this, my comrades, and I promise you: I will not only render his deviltry inert ... but I will entertain you in the process!"

The crowd murmured nervously as he withdrew a massive key ring from the hem of his trousers and held it aloft. "Look, see, as a former servant aboard this vessel, I hold the keys to the prefect's private reserve right here, in my very hand. Even now, our leader—having shored up what is now *our* ship and dispatched of the remaining ferrymen—comes to join us, for a toast! So verily I say unto thee, let us mark our victory here not just with the enemy's liquor ... but with the blood sacrifice of one of His chief myrmidons!"

And such was the totality of the young man's enthusiasm and delivery that, incredibly, and almost immediately, the mob began chanting: "Sihadi! Sihadi! Sihadi!"

The teen—who could have seen the seasons begin anew only nineteen times at best—for his part, seemed entirely expectant of all the praise and smiled only a little. Mostly he had become intent upon staring Dravidian down in some juvenile test of wills, and it was during this exchange that the ferryman noticed the youth had no weapon, but held only a slim flask in his left hand and an unlit torch in his right, which he now ignited. He also noticed that the boy had been wounded recently, for one of his arms was swathed in a worn, blue rag and lashed crisscrossed with a length of fraying leather.

He began to creep toward Dravidian, stifling further observation, and the ferryman jerked his leg against its chain—which caused the great steel ball to rock this way and that on the surface of the plank but to move only a little.

"Please," Dravidian pleaded, gripping Rosethorn tightly. "I do not wish to kill you ..."

Sihadi only grinned, his eyes wild, even as he drew still closer, weaving like a cobra.

Dravidian's belly burned with that terrible flame which always proceeded an act of violence; that flame that was fear and anxiety and aggression all at once. He would kill the youth in three breaths. But just as he feared he must strike or perish, Shekalane cried out from crowd: *"Sihadi!"* —and the boy stopped ... even as Dravidian scanned the throngs to find Shekalane breaking free of her captors and stumbling toward them in what appeared to be stark desperation.

No. Not desperation. *Revelation.* Nor was she alone, for standing there studying the youth's face, Dravidian realized it, too. Indeed, the chanting of the mob seemed to dwindle away to nothing in his consciousness as he truly examined his opponent's physical characteristics, and he felt awed—not by the fact that the boy seemed like a veritable statue sprung to life, or that his tanned, sweaty skin was like polished bronze beneath the golden-red light of the burning and dying orb, or that his handsome face and robust physique reminded him of the marble athletes found in the Grecian gardens of the capitol, or even that he was poised in a similar manner to those perfect men with their shotputs and discuses—but that his greenish brown eyes and the subtle folds around them and even the set of his mouth were identical in every way to Shekalane's.

XVII | Convergence

And yet there was more. For, as the wind blew hot and sweltering, buffeting their hair and billowing their clothes, and swishing between them like a whistling wall, Dravidian looked at the blue scarf secured about Sihadi's upper arm and realized that the fire-eater and Shekalane's lost husband were, had been, one in the same ... and that he, personally— Dravidian of the ferrymen—had been the very man who'd torn their family apart.

"I see you remember," said Sihadi.

And then, slowly and deliberately, he unstopped the flask, after which—and had Dravidian but blinked he would have missed the action entirely—quaffed a quick draft from the vessel before discarding it over the side. Then he lifted the torch to his lips, breathed deep, and blew—and the fire leapt from his mouth ... causing Dravidian to block it with Rosethorn without even thinking.

She went up in flames as though made of dry grass, shrieking, and when her hilt singed his hand he cursed and let go.

The weapon fell smoldering to clatter at his feet, and he watched in utter horror as the swirling smoke began to clear, revealing at last but a black and brittle husk.

From the very base of the platform there was an anguished cry: *"Dravidian!"*—and he looked down into the mob pressed all about them to see Shekalane wedged tight between two burly conscripts. He had not the time to even speak before one of the crude raiders closed a bloody hand about her mouth, and the other snaked an arm around her waist, and she was dragged from view to be swallowed by the crowd.

When he turned to face Sihadi again, he saw that he, too, had been regarding her, and even now his face bore a queer expression—had he recognized her? No, no—her hair had fallen mostly over her face. He'd felt something, perhaps, but not that. Still, he was vulnerable; and Dravidian steeled himself. An instant more and he would have attempted to grapple with him—though the ball and chain would have thwarted him, surely—but the boy whipped his head around and looked at him with such mortal disdain that Dravidian half expected him to spit in his face.

"By the Lucitor," he marveled, unbelievingly. "A *woman?*"

He brought a bare foot whistling up hard into Dravidian's groin, knocking the breath from him all over again, causing him to fold like a collapsible dagger and to crumple to the gangplank. "You, who has murdered many? Some, surely, even with their unborn children? You, who has widowed and orphaned still more? *You,* ferryman?" The youth's tone was full of hurt and his voice quavered, betraying a deeper rage.

Dravidian struggled for breath in the fall of his shadow. "I ... have often shared ... your pain ... and ... your anger."

The boy wrapped his hair up in his fist and drew him closer. "And you shall share more—*Dravidian*—you shall share more." He pointed to the faded blue scarf secured about his arm. "You murdered a great man that day ... and I think you know it. For he would have addressed you ... he would have demanded that you acknowledge his humanity. Nor would he have resisted—for never would he have brought such a dishonor upon his family. Why then did you do it? Why then did you kill him, Dravidian of the ferrymen?" He shook him once violently and Dravidian felt locks of strained hair pull loose from his scalp, like roots from wet earth. "Speak!"

"He ... suffered a heart attack ... I—I was trying to save him ..."

Sihadi grinned as though insane. "Trying to save him ... since when has a taker ever saved anyone?" His tone changed abruptly: "Ah, is that it, then? You are a hero? You, who has served with such distinction in the Lucitor's Army of the Dead!"

Dravidian stared at him through half-open eyelids. "I ... didn't choose ... to be a ferryman. You ... of all people ..."

"And they didn't choose to *sacrifice* themselves to the Lottery—not my father, certainly, nor my mother, who, I am given to understand, died shortly after my own selection. Enough. I leave you to Valdus or the conscripts— whomever gets to you first."

He dropped him to the ash-strewn gangplank and strode back to the platform, and Dravidian was able to lift his head just long enough to say, "The woman ... who called out our names ... She ... is your mother come again."

Sihadi had hardly had time to turn to back around when the entire deck erupted into chaos—for wide swaths of conscripts had begun falling all about—and when Dravidian at last focused he saw the blades of tens of scythes cresting the crowd like threshes of pure light, and knew the ferrymen had begun their counterattack. What's more, there was a clamor of activity near the stairwell—which, on closer inspection, revealed itself to be centered on Valdus (who was clad all in green and thus easy to see). And yet he and the men around him seemed not so much preparing to fight but rather shoving their way through the throng in idol desperation—terror, actually—almost as if—

There was a tremendous explosion which blasted Dravidian into the air only to, miraculously, deposit him right back onto the gangplank—which dropped away suddenly as he pawed at its splintered surface (even while groping for his dead sword, which called to him, somehow, as though reaching into his mind).

And then he was falling through the sweltering void—faster and faster and faster yet—still reaching for Rosethorn, who was but a black shape in the distant sky.

XVIII | Into the Depths

He quickly worked his mask around and sealed it to his face —its emergency oxygen reserves would buy him a little time, at least— before the steel ball broke the surface with a great, smacking noise ... and he was instantly engulfed in icy froth. He bent in the vacuum without delay, reaching blindly for the heel of his boot, and when he'd run across it he cupped its smooth rubber in the palm of his hand and pushed at it desperately.

But neither the boot nor its collar of steel would budge. (He had hoped in some obscure way that he might work the trappings free now that they were submerged in water—now he realized that such a hope had been obscure, indeed.)

He sank. And as he sank the foam surged past his shoulders ... like a white cloak of bubbles to replace the black one he'd lost to the mob. He could see but dimly as the pockets of air twirled up past his face and burst, until a great darkness reared up like a giant hand and closed its black fingers irrevocably about him.

He fell through the void but a moment longer before hearing a muffled impact and feeling his boots touch down on something flat—a plateau of some kind, for the River Dire would run much deeper. Still, it was deep enough for him, for his ears popped and protested and his skull seemed about to explode from the pressure.

He yanked his leg against the steel chain but to no avail. Through throbbing ears he heard it rattle in the deep—a thick, crunching sound like shoes in the snow. Vigorously he attacked the shackled boot again, but out of blind panic or grim determination he could not have said. And though he pushed and yanked and tore at it wildly, it became clear to him in the shortness of his breath that he merely prolonged the inevitable.

And so he tilted his head with the hair swirling about him and looked to the glimmering surface, resolving to die with his face toward the light, however distant that fiery, flickering light seemed to be, and wasn't sure if he was grateful for or resentful of the mask's special lenses, for it seemed as though he stared through a sheet of purest glass.

He could see, and what he saw was the ceiling of his coffin. There was no peace, no beauty, no stream of recollection. It was a drab and awful moment he could not have imagined in the worst of his nightmares.

And then he beheld two things, and in beholding them, felt a sense of hopefulness steal over him he could not explain.

The first was recognition of the organic sword Rosethorn (for her water-rejuvenated, oil slick-colored, nearly black surface had rendered her all but invisible before) ... still high above him but lowering steadily, all the while twirling horizontally and gleaming as though made of night and stars. The second was a glimmer of pearlesque light—which danced at the very edge of his vision as if someone had kindled a torch in the depths—so that he dropped his chin to find the water before him aglow with blue-green fire.

We have something to tell you, Dravidian, came a voice, not through the water but directly into his mind. *Mark it well.*

And there, amidst a vortex of water spores which swirled like glitter, hovered an emerald-skinned ignudi—the likes of which he'd never before seen—who sat upon a throne of her own blue-black hair, some of which but danced in space and some of which strayed wiggling over her body, kissing her thighs and swirling around nipples, like the warm breath of skillful lovers. She bore gills at her neck which moved and pulsed, and the delicate fans which grew from her back—now strobing gracefully to balance her in the water—were not wings such as Milkweed's but *fins.* Yet the strangest thing about her was how she created her own light amidst the darkness of the void, for she glowed from head to toe with an ethereal incandescence—which he'd hardly had time to appreciate before she suddenly flitted away, casting off gentle sparks in her wake.

What happened next happened very fast. She swam quickly to where a black shape floated, and when the light of her body bled glowing over its surface, he was able to see familiar armor plating bobbing in the current. It was Blotto's pale, bloated corpse, turning in the darkness like a murderer hung from the neck.

She spiraled down around his body and fluttered to a halt by his feet, where she turned her slanted eyes to face him in the murk and blinked once—before something reared up from the blackness to coil about the dead man's ankle ... and she skewed to the side but stopped short of fleeing, and he saw by her light that a gaggle of oil slick-colored tentacles had begun slithering around the corpse's legs—racing up his body until the longest of them had locked about his throat and constricted, causing the yellowed sausage of his tongue to loll out the side of his mouth.

Again came the voice: *Look, see, the roots of the War Tree have come for their prize—hungry as always to claim the fruit of Rosethorn's wrath, and to reclaim if they can the sword herself.*

The glowing ignudi darted toward him suddenly and hovered before his face, her soft luminescence flaring brighter than ever, and the gloom all around him was briefly lit as though by the sun of Thesea itself. *Know that every time the sword is used the War Tree—upon which it was born and where it once hung like fruit with its brothers—awakens. Know, too, that in addition to claiming the bodies of those killed by the blade, the Tree will seek for you, its wielder—for its roots, which are not really roots, penetrate all of Ursathrax. Finally, you must know—and this is the chief thing we have to say—that, although in using the sword you fulfill your destiny as the One Who Ferries All, you also destabilize the world. Mark this part well: By matrimony with the sword you both acquire the power to save Ursathrax's people AND accelerate the process of her destruction.*

There was a tugging at his shackled boot and he looked down to find a tentacle wrapped about his ankle.

Now, quickly, Dravidian! Strike and fear not. And in saving thyself, save the world.

And then she was gone from his immediate presence, having darted to one side to hover in the darkness; and he lifted his hand—into which Rosethorn settled like a velveteen glove—and proceeded to smote the strange appendage and the chain about his ankle combined ... so that they fell away even as the squeeze on his lungs became too much, and he shoved off for the surface, glancing to Blotto one last time while noting that the roots had almost entirely entombed him, crushing him, it seemed, so that when his head folded back like an octopi sack Dravidian saw that only his face remained exposed.

Slowly the body was drug into the deep, its countenance shrinking, its eyes bulged as if the balls themselves had become filled with water, or perhaps only the fear of the dead; whatever filled them, it had left no more room for ambition—of any kind. And then the light of the ignudi spun away in consecutively smaller circles until it, too, had vanished completely—and all was dark again.

XIX | Betrothed to the Blade

He turned and kicked for the water's ceiling, unable to endure the void any longer, as the cold foam surged like molasses around his limbs—making every exertion seem double what it should be and his lungs feel as though they would implode amidst the vacuum (for the mask's reserves of air were well depleted). A storm of sparkling dots began to swirl before his eyes, and—just as it seemed he would lose all consciousness—he burst into the red-orange world of men yet again: where he released his mask and swallowed the sky in great, greedy gulps—even as the water shot skyward to rain down around him and the dying orb burned hot and cloying on his face and the chilly droplets pattered his dead-blue skin.

When he'd quenched his need for air at last, he turned to face the burning, sinking dragger—and found that it was no longer above him but perhaps half a mile away. The people along its deck were but tiny, black dots, visible to him only because of their numbers and activity (for they were fighting, clearly); meanwhile, alone amidst the rushing waters, he was surely invisible to them.

Shekalane, he reminded himself. *She is still in danger ...*

Only then did he think to examine the blade, and saw that the swirling currents of the River Dire had indeed restored her fully so that she shown with a life that was bountiful and intense; further, she had morphed her composition so that she could now float rather than sink. And yet he himself was exhausted and shaken, so much so that he had to hook his arms over the length of her body and lay his head down against the flat of her blade briefly, feeling as though he could sleep for all time.

Moments later there came a sound like muddy earth squelching under foot, and he half-opened his eyes to find that, should he fall asleep, he would not have to worry about letting go of his buoy. Indeed, the River Dire could no longer harm him. For Rosethorn had sprouted two oil slick-black vines, which bound his arms gently to her sweet-scented blade.

XXI | Synergique Amore

My son lives, thought Shekalane, numbly, as she struggled toward him through the battling crowd—the blood of her would-be rapists still drying upon her clothes. *And yet he is about to die.*

How could it be otherwise when the raiders piled upon him one after another—for he had turned against them immediately after the second explosion—and now sought his every artery with their pikes and swords and knives? No, she would never reach him in time—even if she did, what good would her little blade possibly be against such a seething throng?

For the world had gone mad, and seemed to move like molasses in her state of shock and confusion. The ship was sinking, that much was clear—nor did anyone, save the slaves, seem to care; for they were all of them, both the revolutionaries and the ferrymen, intent only upon killing the other. Where was Dravidian? Where was Valdus?

Where was herself? For, indeed, it was she herself who had gone missing—become paralyzed—even as one of the raiders lifted his hatchet to smite her son's head ... and was smote himself by a masked, sopping-wet Dravidian, who cleaved the man's arm in two with the strange, rainbow-black sword—only to follow up with a deadly cross-stroke, which struck the soldier's head clean from his body.

What followed was a blur of carnage as Dravidian cut down her son's attackers in a way she wouldn't have thought possible—almost as if the sword itself guided his actions—until the immediate threat had been vanquished and he was scooping up a scythe (presumably his own) from the deck and extending a hand to Sihadi ... who lay wounded upon his back, looking as confused as she felt— before taking the hand offered and being righted so that the two men she loved most in all the world stood together as newly-bonded allies. Nor was that the only thing that so touched her about the sight, for she saw that her son still wore about his arm the very same blue scarf which had been her late husband's trademark.

But then came a new rebel, and another, and another, who fell upon them with their blades flashing even as Sthulhu (for it had to be) joined the fray, pecking and scratching at their attackers furiously, after which Dravidian snapped: "My gondola, run for it!" —and the three of them, supporting each other, rushed through the crowd toward it.

But Dravidian did not climb into the boat with them, only looked over his shoulder as Valdus himself lifted a piece of burning wood and touched it to Sthulhu's wing—which immediately caught fire and sent the raven careening about the deck ... until he fell flopping and kicking on top of the dragger's gunwale, and at last fell overboard completely ... even as a burning section of scaffolding fell between them and Valdus' forces.

And it was at that moment that Shekalane's heart froze, for she could tell by the look in Dravidian's eyes that he had decided upon a course of action, one that would surely separate them again ... only this time, perhaps, forever. Thus she could only look on in horror as Dravidian removed the platinum key from around his neck and scooped up the map-scabbard from the boards and handed them to her hurriedly, saying, simply, "Boat: shields on."

"Wait, what are you doing?"

He picked up a great shield from the deck and slid his free arm into it. "Buying time."

"You can't be serious ..."

"I will take another boat and join you when I can. Hurry!"

"That's crazy—look, see, the scaffolding will stop—"

"The scaffolding is already burning out. You must—"

"But they'll—"

"Hold!" cried Valdus suddenly, and when she looked beyond Dravidian she saw that the battle between the rebels and the ferrymen had largely been won ... that most the remaining ferrymen were now prisoners of her former lover, who eyed her maliciously. And yet the fighting continued in small pockets everywhere.

"I said, 'hold,' damn you! I want that ferryman dead. Archers! Where are you?"

"Shekalane, *please,*" Dravidian urged.

She could only shake her head in disbelief. At length she looked at the gunwale, which was littered with smoldering black feathers, and then back at him. "Revenge, Dravidian?"

He appeared to consider this. "Honor," he said with finality. "For Sthulhu." Then he reached for the derrick's control panel and triggered the release mechanism. "I'll hold them off while the boat descends. Now go!"

But something came over her then, something she could not have explained were she given a thousand hours to do so, and the anger welled up in her so quickly that she very nearly struck him across the face. "Don't be a fool like Valdus. There's too many of them. They will cut you down and still climb through the shield before the boat ever touches the water."

He moved to turn away and she stopped him by the shoulder. "We must do this together, Dravidian. As we have from the beginning. The cables need to be cut simultaneously, or we'll never get away, and Sihadi is too weak." She placed a hand on the side of his facade. *"Synergique Amore,* do you remember?"

Dravidian stared at her, the wind blowing the hair across his mask.

"The archers are assembled, my lord," she heard someone say who was out of breath—to which Valdus responded, simply: *"Then kill him."*

At which point Dravidian stepped into the gondola, and, looking at Shekalane as the arrows bounced and clinked off the shields, whispered *"Synergique Amore ..."*—as he unhooked the scythe from his belt and handed it across to her.

XXII | The Revolutionary

She took it and triggered the blade, then quickly moved to the opposite end of the boat where she held it against the rope ... even as Valdus shouted, "That's it, men, hurry!" —and Dravidian looked sideways to see a group of men with a plank rushing toward the burning (and rapidly collapsing) scaffolding.

Therefore, it was with more than a little urgency that he placed Rosethorn's blade against the rope nearest himself, and, in a surprise to all, addressed Valdus directly: "Valdus, listen to me. All of you, listen to me. Rebels, conscripts, brownies, slaves. Ferrymen. We are on the same side, in the end." He glanced at Sihadi, who acknowledged his look with a nod. "For none of us have escaped the heel of the Lucitor's oppression. We can work together to destroy Him and to save Ursathrax ... or we can continue to destroy each other. You have a choice, Valdus. *We all do."* This last was addressed to Pepperlung, whom he had spied among the prisoners. "Search your hearts, and consider an end to the killing. Perhaps a new revolution can begin today: a revolution rooted in unity, and compassion. Perhaps it can begin with you. Working together." He looked at Shekalane who met his gaze, readying her blade. "Now get to the boats while there is still time ... and consider it, a New Revolution!"

And then he nodded to his *Synergique Amore* ... who drew her blade across her rope at precisely the moment he severed his—sending the gondola plummeting toward the water.

XXIII | Different Paths

"Sihadi!" cried Shekalane—as the boat hit the water and very nearly capsized, rocking so violently that the youth was

catapulted clear to bounce off the side of the dragger, which he reached for from the roiling froth; and, finding purchase on the ragged edge of the hole left from the blast, pulled himself to safety.

"Sihadi, my hand!" shouted Dravidian—too late, for the current was already drawing them away, and at a rapid clip.

"Swim, Sihadi, quickly!" screeched Shekalane ... but the boy only shook his head, realizing, as did Dravidian, it seemed, that the distance between them was already too great; more so, there was a look upon his face now that Shekalane immediately recognized—for it belonged wholly to his father—and it said, simply, and without compromise: *I love you ... but I am compelled along a different path. Forgive me.*

And then he shouted: "I will lead them ... unify them! I am the perfect man to do it." He stood suddenly and steadied himself. "Who better than someone who has walked on both sides? For I am strong, like my father, and the wound is not so bad. Worry not, dear mother. We shall see each other again—and we shall do so in a free Ursathrax!"

"No, no!" cried Shekalane—who immediately moved to jump overboard but was quickly stopped by Dravidian, who held her fast as the dragger began shrinking away, and who told her: "The current is too strong—you'll never make it! Plus there are boar eels in these waters, if they haven't been attracted by the blood yet they soon will be. *Let him lead them, Shekalane ... while we forge ahead and find the control room. It is the only way.*"

"The what? *The what?*"

"The *Imperium Locus*, remember? Jamais said that it could be found at the end of Ursathrax. He said it was the only way, Shekalane."

And, curiously, this spoke to her in a way she could not have defined, so that she immediately shouted out to her son: "The keys around the necks of the ferrymen will open the arches to the Forbidden Channels ... find one as quickly as you can and guard it with your life. Also, salvage a mask if you are able—its com-link may allow you communication with us so long as its power and that of Dravidian's holds out." She glanced at Dravidian, who nodded affirmatively. "Godspeed, son! And guard thyself!"

He waved at her and then leapt to the top of the hole, which he gripped long enough to pull himself above it and begin climbing toward the gondola derricks, which had sunk to within twenty feet of the water, and Dravidian told her, "He will secure a key and a mask and escape in a boat, I promise. He is a brownie, Shekalane, and one not far removed from the promotion to ferryman ... he will make it."

And so it was, for after several moments she saw him reemerge on the deck of the dragger wearing a ferryman's mask and bearing a gold key around his neck, before she was distracted by the sight of Valdus himself, standing alone at the gunwale and holding the prefect's severed head, which even from this distance she could see dangled sparking wires, and thus she knew what he knew—that that against which he had sought such bitter revenge had, in the end, been nothing more than an illusion ... a robot. A lie.

Nor was that the last she saw, for before they rounded the bend of the world and the dragger had disappeared from view, she saw that enormous, black tentacles had risen from the depths and begun pulling the ship into the River—leaving only wreckage and a scattering of boats upon the suddenly stilled water, one of which contained a lone figure which stood as if in defiance and waved at them ... with what appeared to be a blue scarf.

XXIV | The Boar Eels

Within moments of mounting his dais and gaining control of the gondola, as well as switching on the audio receiver of his mask (which had been off since they'd entered the Forbidden Channels), Dravidian informed her that Sihadi had, indeed, made contact, and that while he was preoccupied with coordinating an escape for the battle's survivors—for the Lucitor would be sending reinforcements even now—he would contact them again at first opportunity. Then, as a cloud of ignudi descended upon them seemingly out of nowhere, and Milkweed herself landed cooing upon Shekalane's shoulder, he hastened to tell her one more thing: that the power supply of his mask was orb-based; which was to say, it received and stored energy from the radiance of the sun orbs, and therefore they might—in theory, at least—remain in contact with her son indefinitely.

"By Thesea, I ... I just can't ... I don't believe it," she muttered.

And such was her joy at how this and everything else had so unexpectedly turned out that she ran to Dravidian and embraced him, yet did so in such a forcible manner that she knocked him completely off balance, after which, with what seemed a tumultuous splash, they hit the dark water together.

His mask came away as the cold foam surged around them and he groped for it with little success. He could hear the breathlessness of her laughter even before breaking surface, and he wanted to call out to her desperately, to warn her, but by the time he was able to purge his mouth of froth she was upon him, taking his head in both her hands and closing her lips about his own with ravenous delight. He offered little resistance before succumbing to the moment and pulling her against himself with blind and total abandon. The ignudi hummed and purred nervously above them, stirred into a fluttering frenzy by their crash against the water, and so deliriously impassioned was he that he forgot entirely about the inevitable rush of the boar eels until he saw the spiny scythes of their dorsal fins bearing down upon them.

He had but the space of a breath to push Shekalane clear and lash out at the beasts with his wet and shining scythe (for he did not intend to use Rosethorn, who hung at his back in Jamais' map-sheath, again anytime soon). The first of them wailed as the weapon's great blade sliced into its flesh, rending it crosswise and spewing blood and entrails forth in a rolling crimson cloud, and Shekalane began to scream. He swung at the beasts wildly as she paddled for the boat with desperate, pounding strokes, even as pain singed his thigh and he realized with wide-eyed horror that one of the monsters was nuzzling its tusked snout into the meat of his leg. He cried out as he felt its leathern tongue begin to lap up his blood.

He struck and struck and struck again but the beast would not relent its hold. Finally, having clambered into the boat, Shekalane grabbed at him at last, but their flailing hands could only miss each other in their panic. He realized death was certain when he noticed still more beasts approaching from the south.

So it was over, then.

And that's when Sthulhu seemingly appeared out of nowhere (his feathers all burned off so that his artificial nature of robotics and black steel was revealed), and, hovering, guided Shekalane's hand into his own. After which, Dravidian pumped and kicked his legs frenziedly until at last he and Shekalane lie in the boat together, their chests heaving and their hearts racing, staring up at the *orbis lunae* (for they had moved into a new curve of the world, with a new orb, and had left the burning one behind).

He looked at her sidelong and found her eyes gazing back at him. They stayed that way for a span of three breaths or more, and, finally, she held up a trembling, languid hand— from which dangled, dripping, his ferryman's mask.

He cupped her cheek and leaned toward her—pecked her lips with his own. Then, after drawing back, he turned toward Sthulhu, and said, "Thank you, my friend. I feared you were lost."

"Sthulhu ... lost. Now ... reunited with master ... found. *Caw!*"

"Dravidian," whispered Shekalane, her voice full of wonder. "Look ..."

And, looking, he saw that the ignudi had not fled, nor had Milkweed so much as stirred from Shekalane's side. And noticing their amazement, Sthulhu elaborated, "Milkweed ... rescue. Sthulhu ... owe debt. Sthulhu ... not hurt."

Something about this touched Dravidian more than he would ever admit, for it seemed that, for the first time since he was a boy, he had a kind of family. And giddy with the sentiment, he leaned toward Shekalane once again.

Her eyes bloated and she screamed, and it wasn't until he felt the boar eel's hot, wretched breath against the side of his face that he realized the creatures were slithering free of the dark, roiling waters and mounting the wildly rocking boat.

He slashed at the closest one and its face fell in halves. But the others only flopped and wormed determinedly over its fresh and steaming corpse. He swung again, but one of them caught the scythe's tang just below the curved blade, and, yanking its head, snapped the fragile piece in two, removing the weapon's killing end and sending an electrical shock running up its grip.

He discarded the handle and was able to scramble to his feet before they fell upon him, and he stumbled backward as they approached with his hands out-stretched, knowing full well he could not possibly last long against their tusks and fangs without the reach of the scythe.

"Dravidian!" Shekalane shouted.

He whirled around to face her, assuming it would be the last time he would ever look upon her face. But she threw something to him; and when his hands grasped its shape he knew they would survive.

For he held in his hands the truest of a ferryman's tools. That which was nothing of what it could be if not wielded by a true ferryman.

He held in his hands the Ferryman's Oar: an oar unlike any other, for the edges of its paddle were sharpened like killing steel, and the hollow of its shaft ran with that most perfect balancing agent—Mobius Mercury.

Thus he spun on the encroaching beasts with a near maniacal sort of energy, and as Shekalane took cover behind him, he swung the great oar to and fro with wide, whistling strokes—smashing the beasts aside as they advanced and knocking them squealing and bleeding into the water. He was more than what he might have been had he fought the beasts alone, for the thought of protecting Shekalane inspired him to greater strength.

Singing elatedly, the white ignudi and her sisters swooped and soared in circles above them, as if celebrating the victory. And, by the time the last monster splashed headless into The River, causing great plumes of froth and spray to geyser high and slap back down—the elfemales were as soaked as Dravidian and Shekalane.

And then all was silence save for bubbling water and distant loon song, and the creaking of the boat beneath their feet. Yet he remained ready with the oar for several moments, staring at the swirling water and the clouds of blood within. When he was certain at last the eels had been vanquished, he turned to check on Shekalane.

Neither of them could see very well through the drenched locks of their hair. But he could see she was holding his mask in her hand, and looking at him oddly. It appeared she was either going to cry or get ill. She dropped the mask suddenly and ran to him, and as his oar hit the deck they clashed.

Surely neither of them had ever clung to another so desperately. They were sopping wet and freezing, and their hearts pounded between their pressed bodies like thunder—but they were alive, and they were free, and their racing blood and gooseflesh were but glorious testaments to that.

And at last the turmoil in their veins gave way to an exquisite calm like sleep, and they were able to speak again, though little needed to be said.

"Shekalane..." he rasped into her ear as though a vampire. *"Run with me."*

"To the end of Ursathrax," she said, and closed her lips about his own.

XXV | Wrapped Around Him

She recalled the treasure cove and the vision she'd had of them lying naked in Dravidian's gondola—floating lazily downriver while lying on their sides, he behind her (and fully inside her), holding her in his arms, thrusting his hips slowly in and out, while she pressed her haunches against him—ground them into him—her face contorted in ecstasy.

And all she knew, as at last he reclined on the boat's plush bench and she fondled and stroked his sexual organs (even while admiring their sheer beauty and symmetry ... the firm, walnut-textured testicles, the long, broad shaft with its spider web of veins, the mushroom cap-like blue head), was that she wanted him inside her once and for all ... wanted to mount him like a stallion and ride him to the end of the world; and to keep him there even after he had poured himself into her—keep him there for as long as it took to rekindle his steel and do it all again.

And so she straddled his legs and climbed on top of him, placing a knee on either side of his hips, and, ignoring his efforts to tease her by rubbing the tip of his cock back and forth over her labia, placed her pink hand over his dead-blue one on his shaft and guided the tip into her folds, pushing until the curly flesh gently gave way, then withdrawing slightly, then pushing again, until, inch by inch, she had completely taken him in.

His first thrust was gentle but surprisingly painful, as though he'd somehow gotten bigger since their last encounter, and she gasped as he bumped against her cervix—enough that he immediately moved to withdraw but was held fast by the tightening of her muscles. And then she began grinding him, moving her hips back and forth— slowly, fluidly, like a belly dancer—her intensity increasing with each counter-thrust so that her clitoris meshed against his shaft in often delightful and unexpected ways. And so it was that she felt stirring in her body all the old familiar sensations, to the extent that she had to catch herself before she started bouncing up and down like an inexperienced girl (for she knew the damage a woman could do to a man were she to get reckless), and, feeling him alternately grip her hips and her waist and her buttocks as he bucked—sometimes savagely—had some sense of the urgency he was feeling, as well.

She bit her lower lip as they settled into a groove, finding the warmth of his friction and the fullness of his girth satisfying beyond measure, and had to fight from deliberately slowing her pace to prolong the pleasure—for he wouldn't be long, of that she was almost certain, and it occurred to her that they had never come together ... and that she wanted that, desperately, however gifted he had proven to be with his tongue and lips and—occasionally, albeit gently—his teeth.

But, by Thesea, the thunder of him in her loins! She never wanted it to end, wanted only to stay in this unreal state between reality and another dimension entirely for as long as she possibly could, and she ground him almost violently as though doing so might prevent him from coming, and that's when the first waves of her own release started shuddering through her small frame like a series of Ursaquakes—and she fell forward and braced herself with a trembling hand on his chest, only for him to rear up suddenly and take a breast into his mouth, then the other, which he kissed and sucked and swirled his tongue around and bit gently, before he pushed her knees out from under her and clasped her body to his own and rolled them over on the bench so that she was beneath him, at which point he slapped the palm of a hand against the back of one of her knees and began sliding his steel further and further out before each fluid and undulating new thrust, and she looked down at her wiry-haired mound to see his dead-blue cock plunging into it again and again and again, vanishing and reappearing, smiting her without mercy, causing her to grope at his buttocks furiously and to rake her green nails along his back and to growl, finally, "Fuck me, my demon-lover ... my sweet Dravidian ... my Shadow come to tame me. Make love to me. Come inside my house ... and haunt it forever more."

And then she was convulsing as though possessed, coming again and again, and he came too, so powerfully that it seemed his seed shot through her like a bolt of lightning, and she bit her lower lip so hard it drew blood, which she licked at, tasting salt, feeling somehow that they had closed a circuit—truly closed it, at last—unified a field, completed a circle, exploded out the back of an all-consuming singularity to create a new universe of which they, combined, were the Godhead. At which point she whispered, "Black hole ... white fountain." —and then fell asleep in his powerful arms.

XXVI | Epilogue

They drifted beneath the *orbis lunae* for a long while. Shekalane sat on the crimson bench—which was stained almost black with water and gore—and gently teased the albino ignudi perched atop her finger. He, on the other hand, leaned forward on a ragged knee at the boats stern, gazing into the dark water and contemplating what path to follow now that the wind which guided everyone's lives had changed its direction for him.

And Shekalane.

He looked at her now, and she looked back. Staring at her, he recalled something he'd said to her once, about how life was a selfish thing, and he ruminated over her response—that love was a selfish thing, as well. And it seemed to him that there was a hard kind of truth in those words. It was, he supposed, at least, something a man could believe in ... because it was so imperfect. And yet, what lay before them—chiefly, the navigation through all the worlds of Ursathrax until they came to the *Imperium*

Locus—that would require a different kind of love: a love for Ursathrax herself, or at least her people, the kind of love Jamais had had and tried to impart. A love that, in the final reckoning, Dravidian wasn't sure he possessed.

But then he remembered something else Shekalane had said, when they'd stood in the portal between worlds shortly after beholding Thesea: *Is it up to us to save them? Are we responsible now?* To which the answer, of course, was 'yes.' It had to be. How they would do it, how they would locate this control room at the end of Ursathrax, much less decipher its mysteries enough to open the *Cyclopean Porta*—the doors between worlds—much less find the way back to Thesea (only to convince the denizens of any number of realms that they must follow them to freedom or else die in Ursathrax's inevitable collapse), he did not know.

He recalled the water ignudi's words: *By matrimony with the sword you both acquire the power to save Ursathrax's people AND accelerate the process of her destruction.* And this enigmatic phrase: *The One Who Ferries All.* What did it mean? Again, he did not know. He only knew that he had not to face the labyrinth alone, for Shekalane and Sthulhu and Milkweed would be with him, and so long as that was the case he would always find the strength required of him—even should Valdus (if indeed he lived) pursue them to the ends of the earth.

Silently, he picked up his mask and swung its loosened strap over his head, allowing the demon-faced façade to dangle at his back. Then, taking up his oar, he began assisting them downstream ... toward the next archway and *Cuniculum Amoris* ... and beyond.

Somewhere above them, a raven called. And an instant later its shadow appeared overhead. Peering skyward, he followed the raven's progress across the blackened glitter-dome of the evening sky—fearful that the shadowy courier might even then be rushing back to the Lucitor with news of his treachery. It raced along against the backdrop of crowded stars, a stark silhouette, a shape in moonlight, and it passed into the black space which was the maw of one of the jagged rents in the sky ... and was swallowed up. The raven entered, but did not come out.

Yet he could still hear its calls somewhere above. More so, in fact, for they had become echoed and magnified, and soon seemed to fill the sky like a cackling chorus of mad gods.

He would later realize it had been as good as omen as any for what lie ahead.

The End

After Note

The astute reader may have noticed that some of the prefect's language in *Black Hole, White Fountain, VIII / Questions,* sounds familiar. This is because I have incorporated parts of *The Brothers Karamazov,* by Fyodor Dostoevsky, into his speech; the implication being that, despite the prefect's repetition of *Ego non mentior* (I am not a lie); he is in fact drawing his speech and indeed his whole identity from the text (as is befitting, perhaps, a robot). As for whether this is a justified use of another author's work (to suggest an artificial lifeform's imitation of the living) or a brazen act of theft on my part is for you to decide.

–WKS

Behind a Pale Mask

(A non-canonical Ferryman Story)

... being a tale from the self-exiled ferryman Dravidian's autobiography, *Diary of a Ferryman;* of those days when he did wander doomed Ursathrax alone with but the organic sword Rosethorn for companion—and a collection of maps bearing a secret knowledge as his guide.

Already the dying world about him had begun to show signs of a violent upheaval, quaking and changing almost as if in reply to Dravidian's own metamorphosis from ferryman to wanderer.

It would be an hour in which he inspired many enemies both above and below the earth, and in which he would gain his first real presentiments as to the role he would play in the shaping of Ursathrax's future.

He was to encounter one such enemy in the starry tangle of the Tinsel Forest—in the form of the actor, Fenris-Wolf, who would be but one of many more to attempt the slaying of the dark-cloaked renegade known in some quarters already as:

Dravidian—pale-skinned ferryman, yellow-eyed lover, Servant of Death turned traitor.

Prologue

I was beginning to learn, at some cost, the difference between being a ferryman and a wanderer. As a ferryman, I'd suffered but sore shoulders and alienation. As a wanderer and a vagabond, I was to suffer blistered feet and trembling cold and fear as I had never known, only inspired.

But in the days of walking which followed Shekalane's disappearance, I had yet to experience those things which would later wake me shivering in the night, turning to Rosethorn for comfort—as I have turned to her always, whether I knew it or not—since that day she was delivered to me on the deck of the

Vorpal Gladio. To the contrary, cavalier in the knowledge I'd nothing left to lose (including my own life), I had taken my leave of the place of Shekalane's betrayal, and forged ahead into the moon-drenched night, having nothing, really, but the shadow of a plan, and hoping, mostly, just to keep moving and to perhaps thwart my inevitable capture a while longer.

I'd carried with me all my possessions, those being but the accouterments as ferryman worn upon my person, the organic sword Rosethorn at my hip, and the maps of Ursathrax stored so ingeniously in Jamais's scabbard. My scythe, the platinum key, my gondola—even my familiar, Sthulhu—had all vanished with Shekalane.

Real fear would come later, when I had forged a future as well and had much to lose.

Still, the going had been perilous ...

Though I believed Shekalane had betrayed me, I'd been unable to write off the possibility of her capture. And if she *had* been taken, then following the immediate banks of the River Dire could have likely led to my own capture, as well.

But in Ursathrax, one seldom had a choice—as I have said in previous chapters. In most places, there was but The River itself, a pair of slim banks, and then the East and West Walls looming straight up on both sides. So, I'd had to travel from the place of betrayal to the Tinsel Forest along those very banks, beating a path through the bramble whenever possible to avoid being spied from The River. I had heard distant sounds on several occasions, and it is possible that these might have been the splashing of oars. I'd noticed no lanterns, but this brought me little comfort. My pursuers would no doubt have doused them as to render themselves invisible to me.

After a time, the West Wall had gradually curved away, and I'd moved inland away from The River to find myself skirting the fringe of the Tinsel Forest. I'd maintained a course which ran parallel to The River, however, as the less populated regions of the Far south were still my objective, and I could see no reason to venture deeper into the forest of lights.

But after stopping to rest and consider the maps as to what lay ahead (using the glittering trees for illumination), I'd elected to change directions. Away from The River Dire, and straight for the West Wall.

I'd learned from the scrolls that something known as a "Relief/ Maintenance Lodge," a term I'd never heard, lay just beyond the Tinsel Forest, where the West Wall began its rocky climb skyward. However, the map had not been entirely clear as to whether this lodge lay at the foot of the wall or stood near its summit.

The discovery had only reinforced my belief that I held in the scrolls a secret knowledge to which few in Ursathrax were privy, yet I did not equate it with survival or destiny yet. I knew only that this "Relief/Maintenance Lodge" would be a place of which few if any could be aware, and that it sounded like a place of rest and perhaps even fresh water, where I might replenish myself as well as Rosethorn—who's color would begin to fade all too soon—if in fact she survived the journey.

Again, as I have said in previous chapters, there were very few places along The River Dire where the land extended for any length before meeting the Barrier Walls. Jaskir, the city on whose shore I'd first betrayed my duty as ferryman, was one such place. The Tinsel Forest was another.

It is here, Dear Reader, that I begin the tale proper, recounted with as much honesty and clarity as a man such as I can ally. If it seems overly dramatic at times, I can only implore the reader to turn an eye toward their own past, to those times in which important events took place, and ask themselves if these events were dramatic to them. Life is drama, Dear Reader. And this bit of drama is but a bit of my own life.

1

I secured the chart and returned it to my boot. I'd discovered a dirt path about a dozen or so miles into the forest, which seemed to have been running FarNorth to FarSouth before I'd met with it, and which now curved abruptly to run roughly west, where the great and distant West Wall loomed like a hazy giant. I had not been able to locate the trail on the map at all, and so I could only assume it had found its origin after the map had been quilled.

Besides the Tinsel Forest and the main roads connecting its few scattered townships (which I had to avoid at all costs), the scroll had shown nothing more in this area save the enigmatic and isolated Relief Lodge itself. The path began nowhere and went nowhere, for all I knew. I had but the West Wall to aim for, however, hence I wasn't particularly concerned by the matter. I could simply turn off the trail if necessary.

I did know the trees were still dotted with lovely lights, just as the night sky above them was still dotted with stars (and blemished with few holes), and so I followed the much-trodden path through the dark wood and twine and thought only of beauty and music as the great trunks passed me by. Fortunately, as I am not the sort of man inclined to croon to myself while in leave of others, the symphonies raged only in my mind, and my passage through the forest was silent.

A false summer had set in upon Ursathrax, and the forest was neither bitterly cold nor particularly warm. My garments were such that I was comfortable in this environment, which was indifferent in temperature just as it was indifferent to my presence.

Concealed like a chameleon in the shadow of my cloak's broad hood and my other accouterments as ferryman, all black as the night save perhaps a glimmer of pale bone at my face and hands, I felt a sense of conformity I had never experienced. Here, at last, a man born unto the ferrymen and fitted with mask and brand could indeed become invisible if he wished. And Dear Reader, if you have followed me this far into the chapters of this account, then you must surely know that I wished it beyond all imagining.

Relishing the thought, I no longer merely walked through that forest of lights, I in fact *strolled*. And as I strolled, I conducted an opera the likes of which Ursathrax had never heard (not even at the ill-fated Aria of Alta Forte), and of course never would, for it was the crude product of my happy delusion alone. As I have admitted often, I possess few talents beyond the turn of an oar or the use of a scythe.

And then I heard the distant chimes of real music and stopped dead in my tracks.

It sifted through the starry elms like an invisible fog as I listened, and, peering FarNorth, I noticed quite suddenly the glow of strung lanterns farther up the path.

I wasn't alone.

The thought was an alarming one, for the news of my treachery had undoubtedly spread in the weeks since Shekalane and myself had first fled our dark obligations. I could now look to strangers with only a profound sense of distrust.

Death may bring peace, but its shadow can only bring fear. And I was a shadow in more ways than how I moved through the forest unseen. I was a shadow of what I had been before Shekalane, for whom I'd let desire cloud duty and ceased to be a ferryman. Now I was anathema to both man and ferryman. No longer Death, merely its shadow. A symbol of fear but not authority. And in the final reckoning, men destroy but two things; that which they fear, and that which they feel they can.

Yet as I drew closer to the music and bobbing lanterns, I came to realize that what awaited at roadside was in fact a miniature bazaar. Such was the distance that I could discern few details. I saw only a garishly-painted coach with a tip-out canvas, and beneath the canvas a crude, wooden table which appeared cluttered and overburdened. Yet, oddly, there was no sign of a mule to pull the wagon.

I ducked into the shrubs and crept closer.

A moment later, peeking between two ferns (like the villain of a puppet show, I mused), I was able to observe a sole peddler sitting motionless behind the table, his head slung back in sleep and his regressed mouth hung agape. It was as if he'd nodded off while gazing at the glittering baubles suspended overhead.

The man seemed very old, indeed. His frail, knotted arms dangled impotently at his sides, the skin besieged with deep wrinkles and liver spots. His fingertips just slightly touched the head of the monkey at his feet, which cranked its music box intently and seemed oblivious to all else. I noticed that one of the peddler's fingers, the second to the smallest, had been severed at its base. It seemed cauterized and tied, but from a distance I could not be certain.

Considering his age and the depth of his slumber, I could not help but wonder what his reaction might be if he were to awaken suddenly and see me watching him from the parted brush, a white-faced demon cloaked in shadows. Hastily, I scanned the remainder of the area, hoping to find food or at least some clothing of a less conspicuous nature, but found nothing more than useless trinkets and strings of costume jewelry, which littered the long table and dangled from the edges of the dowel-stiffened canvas above it like wind chimes.

Then, as I was about to abandon the search, I spied the bloated belly of a wineskin hanging suspended from the rear of the wagon.

As if in thirst, Rosethorn seemed to quiver at my side. In the semi-light of the lanterns, it was difficult to judge whether her color had begun to fade or not. When her degeneration did begin, she would whither rapidly.

"Aye, Rosethorn," I whispered softly. "It may be water. We must get closer."

I backed away from the hedge, taking care not to crush any twigs underfoot or disturb any stones. A slash of pearl blue moonlight revealed a shuffle of boot prints in the dark soft soil which were not my own. Apparently, I had not been the first to watch the peddler from the shadows.

Turning away, I pulled loose the bonds at my elbows and shirked off my gloves. Tying the bonds together, I hung them from the little hook at the bottom of the black girdle so that they dangled readily at my right hip, then decompressed my mask and swung the fearsome facade around to my back.

Reaching into my right boot, I drew up the gold circlet sheathed there. We of the ferrymen, from whom The Lucitor demanded a kind of hideous flamboyance (hence the injections to pale our skin and yellow our pupils), were allowed to cut our hair only once in a year, and such a circlet was often carried as a matter of survival. A storm on the River Dire could easily turn so much hair into a thousand tiny daggers. I placed the shining crescent on my head, then glanced about in search of a walking stick. I found a reasonably straight branch close at hand and snatched it up.

When I had aligned myself with the wagon, I would lower the circlet down over my eyes and stumble forward as if blinded. It was, of course, an absurd idea. But I did not wish to frighten the old man unnecessarily. And, surely, the flash of a ferryman's yellow pupils in the night would do just that. I threw back my hood before moving on, as to ensure the visibility of the makeshift visor once it was in place.

I was a fugitive to be certain, but not a scourge, as yet. If indeed it was water, I would take only what was needed to restore Rosethorn and wet my own throat. I would attempt to do so without waking the peddler, and if I failed in that I would ask. Knowing me as but a thirsty and disabled traveler and not a ferryman, I was certain he would oblige.

I crept back along the hedge to where I'd left the path, yanking the black ferryman's cloak around to face forward, concealing as best I could the exquisite, cruelly configured garments of seamless ebony which could only mean one thing to all who viewed them.

Then, stepping onto the path once again, I approached the peddler in the woods.

2

Dead.

This much seemed certain when, upon noticing my arrival, the little monkey in its red and gold hat and vest leapt hissing and screaming into the darkness of the coach—yet stirred the old man not at all.

But was he in fact dead? If he was, he was only recently so, surely. His color was still that of the living, unlike my own, and the air about the carriage was not rancid with decay but sweet with fragrance and perfume.

I stooped and drew up his hand. The veins were nebulous and clearly defined, exposed as they were by the aging of the skin. Testing the artery, I found no pulse. I examined the stub of his missing finger before allowing the twisted crook of hand to fall, and found that it had been crudely cauterized, but not tied.

The wagon rocked back and forth as it could not have done from the monkey's weight alone. There was someone else inside, then, and it seemed they were coming out. I lowered the circlet down onto the bridge of my nose, covering my eyes.

"Ah, yes, indeed. I see now why little Joyung was so frightened ..."

The voice had come from the wagon. Instinctively, I cocked my head back as to peer beneath the visor, and saw a man older than myself yet young nonetheless leaning against the rear of the coach, his head only inches from the wineskin, and his arms folded in front of him. There was an exquisite black cane wedged between his arms and his chest, just below the handle of which shown a single cut ruby which blinked in the dark like a cat's eye in shadow. He was a tall, well-dressed man sporting a neatly-trimmed black beard and a high-hat of the same color.

The thought was but a fleeting one, but it struck me as odd that the monkey had not followed him out of the wagon.

"Death has come to claim its own," the sharp-dressed man nearly whispered, and strode forward with a gleam in his eye, twirling the cane as he walked. "What'll it be, ferryman? A few trinkets for the children? Some finery for the lady, perhaps?"

I looked to him with sour surprise. Then, feigning insult, said, "Who would call me a Ferryman?" My hand had come to rest on Rosethorn's pommel.

The stranger emerged from half-light and shadow into the multi-hued glow of the lanterns.

"You may call me Fenris-Wolf." He smiled disarmingly, and his teeth gleamed white and perfect in the lamplight. "... for now. I am a man of the method, you see. An actor. And a better one than you, thank the Lucitor! *Gah* ... blind?" He grimaced. "Anyway, having been refreshed as to what truly bad acting is, I shall classify myself further by saying I am a *good* actor. A, ah, traveling thespian, if you will. Though it seems likely that when I travel next, I shall be forced to do so without my bread and butter." He made a gesture toward the wagon. "My mule, as I'm sure you've noticed, has, ah, taken leave of me. Ran off in the night. Got spooked by a loon, perhaps, who's to say ... damn fool animal. No matter. You and the cadaver are the only passersby I've had since setting up here. No doubt I can walk all the way to Jaskir and return mounted before there's any danger of thievery."

He shook his head, dismissing the issue. "I've no company, preferring instead the art of soliloquy and monologue. Joyung there is my only companion. We travel from town to town, up and down the banks of the River Dire, he making his music and I pacing the planks of whatever makeshift stage the sale of my baubles allows me to commission. When the performance is done, I send Joyung into the crowd with my hat, which, as you can see, has ample space for coins."

His dark eyes dropped to where my hand rested on Rosethorn's pommel. Only the flowery hilt was exposed, the rest of the weapon remained hidden within the folds of my cloak. His eyes flashed and then he shrugged as if in disinterest.

"Ah, but how rude it is to talk only of one's self when in the company of a stranger as fascinating as you, boatman. You must tell me what it is that brings you to our Tinsel Forest, and without even your scythe to defend yourself."

"You know me to be a ferryman," I said, pushing the circlet up and over my forehead. "How?"

"Why, by taking one look at you, that's how! You've no mask, that much is true, nor have you a scythe, as I've said ... you've the cloak, all right, but that can be purchased at even the lowliest of costume shops; I've one just like it in my wagon here, in fact. No, this is something in the face itself. It's an aura." He paused, appraising me coldly. "You've the heart of a ferryman."

After a moment I replied, "I knew a woman once who said the very opposite."

"A woman, eh? She must have feared you very much."

I glanced to the dead man and back. "I'm unfamiliar with the habit of posing corpses to safeguard one's merchandise," I said dryly.

"Ah, yes. Well, I fear this old fellow became a bit too enamored with those ignudi in amber you see there ..." The thespian alternately picked at and smoothed the feeble tufts of hair at the back of the old man's head. "I can't imagine how he made it this deep into the wood, nor where he might have been heading."

I raised an eyebrow; neither could I.

Lifting a boot, I kicked at the earth beneath me. The topsoil broke easily, giving way to moist, black dirt and insignificant stone.

"The soil's not too stony," I said. "Why don't you bury him?"

The thespian circled around to regard the old man admiringly.

"What? And lose so fine a scarecrow? Dear ferryman, I think not."

The man's manner repulsed me. Demons we may be, still, we ferrymen are taught from birth to respect death, not make folly of it. Perhaps that's the difference between those reared in its shadow and those reared away from it.

You do not live in the shadow of the Lottery ...

Shekalane's voice, alive in my head as if it were yesterday.

And my own voice, replete with the tenor of that quiet glade in Flax, saying, *We all live in the shadow of the Lottery, Shekalane. Even we Ferrymen. I feel its darkness now as I must ask you to accompany me to The River.*

In the end, of course, everyone lives in the shadow of death. Just as they live in the shadow of their past.

All of which has nothing to do with standing in the shadow of a fool, which was exactly what I had been doing. I elected to do so no longer.

Gesturing at the wineskin, I said, "Before moving on, I would petition your charitable nature with respect to that wineskin there. If it be filled with water, that is, and not wine."

The thespian's eyes darted to the skin and back. His dark pupils flashed as they had flashed upon Rosethorn's hilt. "Ah, but Sir Ferryman ... I am not a charitable man, by nature." He wetted his lips. "Surely you've *something* in trade."

As I might have expected, his greedy gaze shifted to Rosethorn again. I gripped her handle and swung my hip away. "She is not for sale," I said.

The thespian's breath seemed to hitch once and then he was silent, regarding me with disbelieving eyes. It occurred to me then that for a man such as Fenris-Wolf, a refusal to barter was, perhaps, the most devious crime of all.

Then his attention dropped yet further to the very ground beneath me, and looking there myself I saw that small dead leaves were spiraling down to autumnize the forest floor. But it was not Fall in Ursathrax, rather it was nearing the end of winter, and the leaves had fallen not from the starry trees above but from the darkened folds of my own cloak.

Rosethorn was dying.

3

Fenris took a threatening step forward, and the dimensions of his boot struck me as familiar. I waved him back.

"I'm warning you, thespian."

If he heard me at all, he ignored my words. The whites of his eyes quivered as he said, "What sort of deviltry is this ...?"

I moved away from him slowly, saying, "I'm taking my leave of you, peddler. You would be well-advised not to come any closer. Nor to follow me when I am gone."

He stepped forward. "Wait! Ferryman!" His voice was trembling and near desperate.

I continued to back away.

He hurried back to the wagon and I flung wide my cloak and drew Rosethorn, fearing he sought a weapon. Instead, he snatched down the wineskin and advanced toward me, holding it high, pleading, "I've water, ferryman ... see here? Water! W-water f-for your sword there, which certainly looks as though it could use a drink, doesn't it?"

I spared a glance toward the blade, held wide and vertical at my side, and could see by the lamplight that it was so. The vibrant green hue it had taken on that morning (for Rosethorn changed her colors just as women change their clothes) had faded to a deathly ashen gray and the rosebuds about her hilt had withered and fallen free.

But she was still alive and rigid enough to fight without shattering, and the thespian seemed to appreciate this. And though he continued to inch forward slowly, I was moving, as well, and he made no attempt to bridge the considerable gap between us.

I might have paused in my narrative here, Dear Reader, if indeed I had moved on down the path without incident as I had hoped. But such was not to be the case on this day of my journey, and seldom would it be in the future. For so preoccupied with keeping the peddler in sight was I—that I stumbled like a fool over an above-ground root and fell to my back on the forest floor.

I'd but the time to sit upright before the peddler fell upon me, his black cane a blur as it rushed toward my face. Grasping Rosethorn at hilt and tip I brought the blade up, blocking the blow. He struck twice more and twice more the flashing black cane with its bloody glint of ruby smashed against Rosethorn.

I claim no particular talent for combat, especially that outside the scythe, nor am I uniquely quick or agile; but I was able to roll clear of his attack, then, and managed somehow to gain my feet before he was able to press again. He spun on me, cane uplifted, and, feeling a rage both exquisite and sudden, I rushed at him swinging Rosethorn wildly. Gold dust flew from her blade like floating pollen as it swished through the air.

It was a crude approach but effective. The peddler's cane had only half the reach of Rosethorn, and he could but defend himself feebly as he staggered back over the grass, forced closer and closer to the wagon as I pressed the assault.

Then his back collided with the coach and I pinned him there at last, holding Rosethorn at hilt and tip with the flat of her blade pressed tight against his throat.

Our eyes met close and struggling for breath I said, "As I'm sure you've noticed, Sir Fenris-Wolf, I'm a Ferryman in some need of water. I am free of The Lucitor' s service and thus I am free to kill you, if I wish. You said you were not a charitable man. Look upon a desperate, provoked man then and give him what he asks, or he shall slake his sword's thirst with your blood."

As I have said, I was beginning to learn, at some cost, the difference between being a ferryman and a wanderer. The first cost of such transitions in almost always innocence.

"Drop the cane," I commanded, enunciating it by pressing the male edge of my blade tight against his jaw.

He did so without hesitation, and I heard the wand bend the grass at our feet. I kicked it away and released him, pivoting Rosethorn's tip around to prick at his chest. He glowered at me as I backed away—but made no move to attack.

I moved off and snatched up the wineskin. I knew he couldn't be trusted to stand by while I slaked Rosethorn's thirst, so I swung its band over my head and took my leave of him, watching him over my shoulder every few strides.

A moment later he called out to me. "Ferryman!"

I turned to regard him.

"... did it do her any good?"

I must have looked confused.

"That woman's appraisal of your heart," he added. "Did it save her from the Lottery?"

I could only stare at him blankly, then turned and took up the path again into the woods.

4

Only after putting a considerable distance between the peddler's wagon and myself did I pause to restore Rosethorn.

The path had dipped between two great faces of craggy rock and tumbled deadwood, and I climbed the slope of one of these faces in the hopes of gaining a vantage point—from which I intended to maintain a vigil while my parched and avid sword drank deeply of Fenris-Wolf's wineskin.

Parts of the incline were sloped while others were near vertical, and so the climbing was at times relatively easy and at others perilous. But my soft boots were well-suited for gripping the rock or balancing myself upon sticks of frail deadwood, and I groped for handholds as I ascended with hands that were naked and keen and unencumbered by the leather river gloves. Only once did they manage to misjudge the stability of a particular outcropping, and only once did I sway precariously with only the grip of one hand and my placed boots to hold me.

Reaching the top of the incline, I found a suitable perch amongst the jumble of boulders and sat down in the shadows. Breathing heavily, I reached into my cloak and took out the wineskin, pulled its cork. Cool water bubbled from the opening and coursed through my fingers. I laid Rosethorn across my lap and began emptying the wineskin's contents over her blade. The water splashed along the dead husk of wood-like material and the weapon shimmered in the moonlight as if it were lacquered. I lavished most all of the skin's capacity upon her, saving but a few swallows for myself, then replaced the stopper and returned the skin to the folds of my cloak. And then I leaned back against the cold stone and waited.

From my place at the top of the slope, I was able to see the entirety of the Tinsel Forest from directly below me to the ghostly gray glow of the East Wall beyond. Looking to its darkened foothills, I could discern on occasion the glimmer of light or the flash of green froth—the vignettes made tiny by the many miles between us—the River Dire.

It was a pleasant discovery and a lovely sight from my position above the forest's canopy. Yet it brought with it fresh memories. Recollections of days spent working the oar and saluting my brother ferrymen when perchance we passed. Days of alienation, yes, but from commoners and not my peers. They were the days when I had belonged to The Brotherhood of Death, rather than the solitaire of Life.

And sitting upon the rocks, awaiting both glimpses of the River's activity and the recovery of my sword, I realized I missed that world more than I had allowed myself to admit. And I found myself fantasizing that I had not saved Shekalane, and that even now I could look to The River and see myself standing in the bow of my boat, a hooded silhouette with my scythe at my hip and an oar in my gloved hands.

But Shekalane and myself fell embraced to the furs in the mirror of my memory, overwhelming the vision like clouds of swimming glitter in an overturned picture-globe, of the kind Fenris might sell. And I saw Shekalane as I had seen her in my vision, staring down at me as we made love with the green vales dancing behind her. I saw her in the place of betrayal—Braklyn—when she had looked to me with what seemed love in the instants before our separation, when I had ordered her to run for the boat while I did battle with The Antika.

I saw her as I had always seen her ... through loving eyes.

The images engendered still more speculation as to why she had betrayed me. Surely our chances would have been better if we had remained together, with she posing as my charge when necessary, and I, of course, as her ferryman. If she was spotted alone behind the oar of my boat, by a raven or indeed another ferryman, she would only be captured and put to torment all the sooner. And though I couldn't measure the likelihood of a raven having already informed The Lucitor of our flight, it seemed impossible that He could have dispatched other ferrymen in time to capture her at Braklyn.

Deliberating thus, I sat below the stars and stroked Rosethorn's length as I had once stroked Shekalane's hair.

5

I am not sure why I awakened so suddenly, perhaps it was in response to the cry of one of the loons Fenris had spoken of earlier.

Gazing out over the roof of the forest, who's star-speckled elms had seemed the reflection of the evening sky in an un-rippled pond before I'd slept, I saw that a fog had rolled in from The River beyond and cast the whole of the wood into a swirling gloom. The fine points of light which traced the thick trunks and cluttered the branches had swelled into nimbuses by their meeting with the fog, and it now seemed as if I sat at the center of the cosmos itself, in a time of great upheaval and with exploding stars all around.

The great, misty void was silent but for a single sound, and this not so much a sound but more the hint of one. My only impression was of fluttering wind and vague movement.

I looked to where Rosethorn lay in my lap and saw with some relief that she was restored of her formidable beauty. Sweet-scented roses had again sprouted where the guard joined blade and hilt, these new ones of a color that was not blue nor silver but rather a striking, inexplicable hybrid of the two, and her blade shown white as dogwood petals in the ample light of the moon (which was always full in Ursathrax) and was slashed with streaks of flowing gray and black, like storm clouds seen from a distance.

The fluttering sound drew closer as I inspected her restoration, and realizing it was a "fluttering" sound, like that of wings and not merely the whipping of wind, I peered into the gloom half-expecting to see Milkweed zig-zagging toward me in the night. The little, white ignudi had taken her leave of Shekalane and sought me out, I dared to dream, perhaps to warn me of an impending danger. Indeed, I half-expected Sthulhu himself, come again to prove that they had not all betrayed me.

But what emerged like a specter through the clouds of churning mist was not by any measure comparable to the miniaturized and fleet-winged elfemale I had befriended in my prior life, or my familiar Sthulhu.

It burst into view as the prow of a ship cuts through a fog bank, revealing itself to the shore. It seemed at first an enormous bat, comparable in size to the peddler's wagon and perchance even bigger, but it was not a bat. And then as it drew closer it seemed almost a lizard, its flesh covered in scales where it was not covered in hair, and its face that of a saurian boasting rows of jagged teeth and unfeeling eyes seeming red in the night—yet it was not a lizard.

And at last it seemed to me to be more of a monkey, with gangling arms and little bent knees, an absurd, extravagant creature having mammoth wings yet barely capable of flight. I thought fleetingly of the thespian's monkey—then the bat-creature was upon me, and I'd no time to think of anything but lifting Rosethorn in defense.

I managed to scratch it with the tip of my blade as it lighted on the rocks beside me with a great weight, crumbling the lesser stones and causing crushed sediment to hurl over the edge of the incline and cascade down the slope.

Its saurian jaws snapped, and its simian arms groped, and I swung and stabbed at it with Rosethorn, knowing not at all how I might defeat such a monster.

Its breath blew in my face as it exerted itself to fang me; hot and cloying and seeming to reek of wet fur. I wounded it once, raking my blade across its heaving, reptilian chest, leaving a wake of furrowed flesh and swelling blood.

It leapt at me from its precarious perch and I stumbled toward the edge, lifting Rosethorn with a hand at each end and holding her before me horizontally, to shield my face. Holding itself aloft before me with what seemed a great effort of its pounding wings, the beast pushed and scratched at me wildly. And then, just when it seemed I should be cast over the side to tumble and bounce helplessly down the jagged rocks, the behemoth's claw-hands smacked against the flat of my sword and its long fingers curled tight, locking the weapon in its grip. I saw a flash of ruby as I held on tight.

Its wings strobed in the moonlight, beating against the air, whipping and snapping like war banners in the wind. The beast made an effort to propel itself forward, reams of gooey drool spilling from its panting maw to patter in my hair. Its actions bent me backwards over the drop, and I realized I could not relent Rosethorn even if I wished, for she was all that held me from tumbling back-first down through the cruel stone and twisted deadwood.

Again I saw a blur of ruby as the creature's hands continued to try and wrest my weapon from me.

It succeeded in gaining forward momentum, then, if only a little. I heard my boots being drug along the rocks near the edge, their soft soles scraping over pebbles and fine sediment, stirring clouds of choking dust.

It turned its saurian head to gaze at me through one black eye, which caught the moon and blazed red as a ruby. And then it revealed its intelligence and purpose by whirling about and backing up unexpectedly, forcing me to do likewise. I was suddenly facing the East Wall again, still gripping Rosethorn. And with profound dismay and a grinding admiration for my opponent's cunning, I realized what my attacker had done.

I'd been presented with the opportunity to survive—if I but relinquished the sword Rosethorn.

There was a tremendous rumbling somewhere distant as a part of Ursathrax spasmed. Thunder cracked above us although there was no rain, nor even so much as a cloud, and the sound was deafening. Giant cymbals clashed together in my ears.

Engulfed in the flashing shadow of great, leathery wings and my own long hair flying all about, I peered downward to where the little path cut through the crevice, the image seeming to spin below me for such was the height, and saw a school of random peddles spiral down to vanish in the haze.

There was another rumble and another *crack!* and another smashing of cymbals in my ears.

I breathed deeply.

If my opponent took flight and me along with him, weight him down I could but, I would not be able to hold on forever.

The great wings beat harder, jerking me forward. My boots were drug along the gravel until my toes overhung the ledge.

My mind swooned with the import of the choice I had to make and the dizzying drop which yawned below me, and I very nearly fainted.

The hovering shape squawked above me, and I knew what I had to do. For all my supposed indifference to the matter, I did not want to die—yet. And in fact, *I did not want to die.*

I let go of the sword.

Its captor rose rapidly, leaving me to rock and sway at the cliff's edge, swinging my arms in desperate circles, my wide eyes riveted to the plummeting abyss below. The stealer of Rosethorn flapped his great wings and vanished into the gloom.

And then I fell to my back on the rocks behind, gasping for breath, and my heart seemed to pound against my ribs as I lay gazing at the stars, chest heaving.

Through a window in the clouds of mist, I saw that there was a new rent in the sky several miles FarSouth. Licks of ruby lightning seemed to dance along its edges as I watched, and handfuls of showering sparks fell from its starless black maw to plummet, sparkle and vanish like the tails of shooting stars or the glowing ruby embers of spent fireworks. Then the schism fell utterly dark and it was over. The Map Makers had a new guide-post.

A cool breeze caught the edge of my cloak and it fluttered in the moonlight.

The full moon which would become the sun (and in fact was already showing signs of brightening) shown fat and distant to the FarSouth, and staring at it, it came to me.

My mind began moving very fast, then, all the observations and bits of theory bleeding together and coalescing to form at last an answer. And, however insubstantial or unproven it might have been—I believed it.

I hadn't solved the mystery of Ursathrax.

But I thought I'd solved the mystery of The Peddler in The Woods. And I knew now how to regain Rosethorn.

6

Flies took lite and scattered as my shadow fell thread-like over the old man's corpse—now spilled forgotten to the ground.

I'd followed Fenris' footprints only to find that the thespian's wagon was gone. In its place was but a rectangle of yellowed, sun-starved grass and a thin scattering of abandoned baubles.

I nudged the old peddler over with a boot. His corpse lolled onto its stomach to lay with its withered face against the grass, and I looked at the torn, blood-stained robes on its back and the pierced flesh between his shoulder blades and nodded in confirmation.

It was just as I'd thought. The old man had been fatally stabbed.

Hoofprints and wheel-tracks led away down the trail, back toward the River Dire, and I stepped over to them.

Brushing aside my soiled cloak in a little plume of dust, I knelt and furrowed through one of the prints with my finger. The impressions seemed fresh, the tromped soil moist and dark—unparched yet by the early morning sun. I was about to stand when I glimpsed something pale at the edge of the trail, something which lay in the shadow of the shrubs, crawling with black ants. I crept forward on my hands and knees and leaned over it.

It was the old man's finger, drained of blood and riddled with little holes through which the tiny insects came and went like busy little coal miners. The blue knuckle was lacerated and there was a faint band of whitened flesh near the digit's ragged end—a thumbnail's length from where the cloven bone protruded from the darkly crimson grist.

Very well, Fenris-Wolf, I thought bitterly. *You've earned my contempt.*

I stood up, breathing deeply.

He couldn't have traveled far in the time it had taken me to return from the summit. And he'd be moving slowly in his present incarnation while I was unencumbered. I would meet up with him promptly and take back what was mine, and then I'd attend to the matter of his dying. But first I had some work to do.

I finished raking the loose dirt and pebbles back into the hole, dismayed somewhat that the contents removed to make the hole proved insufficient to fill it. Then, hacking as if with pneumonia in the clouds of dust my efforts had produced, I reached for the crude, bark marker, and stabbed it into the earth at the shallow grave's head. It's hastily etched inscription read:

Here lies in loving peace the Peddler in the Woods—whose humble wares like starry elms once brightened the midnight dreary, and who for sixpence would lighten, the loads they were fight'n, making friends of all travelers weary.

It was a play on a limerick I'd recalled from my youth, or so it seemed at the time. Now I am no longer certain. And below it I'd scrawled:

Except for the actor, Fenris-Wolf. Who slew the peddler so he might steal from him, and but live to slay and steal again.

But not for long. Such was my oath to the old man I'd never known, tendered in the silence of the forest cathedral, who's canopy was speared with rays of gold light even as stained glass may be speared with rays of bold color.

The earth seemed to rumble, then, drawing me from my reverie. It was a mammoth, distant, almost subterranean sound, a quaking and a cracking and an emergence into light, and then it was gone—over the treetops and into the hills.

It was time.

Still kneeling, I drew from my tunic the little drawstring pouch I'd found spilled in the grass where the wagon had been, when I had endeavored to collect the remaining trinkets and deposit them in the shallow grave to be buried with the peddler. Upon inspecting its contents, I'd discovered it to be the thespian's make-up bag. The creams and oils it contained had seemed plentiful except for one; a fleshy-blush hue whose flask had been almost entirely depleted. It had occurred to me that perhaps Fenris had used that particular pigment to liven the pale of death which the old man would have developed after his murder.

Now I spread the bag open again, and shook out its contents onto the path. Locating a decanter of black ruse, I twisted free its cap and began slopping the paint onto my arms and face, around my eyes, down my neck, until it was gone.

Then I discarded the empty vessel and stood.

Pushing the cloak back over my shoulders, I took up my mask and gloves. I pressed the facade against my face and touched the pad at my temple, sealing it snugly. It wasn't until I was lacing up the elbow-length gloves of tendon, bone and leather that I thought: *We are both actors, Fenris-Wolf and I.*

Sunlight danced along the strips of bone woven into the gloves and I thrilled at the thought of my own ritalimortis-injected eyes glaring wide and lunatic within the skull mask's blackened, down-slanting eye-holes.

He had played his role well, the thespian.

Somewhere distant the earth rumbled again, and I fear my lips curled into a sardonic grin behind the mask's wolfen sneer.

Now it was time for me to play mine.

7

The carnage was near total—a splintered section of wheel here, a flaming piece of wood there, and the smoldering remains of trinkets and costumes spread all about. The stores of kerosene for the lanterns had ruptured, spraying the fluid everywhere, and an unfortunate spark had set what remained of the wagon aflame.

All that was visible of it now was its flaming hindquarter, its doors hung wide—broken, splintered, and charred of their once colorful decor. A column of black smoke rose curling and billowing from the half-buried, fire-gutted interior, obstructing the spill of light through the treetops and casting my masked face in shadow.

Circling around, I found the trail besieged with familiar sinkholes, and recalled the rumbling I'd heard from the peddler's gravesite. It occurred to me now that it, too, had seemed vaguely familiar, different in temperament from the death groans of Ursathrax herself, which I'd heard most recently from the top of the incline the night before.

What had happened became clear. Fenris had been attacked (probably by a band of cutthroats who'd reasoned that plundering the goods of a sole peddler would be too easy to resist) and had employed Rosethorn to slay his attackers. And then all hell had broken loose, for such was the curse and the power of wielding her.

By slaying the men with Rosethorn, Fenris had unknowingly tipped off the forces at work to reclaim her—the forces of earth and root and yet, *not,* for everything about the blade was alien—and the great, questing tentacles had surfaced from below to claim the bodies as well as the sword. When that had happened no inch of soil would have been safe.

The bearer of Rosethorn learned quickly to refrain from killing lest the very earth rise up in anger, searching blindly for its stolen child. Only the man with the mercy (or the cruelty) to but wound his opponent would hold her for long.

Then, through the whisper of these thoughts, there was the sound of rushing water.

I stood motionless and listened, even as glowing embers floated and fluttered up from the wagon's charred ruins to dance about me like a ballet of fireflies. Through the crackling and popping of burning wood I discerned that the airy gushing of water lay east of me, back amongst the tall grass and tangled roots of the untrodden wild. And I was able to discern, also, the nature of the water's movement: it was falling. The sound I was hearing was that of cascading water crashing against rocks.

... rocks!

Safety.

The discovery both excited and dismayed me—excited because it tipped me off to Fenris' whereabouts, dismayed for had I been more attentive while passing this way the first time, I could have replenished Rosethorn and passed the thespian by completely.

Yet the map had shown no brooks, streams or tributaries whatsoever in the Tinsel Forest. Probably the chart was too old, predating both the channel I heard as well as the path.

The realization only increased my fascination with the printed relic I'd found amidst Jamais' hand-drawn documents. For example, what was a "Maintenance Lodge?" What were the interconnecting blue lines threading through the one nearby and other designations like it throughout Ursathrax? If they were to symbolize roads of some kind, why then had I never seen these roads, even though I was completely familiar with some of the locations depicted as having them? There were no rent outlines for schism-navigation—could it be that old? Predating even the degeneration of the sky?

Fenris, I reminded myself. He was undoubtedly near and my immediate concern was to regain Rosethorn.

A quick scan of the hedges told me nothing, and I reprimanded myself for my ignorance. The tangled greenery would have only slowed him down, and Fenris would have had other avenues of reaching those rocks readily available.

However, unless he had slithered upon his belly (appropriate but unlikely) he could not have traveled far. Examining the forest's canopy, I saw that it gradually sank as it tapered away toward the sound, becoming so thick and overgrown that it would have made flight nearly impossible. Using my gloves to clear the way, I left the path and followed the subtle sound deep into the brush.

Few sunbeams strayed so deep as I. The path was quickly covered over behind me and ahead there was only tangled root and earthen hues, and things which moved about my feet (now hidden), which made no sound but brushed against an ankle from time to time and set me shivering with revulsion.

At last I burst upon a clearing. Unlike the veritable tunnel of darkness before, the glade into which I emerged was airy and moist and illuminated somewhat by falls of golden sunlight, which pierced the high ceiling and spotted the water of the roaring, turquoise falls with ragged patches of amber. Studying the great canopy, I smiled behind my mask.

Fenris had to be close. The high ceiling of the clearing was hung with tapering stinger-vines.

Nothing the thespian might become could survive the sting of such vines. Prefect Asmodeus had warned us repeatedly of such dangers, and though I disdained the teacher I valued his teachings more than ever.

That was why the water was turquoise. It was poisoned by the stingers. The vines were parasites. They were not part of the trees, but rather a separate entity, which fed off them just as tapeworms feed off the food ingested by the host. By merging with the host-tree, the vines could tap the roots of the larger organism and grow fat on their water. During fall the stinger-thorns fell from the vines just as leaves from a maple, tainting the water with their poison, which would ultimately be absorbed by the host-tree and over time that tree would die.

It occurred to me without real summoning that the parasite or the disease was one of the Lucitor's most imperfect creations, for by living off the host it slowly sapped that host of life, thereby destroying its own environment and thus itself. Yet was it not likewise with man? There, too, the debt incurred by living could, ultimately, only be paid by death.

I dispelled the thought as an unnecessary gloomy one and moved forward, passing through the slanting shafts of sunlight and the swirling motes of dust, pollen and misty spray they illuminated, and mounted the wet rocks alongside the falls.

I climbed up and up, the cascading water dotting my mask and clothing.

The dead trunk of a great tree had fallen across the transom higher up. Finding no trace of my quarry on this side of the falls, I tested the log's stability by shoving at it, the pungency of wet bark filling my nostrils, and found it to be solid. Not really thinking of the danger but only of regaining Rosethorn and exacting revenge on the thespian, I mounted its slickened wood and began inching across it slowly, the turquoise water raging past.

Of course, I tried not to look down, and of course I failed. In part because the log was considerably longer than it was wide—and I had to place my steps carefully, and in part because of the grim curiosity which drives us all to look down when we know we should not.

The strange waters plunged down below me to bash against the tumbled rocks, and it seemed to me I stood at the edge of the crevice around the path all over again.

At last I gained the opposite side and leapt to the boulders in which the tree's giant branches had become wedged. I stood gazing down at the rapids for a moment, my heart beating rapidly, and then turned to find an avenue of ascent up the remainder of the fall's stone border.

Rounding a wall of craggy rock, I nearly tripped over the outstretched legs of Fenris-Wolf himself.

8

Our eyes met, and he moaned in agony, writhing and twitching as he lay with his back against the stone, Rosethorn clasped desperately against his chest, which was swathed in fresh bandages.

"I see you managed to hang on to the sword and your hat," I said dryly. "If not your courage." I glanced to the bushes and saw a black shaft with a brass tip protruding from beneath. "Or your cane."

His breathing harsh and ragged, he managed, "Is it not enough that I already lay poisoned and dying ... must Death gloat over me as well?"

"Gloating is for petty thieves and buried baubles, thespian." Dropping to my knee beside him, I held the small knife I kept in my boot to his throat and reached for the sword, adding, "Not Ferrymen."

He allowed her to slip free of his embrace without protest. Looking to his trembling hands, I did not find the ruby ring I had expected—only a pale stripe around the smallest finger of his right hand. Hastily I searched his pockets, but found nothing.

"Where is it?" I demanded.

"Your sword? Why, it's right there, you silly ghoul! Have you gone mad?"

"The ring, Fenris." I scraped his throat with the knife, opening a light wound which swelled blood immediately. "Where is it?"

The thespian gasped, jolted by the pain.

"What *ring?*" he blurted, spraying spittle.

"The ring you stole from the real peddler. The ring set with a single ruby, capable of transforming its wearer into whatever he wishes."

"Gah ...! Babbling fool. Do you even know what you're saying?"

"Yes, Sir Fenris-Wolf. I fear I am quite focused on this."

"Then explain your ramblings, ferryman, and be done with me. And take your weapon when you go. It is as I said—deviltry. It can only be wielded by demons."

"Very well, thespian. I shall explain. After all, what better audience is there than a man both paralyzed and dying? I must begin by applauding your absolute mastery of deception—but alas, you are only a deceiver. You've the heart of a con-artist, not an actor. And so you make the same mistake made by all who would use an artform only to gain money ... you underestimate your audience. You put on a remarkable performance, to be sure, but what else should I have expected from a misguided thespian than just such a performance? You'll recall my reference to the woman in my past and her opinion of what kind of heart I had. It prompted me to remember how she tricked me by deceiving me with the obvious. You sought to do the same, but when you told me you were an actor, my experience left me no choice but to assume you were acting from that point on.

"I noticed you'd no mule to pull your carriage. You told me it had run off, but such is hardly the nature of an ass. Again, you were acting. You'd no mule, because the real peddler in the woods had needed none. He was his own mule. Using his ring, he could transform himself into a giant ox if he wished.

"Also, before I approached the old man's corpse, I took effort to observe the camp from the hedge alongside. And while there I noticed footprints other than my own in the mud at my feet. Later, I noticed that the boots you wore might have made a perfect match. You discovered the peddler in the woods and did as I did, you hid in the bushes to watch him. The timing was so that you must have witnessed him using the ring, so you slew the old man by knifing him in the back and, upon finding the ring would not slide over his knuckle, you severed the peddler's finger and pulled the ring free so that you might wear it.

"You seemed a gentleman, hardly a murderous cur, and so I needed a motive. Who but an actor would have this motive? Would not an actor long for a ring which might transform him into whatever role he wished? You said you were a 'man of the method,' the art of becoming the role. And whoever wears that ring becomes what he wishes. Oh, how you must have ached to possess it! Just as you ached to possess Rosethorn. Its sell might have bought you your own coliseum in which to perform! But surely, you'd never sell that ring."

Fenris glared at me accusingly.

I shook my head. "No, Fenris. I do not want so mighty a ring for my own. I have all the might I can possibly shoulder in Rosethorn. But since a man such as you should not possess so much power, since you would only use it to rob from and do further harm to myself and others, I have no choice but to extract it from you now by whatever means necessary. You must give me the ring ..."

Fenris said nothing.

"I implore you, thespian, " I urged, "I can make your final hours extremely unpleasant."

The thespian groaned.

"Lost," he exhaled at last. "Lost with the wagon."

I scraped him again, deepening the wound.

"You're lying."

This time he cried out, grasping me about the wrist and kicking at me impotently. Tearing away from him, I stood erect and stepped on his neck, allowing the tip of Rosethorn's blade to come to a rest upon his chest, just above his heart. His blood swelled up the sides of my boot as I brought all my weight to bear upon his torn throat.

"Tell me where it is."

Finally, he gasped, "F-fell into the water. It—it's miles downstream by now. Please ..."

I stared down at him through the mask's slanted eyelets. His eyes shown wide and rabid with terror, bulging from his pallid, blue-tinted face like the stools of mushrooms sprouting up from the forest grass, and the thick veins which webbed his forehead stood out like swollen worms. And though my heart was such as cold steel toward him, I knew a pity for the man I cannot explain, and thus I released him from his bondage and lifted the sword away from his heart.

"It is not your fault that you are a maggot, Fenris. No more than it is mine for being a Ferryman. The Lucitor has created his poisons and parasites both in the trees as well as among men, and I shall not hold you accountable for the mystic logic of your creator. I have heard it said that there is no justice inherent in the world, there is only irony. And it seems ironic enough that you should die by a parasite's poison, just as others have died by the poison that is yourself. I wish you no further malice, thespian. Godspeed your journey down the true River of Death."

Turning from him, I made for the fallen tree once again.

"Ferryman!" he called after me.

I stopped but did not turn around, perking an ear over the rush of the falls.

"We are both actors," he wheezed.

I nodded, gripping Rosethorn, and stepped onto the log.

9

How it happened I cannot say. Perhaps it was only because I'd fallen to reverie while crossing the trunk. More likely Fenris had *merged* into some creature of silence and stealth and followed me, like a gaining shadow, until he was close enough to strike—in man-form, with his ruby-set black cane, which no longer shown of ruby at all.

I had not yet sheathed Rosethorn and was able to spin upon him after the blow and lift her to block his follow-up. Grappling with him in this manner, with Rosethorn pitted against the now rubyless cane and his dark eyes pitted against the pale of my own, I noticed the exquisitely-crafted ring of carved obsidian wrapped about his smallest finger—set with a single, flaring ruby, and seeming to swirl from within with restless gases as if it were alive.

"'Twas a splendid review, ferryman," he hissed through the cross of our stalemated weapons, "but the performance is far from over."

He stepped back suddenly and brought the cane rushing up toward my stomach. Its pointed, brass tip caught me just above the navel and I was doubled over instantly. I could only gasp for breath in the slim seconds before his black, vinyl boot hit my mask at the mouth.

The blow snapped my head back and for an instant I saw only the forest's canopy. Then the sole of his boot pressed down upon my throat and he loomed over me a glowering madman, like a veritable demonic carnival promoter in his black suit and tall hat.

"Did you actually presume that only those reared in the Lucitor's service would know enough to avoid mere stinger-vines? How unbelievably arrogant you are, to think I would fall victim to such a fool's end, much less allow you to escape with your sword—a most powerful and mystifying weapon, indeed!"

He increased the pressure against my throat and I could but gasp and struggle uselessly beneath his boot.

He continued: "How it tasks me to think that the finer nuances of my performance should go unappreciated. Did you think that I would allow such a priceless find to simply rattle about in my pocket? What of my artful juxtaposition of the ring on the old man's cane, eh?" He clomped at my throat. "What of my carefully selected attire which would lead one to believe I indeed sported a cane?" He clomped again. "What of my stint as monkey which warned me of your approach?"

I could only choke for air as he clomped again and again. "Eh, eh, eh?"

He glared down at me with sparkling eyes. "And now, my gruesome and wayward friend, you will impart to me that sword, and enlighten me as to how you control it." He smiled almost sympathetically. "Or I shall kick you from this log and watch your leprous body explode upon the rocks."

The treetops had begun to swirl and fade above me, and he was but a blurred image as he shrugged and added, "And that would be an unsavory thing for me to have to witness on such a beautiful and sunny day, would it n—"

And suddenly he was choking.

At last, the pressure of his boot against my throat relaxed and my opponent swam back into focus.

He was being strangled by Rosethorn. Thick and leafy vines had sprouted from her blade and coiled about his neck, and were constricting.

It was all the chance I needed. I brought a boot up without delay and struck him in the loins. He fell to one knee over me and I was able to strike him again—in the mouth, with the bone-plated fist in which I gripped Rosethorn.

As I have said in chapters past, I possess little muscle save that of my arms and shoulders—from rowing on the River Dire (in one form or another) since before my adolescence, and since that is where my sole physical strength resides, I was able to dislodge a tooth at least and leave his lips both ruptured and bloodied.

"Release him, Rosethorn," I said, and immediately the ropes about his neck snaked free.

He was still disorientated by this sudden and undoubtedly unpleasant turn of events as I shoved him over the side.

I scrambled to my feet on the trunk's slick, fraying bark and brandished Rosethorn as if to convince myself I still held her. The vines which had attacked Fenris retracted, returning to the blade and coiling about it to finally merge like water back into the whole.

Sucking in moist air with deep, ragged inhalations, I felt the tickle of river-spray against my lips and realized my death mask had sustained damage at the mouth. Perhaps it, too, had lost a tooth or two. Nor was it for the first time that I owed the gruesome façade my gratitude. Yet even as this flashed through my mind, the thespian returned to continue the fight; for the saurian, the monkey, the bat, the *thing*, rose up beside me without warning—its massive saurian jaws snapping, its great leathery wings pounding, and its yellowed fangs careening off my mask, sending me stumbling back along the trunk.

It lighted upon the log several feet away, and I watched as its left hand touched the ring and twisted it around once. The bat creature seemed to melt and shift colors and finally morphed into an entirely new menace.

Of its appearance I can only say this: It was shaped like a man and yet clearly it was not, for it was covered head to toe in long, spikey hair (itself voluminous enough as to be absurd), and this hair was all white save several jagged, zig-zagging black stripes, which lashed across its body like the markings of a zebra. Indeed, the only parts of the monster not concealed by this hair were the talons at its hands and feet and the giant red orbs it claimed as eyes. It charged at me along the trunk and, anticipating, I swung Rosethorn in both hands—striking the thing in its side and wedging the blade deep. The beast which was Fenris howled like a banshee and reared back, still stuck to the organic blade, and when I looked down I was not really surprised to see that she had sprouted crooked thorns after impact, which had dug into its/his flesh and entrapped him.

He swiped at me with his black claws and I ducked my head from side to side to avoid them.

"Release him," I commanded.

The living sword only seemed to growl and snarl and wedge herself deeper.

"Rosethorn!"

Grudgingly, the thorns retracted, and I pulled the blade free.

Fenris seemed to hesitate.

"Careful, thespian ..." I smiled sardonically. "She bites."

Fenris retreated several paces, hissing and snorting. Then he morphed again, this time into his most hideous incarnation yet, for he stood before me now not man nor devil but something in-between. His face was the thin, tapered skull of death itself, the enshrouded eyeholes large and slanting beneath down-swooping brows of cracked bone, and when he turned his head the shadows skewed to reveal bloodless whites and yellow pupils—narrowed eyes, set in blackness. In short, he was me, identical in every bitter detail.

And like me, he now held a replica of Rosethorn in his right hand.

10

"Aye, ferryman," he growled in my voice, "she does bite at that. But so does her *bitch sister.*"

And then he leapt at me, howling, swinging the ersatz Rosethorn this way and that, and I was forced back along the slim width of tree trunk capable only of defending myself feebly from his relentless assault.

The twin blades struck and smashed repeatedly against each other, seeming to curse and snarl like jealous, grappling women, until I stumbled blindly from the log's end and fell twisting to the wet rocks at the side of the falls. Fenris leapt upon me without even thinking, and I extended Rosethorn straight out. He fell upon her blade and its glinting tip was driven through his chest and out his back.

That's when I realized with horror and revulsion that she had sprouted crooked thorns along her blade while passing through his body, thorns which curved and pointed away from her hilt, and in doing so had drug out most his innards—which now hung steaming and bleeding from her tip.

Soaked in sweat and breathing heavily, exhausted, I gazed into my own eyes and watched as the life began to flicker within them. A shadow passed over us which I assumed to be a bird of some kind. My own yellow pupils rolled up white.

An intense panic took hold of me and I threw him off—pulling on Rosethorn's hilt, her blade sliding free without protest—and I sat up and began scooting away. I didn't stop until I'd brushed up against the trunk of an elm, where I remained with my back against its bark for what seemed a very long time.

My eyes never left Fenris.

At last, his body morphed while I watched, and he returned to his true form, thus confirming what I'd come to suspect.

There was a limit to how long the transformation could last. Also, supposing the transformation was allowed to run its full course, the ring would need time to recover from being drained so thoroughly. After all, why would he have killed me to obtain Rosethorn if he could have created his own lasting replica? Yet, if it could replicate things such as Rosethorn as well as creatures, then was it not indeed a ring of creation and not merely a shape-shifter? What were the limits of its power, if there were any at all?

A faint groan drew me from my reverie and I realized it had come from Fenris himself. Unbelieving, I stood up.

Returning to where he lay, I knelt beside him in a state of shock. He was still alive, and aware—somehow. This seemed unthinkably insidious—even to I, a ferryman and a traitor. And no matter the dread enemy he had proven himself to be, it was more than I could bear to watch a man dying so slowly like that.

I did not think to be wary of the roots which sought Rosethorn as I stood and lifted her high above my head. And I did not feel like a monster as I drove her blade through the center of his skull, but Dear Reader, how I wished I could have. Monsters do not feel the sickness of the slaughter, nor do they feel remorse. They do not feel guilt over having "won," and they do not kill out of mercy or pity.

They kill only because it does not occur to them to do otherwise. They haven't the capacity. And in this sense, they may well be like children in their simple innocence. But is it a hard heart or a soft one which kills out of mercy? Reader, I cannot say, for I haven't the answer. I know only that mercy is what drove me to deliver the final blow as I did, just as mercy tainted with lust had driven me to spare Shekalane and thus set me on the road to my inevitable torment and death, or so I believed at the time.

But an act of mercy was not to be the summing up of this matter, as it had been with Shekalane.

I am not a healer, and so I do not know how such things as follows might occur, or indeed if they are even possible outside the realm of magic or miracle, but this is what happened:

The sword plunged deep into the thespian's brain, to no doubt sink into the soft earth beneath, and his blood dotted my skull-mask as well as my cloak, and then his eyes sprang wide open, and they glowered at me, and, somehow, he managed to reach across his pierced chest to the ring—and turn it round once more.

To become a Regenerator.

There was little known about these half-human earth-dwellers due to their utter rarity in modern and decaying Ursathrax. Like so many of the world's biological mysteries, they were ancient creatures elevated to near mythical status by the extrapolations of playwrights and poets throughout the millennia. But they were said to have the ability to control their own matter in such a way as to literally pull themselves back together if mutilated or dismembered.

And such is exactly what this one did, while I watched in slack-jawed disbelief. The creature's innards seemed to reel themselves in of their own volition and its hairless, blue-gray flesh merged together to become whole again. Immediately I tried to yank my blade from its head but Fenris twisted the ring round again and became still another monstrosity—something without name and little shape, something resembling nothing more than a giant mass of gray jelly—which held Rosethorn like a vice and would not relent no matter how desperately I pulled.

It made a tremendous squelching sound which gurgled and smacked, and I looked to Rosethorn to find her being drained of all color and vitality with frightening speed—her delicate petals browning and falling free, her blade seeming to whither, while she whimpered softly and quickly degenerated into a deathly husk of deadwood.

I was defeated.

I knew this in my heart without any hint of doubt. And so I released my grip on her now brittle hilt and leapt back from the gulping blob which was Fenris reborn.

And a raven cawed.

Then another, and another, all from different directions.

I looked to the treetops as I stumbled backward, my heart pounding, and their twisted branches seemed to whirl about me dizzyingly, faster and faster ...

The dark birds were soaring in from all directions to alight in the trees, where they perched disinterestedly upon the sullen branches and regarded me accusingly with their red, blinking eyes, like a coolly decided jury.

The Lucitor had found me.

11

There was a sudden, unyielding push of stone at my back and I knew I could retreat no further. I sank against the rock wall, sliding down it to sit exhausted and helpless upon the soil.

Fool! I cursed myself. The shadow which had passed over my doppelganger and I had been that of a raven come to find me. It was truly all over now.

I looked to the blob of gray matter in which Rosethorn was still imbedded with hopeless indifference, watching as it shifted and twisted upward and became Fenris again, whole of body and exactly as he had been upon our first meeting, dressed in his long-tailed suit and tall, black hat. Rosethorn's husk had fallen to the rocks and now lay silent. Ignoring her, he moved to the spot in which I'd found him earlier and snatched up his cane. Then he slid the ring from his finger and reinserted it into the little hole beneath the handle. He strode toward me, swinging the brass-tipped wand casually.

"There's men who will spy a ring such as mine from across the length of a pub," he said, "and follow him to his inn so they might cut it from him in his very sleep." He laughed coolly. "A cane seldom attracts such scrutiny."

His shadow fell upon me and he came to a halt.

"They say that one should measure a man by his enemies, not his friends," he said, seeming newly invigorated, and added, "If this is so, then what am I to make of you, dear boatman? You who would seem to have no friends at all, and claims the Lucitor Himself as his dire foe!"

I could only stare up at him helplessly as he continued.

"He spoke to me, ferryman, did you know that?" He broke into a sudden shout, "At the instant of my dying He spoke to me and commanded me to apprehend you!"

His thespian's voice boomed throughout the woods.

"Dravidian! Of the Brotherhood of Death! Once a ferryman but a ferryman no longer! Lustful traitor to the Lottery! Fornicator!"

I reeled beneath the weight of his words, defeated, discovered, hopeless. My eyelids flickered, and I feared I would faint.

The thespian paced his stage.

"And though I be dead by your traitorous hand," he now almost whispered, "He rekindled the spark which gives life, His spark, His creation, and lifted me up so that I might serve Him by capturing you—Dravidian, who's name shall come to mean infamy and betrayal of duty to all future generations of Ursathrax."

He waved and made gestures with his hands as he spoke. Watching him through half-open eyelids in the darkness of my damaged mask, I saw the Lucitor's ravens solemnly looking on, as if to concur. It occurred to me even in my delirium that the thespian was making good on the presence of what would surely be his ultimate audience—the Lucitor Himself.

He lifted the steely tip of his cane and pressed it against my throat. "And now, my good ferryman ..." He smiled sardonically.

"I shall escort *you* down the River of Death, where torment awaits your audience."

The ground beneath us started to rumble. There was the wet, cracking sound of tangled roots shifting and buckling somewhere below.

Fenris glanced about nervously.

The entire congregation of ravens erupted into flight as the rumbling became a trembling and then a quaking and suddenly snaking black roots—tentacles, *things*—punched up through the soil and coiled about Fenris' ankles. He snapped his chin down to look at them.

"What's this ...?"

The roots yanked violently and he was drug into the ground, nearly to the knees. Several breaths passed before I realized what was going on. The thespian, though resurrected, had nonetheless been dead, if only for an instant. That had been all the roots needed to zero in on Rosethorn's presence.

She was safe, I hoped (if indeed she lived at all), where she lay upon the rocks by the falls. But there was no fresh water for some distance yet, and even if the roots did not find her, she would surely be forever lost by the time I reached the Relief Lodge or a village.

Fenris was wailing, and re-focusing on him I saw that he'd been tugged still deeper, nearly to his thighs.

Marshalling whatever strength (both mental and physical) I still possessed, I leapt forward and grabbed for the thespian's arms, for the roots had snaked up and over his legs and torso, and I was able to cut at them with my knife and sever them. The sections fell away to writhe and flop about on the shaking ground around us.

I pulled Fenris from the churned soil, and, while he was still somewhat disorientated, clubbed the cane from his grip with my left hand and straight-armed him with the right, smashing him in the nose as I kicked his feet out from under him. He fell to the dirt and I stepped over him, making for Rosethorn.

Bounding over the heaving grounds, I snatched her up and returned to my fallen nemesis. More roots had sprung up around him and were taking hold of his appendages once again. I dared not employ Rosethorn, for she would surely shatter in her dry and brittle condition, so I lopped them in twos with the knife and dropped to my knees over Fenris.

Extending my blade underhand, I touched his throat with its tip. His nose seemed broken and spidery rivers of thick blood were coursing down over his mouth and chin. He focused on me and spat, cursing. His saliva splatted against my mask just beside the eyehole and I felt a tiny drop enter my eye.

Calmly, I said:

"I am proposing a truce, thespian. Hear me out. I am prepared to offer you a slim chance at life, as well as a learning opportunity. I believe my sword to be still living in spite of your efforts otherwise, yet her death is inevitable if I do not find water immediately. I cannot allow this. I need her as you need that ring, and so I am prepared to barter as you would have liked me to from the beginning. Are you with me?"

The actor's eyes shown with a familiar dark twinkle.

"Good. You're going to like this, Fenris, for if you agree to my terms—and you must—and, of course, if you survive what I'll require of you ... I will spare you your life *and* allow you to keep the ring." I smiled and lifted an eyebrow behind my mask. *"Hmmm?"*

He nodded and grunted like a true business partner.

I patted him on the cheek. "Aye, bully for us. Very well ... I've need of your assistance with a certain experiment I wish to perform. The scholars theorize that nearly three quarters of the human body consists of water alone ..."

12

When the heaving earth and questing roots had become too much of a bother, I'd drug Fenris to the safety of the rocks and after a time the tentacles had given up and retreated into the soil.

He sat there now with his back against the stone and his eyes staring pale and empty from his parched and shriveled skull. But he was not dead as of yet.

I'd allowed Rosethorn to drink of him until fully restored, and she now resided once again in her sheath at my side, her hilt abloom with roses and dogwood petals and her blade having changed to the most vibrant green I had ever seen.

Using a strip of black cloth I'd torn from my cloak, I bandaged the thespian's wound at the shoulder and removed the ruby ring from its clever place beneath the cane's grip.

Displaying it several inches from his face, I said, "Your ring, Sir Fenris-Wolf."

One of his tiny, withered arms managed to lift off the stone about an inch or perhaps two, but only for an instant, and then it slumped back down. He could only move his colorless lips slightly, opening and closing them feebly. After a moment I realized he was speaking, however faintly, amidst the roar of the falls. I bent close and listened.

"Put ... it on ... my finger."

I could only shake my head gently.

"No, Sir Fenris-Wolf. I'm afraid that wasn't part of the bargain. You'd only be in pursuit of me at once, in whatever guise, though surely the Regenerator would come first."

Delicately, I opened his mouth a share wider and placed the ruby ring inside. Then I put my knife to his throat and said, not unkindly, "You must swallow the ring, Sir Fenris. You have some hope this way. If you can remain alive long enough to reclaim it from your stool, then it is possible you might succeed in getting it on your finger ... with your teeth if need be. Hurry Fenris and swallow without delay ... there may still be time."

A moment passed, and I heard his throat click like dry leaves. His eyes blazed and using what seemed his last breath he managed to say, almost clearly, *"Have you no heart?"*

I stood and rested a hand on Rosethorn's hilt.

"Of course, Sir Thespian. I've the heart of a ferryman, as you said so yourself."

Then I left him at the edge of the falls and re-crossed the fallen trunk, heading back toward the trail somewhere west.

Epilogue

The remainder of the day was spent beating the path toward the ever-growing West Wall, and the mysterious Relief Lodge I hoped to find there.

I walked briskly for fear of pursuit, not, of course, by Fenris, but by other ferrymen who, even now, were undoubtedly enroute to reclaim their doomed berserker—having been informed of my location by the silent ravens that I hadn't even noticed until it was too late. And though I was convinced at the time my flight would be ended soon and that my torment was imminent, I felt good in knowing at least some justice had been done in the world, or, if not justice, then at least an irony.

Before taking my leave of the thespian entirely, I'd fashioned a tombstone of dry bark and straight wood much as the one I'd erected for the real peddler earlier that morning, and secured it between the rocks at his feet. In Fenris' dark blood, I'd written:

Here lies the actor, Fenris-Wolf, resurrected by the Lucitor only to be cut down again by the ferryman's scythe. Here lies the murderer of the Peddler in the woods.

I would think no more on the violence and spite of the whole dark affair for many months. Saying goodbye to innocence is perhaps the easiest part of growing up, for it leaves in the night and is not often missed until many years later.

However, I was beginning to learn, at some cost, the difference between being a ferryman and a wanderer.

The End

About the Author

Wayne Kyle Spitzer is an American writer, illustrator, and filmmaker. He is the author of countless books, stories and other works, including a film (*Shadows in the Garden*), a screenplay (*Algernon Blackwood's The Willows*), and a memoir (*X-Ray Rider*). His work has appeared in *MetaStellar—Speculative fiction and beyond,* *subTerrain Magazine: Strong Words for a Polite Nation* and *Columbia: The Magazine of Northwest History,* among others. He holds a Master of Fine Arts degree from Eastern Washington University, a B.A. from Gonzaga University, and an A.A.S. from Spokane Falls Community College. His recent fiction includes *The Man/Woman War* cycle of stories as well as the *Dinosaur Apocalypse Saga.* He lives with his sweetheart Ngoc Trinh Ho in the Spokane Valley.

Ingram Content Group UK Ltd.
Milton Keynes UK
UKHW011108310323
419467UK00004B/186